Allen Putnam

Witchcraft of New England

explained by modern spiritualism

Allen Putnam

Witchcraft of New England
explained by modern spiritualism

ISBN/EAN: 9783337334093

Printed in Europe, USA, Canada, Australia, Japan

Cover: Foto ©Andreas Hilbeck / pixelio.de

More available books at **www.hansebooks.com**

WITCHCRAFT OF NEW ENGLAND

EXPLAINED BY

MODERN SPIRITUALISM.

BY

ALLEN PUTNAM, Esq.,

AUTHOR OF "BIBLE MARVEL WORKERS," "NATTY, A SPIRIT," "MESMERISM,
SPIRITUALISM, WITCHCRAFT, AND MIRACLE," "AGASSIZ
AND SPIRITUALISM," ETC.

SECOND EDITION.

BOSTON:
COLBY AND RICH, PUBLISHERS,
9 Montgomery Place.
1881.

CONTENTS.

5

CONTENTS.

APPENDIX.

PREFACE.

" The nobler tendency of culture — and, above all, of scientific culture — is to honor the dead without groveling before them ; to profit by the past without sacrificing it to the present." — EDWARD B. TYLOR, *Primitive Culture.*

MOST history of New England witchcraft written since 1760 has dishonored the dead by lavish imputations of imposture, fraud, malice, credulity, and infatuation ; has been sacrificing past acts, motives, and character to skepticism regarding the sagacity and manliness of the fathers, the guilelessness of their daughters, and the truth of ancient records. Transmitted accounts of certain phenomena have been disparaged, seemingly because facts alleged therein baffle solution by to-day's prevalent philosophy, which discards some agents and forces that were active of old. The legitimate tendency of culture has been reversed ; what it should have availed itself of and honored, it has busied itself in hiding and traducing.

An exception among writers alluded to is the author of the following extract, who, simply as an historian, and not as an advocate of any particular theory for the solution of witchcraft, seems ready to let its works be ascribed to competent agents.

" So far as a presentation of facts is concerned, no account of the dreadful tragedy has appeared which is more accurate and truthful than Governor Hutchinson's narrative. His theory on the subject — that it was wholly the result of fraud and deception on the part of the afflicted children — will not be generally accepted at the

9

present day, and his reasoning on that point will not be deemed conclusive. . . . There is a tendency to trace an analogy between the phenomena then exhibited and modern spiritual manifestations." — W. F. POOLE, *Geneal. and Antiq. Register,* October, 1870.

While composing the following work, its writer was borne onward by the tendency which Poole named. Survey of the field of marvels has been far short of exhaustive — his purpose made no demand for very extended researches. Selected cases, representative of the general manifestations and subject treated of were enough. The aim has been to find in ancient records, and thence adduce, statements and meanings long resting unobserved beneath the gathered dust of more than a hundred years, and therefore practically lost.

The course of search led attention beyond overt acts, to inspection of some natural germs and their legitimately resultant development into creeds, which impelled good men on to the enactment of direful tragedy.

Examination of the basement walls — the foundations — of prevalent popular explanation of ancient wonders, forces conviction that they lack both the breadth and the materials needful to stability. Modern builders of witchcraft history have either failed to find, or have deemed unmanageable by any appliances at their command, and therefore would not attempt to handle, a vast amount of sound historic stones which are accessible and can be used. Lacking them, these moderns have let fancy manufacture for them, and they have builded upon blocks of her fragile stuff, which are fast disintegrating under the chemical action of the world's common sense.

We proposed here an incipient step towards refutation of the sufficiency and justness of a main theory, now long prevalent, for explaining satisfactorily very many well-proved marvelous facts. Some such have been presented on the pages of Hutchinson, Upham, and their followers; and yet these have been either not at all, or vaguely or ludicrously, commented upon, or reasoned from. Very many others, and the most important of all as bases and aids to an acceptable and true solution of the whole, are not visible where they ought to have conspicuous position. Presentation and proper use of them might have caused public cognizance to topple over the edifices which it has pleased modern builders to erect.

It is not our purpose to write history, but to give new explanation of old events. The long and widely tolerated theory that New England witchcraft was exclusively but out-workings of mundane fraud, imposture, cunning, trickery, malice, and the like, has never adequately met the reasonable demand of common sense, which always asks that specified agents and forces shall be probably competent to produce all such effects as are distinctly ascribed to them.

Persons who of old were afflicted in manner that was then called bewitchment, and others through or from whom the afflictions were alleged to proceed, are now extensively supposed to have possessed organizations, temperaments, and properties which rendered them exceptionally pliant under subtile forces, either magnetic, mesmeric, or psychological, and who, consequently, at times, could be, and were, made ostensible utterers of knowledge whose marvelousness indicated mysterious source, and ostensible performers of acts deemed more than natural, and which, in fact, were the productions of wills not native in the manifesting forms. The special forces that produced bewitchment and are put in application now, do not become sensibly operative upon any other mortals than peculiar sensitives; and their action upon such is often most easily and effectively manifested through aid obtained from other similar sensitives. Selections of both subjects and instrumentalities were of old, and are now, controlled by general law. Steel needles and iron-filings are not selected by the magnet's free will when it forces them to leap up from their resting-places and cleave to 'tself. Seeming levitation possesses them, and an invisible force takes them whither gravitation, their usual holder, would not let them go. It is upon steel, not lead — upon iron, not stone — that the magnet can execute its marvelous liftings. Nature's conditions fix selections. The organizations, temperaments, fluids, solids, and all the various properties, are, to some extent, unlike in any two human bodies whatsoever, and the range of the differings and consequent susceptibilities is very wide. A psychological magnet in either the seen or unseen may have power to draw certain human forms to contact with itself, and to use them as its tools, and yet lack force to produce sensible effects upon but few in the mass of living men. Where its action is most efficient, it controls the movements of what it holds in its embrace — takes a human form out from control by the spirit which usually governs it, and through that form manifests its own powers and purposes. Both the reputed bewitched and bewitching may severally have had but little, if any, voluntary part in manifesting the remarkable phenomena that were imputed to them. Where physical organs are used, the public is prone to deem the performances intentional acts by those whose forms are operated, while yet the wills of those whose forms are visibly concerned in marvelous works may have been formerly, as they often now are, little else than unwilling, and in many cases unconscious tools.

The afflicted — in other words, the bewitched ones — may have actually perceived, — they no doubt often did, — and also knew, that the annoyances and tortures they endured were augmented, if not generated, by emanations proceeding forth from the particular persons whom they named as being their afflicters; and these afflicters may have been all unconscious that their own auras were going forth and acting upon the sufferers.

The chief non-intelligent instrumentality employed in producing miraculous, spiritualistic, necromantic, and other kindred marvels, is now generally called psychological force — force resident in and put forth from and by the soul — from and by the will and emotional parts of a living being; it is the force by which some men control with magic power not only many animals in the lower orders, but some susceptible members of their own species; it is a force deep-seated in our being, and may accompany man when he leaves his outer body, and continue to be his in an existence beyond the present.

The usurping capabilities of this force were strikingly set forth by the illustrious Agassiz in his carefully written account of his own sensations and condition while in a mesmeric trance induced upon him by Rev. Chauncy Hare Townshend. The great naturalist — the strong man both mentally and physically — says that he lost all power to use his own limbs — all power to even *will* to move them, and that his body was forced against his own strongest possible opposition to pace the room in obedience to the mesmerizer's will. Since such force overcame the strongest possible resistance of the gigantic Agassiz, it is surely credible that less robust ones, in any and every age, may have been subdued and actuated by it. — See page 385, in *Facts of Mesmerism, 2d Ed. London,* 1844, *by Rev.* *Chauncy Hare Townshend.*

Those who were accused of bewitching others were fountains from which invisible intelligences sometimes drew forth properties which aided them in gaining and keeping control of those whom they entranced or otherwise used. Also from such there probably sometimes went forth unwilled emanations that were naturally attracted to other sensitives, who perceived their source, and pronounced it diabolical, because the influx thence was annoying. Impersonal natural forces to some extent, and at times, probably designated the victims who were immolated on witchcraft's altar.

Citations of evidences and proofs from early historic records, that other agents and forces had chief part in producing New England witchcraft than such as modern historians generally have recognized, together with exposition of legitimate and forceful biases proceeding from articles in old-time creeds, will exhibit our forefathers in much better aspects than they wear in intervening history; will halo in innocence some of their wives and daughters, around whom historians have cast hues appropriate only to most villainous culprits; and also will manifest sadly misleading oversights, shortcomings, and sophistries by some whose writings have done much in forming the world's existing erroneous and harsh views and estimates.

Certain operative, world-wide, and daily occurrences in the present age, unaccounted for, and often sneered at, by adepts in prevalent sciences and philosophies, seem to have fair claims for general, candid, and most rigid scrutiny. Even if despised and contemned of men, they nevertheless are widely and most efficiently working for the world's good or for its harm. Testimony to their positive existence is vast in amount, and much of it comes from witnesses whose words upon any ordinary matters would be absolutely conclusive.

Something more than twenty-five years ago, mysterious raps on cottage walls and furniture were traced to cause which, while invisible and impalpable, could count TEN. A trifle, was that? No; for its teachings and influences have gone forth widely, and have worked efficiently. They have broadened nature's domain as conceived of by man, have opened up to him new fields of study, and have furnished him with a vast amount of new views and speculations, which are permeating creeds, philosophies, sciences, explanations of history, and most things appertaining to the welfare of civilized society. Well may they have thus efficiently operated, for they have claimed to be, and their potency indicates that they have been, moved onward by forces greater than pertain to incarnate men.

Raps by invisible rappers; liftings of tables, pianos, &c., by invisible lifters; music flowing forth from pianos, harmonicons, and other instruments having no visible manipulators; pencils writing legibly, instructively, eloquently, when no visible hand held and moved them; levitations of tables and human forms; transfer of

books and other objects from one side of rooms to the opposite by
invisible carriers; hands of flesh grasping and holding live coals
of fire with impunity; raisings of human forms from floor to ceiling
overhead, and holding them there by invisible beings; impressions
of recognized likenesses of departed mortals upon the plates of
photographists; presentation of moving and palpable hands and
arms where no body is present for their attachment; materialization
of entire forms of the departed, and the speaking and moving of
the re-clad ones so exactly as in life as to be distinctly and unmis-
takably recognized by their surviving relatives and familiar acquaintances; — these phenomena, and many others kindred to them,
admit of being, and we ask that they may be, viewed apart from
any and all verbal or written communications by spirits, and apart
from the character, standing, and habits of spiritualists. Such
presentations as have just been specified may be looked upon as a
class by themselves, and as being worthy the attention and closest
scrutiny of devotees to the physical sciences and all logical minds.
Even though they have emerged into view from a modern Nazareth,
the obscurity of their place of issuance is not conclusive against
their virtue to enlighten man, and broaden the extent of human
knowledge.

When, in days to come, some abler and more polished pen shall
apply, in the solution of witchcraft marvels, a theory that shall be
based on the classes of agents, forces, &c., which are now evolving
modern marvels, its fitness and adequacy will attract wide attention,
and command general acceptance. Our work, of course, will fall
far short of such results, for he who here writes possesses no com-
manding powers, — never had much taste for historical and antiquarian researches, — has for many years last past found himself much,
very much, more prone to be seeking for mental and moral wealth
in oncoming than in receded times, — possesses only moderate skill
and less than moderate facility in literary composition, — has spent
the greater part of adult life in pursuits which debarred him not

only from much perusal of books either historical, literary, or scientific, but also from much converse with well-cultured society.
Therefore, necessarily, his whitened locks and waning forces find
him consciously deficient in nearly every qualification for either a
good historian or good expounder and applier of any theory pertaining to profound and intricate subjects involving occult agents
and forces.

Then why write? Perhaps vanity is strong among our motives.
Nearly as far back as memory can take us, we heard from a grandfather's lips accounts of what his grandfather and others did and
suffered when witchcraft raged in our native parish, and threatened
trouble to those occupying the house in which we were born and
reared. From boyhood onward the subject has never been new to
us. We received an early impression, and since have ever felt, that
works more than mortals could perform had transpired there. But
who the workers could have been was long a doleful mystery.
Their doings made them far from pleasant objects of contemplation.
In common with most other natives of the place, we formerly were
very willing that the dark matter should slumber in obscurity —
were indisposed to draw attention to its aspects and character.

But not so in later years. Most people on the spot, however,
now are probably averse to its consideration. Less than three
years ago, a parish committee of arrangements were very solicitous
that this dismal subject should receive very little notice at their bi-
centennial celebration. Their wishes and ours differed widely.
What courtesy withheld them from forbidding, courtesy withheld
us from doing extensively. We just opened there; and now, in
continuance, here say that we longed then, on the spot where he was
born, to wash off from their most notorious child much black dye-
stuff in which the world has dipped him, and let them look upon a
fairer complexioned and more estimable personage than they have
deemed that far-famed native. We are vain enough to hope, that,
in this continuance of our speech, we shall adduce facts and views

which will present Salem witchcraft in new and less dismal aspects, and dispel what seems to dwellers where it transpired a "cloud of darkness." Aside from vanity, we have been moved by definite desire to give both the people of Danvers and many others, opportunity to learn facts and truths as yet perceived by only a few, which give a character to the great witchcraft scene, vastly less disreputable to those concerned in it than does such as has been presented by prior expounders, and extensively accepted as plausible by the public. Teachings of spiritualism have luminated the places where witchcraft has been sent to slumber; and facts now come into view which reveal beneficent results where none but baneful ones have been apparent. Perhaps willingness to show that spiritualism has been an illumining force to us, and may be so to others, has place among our motives.

Opportunities for studying spirit manifestations came in the writer's way more than twenty years since, and have been recurring quite steadily down to the present hour. Release, long ago, from cramping mill-horse rounds of professional life and thought, and consequent freedom to live and move relatively aloof from annoyances and fears which known or suspected attention to unpopular and tabooed matters is apt to bring, permitted him to be a more open, avowed, persistent, and studious observer of these marvelous works than could most other persons *comfortably*, who had spent early years in academic and collegiate halls. Unhampered by dread of slurs, innuendoes, hints, or growls from either parishioners, patients, or clients, he sought, found, and strove to use thoughtfully, critically, and religiously, extensive and many varied and often very favorable opportunities for estimating the force and value of alleged evidences and proofs that we, all of us, are ever living in the midst of agents, forces, conditions, faculties, powers, and susceptibilities, acting upon or residing in ourselves and our neighbors, which common observation and science have not generally recognized. Thus, as he judges, clews have been acquired to such knowl-

edge as promises, in days not distant, to furnish not only a solution
of ancient witchcraft that will stand the tests of time and common
sense, but cause human physical science to bring within its embrace
agents and forces which have heretofore escaped its recognition.
The varied phenomena of spiritualism, witchcraft, and miracle are
all *within* nature.

Modern spiritualism, fraught, and all alive, as it is, with evidences, and some sensible *proofs positive*, of a future life, is to-day
more efficient in retaining faith among thinking men that a life
beyond awaits them, than any and all other forces in operation, or
that man can apply.   Science — yes, an advanced *science*, based on
observed, proved, and provable facts of spiritualism, ancient and
modern — is the only power we see that can stay the hope-crushing
inroads of the bald materialism which is now dogging the advancing steps of physical science and liberal culture throughout enlightened Christendom.

Perception of strong indications, more than twenty years ago,
that keen intelligence wielding strange power was evolving before
human senses, raps, table-tippings, and the like, — which intelligence, if properly invoked and treated, might become one's helpful
teacher, — induced the author to use as well as possible each occurring opportunity for increasing his acquaintance with the strange
visitants, not doubting that in the end he should gain wherewith to
instruct and benefit both himself and his fellow-men, enough, and
more than enough, to richly compensate for whatever loss of caste,
favor, or reputation his course might occasion.   During his well-
meant, protracted, and reverential searchings along the faintly twi-
lighted borders of spirit-land, ever and anon he has been catching
glimpses of laws, forces, conditions, and agents, which earth-born
beings — the embodied and the disembodied — can, and limitedly
now do, conjointly use for reciprocal communings, and for mutual
helps toward improvement, elevation, and bliss — for social, intellectual, moral, and religious growth.   He means *mutual;* for those

who have escaped from the flesh are helped by intercommunings with mortals. The reward is ample.

His immediate topic is only witchcraft; but light which he seeks to make bear on that, penetrates below all perceptible phenomena, down to the question which underlies all others pertaining to man's highest interest, viz., Does *animism exist?* Or, in other words, is there in nature, or in God, or anywhere, an animating principle, which, having had individualizing connection with an organized material form, will retain its consciousness and individuality after that connection shall have been dissolved? Who but visible or audible spirits, proving themselves to be such, can give decisive response to that momentous question? Who but they can stop the advance of and effectually cripple that growing materialistic faith which laughs at and tramples over everything save *demonstration,*—demonstration either scientific or sensible,—but is at once and permanently palsied when it encounters that? Man knows of none else who can.

The world as yet is little conscious of the real nature, power, and worth of spiritualism, or of its own need of help obtainable from no other perceptible source. Therein lies enfolded not only charity and justice for our remoter fathers, and correction for later commentators upon them, which may be brought forth and applied in the present work, but also PROOFS of man's survival beyond the tomb.

Threescore years and twelve are saying, Spend no more time in general preparation for your labors, because dangers yearly thicken that your perishing outer man must forever leave undone what it fails to accomplish soon. Your future "footprints on the sands of time" will be but few; therefore now start in right direction, and, as best you can, mark the path you travel, and thus give some guidance to future wayfarers journeying toward the goal at which you aim, but lack power to reach.

.ALLEN PUTNAM.

Boston, 426 Dudley Street.

2

REFERENCES.

The principal works quoted from and referred to in the following pages, are —

Salem Witchcraft, edited by S. P. Fowler, of Danvers; H. P. Ives and A. A. Smith, Salem, 1861. This furnished the citations from Calef, and most of those from Cotton Mather. References are to this edition.

Hutchinson's History of Massachusetts. Boston edition 1764 and 1767.

Upham's History of Witchcraft and Salem Village. Boston, Wiggin & Lunt, 1867.

Woodward's Historical Series, embracing Annals of Witchcraft in New England by Samuel G. Drake, furnished the citations from Drake.

New England Genealogical and Antiquarian Register, October, 1870, p. 381, was the source of extracts from W. F. Poole.

EXPLANATORY NOTE.

A subject mysterious as ours will need for its ready comprehension some general knowledge of the imputed attributes and doings of witchcraft's special DEVIL, and of supposed aids and hindrances to his getting access to the visible world; also of demonology and necromancy, of biblical witch and witchcraft, of Protestant Christendom's witch and witchcraft, of spirit, soul, and mental powers, of miracle, spiritualism, Indian worship, and the like. Therefore we wrote out brief dissertations upon those subjects, with a view to have them constitute an opening chapter. But they are somewhat dry, and would, perhaps, keep many readers back from less thought-taxing pages longer than their pleasure will permit. Therefore we postpone presentation of what usually is placed in front, at the same time advising each one who desires to read this work as advantageously as possible, to turn first to our Appendix.

In form of definitions, at the close of the dissertations, we placed a summary of some past conceptions, designing thus to indicate, compactly, special stand-points for explanation of witchcraft, on which some of our predecessors have severally taken position. We insert it here.

DEFINITIONS.

Biblical.

DEVIL, or SATAN. Any opponent or antagonist, whether seen or unseen.

WITCH. Employer of mysterious acquisitions in teaching *heresy*.

WITCHCRAFT. Using mysterious acquisitions in teaching *heresy*.

21

By Cotton Mather.

DEVIL. Heaven-born, fallen, mighty, malignant; and yet *dependent on human help* to act upon physical man or anything material.

WITCH. A *covenanter* with the devil.

WITCHCRAFT. Helping or employing the devil to do harm—either.

By Robert Calef.

DEVIL. Heaven-born, fallen, mighty, malignant; but *independent of man* in action upon this world.

WITCH. Seducer of men from worship of God " *by any extraordinary sign.*"

WITCHCRAFT. "Maligning and impugning the word, work, or worship of God, and by any extraordinary sign seeking to seduce men from worship of Him."

By Thomas Hutchinson.

DEVIL. (None, as witchcraft enactor.)

WITCH. (*By inference.*) A woman possessing "a malignant touch," or "a crabbed temper," or being "a poor wretch" or "bed-ridden;" also, "a cunning child."

WITCHCRAFT. Producing "pains," "nausea," &c. Scolding, playing tricks.

By C. W. Upham.

DEVIL. (Not specially concerned in witchcraft.)

WITCH. (*By inference.*) Subject acted upon by a girl or woman trained in a school for practice "in the wonders of necromancy, magic, and spiritualism."

WITCHCRAFT. Suffering from the tricks and malicious purposes of girls schooled in magic.

By us.

DEVIL. (Not specially concerned.)

WITCH. A medium or a human being whose body becomes at times the tool of some finite, disembodied, intelligent being, or whose mind senses knowledge in spirit land.

WITCHCRAFT. The manifestation of supernal knowledge, force, and purposes through a borrowed or usurped mortal form; or the giving utterance to knowledge sensed in through one's spiritual organs of sense.

Our purpose is to adduce strong evidences from the primitiv records of American marvels, that lesser beings than the devil of Mather and Calef, and more powerful ones than the operators designated by Hutchinson and Upham, were actual performers of the principal manifestations that have been known as witchcrafts. Those whom we shall present were earth-born, on either this planet or some other, had previously passed out from encasements of flesh, but obtained control of and actuated physical forms belonging to embodied children, women, and men. Such beings, graduates from earths, are as varied in character and purposes as the survivors on their native planets, as varied as mortals are to-day. They may have ranged in character from dark devils up to bright angels, and have come, and gone, and operated by natural, though occult, forces and processes; they being as free to use such as we are the forces and implements of external nature. Many of our positions will be based upon psychological powers and susceptibilities which are far from being generally known to pertain to man; and we may fail to keep always within the bounds of things credible to-day, but yet shall never consciously go further than observed or credited facts will sustain us. If successful, we shall show that benighted man formerly, in good conscience, made certain events fearful curses, which, when rightly understood and used, may become gladdening and rich boons to mortals.

WITCHCRAFT MARVEL-WORKERS.

BRIEF notice of several authors to whom the present age is indebted for knowledge of most of the facts and beliefs which will be presented in the following pages, may be appropriate here. Their competency, traits, and circumstances, as inferred chiefly from their writings pertaining to witchcraft, are all, or nearly all, which we propose to state.

Two of these who lived in witchcraft times, a third in an intervening century, and a fourth in our own age, viz., Cotton Mather, Robert Calef, Thomas Hutchinson, and Charles W. Upham, will severally be noticed, because their works have been specially instructive and suggestive, and have had very much influence in shaping public opinions and conclusions in reference to the mysterious matters under consideration. Each of the above-named authors either lacked, or failed to use, some light which is now available for disclosing contents in vailed recesses of nature — light beginning to shine in where darkness long brooded, and to elicit thence such knowledge as promises to show that the theories of most witchcraft expounders have been such as now may be, and should be, superseded by more broad, sound, and philosophical ones.

25

The writings of the first two named above are eminently important, because they disclose very distinctly
many highly operative beliefs and methods which
were prevalent when marked witchcraft phenomena
were actually transpiring, but are obsolete now.   We
cannot, perhaps, do better than forthwith present
those two combatants, Mather and Calef, in actual
conflict over the last described case of seventeenth
century obsession.   Out of this case came open conflict in the very days when such marvels were living
occurrences.   Further on we may notice these two
men, *as men*, more particularly.   Here we take them
as contestants about phenomena attendant upon Margaret Rule in 1693; hers, the last of our cases to
occur, will come first under our inspection.   Our
quotations will be mostly from the earlier pages of
" SALEM WITCHCRAFT," edited by S. P. Fowler.

MATHER AND CALEF.

IN 1693, Mather wrote an account of afflictions
which Margaret Rule, of Boston, then about seventeen
years old, began to endure on the 10th of September
of that year.   This production drew forth the first
open shot at the then prevalent definitions of witchcraft — at the assumed source of power to produce
it — at the adopted methods of proceedings against
it, and at treatment of persons on whom that crime
was charged.   '
Robert Calef, called a merchant of the town, either
listened to statements or received written ones, made

by other persons who had been present with Mather
around this afflicted girl at her home during some
scenes which the latter had described, or he was himself a witness there. From data early obtained he
furnished a version of the case which disparaged
the minister's account, and questioned the propriety
of some of his proceedings. Calef's was in itself
a rather meager production, not putting forth the
whole or even the main facts in the case, but indicating that in this, that, and the other particular,
Mather had misstated or overstated, and that some
of his own acts might be indelicate or improper.
This production so incensed Mather that he openly
pronounced Calef "the worst of liars," threatened
him with prosecution for slander, and actually commenced legal proceedings against him.

In a subsequent letter, September 29, Calef re-
spectfully asked Mather for a personal interview in
the presence of two witnesses, in order that they
might discuss and explain. Mather intimated willingness to comply with the request, but dallied, till
Calef, November 24, sent a second letter, in which,
rising at once above the comparatively trifling question whether himself or Mather had furnished the
more accurate and better report, he grappled with
fundamental questions pertaining to the devil, witchcrafts, and possession, and set forth distinctly some
points which, in his judgment, needed discussion
then ; for on them he dissented from Mather, and
probably from a majority of the people amid whom
he was living. In much of that letter, Calef, or whoever composed it, manifested discriminating intellect,
clear perception of his points, firm will, together with

strong desire and purpose to labor earnestly for acquisition of knowledge by which either to convince
himself that his own positions were unsound, or to
better qualify himself to reform some prevalent faiths
and practices. The Bible was his magazine, and
implements, weapons, or stores from any other source
he deemed it unlawful to use for defining, detecting,
or punishing witchcraft. Bowing to the Scriptures
in unquestioning submission, he took them as guide
and authority. In the outset, frankly and definitely
stating his own belief, he, in an apparently manly
way, sought manly discussion.   .

He believed, page 62, that "there are *witches*,
*because the Scriptures plainly provide for their pun-
ishment.*" The only known definition of *witchcraft*
that to him seemed based upon and fairly deduced
from the Scriptures, was "a maligning and oppugning
the word, work, or worship of God, and, *by any extraordinary sign*, seeking to seduce from it." He believed
"that there are possessions, and that the bodies of the
possest have hence been not only *afflicted*, but *strangely
agitated*, if not *their tongues improved* to foretell futu-
rities; and why not *to accuse the innocent* as bewitching them? having *pretense to divination* . . . this
being reasonable to be expected from *him who is the
father of lies.*" This witchcraft assailant, therefore,
was a protestant not against belief that the father of
lies sometimes *possessed, afflicted, and strangely agitated human beings, and also controlled their tongues to
prophesy, to accuse the innocent, and to pretend divination.* His protest was against unscriptural definition
of witchcraft, and against those kinds of evidence,
rules, and methods used for its detection, proof, and

punishment which made his age pronounce guilty and
execute many who could not possibly be found guilty
of that crime, where its scriptural definition was adhered to. He was not a disbeliever in witchcraft of
some kind, nor of action upon men by some invisible
intelligences in his own day. He and Mather both
were believers in witchcraft outwrought by super-
nals, but differed as to what might or might not constitute it, and therefore, also, as to the extent of the
prevalence of the genuine, article. Calef seemingly
believed in *possessions*, — that is, in control by spirits of some quality, — but was unwilling to concede
that such control was *witchcraft*, as many people at
that day did, though Mather may not have been one
among them *abidingly*.

The pith of Calef's definition of witchcraft was,
*seduction of men from the worship of God by manifesta-
tion of extraordinary signs ;* while Mather said, *covenanting with the devil made one a witch*, and co-operative action with *him* in harming men constituted
witchcraft. The former demanded evidences of seduction of men away *from worship of God*, while the
other could rest on evidences of *visible harm to man ;*
therefore Mather found cases of witchcraft much more
abundant than Calef was required to or would.

Another practically important item on which they
differed was the immediate source of the devil's power
to act upon visible man and matter. Calef claimed that
" it is *only the Almighty* that . . . can commissionate ·
him to hurt or destroy any ; " while Mather said, " I
am apt to think that the devils are seldom able to hurt
us in any of our exterior concerns without a commission *from our fellow-worms*. . . . Permission from

God for the devil to come down and break in upon
mankind must oftentimes be accompanied with a
commission from *some of mankind itself.*"

Both of them conceded a commission by God to
the devil. But we doubt whether his commission
was ever more special than that which every created
being, in either material or spiritual abodes, constitutionally holds at all times, to avail himself of whatever natural laws or forces his inherent powers and
attending circumstances enable him to control. Words
are often used which obscure proper, if not intended,
meaning. Commission from God means no more than
constitutional capabilities to perform at times certain
specified things when conditions and circumstances
favor command of natural forces. That special powers are often conferred upon mortals by some supernal
beings whose recipients are prone to ascribe the gifts to
omnipotence is obviously true ; though their increased
abilities are only bestowments by finite invisibles.

What witchcraft was, and *who* commissioned the
devil, whether God alone or God and man jointly,
were the two most prominent questions about which
those contestants differed. They agreed that the
devil enacted both witchcraft and possession, but
Calef's beliefs necessarily caused him to regard vast
many cases as only simple possession, which Mather
could, if he saw fit, regard as witchcrafts ; and he
sometimes seemingly did, when called to act publicly
in connection with them. Mather at home and Mather abroad were not always in harmony.

Without designing, either here or subsequently, to
make full presentation of the case of Margaret Rule,
we shall freely adduce many parts of the record of it

as helps in exhibiting leading positions and traits pertaining to the parties who crossed intellectual swords over them.

Mather states, page 29, that "upon the Lord's day, September 10, 1693, Margaret Rule, after some hours of previous disturbance in the public assembly, fell into odd fits, which caused her friends to carry her home, where her fits, in a few hours, grew into a figure that satisfied the spectators of their being preternatural. A miserable woman who had been formerly imprisoned on the suspicion of witchcraft, and who had frequently cured very painful hurts, . . . had, the evening before Margaret fell into her calamities, *very bitterly treated her, and threatened her.*" That briefly antecedent treatment of her by a person who "had frequently cured very painful hurts," and therefore, and for other acts perhaps, been accused of witchcraft, is very important in its psychological indications, and is worthy of being borne along in the reader's memory. The wonderful *curing of painful hurts* — that is, her beneficence — had caused her imprisonment.

"The young woman," continues the reporter, "was assaulted by eight cruel specters, whereof she imagined that she knew three or four." She was careful, under charge from Mather, "to forbear blazing their names," but privately told them to him ; and he says, "they are a sort of wretches who for these many years have gone under *as violent presumptions of witchcraft*, as perhaps any creatures yet living on the earth." Specters known by her might, in some connections, mean persons whom she had known before their death, whose spirits now became visible ;

but since she gave the names of living persons as
being then seen, it is obvious that she did not regard
her tormentors *as bona fide spirits*, but only effigies
manufactured, presented, and vitalized by the devil.

The psychologist will not overlook the fact that
persons whose specters were here presented were
such as had in some way previously aroused suspicion that they were witches. It was imprudent
at that day to "blaze names," because of very prevalent belief that the devil could present the specters
of none who had not made a covenant with him, and
the bare fact of annunciation by a witched person
that she saw the specter of any individual whatsoever, was then conclusive proof to many minds that
the said individual had made covenant with the evil
one, and therefore was a witch, and must be put to
death.   Mather cautioned the girl not to give names
to the crowd around her bed, "lest any good person should come to suffer any blast of reputation."
Neither Mather nor Calef denied the devil's power to
bring forth apparitions of the *innocent;* and neither
reposed full confidence in or justified the use of
spectral testimony generally, though very many people in those days did.   The point we desire to mark
is this: that Mather's account is in harmony with
modern observation in giving indications that spirits,
apparitions, or appearances of highly mediumistic persons are more frequently seen than those of unim-
pressible ones — if such are not, and we believe it is
so — the class generally thus presented : — such persons, that is, the mediumistic, are more frequently
than others seen by the inner or clairvoyant eye.
This fact begets at least conjecture, that it is prob-

ably psychological law, and not the devil's or any
one's else *choice*, which determines who shall or may
be seen as specters. Persons seen in this case had
previously manifested powers or acts which caused
them to be regarded as witches. Around most persons, who in the sequel of these pages shall be found
appearing as specters and as bewitching and tormenting others, will be found signs that they were very
like such as to-day are called mediums.

"They presented a book and demanded of her
that she should set her hand to it, or touch it at least
with her hand, as a sign of her becoming a servant
of the devil;" upon her refusal to do that, they confined "her to her bed for just six weeks together."
True answer to the question whether an accused one
had signed the devil's book or not, was eagerly sought
for in all trials for witchcraft, because if such signature had not been made by the person on trial, he
or she *might* be innocent; while if it had been, guilt
was already consummated, and death was deserved.

"Sometimes there looked in upon the young woman
a short and a black man, whom they (the specters)
called their master. They all professed themselves
vassals of this devil, . . . and in obedience to him
. . . she was cruelly pinched with invisible hands, . . .
and the black and blue marks of the pinches became
immediately visible unto the standers by. . . . She
would every now and then be miserably hurt with
pins, which were found stuck into her neck, back, and
arms. . . . She would be strangely distorted in her
joints and thrown . . . into convulsions." Such things
are stated as facts, and were not contested in the day
of their occurrence — not even by Robert Calef.

" From the time that Margaret Rule first found her-self to be formally besieged by the specters, until the ninth day following, namely, from September 10th to the 18th, she kept an entire fast, and yet she was unto all appearance as fresh, as lively, as hearty at the nine days' end, as before they began ; during all this time . . . if any refreshment were brought unto her, her teeth would be set, and she would be thrown into many miseries ; indeed, once or twice or so in all this time, her tormentors permitted her to swallow a mouthful of somewhat that might increase her mis-eries, whereof a spoonful of rum was the most con-siderable ; but otherwise, as I said, her fast unto the ninth day was very extreme and rigid."

Protracted fastings without consequent exhaustion have been common with the mediumistic in all ages. Moses, Elijah, Jesus, each fasted forty days ; many mediums in our midst are often sustained for long periods by absorptions of nutriment in its elemental state into the inner or spirit organism, from that in-visible storehouse of food from which trees obtain much sustenance, and whence once came loaves and fishes in Judea ; from the inner thus fed, the outer man receives supplies ; at least, spirits state such to be the process.

" Margaret Rule once, in the middle of the night, la-mented sadly that the specters threatened the drown-ing of a young man in the neighborhood, whom she named unto the company ; well, it was afterward found that at that very time this young man, having been prest on board a man-of-war then in the harbor, was, out of some dissatisfaction, attempting to swim ashore ; and he had been drowned in the attempt if a boat had not seasonably taken him up. It was by computation a minute or two after the young woman's discourse of the drowning that the young man took to the water." This account, if taken literally, reveals her prescience of a definite approximating event, also knowledge of the person whom it threatened, the place where it would act, while neither outward perceptions nor any embodied mortals could help her to such knowledge. It is not stated that either the outer or inner set of her perceptive organs directly sensed danger tending towards the young man. The report of her words is that " the specters threatened the drowning ; " from this it seemingly follows that her inner sense, either of hearing or of vision, learned either the intention of spirit beings to purposely expose a particular man to danger, or they saw the oncoming of danger to him, and spoke of it to her.

This occurrence through the impressible girl was left unnoticed by Calef ; his silence approximates to concession that the main facts here stated were not refutable in his day.

" Once," continues the narrator, " her tormentors pulled her up to the ceiling of the chamber, and held her there, before a very numerous company of spectators, who found it as much as they could all do to pull her down again." That statement is distinct and needs no comment here, but may receive further notice when we shall adduce the attestation of other personal witnesses to its actual truth.

Again Mather says, " The enchanted people have talked much of a *white* spirit from whence they have received marvelous assistances, . . . by such a spirit

was Margaret Rule now visited. She says she never
could see his face, but that she had a frequent view
of his bright, shining, and glorious garments; he stood
by her bedside continually heartening and comforting
her, and counseling her to maintain her faith and
hope in God. . . . He told her that God had permitted her afflictions to befall her for the everlasting
and unspeakable good of her own soul, and for the
good of many others." Hers was very strange experience to outflow from *delirium tremens*. It seems to
us very much more like inflowings of heavenly peace
from vision of the blessed. Obviously at times there
flashed forth glorious brightness during witchcraft's
dismal night.

Mather stated these and some other very significant
facts, which Calef omitted to grapple with or to gainsay in his version of the scenes. Omitting to extract
more from Mather, we will now look at Calef's account. He commences a letter to Mather in which,
referring to his own previous production, he says,
" having written '*from the mouths of several persons*,'
who affirm they were present with Margaret Rule the
13th instant, her answers, behavior, &c." Calef
therefore probably was not himself a witness of the
scenes he described, but received his account from
the mouths of several other persons. One of them
apparently wrote, and Calef, adopting the statement,
says, " I found her of a healthy countenance, about
seventeen years old, lying very still and speaking but
very little." Soon the Mathers (father and son,
Increase and Cotton) came in. The son shortly
began to question Margaret and get replies. Their
colloquy was commonplace mostly, and need not be
quoted; but some things then *done* we shall notice.

Margaret went into a fit, and Cotton Mather " laid his hand upon her face and nose, but, as he said, without perceiving any breath. Then he brushed her on the face with his glove, and rubbed her stomach, and bid others do so too, and said it eased her ; then she revived." Shortly again she " was in a fit," and was again rubbed. " Margaret Perd, an attendant, assisted Mather in rubbing her. The afflicted spake angrily to her, saying, ' Don't you meddle with me,' and hastily put away her hand. He then wrought his fingers before her eyes."

Such things, presumably, were stated correctly as matters of fact observed. Were these doings by Mather foolish and useless? Different persons will answer variously. In the eyes of most New England people to-day, they may seem to be so. In part they appear to us ill judged and harmful, though well meant and partially productive of the effect desired. When Mather could perceive no breath, he naturally became solicitous to set her lungs in motion, and by his rubbings probably soon accomplished that. The observations of many moderns have taught them to welcome, at times, stoppage of the external breathings of good mediums, deeming that indicative of free, but imperceptible, breathing by the inner lungs, which process sustains the person physically, while the spirit roams and recreates in spirit-land. Yes, to *welcome* it, as watchers by the restless sick welcome the advent of sleep to the sufferers. Once we probably should have acted, in like circumstances, much as Mather did ; but now we might often leave such a patient unacted upon for a time, even though breathless to our external perception, because of belief that action like Math-

er's might be as unwise as would the awakening of a
sick one immediately after the commencement of a
nap. His motions of the fingers around her eyes
might tend to produce the same effect ; that is, to .
draw her out of a state of *rest* and joy, provided the
outer breathing was imperceptible. Rubbings and
motions of the hands, however, are often very serviceable in removing influences which are distressing,
whenever the entranced one is conscious externally, as
Margaret probably was in the *second* fit, but perhaps
not in the first. For in the second she detected difference between influences upon her from Mather and
those from Miss Perd ; the former were agreeable and
welcome, the latter annoying and offensive. Systems
sensitive enough to detect the qualities and influences
of magnetic emanations from all human beings, yes, all
animals and most minerals, that come in contact with
themselves, are greatly soothed by absorption of unconscious properties from some, and irritated by those
from others, though their esteem, respect, or affection
for each class be the same. Qualities of emanations
are, to considerable extent, independent of either intellectual, moral, or emotional states. A babe or
simpleton may be the best of anodynes, while the
cultured saint may be an irritant to a sensitive
medium.

" He put his hand on the clothes over her breast,
and said he felt a living thing." Perhaps he did.
In our day we hear of such presentations as semblances of small living animals around mediums ; but
personally, have not seen or felt such.

" Soon after they " (the ministers) " were gone,
the afflicted desired the *women* to be gone, saying that

the company of the *men* was not offensive to her."
There is not general popular knowledge, that the
magnetisms of all animals are as distinctly male in
one sex and female in the other, as are any of their
organs, nor that to very sensitive persons there come
times and states when their own magnetisms hunger
for food from magnetisms of opposite genders. Some
sensitives feel the action of finer laws and forces than
men detect in their normal condition.

" She learned that there were reports about town
that she was not afflicted. And some came to
her as spies ; but during the said time " (of their
visit) " she had no fit." Few anti-spiritualistic as-
severations are more frequently put forth than this ;
that manifestations rarely occur in the presence of
certain persons deemed specially competent to detect
fraud and imposture, and who visit mediums for the
purpose of exposing them. Unbelief was once a bar
to manifestation of many marvels by Jesus of Nazareth. Also it much obstructs their presentation to-
day ; and probably, therefore, might have done so
when emanating from spies and would-be exposers
around Margaret Rule. But " they can't," is perhaps
often said of spirits when " they won't," would more
accurately describe the fact. As at the Albion in
1857, they would manifest before press reporters,
but not before Harvard professors. They know the
thoughts of each observer, and are often pleased to
bite the biter ; the playfully roguish sometimes find
it fun to catch rogues. " She had no fit " when spies
were present.

" The attendants," September 19, " said that Mr.
M. would not go to prayer with her when people

were in the room, as they" (he and his father) " did that night he felt the *live creature*." Peter of old knew what was conducive to effectual prayer when, at the side of Dorcas, then entranced to seeming death, he " put the bystanders all forth and kneeled down and prayed." Mather no doubt had acquired similar knowledge ; world-wide experience and observation teach that quiet and harmony are needful to the utterance of satisfactory or very helpful prayer.

" Margaret Perd and another said they smelt brimstone. I and others," said Calef's informant, " *said* we did not smell any." The wording leaves it doubtful, perhaps, whether the reporter and his " others," though smelling brimstone, quizzically said they did *not*, or whether they actually failed to smell it. If they did not smell the article, their natural, frank statement would have been, *we did not*. But the wording is, " *we said* " we did not. Our quotation was not made, however, for the purpose of making such criticism, but as a text to the following paragraph.

Spirits sometimes have power to produce in the olfactory nerves of many persons, precisely the sensations which many familiar odors produce. We have personally been refreshed on several occasions by perception of the fragrance of pinks, while we were reclining drowsily on a couch in our own study, no visible person present with us, and no pinks in the vicinity, or in our thoughts. This has occurred quite as often in dead of winter, as when the garden was odorous with flowers. Probably such presentations may be made to some members of a company, while others in the crowd will be insensible to them.

One's non-perception of spirit-born odor, whether
coming from above or below, whether pleasurable
or offensive, does not argue that mere fancy alone
acts upon a neighbor who says he smells such.

On the evening of the 13th some one present, seemingly unacquainted with her habits, put either to a
particular person or to the whole company, this question. " What does she eat or drink ? " And, from
some unnamed source, came this response : " She does
not eat at all, but drinks *rum.*" Neither the question
nor the answer is ascribed to Mather, nor to any one
in particular.

We are surprised-that S. P. Fowler, the intelligent,
just, and charitable editor of Salem Witchcraft, said
in a foot note, page 57, that " the affliction of Margaret Rule . . . was nothing more than a bad case of
delirium tremens ; " statements indicative of her good
morals and habits previous to her affliction were right
before his editorial eyes on pages just preceding his
note, and nothing is found to her disparagement excepting that annunciation by some unknown body
that she drinks *rum.* Statements in her favor, and
absence of any against her in the original records,
convince us that Fowler's conclusion was rash and
not well founded. Mather says that " she was born
of sober and honest parents ; " also that it " is affirmed that for about half a year before her visitation
she was observably *improved in the hopeful symptoms
of a new creature :* she was become seriously concerned for the everlasting salvation of her soul, and
careful to avoid the snares of evil company." Habits
of that kind, during six preceding months, were not
probable antecedents to *delirium tremens ;* Calef's

temptations to have charged bad character for temperance, had there been facts to sustain him, were
probably very strong; but we have found no evidence
that he did so.   An informant of his, when reporting
conversation which took place around her, furnished
the question and response, viz. : " What does she eat or
drink ?   Answer.   She does not eat at all, but drinks
rum."   A fact stated by Mather himself naturally
might tempt any wag, inclined to create mirth, to say
playfully, " She eats nothing, but drinks *rum.*"   He,
Mather, informs us that " once, twice, or so " her
" controllers, for her annoyance or distress," allowed
her to take a *spoonful* of rum.   What more common
than for attendants to offer and urge upon a suffering and agonized person any stimulant or cordial at
hand ?   Nothing.   We will allow that Margaret did
take " once, twice, or so " a spoonful of rum ; but
nothing else that we meet with in the account of her,
gives the shadow of foundation for the charge of *delirium tremens.*   If the charge is true, *delirium tremens* in
that case worked wonders which it is not accustomed
to perform ; to tell correctly, when lying on a bed on
shore at night, that danger of drowning was then
about coming upon a particular young man away
down the harbor, was an extraordinary operation
for that disease to perform ; and still more extraordinary was it, that such disease lifted the body on
which it was feeding, up in horizontal position to the
ceiling overhead, held it there for minutes, and so
firmly that it took several men to pull it down.   Do
such feats bespeak their origin in *delirium tremens ?*
No.   Calling it a case of *delirium tremens* does nothing toward giving rational explanation of the marvels

attendant upon Margaret. *Rum* is the name of a
very unsafe guide, and the name, not the thing,
deluded the annotator to inferences useless, entirely
useless, as helps to explain such phenomena as he
was engaged in elucidating.

Any weakness, sin, or crime which was not charged
upon Margaret Rule by her cotemporaries, it is un-
charitable to allege unqualifiedly against her now, on
the sole basis that in her hours of suffering she drank
a few spoonfuls of rum ; and is especially inapropos,
when, as is the case here, the charge gives no help
toward accomplishing the very purpose for which
alone it should have been made, namely, as an elucidation of the cause of such things as how she sensed
the danger threatening the absent man, and how or
by whom she was lifted up and sustained.

We shall quote no further from the statements of
the two parties, Mather and Calef, made prior to
their coming into distinct conflict. Enough has been
presented to show that Mather stated several facts
which, to the mass of men, must seem astounding —
such facts as bespeak performances beyond what embodied men could enact. The wondrous facts, such
as her prophecy of danger about to wait upon the
impressed sailor — her long fast without pining — her
being lifted by invisible force to the ceiling above
her, &c., constitute the important parts of Mather's
narrative of what he personally witnessed and knew.
On the other side, Calef, adopting the account of unnamed witnesses, omits any allusion to the important
facts in the case, and presents, in the main, different,
and relatively, if not absolutely, trifling accompani-
ments. Calef was complained of by Mather for *omis-*

sions. To this Calef replied, " My intelligence not
giving me any further, I could not insert that I knew
not." The doings of the Mathers, and especially of
Cotton, much more than the manifestations through
and upon Margaret, were detailed to Calef, and caused
him to put forth a very meager and one-sided manuscript account of this case. The clergyman at once
perceived and felt this, and soon sent his opponent
the following affidavits:—

" I do testify that I have seen Margaret Rule in
her afflictions from the invisible world, lifted up from
her bed, wholly by an invisible force, a great way
toward the top of the room where she lay. In her
being so lifted she had no assistance from any use of
her own arms or hands or any other part of her
body, not so much as her heels touching her bed,
or resting on any support whatsoever. And I have
seen her thus lifted, when not only a strong person
hath thrown his whole weight across her to pull her
down, but several other persons have endeavored with
all their might to hinder her from being so raised up ;
which I suppose that several others will testify as
well as myself when called unto it.
    " Witness my hand,   SAMUEL AVIS."

To the substance of the above, Robert Earle, John
Wilkins, and Daniel Wilkins did subscribe that they
could testify. Also Thomas Thornton and William
Hudson testified to having seen Margaret so lifted up
" by an invisible force . . . as to touch the garret floor,
while yet neither her feet nor any other part of her
body rested either on the bed or on any other support,
. . . and all this for a considerable while : we judged
it several minutes." — p. 76.

Before presenting the merchant's comments upon such statements of such facts, we will name again the special reason why we draw protracted attention to the two writers, Mather and Calef. They were intelligent and alert cotemporaries, both in the vigor of manhood probably, for Mather was about thirty years of age, and Calef lived more than twenty-five years after the commencement of his controversy; both probably were cognizant of the main facts pertaining to witchcraft, even during or very shortly after their occurrence in the family of John Goodwin of Boston in 1688, in Salem 1692, and around both Mercy Short and Margaret Rule in Boston 1693. Therefore the controversial writings of these two, both well acquainted with the occurring witchcraft events of their day, but differing distinctly on many points of belief and policy, become, when used in connection, our best accessible source for learning what actually occurred in many witchcraft scenes, what beliefs were prevalent then, what kinds of evidence for convicting of witchcraft were admissible, and what rules governed the courts. Because of their value as teachers upon witchcraft, we desire to have these two men, with their agreements and differings, clearly comprehended.

The merchant sent to the clergyman the following comment upon the chief point confirmed by the affidavits of five or six unimpeached witnesses, viz., the lifting of the girl to the top of the room by invisible power : —

"I suppose you expect I should believe it, and if so, the only advantage gained is, that what has so long been controverted between Protestants and

Papists, *whether miracles are ceast*, will hereby seem
to be decided for the latter ; it being, for aught I can
see, if so, as true a *miracle* as for iron to swim ; and
the devil can work such miracles."

A statement either more aspersive of its author's
own candor, or more indicative of his thralldom to
prejudice, has rarely been made. Either Calef or some
one for him, when treating of the departure of the
community from scriptural interpretation and treatment of witchcraft, when scanning rules laid down
by accredited authors for its detection, and, generally,
when handling creeds, broad principles, and prevalent
usages, wielded a clear, pointed, and forceful pen.
But Mather's facts blunted its point and baffled its
powers. Look at their metamorphosis of the logi-
cian ; he says, essentially, to his opponent, " If your
facts are true, Catholics have the better of us in our
controversy with them as to the continuance of miracles down to the present day. Your facts, if facts,
are miracles, and we Protestants are wrong. Therefore I will not concede them : if true, they are " as
great a miracle as for iron to swim," and prove the
Catholics right. I won't grant them."

What miracle did he concede that the devil can
work ? Was it causing iron to swim ? or was it such
lifting of Margaret Rule as had been sworn to ? Perhaps we are mistaken, but we think he meant to say
that the devil could lift the girl as described ; who,
if he had done so, wrought as great a miracle as God
did when he caused the ax-head to swim where the
prophet cast a stick over it. Still such an operation
in modern times must not be avowed, because that
would give the Catholic advantage over the Protes-

tant! Alas for the clear-headed man when facts
force him to abandon the methods of logic, and resort to those of prejudice! Mather's facts completely
stultified Calef in this case.

We cannot doubt—and who will venture to?—that
he must have known the characters for truth and veracity of Avis and his associate witnesses; must have
known the circumstances surrounding, and the state of
the public mind in regard to them; and yet we notice
no indication that he attempted to impeach any of
them even in thought. He leaves them entirely unnoticed. Yes, where even a very slight intimation or
covert innuendo in some turn of expression pointing
at either credulity or mental weakness on their part
would have been an argument in favor of his views,
nothing of the kind appears in his writings. He
leaves them without characterization — leaves them
unnamed. And since he who obviously must have
known them, and known too how they were generally
esteemed, left their veracity and competency entirely
unimpeached, when impeachment would have been his
natural resort, if justifiable, — only blinding, rash, very
rash, prejudice will prompt any one at this day to
doubt their fair claim to be regarded as truthful and
competent witnesses. Mather had said that "once
her tormentors pulled her up to the ceiling of the
chamber, and held her there before a numerous company of spectators, who found it as much as they
could all do to pull her down again." Such was the
published statement of a learned and able man, much
respected by a large portion of the inhabitants of
Boston, and whose incredulity was not strong enough
to make him distrust the distinct testimony of his

own senses. Therefore, though backed by the testimony of six other witnesses, he is deemed so credulous by many moderns that his word has little weight
with them. Calef's comments upon the case are
jumbled, and not such that we can place much confidence in the accuracy of our own perception of his
meaning; but he seems to have conceded that the
devil possessed power enough to have lifted the girl,
and leaves us privileged to infer his belief in its possible exercise upon her. That generally clear-headed
man's illogical and confused statement is not the least
among marvels attendant upon witchcraft. He murdered logic when attempting to parry the force of facts
sworn to.

He did not impeach the witnesses. Omission to
do that, under the circumstances, argues more convincingly to us, in favor of the literal and exact truth
of the statement by Mather and six others, that the
girl was raised from her bed by invisible powers up
to the ceiling at the top of the room, than would
Calef's own distinct assent to what they affirmed.
He was no *timid* advocate, and since a man as strong
and brave as he, circumstanced as he was, omitted
attempt to discredit either the character or competency of Mather's backers, the presumption is, that
Calef's own sense of justice and the judgment of the
town regarded them as unimpeachable. The girl was
lifted, as they affirmed. What they stated is credible.

We, personally, possess lack of incredulity rivalling
that of Mather. For, when our own senses testify to
us calmly and deliberately, under circumstances which
exclude both illusion and delusion, we are accustomed
to repose very much confidence in the truth and

accuracy of what they say ; and, in illustration of our lack of incredulity regarding what our own senses witness, or, if one prefers different phraseology, in illustration of our credulity, that is, of our ability and willingness to believe what is thus learned, we give the following account of one of our own interesting and instructive experiences : —

Several years ago, from fifteen to twenty, in a chamber of the residence of Daniel Farrar, Esq., Hancock Street, Boston, to which he had invited us and several others, we clasped the left hand of Rollin H. Squires in our own right, took position with him in the center of a large room, several feet distant from any other person or any article of furniture, when, promptly upon shutting off the gas-light, his hand began to draw ours up, gently and steadily, till our own right arm, its hand clasping his, was extended to its full length above our head. Then we moved our left hand across our chest, and it came in contact with the young man's boot at rest by our side, and simultaneously we heard a scratch upon the ceiling above, which was at least ten feet from the floor of the room. Soon he began to descend as gently as he had ascended, and when he had reached the floor and light had been let on, we saw a red chalk-mark at least three feet long on the ceiling over the spot on which we had stood up together. The mark was not there previous to the extinguishment of the light, for the whole company present had been informed that he would have chalk in his hand in order that he might give evidence to all present that he had been lifted up. Consequently all of us carefully observed the overhead ceiling up to the extinguishment of the light.

No reluctance attends our publishing such a narra· tive ; we are less solicitous to win a skeptic's laurels, than to make distinct statement of any facts pertain- ing to occult forces in nature, which we have exper- imentally learned. O, credulity! Thou art a most beneficent helper to knowledge of nature's finer laws and forces, especially of those relatively occult ones which evolve mysteries and exert unrecognized action upon man ; laws and forces which it would benefit him to comprehend and regard.

Scarcely can history or experience furnish a more striking instance of the stultifying and bewildering influence of marvelous *facts* upon a bright, resolute, philanthropic man, who was kept by his creeds and prejudices from liberty and ability to let reason and logic have fair play, than was witnessed in the case . of Calef. Facts are man's masters ; rebellion against them, or disregard of their demands, is sure to bring humiliation upon him.

Calef, whether conscious of it or not, was in an humiliated mental condition when his strong mind, without denying well-attested facts, indicated an un- willingness to acknowledge belief of them, because doing so would settle a long-controverted question adversely to the party which included himself. Seem- ingly nonplused and bewildered by facts, he said, in quasi-concession of their occurrence, "The devil can work such miracles."

Both what Calef said, and what he omitted to say, tend forcibly to produce conviction that Samuel Avis and his five associate witnesses stated "truth, and nothing but the truth." Words or statements from men whose characters were not impeached by a contesting cotemporary, ought to be accepted as true by those who now can know nothing against the truthfulness of lips from which they issued.

Had Calef's mind embraced perception that those whom he and nearly all others then deemed the great devil, and smaller ones, — heaven-born, but fallen, — were in fact what all clairvoyants, then and in all subsequent days, have said they resembled, — and what they claimed to be, — that is, men and women originally earth-born, and then earth-emancipated spirits, requiring no more special permission from the Omnipotent One than man does for using the forces of external nature, — could he have perceived that such beings might be the performers of all the marvelous works of witchcraft, he would have become free to admit possible solidity in some Catholic ground ; free to have set at least one foot upon it, and having done that, he could have dispensed with that heaven-born devil whom he supposed God commissioned, but whom Mather believed man had to help God commission before he could harass mankind ; would have been free to do thus because he then would have seen possibility that other, lesser, or less formidable agents have power to work marvels, would have seen that such could have lifted Margaret Rule, and thus made the words of those who described their wonderful works credible, and exempted himself from attack of Mather at points where the striker was greatest sufferer from the blows.

When attacking some barbarous beliefs and customs of Christendom, Calef was very successful, and became a very great public benefactor ; but he failed, if such was ever his design, to refute the positive occurrence

4

of such marvelous facts as Mather's descriptions set
forth. The general accuracy of the clergyman's allegations was not made questionable by the merchant's
writings, even though he did present the man himself
in some ludicrous aspects, and often attempted that,
when more knowledge of spirit forces and agents than
he possessed would have taught him that future time
might smile at the smiler and the would-be provoker
of smiles.

COTTON MATHER.

THE phases in which the writings of Cotton Mather
present their author are so varied, and the estimation
in which he has been held by subsequent writers is so
diverse, that there is difficulty in characterizing him
to one's own satisfaction. He was neither wholly
saint, nor wholly sinner ; was not unmingled wisdom,
nor all folly. We do not very eagerly undertake to
outline his character. But since, apart from records
of courts, his pen furnished more valuable and more
numerous facts pertaining to New England witchcraft in the seventeenth century than have come
down from any other pen, there seems to be a call
upon us to comment upon his competency and trustworthiness as observer and as reporter or recorder of
facts.

In matured life he had become probably the first
scholar and most learned man in the province. His
mind was bright, versatile, and active, and its application to books, to the demands of his profession,
and to the educational, moral, religious, and political

interests of the public,. was untiring. His attention
was drawn to consideration of marvelous occurrences
while he was quite young, and his records of witchcraft
were nearly *all* penned by the time he was thirty years
old. In 1689, being then only twenty-six, he published a small work entitled " Memorable Providences
relating to Witchcraft and Possessions."

He was a personal witness and an alert observer,
through several successive months, of a rapid and
prolonged stream of marvels, which were manifested
through the children of John Goodwin, of Boston, in
1688, a long account of which he published quite
soon after their occurrence. Four years later came
on the SALEM WITCHCRAFT, and portions of its
tragic and agonizing occurrences were witnessed by
this Boston clergyman. He was present in the crowd
around the gallows when several of the wronged victims to diabolism were executed. And he promptly
furnished an extended account of much which had
just intensely agitated and frenzied not only Salem
and Essex County, but the whole province. The
next year, 1693, brought him opportunity to be much
with and to observe carefully two afflicted young
women in Boston, Mercy Short and Margaret Rule,
whose maladies were deemed bewitchments. He recorded his observations and doings relating to these
two persons, and his accounts are available to-day,
though there is evidence rendering it probable that
he never prepared either record for the press, and
that both have become public without his sanction.

As has been learned from what precedes, Robert
Calef, an opponent of some then prevalent beliefs
and practices concerning witchcraft, found means,

whether honorably or not is perhaps debatable, for putting Mather's account of Margaret Rule before the world. This young woman was under Mather's special watch for several weeks, while she was being acted upon by occult agents and forces; and he promptly recorded for perusal by his friends an account of what transpired around her.

From the foregoing statements it is obvious that, both directly and indirectly, very many facts and opinions, that will be adduced as our work proceeds, will have been derived from Mather's records, and will rest, at least in part, upon his authority. Consequently, his qualifications, as observer, reporter, and recorder, are matters not only of interest, but of some importance.

Though young when attentive to witchcraft scenes, Mather was learned and influential. Probably few other persons, if any, in the colonies were then his equals in those respects. His duties as a clergyman and a citizen, and his inclination also, led him to be an extensive observer of marvelous manifestations; he obviously was a lover of such. And his records show that he was either a closer observer of the minutiæ of transpiring events of that nature, or a more willing and careful specifier of little things pertaining to them, full of important meaning to some readers now, yet probably meaningless to many others, than were most of his cotemporaries; though Lawson, Hale, and Willard were good at specification, and were more cautious commentators than Mather. An ignoring of any participation by spirits in witchcraft scenes has blinded historians in both the eighteenth and nineteenth centuries to some decided merits in the writings of Mather.

The assumption by later commentators that no occurrences whatsoever, which required more than mortal
agency for their production, ever actually transpired
in cases witnessed and described by Mather, has apparently caused them, consciously or otherwise, to
impute to his fancy, credulity, or other untrust-
worthy attributes, many things which a moderate
acquaintance on their part with modern manipulations of occult forces by invisible intelligences
would have suggested to them that possibly, and even
probably, his statements of facts were based on positive observations by his own physical senses, and by
the external senses of other observers. A class of
agents are now at work whose cognition may some
day turn the laugh upon overweeningly wise laugh-
ers at Cotton Mather. This circumscribed view as
to the actual extent and variety of *natural* intelligent agents, and *natural* laws and forces, has caused
them to draw inferences disparaging to Mather's
accuracy in places where more knowledge of the
outworkings of laws and forces which spirits obey
and use, would have given them trust in the essential naturalness and consequent probable occurrence
of nearly or quite all the facts stated in his narrative of personal observations and experiences — we
do not say in the pervading wisdom and value of his
comments and inferences, but in the naturalness and
consequent credibility of his *facts*.

Where forlorn and wretched old women, together
with tricksy and roguish girls, and a few low-lived,
malicious mortals of both sexes are regarded as the
actual authors of all witchcraft phenomena, Mather's
reports of that class of occurrences are an offense —

are a stumbling-block in the pathway of satisfactory solution. So long as his statements are left unimpeached, such agents as witchcraft has of late been imputed to are incompetent to the work ascribed to them. That author, therefore, must needs be discredited; consequently sneer, and slur, and ridicule have been brought to bear against his accuracy and trustworthiness. Some modern commentators have made *savage* use of such weapons upon this original describer of witchcraft scenes. He has been by innuendoes caricatured and metamorphosed to an extent which seems distinctly reprehensible. Brightest minds may sometimes lack knowledge of some existing agents and forces; good men may be actual, though unintentional perpetrators of great wrong, when they depict the characters of some predecessors whose words seem extravagant to such as limit natural actors and forces to those which the external senses and human science have long been familiar with.

Our recent readings have led us to regard Mather as a man of more than common efficiency in acquiring information, and more than common despatch in putting his acquisitions before the public. We find evidences in his works that, if he did not acquire, he put forth both more minute and more extensive knowledge of the marvelous phenomena of his times, than any other person then living in America of whom we have knowledge. Portions of his creeds helped him to frankness in description of marvels. His faith embraced many unseen intelligent agents, both good and bad, moving to and fro among men, ever walking the earth and influencing its affairs both " when we wake

and when we sleep." Consequently he never had
occasion to inquire whether anything whatsoever was
possible which his senses or the senses of other witnesses seemed to cognize. He doubted not that unseen powers competent to anything whatsoever were
around both him and all other human beings. His only
question was, did the thing occur? If it did, it was
proper to describe it as it appeared to its beholders.
How it could occur was a question which he, as
recorder, was not called upon to answer; and he
did not permit it to modify his record. This weakness (?) of his was fraught with latent strength which
becomes beneficent in our day by its revealing to
us the former mysterious irruption upon society of
precisely such *outré* and seemingly unnatural antics
and doings, not only of animated human forms, but
of lifeless household utensils and ornaments, as we
are witnessing. History by him repeats itself to-
day, and to-day's marvels give credibility to his
statements. Mather furnished broader and better
bases for judging of the real sources, nature, character, and extent of witchcraft facts, than we generally get from other persons of his day. Over-
cautious witnesses and reporters often mislead very
widely by failing to tell "the whole truth."

Some of Mather's statements and doings which were
slurred even by his cotemporary Calef, and have been
by later writers also, may deserve more respectful
consideration than has usually been accorded to them.
We are alluding to his manipulations of the afflicted,
and other like acts. These indicate that either his
observances and care of bewitched persons, or his
intuitions, were giving him hints of the existence

of natural laws and special conditions which permit mortals to loose, what he conceived to be, — or at least spoke of as being, — the devil's hold upon human instruments. We apprehend that he had at least vague surmises that some things which we now call mesmeric passes and psychological forces might be so applied by himself as to thwart the purposes and powers of possessing spirits. We are ready to grant that his use of dawning knowledge or of inflowed suggestions, whichever of them it was that set his own hands in motion over the obsessed, and prompted him to influence others to do the like, produced movements so unskillful that they were seldom very efficacious; yet we perceive that he moved in direction toward later discoveries which at this day enable many mortals to exercise much power toward both inducing and abolishing the control of human beings by disembodied spirits. There hang about Mather slight indications that he received some knowledge or some impulses, mediumistically, impressionally, or intuitively. The fact that, though having much to do with both Mercy Short and Margaret Rule during the months of their affliction in the year immediately following the executions at Salem, he refrained from advising or procuring their prosecution, or the prosecution of any whom they named as their afflictors, the facts that prayers, fastings, manipulations, and protracted and unflagging kindnesses and attentions, were his only appliances, and that both the girls were brought back to their normal condition, speak very distinctly in favor of Mather's sagacity and philanthropy, in relation to the bewitched and the bewitchers, that year.

Though we are disposed to credit this prominent man with all the merits to which he has fair claim, we are far from regarding him as without foibles, weaknesses, and traits fitted to mantle the reader's face with smiles. We dissent from many of his notions, practices, and beliefs; we find him often swayed by motives which we are not ready to commend. At the same time we apprehend that many modern critics have paraded his weaknesses, blemishes, and laughable traits out of all just proportion to the notices, if any, which they have taken of his genuine merits.

Mather obviously was vain, egotistical, proud of his descent, greedy of the favor of great men both of the province and abroad, and was ambitious of place and influence. But vanity and egotism are not necessarily incompatible with very extensive learning, nor with great activity and beneficence, nor with presentation of facts and truths both very fully and without over-statement or distortion. He wrote hastily — much too hastily, and loosely oftentimes. More care to verify information and statements furnished him by other people, and more careful expressions pertaining to his own observations, experiences, and opinions, would have rendered him a much more valuable historian than he became. We concede that he was a loose and immethodical writer; but we fail to find evidence that he often, if ever, substituted fictions for facts, or made false statements or great exaggerations. The world is indebted to him for preserving and transmitting much valuable information.

This man's estimation of himself and of his ances-

try often reveals itself in extent and manner which
provoke smiles. Possibly his egotism was competent
to give him a latent notion that quite as much favor
might be. vouchsafed by powers above to his two
eminent grandfathers, Revs. Richard Mather and
John Cotton, to his father, Rev. Increase Mather,
President of Harvard College, and to himself, as
Heaven had in store for. any mortals; and if any
one of the four should be the special favorite of
supernal intelligence, why not himself, in whom the
blood of the other three was combined? If any
quite honorable public position was devoid of an incumbent, or if important literary public service was
needed, who was more competent to fill the one, or
to the performance of the other, than himself? He
wrote both for and of Sir William Phips, but was
not chosen President of Harvard College..

Even egregious egotism is not necessarily incongruous with truth, kindness, charity, devotion, and
great usefulness. With all his faults, we regard
Mather, when compared with most men, as having
been very efficient, well-intentioned, and useful to
the community around him. Propensity to magnify
self and whatever self either puts forth or is closely
allied to, may be prevailingly bridled and controlled
by other strong inclinations, and kept within the
boundaries of truth. Greed for approbation and
commendation by persons holding high official position, and by all others whose characters, attainments,
or possessions gave them influence in society, was
apparently very strong in Cotton Mather, and the
influence of that greed must generally have swayed
him to make no important statements which would

fail to meet with general credence by his friends and fellow-townsmen. His account of the Goodwin family is as full of things hard to be believed as any other portion of his writings; and yet, if he therein permitted himself to make any other than such statements as would receive ready credence by many physicians, clergymen, magistrates, and other influential and truthful persons who had been his fellow-witnesses, and knew exactly the bounds beyond which he could not go on a basis of well-observed facts, he would diminish his fame and favor with the public; and he well knew this. He was not the man to thus put his own reputation at hazard. His very weaknesses render it probable that he has transmitted little, if anything, more relating to that family than Boston, as a whole, was at that time actually believing had just occurred in its midst. It is not wise, not kind, not just to overlook such characteristics and circumstances pertaining to a narrator as would naturally hold his speech within the bounds of credibility. Mather's style and manner, sometimes admirable, are very often' laughable, and are generally loose and unattractive. But these matters of taste and polish are distinct from his facts and truthfulness.

Bad manners, lack of tact, also speech, acts, and omissions unbecoming the gentleman and the divine, mark portions of Mather's treatment of Calef. Whether such were his general characteristics, we do not know; probably they were not. Occupation of the pulpit, as we know by personal experience, may make a preacher exceedingly sensitive to questionings of his opinions on any important matters anywhere. His habit of speaking, week after week, year after year, where none question or controvert, induces extreme sensitiveness in the mental cuticle. If sick and over-worked, Mather may have been easily nettled into other than his usual manners when Calef pricked him by opposing his beliefs, and by covert sneers at some of his actions. In his account of Mercy Short he mentions his impaired health and over-workings.

Unfortunately, as we judge, for his posthumous reputation, Mather was scribe of a convention of clergymen who met and deliberately put forth advice to the courts and government pertaining to evidence and processes which might properly be used at trials for the crime of witchcraft. As scribe, Mather re-duced the opinions of the convention to form for publication, if he had not previously drawn up his own, and at the meeting obtained their adoption. Since the advice of this convention has been exten-sively regarded as disastrous in its results, Mather has been deemed an efficient, if not the most efficient of all promoters of the executions at Salem. We seriously question the justice of such imputation upon him, and we doubt whether the advice of the con-vention incited to the special course of action pur-sued by the courts, though it partially permitted it, perhaps. That advice commended " a very critical. and exquisite caution . . . *that there may be nothing used as a test for the trial of the suspected, the lawful-ness whereof may be doubted by the people of God.*" So far, good. This, to us at this day, looks like a caution to avoid the admission of *spectral evidence*, as it was then called, and distinct statement is made

that such evidence alone was not enough to justify
conviction ; also it looks like a caution against cruel
methods of extorting pleas and confessions. But
the concluding paragraph of their advice, which is
in the following words, *may* have greatly nullified
the softening force of all that preceded it. „ " We
cannot but humbly recommend unto the government the speedy and vigorous prosecution of such
as have rendered themselves obnoxious, according to
the directions given in the laws of God and wholesome statutes of the English nation, for the detection of witchcraft." This advice came forth June
15, 1692, just when the flames of witchcraft at Salem
village had become alarming to the whole community ; when scores of people were under arrest there
upon suspicion of witchcraft, and when the courts
were anxiously seeking to know how to conduct their
trials. The advice seems to us somewhat ambidexter,
holding forth in one hand exhortations to caution and
leniency, and in the other an exhortation to make
vigorous and prompt application of English witchcraft laws and usages which permitted and implied
resort to most barbarous processes, and admitted all
imaginable sorts of evidence. The general impression upon our mind, made by our recent readings,
is, that the clergy generally were opposed to much
reliance upon spectral evidence, and that their advice
was meant to give that impression ; while the civil
magistrates at Salem held a different opinion, acted
according to it, and obtained convictions upon spectral evidence in cases where none other was attainable. It was the civil magistrates, much more than
the clergy, whose opinions, when embodied in action,

outwrought the horrors of Gallows Hill. Therefore we attach less blame to the scribe of the convention, and to the convention itself, than many others have done.

Though the belief is wide-spread in the youthful mind of our day that Cotton Mather was chief begetter of Salem witchcraft, we find no facts to justify belief that any act of his ever had such intent. His chief acts known to us which connect him at all with doings there, were his authorship of the clerical advice just noticed, his presence at the hanging when Proctor, Willard, Burroughs, and others were executed, when he said aloud to the multitude which was being melted by a fervent and touching address from the lips of the doomed Burroughs, " Even the devil may be changed into an angel of light," and his offer to support five or six of the afflicted at his own expense for weeks, provided he should be allowed to treat them by his own preferred process — that of praying and fasting, and keeping them mostly secluded from public observation.

Unexplained, his presence at the execution may be supposed to argue that it was one which had attractions for him — one which it was his pleasure to be present at. But a very rational supposition of Poole places Mather before us there in a different light. Proctor and others had been hardly dealt with by the clergy in and near Salem, and, while confined in Boston jail awaiting the day of execution, they received such attentions from Mather, that they requested him to be present as their spiritual adviser at the closing hour of their earthly lives. Statements by Mather, which his cotempo-

raries never contradicted, are to the effect that he
never attended any trial for witchcraft, that no one
was ever prosecuted for that crime by him, or at
his suggestion, or by his advice ; that his voice and
intentional influence were ever against such proceedings. He also informs us that he made an offer
to support five or six of the Salem sufferers for weeks
at his own expense, if he could have them subjected
to his special charge, so that he could treat them by
methods of his own. Such facts surely indicate that
an ardent and active man like him, ever burning to
take part in most popular movements, was not in
sympathy with originators of the violent and barbarous proceedings which were prosecuted at Salem.
Had he relished them he would have been present at
the trials. The facts give spontaneous birth to a
presumption that some other motive than curiosity to
witness the executions took him to Salem at the time
when we find him there, and the supposition of Poole
that he went there as the comforter and friend of
Proctor and Willard is reasonable, and probably correct. If it be, the motive of his visit was not only
commendable, but was also in harmony with his general doings in witchcraft cases that were more specially
under his supervision, and is in distinct antagonism
with motives which have been extensively imputed
to him. We apprehend, however, that when others
obtained convictions and sentences for witchcraft, he
favored the execution of what he deemed wholesome law.

We regret that he rudely broke the spell which
the hallowing speech and prayer of the saintly Burroughs were bringing upon the witnessing crowd.

But we question whether the special reputed crime for which Burroughs was about to die, caused Mather to allude to him as the *devil*. Burroughs, though a preacher, had not been regularly ordained, or surely not in a way that satisfied Mather; also he was too regardless of the ordinances of religion, and too free a thinker, to suit the taste of the pastor of the North Church in Boston. This was, we think, his great offense in Mather's view; and this caused the latter to say in reference to one who may have been more God-like and Christ-like in spirit than himself, " Even the devil may be changed into an angel of light." That saying, under its circumstances, is damaging to Mather; yet it does not bear against him in matters pertaining to witchcraft, but to those of sectarianism or bigotry.

Mather the *humane* and Mather the *fame-seeker* present very different aspects in their connections with witchcraft. As we view him in cases where he was leader and director, as those of Mercy Short and Margaret Rule, matters were so managed that no one was brought to examination upon suspicion of bewitching them, and Mather's words and acts were uniformly designed to prevent any arraignment. Prayer, fastings, manipulations, and all practicable privacy and quiet were his preferred appliances for closing up the devil's avenues of access, and of barring him off from man. This was Mather the *humane*, was Mather the *practical pastor*. But when the courts and men of influence and high position had applied, as they interpreted them, " the laws of God and the wholesome statutes of the English nation for the detection of witchcraft," the thirster for public

approbation, not only refrained from protest against
bloodshed, but lacked modesty enough to hold him
back from hinting that his own productions might
have helped on the beneficent work which had been
accomplished; for he carefully let the world know
that Mr. *Mather, the younger*, drew up the advice
of the ministers to the court; and after having written out an account of the trials at Salem, he said,
" I shall rejoice that God is glorified, if the publication of these trials may promote such a pious
thankfulness to God *for justice being so far executed
among us*," as the ministers piously expressed in
their advice. This was Mather the fame-seeker,
the ecclesiastic, and the subject of their Majesties,
William and Mary. Mather was not a well-balanced
man. Consistency all round was not conspicuous in
him, yet he was consistent in his own treatment
and management of all his special patients, and also
in his efforts to make it known that himself might
deserve some meed of merit for the murderous course
pursued by the authorities for stopping the ravages
of the evil one.

From early manhood to the close of his life, Mather
was an unfaltering believer in Protestant Christendom's great witchcraft devil, backed by countless
hosts of lesser ones, and he also believed in her
special witchcraft. He had full faith in a devil as
ubiquitous, active, and malignant as his own vigorous and expansive intellect could conjure up; had
faith that extra manifestations of afflictive might,
of knowledge, or of suffering in the outer world were
produced by the devil, and faith also that even that
mighty evil one was unable to afflict men outwardly,

5

excepting either at the call or by the aid of some
human servant who had entered into a covenant
with his Black Majesty. The woe-working points
of this man's faith were, that special covenantings
with the devil were entered into by human beings,
in consequence of which the covenanting mortals
became witches — that is, they thence became able
to command all his powers, as well as he theirs; also
that only through such covenanted ones could he
or his do harm to the bodies and external possessions of men. Therefore, he reasoned, that, whenever extra and unaccountable malignant action appeared, some covenanter with the devil must be in
the neighborhood of the malignant manifestation.

And yet, practically, Mather was not disposed to
let the public get knowledge of the covenanter. His
choice was, to keep secret the names of bewitched
actors, the afflictors of the suffering ones, and to
strive by prayers, fastings, manipulations, &c., to relieve the unhappy sufferers. Had his policy been
adopted by the public, had his example been widely
followed, there would have been no execution for
witchcraft in his generation.

We can — and we are glad that we can — state that
Mather's faith embraced some other invisible beings
than malicious ones, who had access to man. In that
respect he probably differed from, and was favored
above, most of the clergy and church members of
his times; and perhaps his possession of faith in the
ministry of *good* angels made him a more lenient
handler and more patient observer of the afflicted,
than were most of his cotemporaries. His prolonged
attention to Martha Goodwin, to Mercy Short, to

Margaret Rule, and his offer to take care of five or six Salem ones if he could be allowed the management of them, bespeak kindness in him above what was common in his age toward those deemed to be under "an evil hand." He once wrote thus : —

"In the present evil world it is no wonder that the evil angels are more *sensible* than those of the good ones. Nevertheless it is very certain that the *good* angels continually, without any defilement, fly about in our defiled atmosphere *to minister* for the good of them that are the heirs of salvation. . . . Now, though the angelic ministration is usually behind the curtain of more visible instruments and their actions, yet sometimes it hath been with extraordinary circumstances made more obvious to the sense of the faithful."

He was not unmindful and did not omit to record the fact that " the enchanted people talked much of a *white spirit*, from whence they received marvelous assistances. . . . Margaret Rule had a frequent view of his bright, shining, and glorious garments, . . . and says he told her that God had permitted her afflictions to befall her for the unspeakable and everlasting good of her own soul, and for the good of many others ; and for his own immortal glory."

When a being or beings of such glorious appearance present themselves, and when their utterances and influences are elevating and blissful, it is not wise to ignore them. The very laws which permit the advent of low and dark spirits are natural, and can be availed of, on fitting occasions and conditions, by elevated and bright ones ; therefore wisdom invites man to solicit and prepare the way for visits by the latter class.

The courtesy of S. F. Haven, Esq., the accomplished librarian of the American Antiquarian Society, Worcester, Mass., recently permitted us to see a long-lost and recently discovered manuscript, giving, in Cotton Mather's handwriting, an account of Mercy Short. We judge from cursory perusal of a modern manuscript copy of Mather's account, that the librarian had ample grounds for reporting to the society that Mercy Short's was " a case similar to that of Margaret Rule, but *of greater interest and fuller details.*" He further remarked in his report, that " it will be remembered that the account of Margaret Rule was not published by Mather himself, but by his enemy Calef, who by some means obtained possession of it. The story of Mercy Short, from an indorsement upon it, appears to have been privately circulated among his friends, but there is nothing to show that Mather ever intended it for publication." — *S. F. Haven's Report, April* 29, 1874.

Common fairness requires all modern critics to remember and regard the fact that Mather's accounts of Mercy Short and Margaret Rule were never given to the public by himself; that they never received his revision and correction for the press. Because of this they perhaps come to us more alive with the spirit of frankness and sincerity, and with more detail of little incidents. Unstudied records are generally honest and substantially accurate, even if marred by looseness of style and expression, and by statements of wonders.

Our views would require us to refrain from calling Calef *Mather's* " enemy," as the librarian did. He was the enemy of *unscriptural* definitions of witchcraft, and of unjustifiable proceedings against those accused of it; but not, as we read his purposes and feelings, the enemy of Mather himself. He was the enemy of opinions of which Mather was a conspicuous and outspoken representative, and whose writings furnished provoking occasion for an attack upon disastrous errors.

We trust the public may ere long see Mather's account of Mercy Short in print. That, and the one of Margaret Rule, show us very authentically, and we can almost say *beautifully*, the temper of Mather witch-ward, in the spring and autumn of the year next following the memorable 1692. Nothing then inclined him to ways that led to human slaughter. The conditions, seeming acts, and surroundings of those two girls apparently gave him opportunity and power to evoke a repetition of Salem's fearful scenes, in which the modern world has been deluded to believe that his soul found pleasure. If that soul loved blood, it could easily have set it flowing in 1693, and found wherewith to gratify its appetite; but *it did not*.

One of the questions of great importance which received earnest discussion in witchcraft times, perhaps the most important of all in practical bearings, had Mather and Calef both on the same side, and consequently it was not dwelt upon in their controversy. Our reference is to the *validity* of " *spectral evidence*," — that is, of testimony given by those who obviously perceived the facts they testified to while in an entranced, clairvoyant, or other abnormal condition. Some — many — able and good men then maintained that such testimony, unbacked by any other, might justify conviction of witchcraft, while quite as many, equally able and good men, including most of the clergy, maintained that such testimony alone was not sufficient.

Another disputed point was, whether Satan could assume the shape of an innocent person, and in that shape do mischief to the bodies and estates of mankind. The same question, partially, is up to-day — viz., Can any but willing devotees to Satan be used in the processes of spirit manifestations? Our two combatants were not at variance here — both had faith that Satan, the then synonym of *Spirits*, whether good or bad, could employ the innocent in prosecuting his purposes.

On the question whether Satan was obliged to use some mortal in covenant with himself whenever he harmed another mortal, they differed, as has been already shown, Mather claiming that human co-operation was frequently, if not always, needful to any manifestation of witchcraft. But in 1698 he put this among what he conceived to be " mistaken principles." We do not recall any other point on which he expressed change of view, nor do we find him making confessions of personal wrong-doings in connection with witchcraft; neither does he seem to have had cause for either confession or repentance, if kindness, leniency, and good-will to man are not to be confessed and repented of as crimes.

ROBERT CALEF.

ROBERT CALEF, though probably not in advance of many others in detecting and dissenting mentally from the public errors of faith and practice in relation to witchcraft, was first to manifest nerve enough to speak out boldly his own thoughts and those of many others. Backed and aided probably by strong and learned men, he became to Christendom's witchcraft, as Martin Luther had been to its Roman creeds and practices, a bold, outspoken *protestant.* Each of them dared to brave strong currents of popular beliefs and practices, even when the course was encompassed with dangers. Each probably was moved and sustained by firm conviction that truth, right, and justice were on his side; each had nerve enough to stand firm and resolute in his self-chosen post of danger and philanthropy; and each was, to great extent, successful. Luther challenged the pope and his devotees to justify portions of their creed and practices, and Calef did the same to Cotton Mather, as a leading annunciator and expounder of the witchcraft creed. Luther and Calef each conceded that much in the creed of those whom he contested was founded on Scripture, and so far was impregnable; but they saw that many unauthorized and baneful appendages had been put upon true scriptural faith and instructions, and each labored to sever the true and good from the false and bad with which the currents of opinions and events had long been investing them. Neither of them, however, discerned all the errors and pernicious practices which have since become visible. Luther, though he saw, or at least heard, and scolded, and threw his ink-horn at Catholicism's devil, did not discard, but retained, in his Protestant creed, both him and witchcraft as they then existed in the Catholic belief. Calef conceded the positive existence of Mather's great personal witchcraft devil of supernal origin, vast power, and ever-burning malignity, but found him commissioned only by God — never by human witches, as it was then generally believed he was and must be, when he manifested his power through or upon man.

We are much in doubt as to whether Calef was properly *author* of a large part of what he published relating to witchcraft. The articles he put forth from time to time seem to us very varied in style and in merits as to their scholarly and rhetorical airs. It is said, in vol. i. p. 288, Mass. Hist. Soc. Records, that " Calef was furnished with materials for his work by Mr. Brattle of Cambridge, and his brother of Boston, and other gentlemen who were opposed to the Salem proceedings." He may have had — and we conjecture that he had — much help in putting his materials into the form in which they came before the public. We are able to learn very little concerning the man himself. It is usual to style him a Boston merchant, but Mather alludes to him as that " weaver," &c.

Whatever may have been his culture, occupation, character, or social position, he assumed the respon- sibility of what is imputed to him — and we very willingly leave uncontested both his claims to have been author of all that he subscribed to, and to be called a Boston *merchant*.

Calef went into his work in deep earnest, and perhaps from a strong sense of duty to God and man; he perceived that departure from teachings and requirements of the Scriptures, and adoption of opinions, processes of examination, and kinds of evidence which the Scriptures did not prescribe, had occasioned the chief woes of witchcraft, and therefore devoted much time to the work of producing great and needed change in public opinion. He continued for some time to write clearly and forcibly to Mather; but, failing there to get his fundamental questions squarely and satisfactorily met, after months of trial, addressed a letter " to the ministers, whether English, French, or Dutch," upon this subject; this general application, however, failed to bring a response. Next he tried the Rev. Samuel Willard individually, then " all the ministers in and near Boston; " afterward Rev. Benjamin Wadsworth singly; but his success in eliciting replies was so meager, that we apparently may apply to those from whom he sought information the following words which he used in reference to some who had defined rules by which to detect witchcraft, — viz., " Perhaps the force of a prevailing opinion, together with an education thereto suited, might overshadow their judgments." His dates show that his calls for either refutation or assent to his positions were continued for two or three years, and that he was not simply or mainly an opponent of Mather, but an earnest seeker for light. In 1700, his collected correspondence, together with much other matter from Mather's pen and other sources, was published in London, and entitled "*More* wonders of the Invisible World," Mather having previously published "Wonders of the Invisible World."

This clear-sighted, earnest, untiring spirit soon gained the public ear extensively, began to enlighten the public mind, and turn it into new channels of thought and inquiry. Though not a polished, he was an intelligible, logical, and forceful writer in the main, and did much toward accomplishing the reformation to which he devoted his energies.

Calef was a moral hero, and bravely did noble work in bringing flood tides of murderous fanaticism, error, and delusion to an ebb, and in barring channels against their return. His appropriate stand in history's niches may be at the head of Witchcraft Reformers — not repudiators, but *Reformers*.

THOMAS HUTCHINSON.

DURING nearly one hundred years, from about the middle of the eighteenth to that of the nineteenth century, the American public has been content to leave unlifted concealing drapery which the historian Hutchinson threw over witchcraft. His treatment of that subject is plausible and soothing to cursory readers, but superficial and unsatisfactory to minds which test the competency of agents to produce effects ascribed to them. His views have been so widely adopted and so long prevalent, that we must regard him as having been more influential than any other writer in hiding the gigantic limbs, features, and operations of what was

with reason a veritable monster in the eyes of its be-
holders. In him some reprehensible qualities were
conjoined with many admirable ones. Appleton's
New American Cyclopædia states that " Thomas
Hutchinson was born in Boston in 1711, and died at
Brampton, near London, 1780. He was graduated at
Harvard College, 1727. He became Judge of Probate
in 1752, was Councillor from 1749 to 1756, Lieutenant
Governor from 1758 to 1771, and was appointed Chief
Justice in 1760, thus holding four high offices at one
time. In the disputes which led to the Revolution, he
sided with the British government. . . . He received
his commission as Governor in 1771; and his whole
administration was characterized by duplicity and an
avaricious love of money, writing letters which he
never sent, but which he showed as evidence of his
zeal for the liberties of the province, while he advised
the establishment of a citadel in Boston," &c.

The History of Massachusetts by the pen of this man
has sterling merits, and is of great value. That work
and the bestowal of so many high offices upon him indicate that his abilities, acquisitions, and performances
were of high order. His comments upon subjects
which he discussed, and facts which he presented,
were prevailingly fair, and very instructive. When he
perceived—and he generally did—the genuine significance of his facts, reasoned from them all, and allowed
to each its proper weight, he was a spirited, lucid, and
valuable interpreter and guide. But when he encountered and adduced extraordinary facts, which baffled
his power to account for in harmony with his prejudg-
ments and fixed conclusions as to where natural agents
and forces cease to act, he could very skillfully keep in

abeyance the most distinguishing and significant aspects of such troublesome materials. That damaging
moral weakness which let him write letters which he
never sent, for the purpose of exhibiting them as evidence of his support of the popular cause, perhaps
also let him be other than manly and frank when he
encountered a certain class of facts which seemed to
him "more than natural." The whole subject of
witchcraft was nettlesome to him. His pen very often indicated a testy, disturbed, and sometimes a con-
temptuous mover when it characterized persons who
had been charged with that crime ; and concerning
such he recorded many hasty and unsatisfactory opinions and conclusions. A glimpse at the probable and
almost necessary state of public opinion and knowledge concerning spiritual forces and agents about the
middle of the eighteenth century, will detect serious
difficulties besetting any witchcraft historian's path at
that time, and dispose us to look in clemency upon his
hypotheses and conclusions, even though they be far
from satisfactory.

The intense strain given to the prevalent monstrous
creed concerning the devil, when its requirements
were vigorously enforced at Salem Village in 1692, rup-
tured that creed itself ; and no substitute for it under
which the phenomena of witchcraft could be referred
to competent authors and.forces had been obtained in
1767. The public formerly had believed that either
One Great Devil and his sympathetic imps, or embodied human beings who had made a covenant with
him, must be the authors of all mysterious malignant
action upon men, because no other unseen rational
agents were recognized as having access to man. All

acts deemed witchcrafts, therefore, were the devil's. But belief devil-ward had changed at Hutchinson's day. The Great Devil's use of covenanted children, women, and men as his only available instrumentalities, had ceased to be asserted; the fathering of all mysterious works upon him and his had become an obsolete custom. Its revival might not meet kindly reception by the public; it probably would be distasteful to people whom tragic experience had not very long since taught to distrust and disown his Black Majesty's sway over material things, and were also chagrined that their fathers had held undoubting faith in his powers and operations over and upon things temporal and palpable. The devil had been credited with more than he performed or had power to accomplish. Reflection had brought conviction that other intermeddlers existed than purely Satanic ones. And yet the culture and science of those times were incompetent to furnish an historian with any satisfactory evidence that any intelligent actors excepting the devil and human beings acted in and upon human society. Devil or man, one or the other, according to the then existing belief, must have enacted witchcraft. Whether the devil did, had been under consideration for more than seventy years, and public judgment declared him not guilty. What, therefore, was the historian's necessity? He was forced to make embodied human beings its sole enactors. No wonder that the necessity made him petulant when facts and circumstances forced from his pen intimations that mere children and old women were competent and actual authors of some manifestations which, to his own keen and philosophic intellect, seemed "more

than natural." "More than natural" in his sense
they obviously were. A distinct perception that the
good *God's* disembodied children, as well as the devil's,
can naturally traverse avenues earthward, and manifest their powers among men, would have enabled
him to account philosophically for all the mysteries
of those days. But "the fullness of time" for that
had not then come.

C. W. UPHAM.

IN 1867, just one century after Hutchinson, Hon.
Charles W. Upham, of Salem, Mass., published an
elaborate, polished, interesting and instructive "History of Witchcraft and Salem Village." The connection of two such topics as a local history and a general
survey of witchcraft in one work, was very appropriate and judicious in this case, because Salem Village,
which embraced the present town of Danvers and
parts of other towns adjacent, was the site of the most
extensive and awful conflict which men ever waged
in avowed and direct contest with the devil on this
continent, if not in the world. By his course he enabled the reader to comprehend what kind or quality
of men, women, and children they were, among whom
that combat raged.

Upham's history of the *Village* and its people is minute, exhaustive, lucid, sprightly, and ornate. That
work clearly shows that the people of the Village possessed physical, mental, moral, and religious powers,
faculties, traits, trainings, and habits which must have
given them keenness of perception, logical acumen,

both physical and moral stamina and courage, and made them as difficult to delude or cow by novel occurrences as any other people anywhere, either then, before that time, or since. The same properties made them intelligent analyzers of their creed, clear perceivers of its logical reaches, tenacious holders on to what they believed, and fearless appliers of their faith. Holding, in common with all Christendom, the deluded and deluding belief that supermundane works required some human being " covenanted to the devil " for their performance, this people was ready and able to apply that belief in righteous fight. Such a people were not very likely to mistake the pranks of their own children for things supermundane in origin. To suspect them of such credulity or infatuation is to suspect and impeach the truth and accuracy of the very history which makes them so clearly and fully known to us.

The same faculties and acquirements which furnished so sprightly a history of the Village, of course made their impress upon the pages devoted to " *Witch-craft.*" And results might have been as pleasing there as in more external history, had not omission to see and assign spirit causes where spirit effects existed, forced the author to assume that heavy, effective cannon balls came forth from pop-guns, because he had not himself seen cannon in arsenals himself had not visited, and would take nobody's word for it that such had been available.

For his own sake we are prone to wish that our personal friend had recognized that subsequent to the time of his early manhood, when he delivered and published Lectures upon Witchcraft, and pondered upon its producing agents and causes, phenomena, like the marvelous ones of former days, had been transpiring in great abundance all over our land, and that no less a man than Dr. Robert Hare, of Philadelphia, the correspondent and peer of Faraday, Silliman, and others of that class, had, by rigid and exact processes of physical science, actually *demonstrated* that some occult force, moved by an intelligence that could and did understand and comply with verbal requests, repeatedly lifted and lowered the arms of scale-beams, and made bodies weigh more or weigh less than their normal weight, at his mental request. The same had been done by Dr. Luther V. Bell and a band of press reporters in 1857. Such forces, if taken into account by this historian, would have required a reconstruction and vast modifications of his long-cherished theory of explanation, and have called for an immense expenditure of labor and thought.

Ease and retention of long-cherished notions are seductive to man. It was easier for the historian to ignore the discovery that natural laws or forces had always permitted unseen agents to come among us, whose workings the human brain had long, but unsatisfactorily, been laboring to trace to adequate causes, — easier to continue to assume that insufficient causes, lackered in glowing rhetoric, might answer a while longer, — easier to still hug the dream that little girls and young misses, mainly guileless and docile in all their previous days, could and did, without professional instruction and of a sudden, become proficients in the production of complicated schemes and feats rivaling and even surpassing the most astonishing ones of highest legerdemain, of jugglery, and of histrionic art combined, — easier to fancy that these girls rebelled against and set at defiance parental, medical, ministerial, and friendly authority, acted like brutes and villains, turned all things upside down with a vengeance, in the midst of a community clear headed and not easily befooled, — yes, it was easier to retain all these *outré* suppositions than to set aside a pet theory and reconstruct history in conformity with requirements of discoveries which *others* had made in advance of this historian, and by the use of which he could have furnished a truly philosophical and satisfactory solution of all the marvels of ancient witchcraft. Infatuation still lingers on the earth, blinding many bright eyes.

We are hardly sorry that our friend ignored the actual and competent authors — indeed, we are nearly glad that he did so; for his course resulted in presentation of many important portions of New England witchcraft in very lucid, intelligible, and attractive combination, helped a vast many people to perception of the proximate nature and extent of strange things done here of old, and enabled the common mind to make pretty fair estimate of the nature of such forces as were needful to any agents who should perform such wonders.

We cheerfully acknowledge great personal indebtedness to that author for such an exhibition of this subject as shows its mighty influence over sagacious, strong, calm, good, and able men who were living witnesses and actors in its scenes; and shows also that common sense will instinctively feel that the acts imputed to a few illiterate girls and misses were beyond the powers which nature by her usual and well-known processes ever bestowed upon them. Philosophy, sci·

6

ence, and common sense demand causes adequate to
produce whatever effects are ascribed to them. Histories of witchcraft have not met these demands. Previous failure in that respect prompts this effort to
present agents whose powers may have been equal
to the works performed in witchcraft scenes.

The work in hand will necessitate a close grappling
with many of our friend's opinions and processes.
But our grip, however firm, will never be made in
unkindness toward or want of respect for him ;
the object will be · to disclose mistakes, to rescue our
forefathers and their children in the seventeenth century out from under damaging, groundless, needless,
gratuitous imputation of fatuity to the elders, and
devilish ingenuity to the younger ones, and to permit
the present and future ages to look back upon them
with respect and sympathy.

That author is still living, and long may he live in
comfort and usefulness. His biography is not written ; a brief outline of him, solely from this moment's
recollections is here given. Not less that fifty years
ago, we knew him as a student at Harvard, — afterward, for many years, as a respected and successful
clergyman at Salem, — still later, in political office,
especially as member of Congress, — and for many of
the more recent years, as a student and author at
home. He has commanded and retains our high
respect.

The scholar, rhetorician, statistician, fictionist, and
dramatist, all blend harmoniously in him, give an uncommon charm to his " History of Salem Village," and
render it a work which bespeaks wide and abiding
interest with the public. It is no essential part of the

philosopher's specific labors to discover or test *new* agents, forces, or facts. His dealings mostly are with facts known and admitted. Till one concedes the fact of spirit action upon persons and things in earth life, he cannot philosophically admit that spirit forces were ever employed in the production of any phenomenon, but must regard all as purely material or within the scope of ordinary human faculties. Therefore we can, perhaps, with propriety regard our friend as also a philosopher ; but must add, that he either lacked knowledge of or ignored the agents and forces that produced many witchcraft phenomena which he attempted to elucidate, and many others of the same character which he failed to adduce from the earlier records ; which agents and forces must be allowed their actual and full connection with their own effects before philosophy can furnish just, clear, and satisfactory solutions of their source and nature.

MARGARET JONES.

THE great endemic witchcraft at Salem Village in 1692 has been extensively ascribed to the voluntary acts of a few girls and women, who are sometimes credited with having derived much knowledge from books, traditions, weird stories, and the like, and thus obtained hints and instructions whereby they were enabled to devise, and, acting upon the credulity and infatuation of their time, to enact, and did enact, that great and thrilling performance, without supermundane aid. Was it so ? An examination of several sporadic cases which preceded that famous outburst of mysterious operations, may indicate strong need to assign many witchcraft manifestations to causes and forces lying off beyond the reach of man's ordinary faculties, for we perceive in them the operation of powers which he never acquired, nor can acquire, by reading, listening, or by any training processes.

Hutchinson says, "The great noise which the New England witchcraft made throughout the English dominions proceeded more from the general panic with which all sorts of persons were seized, and an expectation that the contagion would spread to all parts of the country, than from the number of persons who were executed; more having been put to death in a single county in England in a short space of time, than have suffered in New England from the first settlement until the present time. Fifteen years had passed before we find any mention of witchcraft among the English colonists. . . . The first suspicion of witchcraft among the English was about the year 1645."

We commence now an examination of several of the earlier cases, and begin with MARGARET JONES.

There is extant, in the handwriting of the judge before whom she was tried, a summary of the evidence adduced against this woman, who, in 1648, was tried, condemned, and executed in Boston for the crime of witchcraft; and who thus became, so far as we now know, the first American victim in Christendom's carnal warfare against the devil. Unconsciously to herself surely, but yet in fact, she may have been, as we sometimes view her, America's first martyr to *Spiritualism*.

The chief knowledge of this case now attainable is furnished by the Journal of Governor John Winthrop, who was both governor of the colony and chief judge of its highest court in 1648, and presided at the trial of Margaret Jones. His position on the bench gave him opportunity, and made it his duty, to know precisely what was charged, what testified, and what proved in the case. The character of that recorder is good voucher for an honest and candid statement as far as it goes. His record states that, —

"In 1648, one Margaret Jones, of Charlestown, was indicted and found guilty of witchcraft, and hanged for it. The evidence against her was, that she was found to have such a malignant touch, as many persons, men, women, and children, whom she stroked or touched with any affection or displeasure, or, &c., were taken with deafness, or vomiting, or other violent pains or sickness; that, practicing physic, and her medicines being such things as, by her own confession, were harmless, as anise-seed, liquors, &c., yet had extraordinary violent effects; that she used to tell such as would not make use of her physic, that they would never be healed, and accordingly their diseases and hurts continued, with relapses against the ordinary course, and beyond the apprehension of all physicians and surgeons; that things which she foretold came to pass accordingly; other things she could tell of, as secret speeches, &c., which she had no ordinary means to come to knowledge of; in the prison, in the clear daylight, there was seen in her arms, she sitting on the floor, and her clothes up, &c., a little child, which ran from her into another room, and the officer following it, it was vanished. The

like child was seen in two other places to which she
had relation ; and one maid that saw it, fell sick
upon it, and was cured by the said Margaret, who
used means to be employed to that end."

Thus much was recorded by Winthrop in 1648.
But the quantum of information relative to Margaret
Jones which historic selection deemed needful for the
public in 1764 had become very small, for at the latter date Hutchinson says (vol. i. p. 150), " The first
instance I find of any person executed for witchcraft,
was in June, 1648.   Margaret Jones, of Charlestown,
was indicted for a witch, found guilty, and executed.
She was charged with having such a malignant touch
that if she laid her hands upon man, woman, or child
in anger, they were seized presently with deafness,
vomiting, or other sickness, or some violent pains."

Those few sharp lines comprise the whole of that
historian's account of this case.   He gives no hint that
the woman was accused of anything but *a malignant
touch ;* therefore he falls long way short of fair presentation of the facts.   He leaves entirely unnoticed
the chief grounds for just inferences and conclusions.
Whether that writer had access to Winthrop's record
we do not know.   But the historian Upham had, and he
states (vol. i. p. 453), " The only real charge proved
upon Margaret Jones was, that she was a successful
practitioner, using only simple remedies."   *The only
charge proved!*   What can that mean ?   There surely
were several other and much more marvelous and significant things just as clearly charged and " proved
upon " her as was her successful use of simple remedies.   The only thing *proved!*   If that thing was
proved, then the same document which teaches this,

also teaches with equal distinctness that five or six other things were proved upon her; and the greater part of these others were difficult of solution by the philosophies of both the historians named above. Turn back to Winthrop's account, and see what was charged.

1. When she manipulated either man, woman, or child, some nausea, pain, or disease was forthwith engendered in the subject of her operations.

2. Her very simple medicines, viz., anise-seed and liquors produced extraordinary violent effects.

3. She told such as would not take her physic that they would never be healed; and accordingly their diseases and hurts continued, with relapses against the ordinary course.

4. Things which she foretold came to pass accordingly.

5. She could tell of secret speeches which she had no ordinary means to come to knowledge of.

6. While in prison, in the clear daylight, there was seen in her arms . . . a little child . . . which at the officer's approach ran and vanished.

7. The maid that fell sick at sight of that child " was cured by the said Margaret, who used means to be employed to that end."

The *only* charge *proved?* If it was proved that "she was a successful practitioner, using only simple remedies," then each one of the other six is just as clearly proved as her successful practice, and by the same document, too. But some of them are more difficult to account for on sadducean grounds, and were left unnoticed. Even the admitted marvel is put forth in distorted form, being so draped as to teach that the woman was a *successful* medical practitioner, while the original record reads that her simples produced extraordinary *violent* effects. No doubt she was in an important sense " a successful practitioner, using only simple remedies." But that is not what the testimony specially stated. The historic evidence is, that her simples produced "*violent effects.*" Her fate teaches that the action of her simples was deemed diabolical. Is that idea conveyed in calling her a successful practitioner ? No.

The case of this woman is vastly more instructive than it has been deemed by former expounders; and since, in its varied features and aspects, it presents many interesting points, we shall dwell upon it at considerable length.

Nothing has been met with in her history which conflicts with supposition that she and her husband, perhaps in or below the middle ranks of society, were laboring for a livelihood amid a clear-headed, sagacious, hardy, industrious community, which had resided twenty years around the mouth of the Charles without any startling witchcraft among them, or any teachers of that art, (?) or skillful co-operators in its practice. Something induced her to lay hands upon and administer simple medicines to the pained, the sick, or the wounded. Whence the impulse ? We can hardly suppose that she had studied medicine. A nurse she may have been — very likely had been — and perhaps had become conscious of ability to relieve sufferings and disease, and may have been known by her neighbors to be willing to practice the healing art. Obviously they became accustomed to submit themselves to her manipulations and medical treatment quite extensively, and at length were astonished at the extreme efficacy of her hands, and the sometimes *violent* action of her simple medicines.

So extraordinary were the effects of her labors that the neighborhood became suspicious that an obnoxious *one from below* was her helper, and therefore she was arrested on suspicion of witchcraft.

What persons would be summoned into court to testify concerning her when such was the charge? Her patients promiscuously? No. Only such among them as had, or as would swear that they had, received suffering or annoyance under her treatment. Search would be made for harm only, and not for any good which she had done. More moral courage and strength than are common would be needed to induce those not summoned, and who had nothing but good which they could say of her operations, to try to get upon the witness stand where witchcraft was the alleged offense. All the testimony, either sought or given, was, no doubt, intended to bear against her; and yet it comes to our view that the sickened maid " was cured by the said Margaret, who used means to be employed to that end." Beneficence as well as "murder will out" sometimes.

The various powers manifested through her are worthy of separate examination.

1. *When she manipulated either man, woman, or child, some nausea, pain, or disease was forthwith engendered in the subject of her operations.* That is the only crime which Hutchinson seems to have found laid to her charge; it is the only one he puts to the credit of her persecutors, and thus he leaves them heavily indebted on humanity's ledger. If the testimony

were not mainly sheer fabrication, some extraordinary
efficacy went forth from her imposed hands, and apparently on many different occasions, too; for the
account stating that effects were similar upon men,
women, and children, indicates that she was an extensive operator.

Mesmer had not then made his discoveries. But
the powers always resided in living forms which he
detected and measurably learned to educe and control. Margaret Jones's system may have been a very
powerful magnetic battery, controlled sometimes by
her own will, sometimes moved by and giving passage-way to impersonal magnetic forces, and sometimes also used by that intelligence outside of man
which Agassiz and Brown-Séquard say (see Appendix) can operate through his organism. Both intensification and mitigation of pains, diseases, and the
forces of medicines are credible results from her manipulations.

As said before, only those portions of the primitive
document which relate to the efficacy of her hands
and her simples, drew forth comments from the historians; they also failed to set forth a tithe of the
significance which was involved in the little they did
attempt to unfold. Such action of hands and very
simple medicines upon the systems of men, women,
and children is not satisfactorily accounted for either
by ascribing it, as one did, to the anger of the operating woman, nor, as the other did, to the simple
medicines acting normally. Such causes could never
have produced effects competent to so startle an intelligent and firm-nerved community as to make them
charge this practitioner with diabolism, and seek her

execution. The implied infatuation and credulity of a generation which could be roused to such barbarity by such insignificant causes is a most defamatory impeachment of the sagacity, manhood, and humaneness of our forefathers. Our witchcraft expounders, we apprehend, have allowed themselves to sacrifice very much that was bright and noble in the past, on the altar of false assumption that modern scientists, or at least that their own wise historic intellects, have explored all the recesses of broad nature, and positively determined that no forces can anywhere exist by which supermundane acts can legitimately be brought to the cognizance of man. The merits of the fathers are darkened, that the arrogance of the children may be labeled Wisdom.

Many men of no mean intellects have admitted that a spirit once came forth from a man " and leaped " on the seven exorcist sons of one Sceva, " and overcame them, and prevailed against them, so that they fled out of that house naked and wounded." The mind which believes that record ought to be in condition to admit that possibly spirits could throw forth power through the hands of such as Margaret Jones which would produce pains, nausea, and disease in those whom the mediums touched, provided the spirits desired such results. It was no unprecedented event in kind, if, through her, some unseen force tortured the bodies of any who, as spies, enemies, mimickers, or rivals, sought an imposition of her hands; not new that torturing sensations should be produced when the magnetisms of the operator and subject were as alkali and acid to each other; nor new that her own spirit of resentment for wrongs either received or

foresensed, thus operated. But favor too might often
induce either her or a spirit through her to produce
violent effects at first, unless our doctors prescribe
emetics and cathartics in unkindness or malice.

Read the following statement, which I have just
written down from the lips of a neighbor whom I
have known well for-nearly or quite ten years, and
whose truthfulness is as complete as that of any other
one whatsoever in the whole circle of my acquaintances : —

" In the autumn of 1869, a woman in South Boston
who knew me, advised one of her neighbors who was
sick of fever to send for me and receive treatment by
my hands. The patient's husband, a robust mechanic,
had little faith in helpful efficacy from ' laying on of
hands.' Still, curiosity or some other motive induced
him and three other men to observe my processes and
their effects. They witnessed very marked contrac-
tions of the sick woman's muscles, and many spas-
modic movements of her limbs. When I ceased
working upon my patient, her husband said, ' Do you
suppose you can affect *me* in the same way?' My
reply was, ' I don't know — probably not ; but if you
desire me to try, I will.' ' Yes,' said he, ' try.' ' Sit
down, then, sir, in the chair where your wife sat.' He
did so, and I operated for a short time without perceptible effect, but was soon impressed to say to him,
' Strike me on the small of the back,' — simultaneously
placing my back so that he could give it a fair, hard
blow, which he was by no means unwilling to inflict.
After his first stroke I called out, ' Harder ! ' After
the second, ' *Harder !* ' After the third, he was in-

stantly cramped up, his arms were hugged in upon
and across his chest, the muscles on them were much
enlarged, intensely hardened, and not obedient to his
will, and he lustily begged, 'Let me down! let me
down! let me down!' while the other men, the sick
wife, and myself laughed till we were exhausted. I
had no will in producing, nor any design to effect any
such results.   J. W. CROSBY.

"BOSTON, April 30, 1874."

2. The testimony indicates that her *very simple medicines, such as anise-seed and liquors, produced extraordinary violent effects.* This is credible. Extraordinary
effects were produced by magnetized handkerchiefs in
the days of Paul, and to-day, even pure water, placed
beneath the hands of some peculiar mediums, or beneath the tips of their fingers, sometimes absorbs or
is made to manifest the medicinal properties of wine,
ipecac, or of other substances desired; and such mediums are often very "successful practitioners using
only simple remedies." The action of what they
administer need not be psychological in any proper
sense of that term: that is, the patient need not
be informed, nor have suspicion, that the water is
medicated thus; though any persons upon whom the
action is very perceptible, probably, must be constitutionally mediumistic. By personal observation we
have learned that water may be so medicated by unseen infusion from unseen source, as to taste like, and
operate like, either ipecac or wine, according to the
properties which some unseen intelligence to whom
needs are transparent, and who can sicken or refresh
at pleasure, has gathered from the atmosphere or else-

where and infused into that water. When public vigilance had been roused to suspicion around this woman, it is not improbable that many persons, belligerent devil-ward, sought a test of her powers, and that some of them (susceptible ones) felt or drank in what caused "deafness, or vomiting, or other pains or sickness"— not improbable that on some of them her simples had "*violent* effects." Persons thus affected would make up nearly the whole class from whom witnesses at her trial would be selected. If she had been generally a producer of only pains and sickness, her practice would soon have dwindled to nothing, and she would have lived on without molestation. "A successful practitioner," simply as such, would never have been arraigned.

Upham detected the significant fact in the case, that her simple remedies were so efficacious as to make her a successful practitioner; yes; — but was simply successful medical practice the chief reason why her neighbors charged diabolism? What amount of success in alleviating the sufferings that flesh is heir to would invoke public vengeance? How much beneficence did one then need to perform before public sentiment would reprobate its author? Could such faculties and agents alone as are normally and ordinarily used, enable a woman to achieve such success in curing diseases, healing wounds, and alleviating pains, as to arouse an intelligent and religious community to arrest and try her for a capital offense against the well-being of society? Never. Did the historian notice his own back-handed imputation of atrocious diabolism upon the population of Charlestown when he led his readers to infer that they persecuted one of their number unto an ignominious death, solely because "she was a successful practitioner using only simple remedies"? Whether he saw it or not, his explanation made her neighbors take the life of this woman because of the good works she had done among them. Some theory · of explanation, which will exempt us from the neces- sity of assenting to gratuitous aspersions of the sagaci- ty and sentiments of justice pertaining to our ancestry in the mass, is very desirable. Margaret Jones was a very successful *healing medium*, and therefore her works were mysteries.

Having noticed the only two allegations in this case which the historians have deemed worthy of specification or had courage to adduce, and having seen that Hutchinson ascribed her persecution to her own · anger flowing out through her hands, while Upham ascribed it to her great success as a healer, we will just note the fact that the former historian generally indicated an abiding apprehension that those who *were persecuted* for the crime in question, were the parties most to be blamed ; while the latter, of- tener than otherwise, throws the chief blame upon the *persecutors*. In this instance the earlier historian makes her anger, — a trait which is blamable, — while the latter makes her beneficence, — a commendable characteristic, — the chief exciting cause to her con- demnation and execution.

We proceed to examine other original charges more difficult to solve plausibly on the hypotheses of Hutch- inson and Upham than were anger and successful med- ical practice ; charges not amenable to any philosophy entertained by those expounders.

3. "*She used to tell such as would not make use of*

her physic that they would never be healed; and, accordingly, their diseases and hurts continued; with relapses against the ordinary course," &c. It is very common in our day for clairvoyance to see, or — more broadly and instructively — it is common for mediumistic faculties to *sense* and feel sure, that the existing tendency of a patient's disease will soon terminate in death, if not checked by some peculiar medicinal agent, often a spiritual one, or one medicated by spirits, which ordinary physicians are ignorant of, will not prescribe, and cannot obtain. The evidence which Judge Winthrop reports, shows that "the diseases and hurts" of recusants to take her prescriptions, not only continued to remain unhealed, but underwent such changes and relapses as physicians and surgeons could not understand. Since such things occurred in accordance with her predictions, we here perceive strong evidence that the woman possessed uncommon susceptibilities for *sensing* coming results. *It is just as clearly proved* that she foretold specific events, as it is that her touch was malignant, and her practice successful. Her marvelous prescience, which was one of her conspicuous powers, the historians failed to set forth. Their philosophy, founded only on such materials as are recognized in man's physical sciences, was too narrow to embrace occult natural agents and forces by which such prescient powers could be drawn or put forth through some human organisms and produce marvelous results. Therefore those expounders let such facts remain undisturbed in the rarely visited closets where they have long reposed.

4. *Things which she foretold came to pass accordingly.* That is, events verified her predictions, and thus

proved her exercise of marvelously prophetic powers.
Should one assume that her verified predictions were
only skillful or lucky guesses, would such assumption
be fair and just toward the people who, as living witnesses on the spot, could know what the things were
which she foretold, and know also with what accuracy
they were fulfilled, and yet deemed them genuine
prophecies? Her accusers could know the facts,
while we, in the main, must be ignorant of them.
We cannot reasonably deny that the direct observers
actually discerned the exercise of genuinely prophetic
powers by her. Some mortals at times can prophesy;
for both in ancient prophetic and apostolic times, and
in our own age, many people have been and are known
to do it. Eternal laws or forces lead some mortals to
sure knowledge of coming events. History and returning spirits both so teach.

"The spirit of prophecy has its source in infinite
truth, and is as much a part of infinite law as any
other manifestation of life; therefore it has a wise
and powerful protection; and they who avail themselves of this spirit of prophecy, *by virtue of the way
and manner in which they are physically and spiritually
compounded*, if they are fortunate enough to place
themselves in harmonious relations to the law, fail
not in prophesying. But if, as is often the case, they
unfortunately place themselves in inharmonious relations to the law, they must, of necessity, fail in part,
if not entirely. It is a truthful saying, that 'coming
events cast their shadows before.' *These shadows* (?)
are, in reality, portions of the events; these shadows
take precedence of the material birth of all events as
they are understood by mortals; they are the basis of

7

that which you receive, and outlast that which you receive; they are the infinite part. Now, then, there are some persons *so constituted* that they perceive these shadows (?) and can judge as accurately concerning what they predict, as the learned astronomer can concerning an eclipse." — *Spirit, Prof. Alexander M. Fisher, of Yale.* BANNER OF LIGHT, Jan. 30, 1875.

5. " *She could tell of secret speeches which she had no ordinary means to come to knowledge of.*" At times, then, she was clairaudient, or was one of those sensitives whose spiritual organs of sensation are at times so disentangled from their material ones, that she experienced a practical annihilation of space and gross matter, which let her, as all unclogged spirits may, be practically present with and listeners to any person anywhere, to whom she was for any reason attracted, and with whom she came into rapport. Conditions admitting cognizance of the thoughts and words of the absent in body are now of daily occurrence with men, women, and children not a few, and therefore were possible with Margaret Jones in 1648 and years preceding. A letter from Captain Densmore, on a future page of this work, will show recent possession of power to hear the voices of living persons whose bodies were very far distant from the hearer.

6. " *While in the prison in the clear daylight there was seen in her arms . . . a little child . . . which, at the officer's approach, ran and vanished.*" *Vanished;* that word intimates that it was a spectral or spirit child — perhaps her own departed one. By whom was it seen? By an officer of the prison, and therefore by one not likely to be her confederate in attempt at imposture. Not by him only; for a chamber-

maid also saw the little one, and was made sick by
the sight; which effect argues against her having had
any complicity in a trick. That testimony to such
occurrences was given in court, is vouched for by
Winthrop, and must have been, or surely should have
been, read by subsequent historians. Their adroit-
ness at leaving certain classes of facts in undisturbed
obscurity, nearly rivals the cunning of agents to whom
they impute the origin and production of witchcraft
manifestations.

The visible presence of that evanescent child shows
very clearly that Mrs. Jones was endowed with some
of the rarer and exceptional properties of mediumship — that she possessed those special elements in
the midst of which spirits could be robed in such
materialized encasements, that material eyes could
discern them. Angels looking and acting like men
(Gen. xviii.) were seen by Abraham and Lot. One
was seen (Judg. xiii.) by Manoah and his wife.
Another by Tobias, son of Tobit (Apoc.); another
by disciples who were walking toward Emmaus
(John xx.); others also by thousands of individuals
in various ages and nations, sporadically. To-day,
distinct perception of materialized spirits in the presence of Mrs. Andrews at Moravia, N. Y., around
Dr. Slade of New York city, and many others are reported almost weekly, and are well attested. In these
modern instances, generally, some special, though simple, pre-arrangements are made to facilitate such manifestations; but we may very reasonably doubt whether
anything of the kind was resorted to by Mrs. Jones,
because, being in prison charged with the awful crime
of witchcraft, the presumption is imperative that she

must have lacked both means and opportunity to
command tangible apparatus either for helping on a
genuine spirit manifestation, or producing an optical
illusion upon her keepers.

Mortal. " How do spirits materialize ? "

Spirit. " You must know the atmosphere is full of
particles of matter. Everything that is in the human
body is also in the atmosphere in fine particles. Darkness renders these particles more quiescent, and hence
more easily managed by spirits. The spirit has a
will point or center which is a spark of the Divine
Nature. When the condition of the atmosphere, of
the medium, and of the circle is proper, the spirit
exerts that will power, and, in accordance with natural law, *attracts to its spirit form* the floating particles in the air, and they condense upon and inter-
penetrate the spirit form or body so as to materialize
it, making bone, muscle, skin, hair — every part, and
making the spirit body, for the time being, a solid,
palpable one. The air contains an immense amount
of matter which can be used by spirits for materializing. We do not, however, usually materialize the
blood. . . . We have to draw a portion of the substance for materialization from the medium, he being
a kind of reservoir where we concentrate our supplies, and it is much more difficult to draw from him
when at a distance, therefore we keep near him." —
Spirit. Disc., *as reported by H. A. Buddington.* BAN-
NER OF LIGHT, Feb. 6, 1875.

A case of much interest and significance was reported to the Boston Post, a daily newspaper, by a
correspondent under date of Newburyport, Jan. 13,
1873. Therein is furnished an account of a spirit boy

showing himself in broad daylight, several times, on different occasions, at a window between an entry and a school-room, to a band of children and their teacher; also of his making a disturbing racket in an unfinished attic over them occasionally for many successive months. Miss Perkins, the teacher, says, " He is a little fellow, about eleven years old, with a pale face, and the saddest, sweetest mouth that she ever saw in her life, looking fearlessly up into her face out of a pair of blue eyes. He retreated into a corner. She followed him, and just as she was about to lay her hand upon him he vanished. No door had been opened, and yet he was gone." The account states that Miss Perkins, " though no spiritualist, is convinced that it " (the racket) " is all produced by supernatural agency, and believes that the apparition she saw was a veritable ghost."

The editor of the Springfield Republican probably consulted the teacher of that school, Miss Lucy A. Perkins, as to the correctness of the foregoing, and perhaps other accounts, which had become public, for she wrote to him, and he published as follows : —

" The account you sent me is true, with a few exceptions. When I first saw the boy, he was neatly attired in a *brown* suit of clothes, trimmed with braid and buttons of the same color. When I reached forward to grasp him, he seemed not like the boy, but vapory, or, as I can only describe it, like a thin cloud scudding across the room; still he seemed to have the boy form. Reports from some of the Boston papers say I fainted ; such is not the case. I knew where I was and what I was about just as well as I know I am writing.

" One day I sent a boy out to hang up the brushes,
&c. . . . He was out about five minutes. After he
had taken his seat, three raps came on the door of the
room where the brushes were hung. He said, ' Miss
Perkins, can I go out and see who's there ? ' I told
him, ' Yes, and leave the school-room door open.' He
did so, and when he opened the brush-room door (I
sat where I could see all) every one of the brushes,
both long and short handled, came falling off the nails
where they were hung ; some struck him on the
shoulders, and the broom directly on the top of his
head. The dust-pan, hanging on a nail at some distance above the brushes, came tumbling to the floor
with a vengeance. It then stood on its handle, then
on the bottom edge, and continued on so till it
entered the school-room, and then it was placed as
nicely against the partition as if I had done it myself. Just as soon as I'd raise the ventilator, a black
ball, like a cannon ball, would begin to roll around
the attic, and make such a noise I would be obliged
to lower the ventilator. One day the room was
quiet as it possibly could be, and all at once some
one in the attic called out, ' Dadie Pike ! ' Dadie
thought I spoke, and said, ' What'm ? ' I said to him,
' Can you say your lesson ? '

" Since the boy affair took place, the attic has been
fastened up ; locks and keys are of no use, however, for there is as much walking up stairs, and
sometimes the hammering and nailing. Once in a
while, sounds as of some one walking will come
down the attic way, go across the entry, and open
the outside door, and be gone perhaps ten minutes ;
after it is quiet again, the door will open, and he,

she, or it will go up stairs. . . . I am not a spirit‑
ualist ; never attended a sitting, in fact, never had
anything to do with a person of that belief, and
never saw any manifestations. Why anything of the
sort should take place where I am, is more than I
can account for."

This case, wherein a teacher and her two score pupils
simultaneously saw a spirit in broad daylight, day after
day and week after week, argues very forcibly that
" the nature of things " permits admission that the
testimony relating to the spirit child in the jail may
be literally true. Laws and forces are now frequently
indicating their existence, which permit the observable
presence of spirits.

Intense yearnings for comfortings, sympathy, and
support in her dark and trying hour, as well as other
causes, may have drawn an angel child — her own or
some other — to the arms of Margaret Jones, whose
history reveals her possession of peculiar susceptibilities and mediumistic properties ; and with her
as a reservoir, materialization of the spirit may have
been accomplished.

7. The sickened maid " was cured by the said Margaret, who used means to be employed to that end."
Kindness and skill successfully put forth to heal the
sick, even while the public was keeping her in a
felon's cell, hang as a luminous cloud over her head,
and betoken something good in her — betoken the
possible source of something different from a malignant touch — yes, of " genuinely successful medical
practice."

We know little of her character ; there is no impeachment of it in the recorded testimony. Her

peculiar powers resulted, no doubt, from peculiar in nate formations of and connections between her outer and inner organisms, and had little dependence upon intellectual or moral qualities. Not her own holi- ness, nor any other common power of hers, enabled her to either intensify or abate painful sensations. Whether sinner or saint was the more prominent in her character, our course and views have no occasion to inquire.

Winthrop's comments say that " her behavior at her trial was very intemperate; lying notoriously and railing upon the jury and witnesses; . . . in the like distemper she died." He gives no particulars, and therefore furnishes no grounds on which we may judge whether any of her statements which seemed to him false, might not seem to us, at our different stand-point of observation, to have been true. Very many perfectly true utterances made by mediums to-day relative to their involuntary and even uncon- scious putting forth of acts and words imputed to them, would be deemed lies by all common interpre- ters who are ignorant of the part often performed by or through that higher set of mental powers which our leading scientists have lately discovered are at the service of intellect not our own. Perhaps she lied; perhaps, too, she was truthful, but misunderstood. In- temperance in her behavior, no doubt, was manifest. But that might spring from various motives. Any spirited person, consciously innocent of a charged offense, and possessing only moderate power of self- control and moderate intellectual stamina, would be very likely to pour forth warm language, and flat and forceful denials of allegations of wrong-doing. Per-

secuted innocence was only a very little less likely —
if at all less — than ill temper or "distemper," to
call forth what might seem to be "railing upon the
jury and witnesses." Neither severe language nor
"intemperate behavior" is necessarily derogatory to
any one's prevailing temper or character, when rushing forth from the lips and limbs of one whose deeds
are being so misinterpreted that beneficence is looked
upon as diabolism, and whose beneficent works are
being made to draw down upon their author an ignominious death.

Possibly words from her lips, and behavior seemingly prompted by her emotions, were manifestations
of the thoughts and impulses of some other intelligence than herself. If so, most scathing rebukes for
her persecution, and for thirstings for her blood, might
fall thick and heavy upon the ears of benighted jurors
and blinded witnesses. Observation has often noticed
most terrific outflowings of denunciations upon blind
guides, through organs of speech not controlled by
their reputed owner. Felix is not the last person
who has trembled under the lashings of inspiration.
An acting out through her form, by another intelligence, a deep sense of wrong she had received, may
have made her seem as mad in the eyes of Winthrop,
as the learning and forceful utterances of Paul did
him in those of Festus.

Evidence produced at her trial shows that Margaret Jones correctly foretold the course of diseases
in the systems of those who declined her prescriptions
— that she foretold other "things which came to pass
accordingly" — that she learned the purport of conversations by the absent or secluded — that a spirit

child became visible in her auras — and that the sickened maid was cured by her appliances. Each and
all of these very marvelous manifestations were just
as distinctly and authentically recorded on paper still
extant, as were those less rare ones which have
been put forth as fair indices of the case. Such
blinking out of sight the most important things pertaining to the person who, as far as is now known,
was first on this side the Atlantic to be executed for
witchcraft, is unjust to culture and philosophy, which
should be furnished with all known facts; is unjust
to the fathers, whose full basis for her prosecution
and execution should be set forth ere just judgment of their doings can be formed; and is unjust
to her whose transcendent powers and effective labors
for healing the sick may have been the main cause
why minds deluded by a false and frenzying creed
devil-ward, were impelled on to barbarously destroy
one who had been and might have continued to be
their benefactress.

She was a natural conduit from the inner to the
outer world, through which perhaps impersonal force
at times might cause supernal knowledge and power
to come into her outer being; through which again,
her own will might suction such, while at other times
unseen persons might inject them through from their
abodes, and even come themselves to aid her in their
application. Nothing harmful was charged against
her, excepting what seemed to be, and were believed
to be, superhuman abilities.

The power that formed her originally, implanted
and developed within her organism unusual capabilities for curing physical disease, for reading the

future, and hearing the distant. There is neither evidence nor foundation for a conjecture that she was ever pupil of teachers of medical science, or of jugglery, nor that she belonged to any mesmerically developing circle. Her acts cannot well have been mere imitations of what she had seen others do, or had read or heard of having been done. She had no teachers, no confederates that were visible and tangible. Indeed, who among men could possibly have taught or helped her to prophesy correctly, to hear the far distant, or to embody a spirit child? Not one — not one. Such performances were only natural evolutions from her inborn faculties, when acted upon by spirit forces or agents, or both. The reader is asked how these manifestations, through our first martyr to it, can *possibly* be explained on the hypothesis that witchcraft was nothing else than the histrionic tricks of sprightly and cunning children, either singly or in combination with the ingenuities and malignities of old women. Such agents, unaided from out the unseen, were most clearly incompetent to project into human view some phenomena which attended upon this consternating seer, hearer, healer, and holder of properties for materializing a spirit form so as to render it visible.

What possible facts or considerations could have induced the humane, intelligent, virtuous, and religious community in which she lived, to seek the life of such a woman, moving, probably, in humble sphere, but, in the main, a doer of good works? The question brings up a complex and difficult problem, viz., How can the seeming stupidity and inhumanity of our fathers be reconciled with their obvious intelligence and humaneness?

Assuming the record of testimony given in court to be correct — and why should we not ? — the manifestations through and around Margaret Jones clearly indicated the outworking there of some abilities which the bodies and ordinary mental powers of embodied human beings do not possess. What then ? Some unseen power must have helped her. What unseen power ? Yes, *what* unseen power ? Experience as then interpreted — religious creeds as then understood — science and philosophy as they then existed — all conspired to give one and the same answer, viz., *The Devil.* That conclusion from the witnessed facts was then inevitable. The devil helped her. What next ? The devil could help no one who had not previously entered into a covenant with him, and he surely helped this woman. Therefore she had made a covenant with him, and in making that she became a *witch.* The law of God which binds Christians says, " Thou shalt not suffer a witch to live." Thus our forefathers saw and reasoned. Steps from facts to the conclusion were few, short, and plain. Feeble intellects *could* take them, and strong ones *must* do so, or reject their life-long creeds. Then a crucial hour was upon them. To distrust and disregard their credal faith or stifle their humanity, one or the other, was the hard alternative presented to strong, good men. Their cherished creed or Margaret Jones, one or the other, must be sacrificed. Which ? Clear heads and life-long affections grasped the creed firmly, and resolved to save it. They let Logic draw her rigid conclusions, and put them forth as rules for individual and public action. Sympathy went down before dominant faith, and man stifled every rebellious

emotion. God's call and law, Christian men then felt,
were paramount to sympathy. In submission to what
they deemed Heaven's will and call they said, "Down,
humaneness — down ! Up, God-derived Faith — up,
in your majesty and might ! Heart must follow whither you lead." Their awful and cramping *Creed devil-
ward* was the chief fountain of bewildering and bru-
talizing force that dragged intelligent and kind men
on to redden our soil with innocent blood, and that
too "in all good conscience."

Look closely at their position. The faith of all
ages and nations had held that occurrences which
seemed to result from supermundane force were produced by disembodied intelligences. Protestant
Christendom was extensively holding that no invisible beings, excepting their Great Monstrous Monk-
made Devil (see Appendix) and his obedient servants,
could by any possibility work upon the bodies and
possessions of men. And none such could work upon
the external world in any other way than through, or
by the aid of, such mortals as had voluntarily made a
covenant with him. Such covenant once formed, the
person making it would be an open door through
which his fearful Majesty, or any imp of his, could
freely enter the outer world and vent his malignity
upon all the region far and wide around his entrance-
place. Her works proved to the intellect of that day
that this Margaret had covenanted to let him enter
and co-operate with her. What, therefore, must be
done ? It was manifest to the people of Charlestown
that through her the great invisible cloven-foot had
found entrance, and was prowling among them.
What was their duty ? They must bar his entrance

promptly. To do it, they arrested, tried, condemned, and executed the Christian traitor who had furnished their great enemy entrance to the Christian fortress. Could firm, true men, holding then prevalent beliefs, have done less?

That prisoner was put to trial before judge, jury, and a public who each and all held the then common creed throughout all Protestant Christendom which is set forth in our Appendix. Witnesses swore that she accurately foretold the effects of medical treatment and other events; that she heard speeches by persons far remote from her; that a spectral child was seen in her presence; that her hands and simples wrought marvels, — therefore, how could jurors avoid conviction that the devil helped her? There was no spectral testimony in this case; outer senses of many persons had learned her supermundane powers. The nature of the testimony was unexceptionable, and its purport distinct and conclusive. The prevalent faith imperatively demanded that the verdict should be — *guilty*. The clear, strong faith of that day, in whomsoever it conjoined with good conscience and courage, put forth mighty power to persuade the good citizen and good man that high duty was calling upon him to gird on heavenly armor and fight for the destruction of this minion and colleague of the devil, even at the smothering of kindlier sentiments in his heart. She was *witch*, and therefore must die. Was that a *deluded* court, representative of a *deluded* people, which condemned Margaret Jones to " hang high on the gallows-tree "? No doubt it was. Delusion led not only our fathers here, but all Christendom, on to deeds of shameful bloodshed. Witchcraft itself, as a whole, is now by most people deemed a " *dark delusion.*" But which, among the human faculties, did that delusion spell-bind, stultify, and make sanguinary?

Were the external senses of a whole community so disordered that the character and dimensions of sensible acts were grossly misapprehended? No. The circumstances amid which the early colonists lived, were certainly as well fitted to sharpen, discipline, and give reliability to the external senses as those which wait upon their descendants in the present century. Whatever eyes saw, ears heard, or touch felt in 1648, was reported to the mind then as accurately as the same senses can report to-day. Witchcraft phenomena were not the fictions of deluded *senses.*

Did that delusion dominate those mental faculties which clothe in words and report what the senses had learned, and derange them so effectually that they would put forth even under oath distorting and exaggerated accounts of facts which the senses had witnessed? We think not. Distrust of the truthfulness and discrimination of ancient unknown witnesses, founded mainly upon the marvelousness of facts they swore to knowledge of, is not a basis that either candor or justice can deem sufficient to sustain a' charge that their testimony was misleading. Wherein. lurks anything which indicates that the witnesses in this case stated anything that was not substantially true? If anywhere, it is probably in modern incredulity that spirits ever colabor with or act upon men. If the time shall come — and there now exist signs that it is near — when the cultured world shall learn that *science* has been unwittingly *generating delusion* by failing to detect and regard the existence of certain occult agents and forces which play important parts in scenes of nature and human society, then a greatly modified opinion concerning the truth of testimony evoked in witchcraft times may prevail throughout the enlightened world. The signs of to-day make it prudent, kind, and just to conceive that ancient *witnesses* were quite as truthful and discriminating as modern elucidators of remote transactions have generally been.

Were the faculties of jurors and judges for comprehending the accuracy, force, and tendency of testimony, and for logically deducing conclusions from proved facts, so deluded as that the whole court, without a misgiving, convicted either on false testimony or illogically? Candor must hesitate to say yes — especially in a case where such a man as Governor Winthrop sat upon the bench. He and his associates in the court may have been as free from any delusion that impaired or perverted their powers of discrimination, or for logical inferences from facts, as any court that has adjudicated since their day. The absolute cruelty and injustice of their verdict and sentence, however, do indicate delusion of some faculties; but not of the senses; not of the capacities to speak truth, and "nothing but the truth;" not of the capacities to sift evidence and to reason logically — not of these.

Their faculties for receiving, containing, holding on to, and obeying an inherited FAITH were the *deluded* ones. In common with all Christendom the convictors of witches had been deluded into adoption, or at least retention, of a woful creed concerning the devil. At that time public sentiment in most countries on the

continent of Europe, and also in both Old and New
England, demanded rigid enforcement of all laws
which that false, mischief-working creed had engendered and recorded in statute-books. Such laws were
plain and imperative ; both jurors and judges, sup-
prèssing sentiment, must yield to logic — must convict and senteuce. By no other course could they be
true to their convictions of duty toward society
around them, or toward God on high. Yes ; an imported monastic-born FAITH, unnatural, erroneous,
and more than barbarous, deluded kind and good
men to feel that they must suppress sympathy, ignore their tender impulses, benumb their hearts,
and, whither God's voice was believed to call, go forward in stern, agonizing resolve to thrust a devil-
helped worker, however good and estimable in outward seeming, to where the wicked one could do them
and theirs no mischief through that mortal ally. Such
was the logical and stern demand of the old deluding
and heart-curbing creed.

Do we wonder in our day how such monstrous faith
could ever have obtained and kept both an abiding
hold and controlling authority in any clear head that
was joined to a kindly heart ? Seeds of faith get
lodgment in the human brain while it is yet too
young to understand or even try to test the nature
and quality of what falls upon it. Whatever the
church and public believe, and have believed through
a long past, is ever dropping its own seed into opening minds, which forthwith germinates therein. This
sends its roots deep into virgin soil, grows with vigor
there, and becomes fruitful of the same old faith during that very early portion of life in which the infan·

8

tile questioning, analyzing, and reasoning faculties
are scarce able to doubt the soundness or excellence
of what thence has grown and matured in close alliance with themselves. Faith's right and fitness to
define duty, and the child's obligation to execute its
requirements, are usually conceded by all the other
faculties. The truer and better the man, the more
surely will he carry out his faith to its logical demands, even though, Abraham like, he have to lay
his dearest on the altar of sacrifice, to lift the knife,
and nerve himself to plunge it into his own child's
heart, unless some voice from on high, more potent
than previous faith, shall bid him hold. Few other
than strong men and true, conscious of being sol-
diers in heaven's army, would march resolutely to
the Devil's living and shotted guns, purposing to destroy them; for their destruction was instinct with,
and inseparable from, anguish to Christian neighbors
and friends. Extremists alone would do that. None
midway between vile demons and men of high faith
in God would voluntarily meet that ordeal.

We do not regard *all* the active prosecutors and
convictors of witches as having been actuated by well-
defined faiths and high principles. When popular
furor sets strongly in any direction, the thoughtless,
the unprincipled, the cruel, the malicious, join in the
rush, and some such often become conspicuous and
heartless agents in confounding confusion and in executing public decrees. Still, nearly all eminent men
of both Europe and America — the leading divines,
jurists, and civilians, the men of culture and of influence — believed that witchcraft and the witchcraft
devil existed, and that witches should be detected

and punished by the processes and laws then deemed applicable in such cases. Therefore, the mass of the people, however ignorant, thoughtless, or rash, when detecting and punishing witches, were only hastening to effect by rough processes and expeditiously, no more than the learned, more orderly, and patient would have felt constrained to accomplish, in the end, from a firm conviction of duty. Good faith and conscientious regard for the public weal actuated and sustained all those "solid men of Boston" and its vicinity, who were the real bones, sinews, and muscles which brought the devil's seeming helper to the gallows.

Whether this impressible and unfolded woman was literally aided in any of her marvelous operations by invisible *intelligences* may be debatable. It is possible that forces subject to no will but her own, and not even to that at all times, may have passed from her into other persons, which relieved some and agonized others extensively. Medication of her simples may have been mainly their natural absorption of elements residing in her system, or which were naturally attracted into and through that peculiar system. Her correct perceptions of the future action of remedies prescribed by either herself or others, and of the future course and result of diseases, may have been obtained by her own inner faculties when partially and transiently disentangled from her outer ones, and sensing in knowledge from the hidden realm of causes. So too she may have been at times so nearly a freed spirit, that she could by her own perceptives accurately sense coming events, and hear the words of far distant speakers. We refrain from denying the possibility that such auras resided in, emanated from, and surrounded her body, that a spirit child coming within them was by natural impersonal forces there rendered visible to external optics. It is possible there was no phenomenon in this case that must be called *spiritual*, excepting the mere *advent* of the child — not its visibility, but its *advent*. If the child was there, then a spirit was there, and it was a case of Spiritualism. All this is possible; but we ask whether it is probable that all works seeming to be hers were produced by blind natural forces and her own will and powers solely? To this our own answer is an emphatic NO. The presence of the child gives force to that response. If one spirit came to her, others could have come.

The old records are nearly or quite devoid of information relating to the intelligence, character, and social position of Margaret Jones. She was wife of Thomas Jones, who, soon after her execution, took passage on board a vessel for Barbadoes. We have met with no indication that they had children — with nothing which alludes to his age, occupation, or standing in society. We find her a practicer of the healing art; but at what age, or amid what worldly circumstances, is all unknown.

Bunker Hill and its circumjacent slopes and lowlands have close connection with the earlier stages of two American conflicts for freedom. There lived, and from thence was taken to prison and the gallows, the first American martyr in a war whose end, obtained forty-four years later at Salem Village, was Christendom's mental emancipation from deluding and dwarfing bondage to a more than savage creed. True, the aggressive hosts — the prosecutors for witchcraft —

were ignorant and unsuspicious of the far-reaching purposes of the divinity that shaped their ends, that beheld and ruled over their blind violence, and made them, all unconsciously and undesignedly, mortally rend a monster-creed whose demands they were slavishly and blindly complying with, and thus, without knowledge of it on their part, procuring for themselves, their children, and all future Christians, new freedom and new incentives for independent speculations and conclusions regarding all matters both demonological and theological. A nightmare of centuries was thrown off from disturbed and horrified Christendom at Salem, and each cramped sufferer could thenceforth draw breath more freely, and commence processes of recuperation and expansion.

The case of Margaret Jones is isolated. It has no traceable connection with any kindred one which either preceded or followed it. Still its origin was in the abiding-place of forces and operators acting invisibly upon the external world, and amidst which all genuine witchcraft, miracle, and Spiritualism have been born.

Her case must be catalogued among the marvelous, though the proving of the nature and character of her offense, erroneously so called, was unattended by the absurdities and cruelties which attach to many cases where spectral evidence was admitted, and barbarous processes were resorted to for extorting a plea to an indictment. As a witchcraft trial, hers was exceptionally inoffensive to modern views of propriety. The testimony throughout was based on experiences and observations by external senses, and would be admissible in any court and any age. The extra-common powers or susceptibilities of the accused were clearly proved. Therefore the monstrous creed which then blinded and tyrannized over all minds took her life legitimately. Good men, humane men, could do no less than pronounce her guilty before the law and before that creed which engendered the law. Before we denounce or even disparage those who condemned her, let us pause for reflection.

"A creed sometimes remains outside of the mind, incrusting and petrifying it against all other influences addressed to the higher parts of our nature, manifesting its power by not suffering any fresh and living conviction to get in." — *John Stuart Mill.*

We requote as follows : —

"The nobler tendency of culture, and above all of scientific culture, is to honor the dead without groveling before them — to profit by the past without sacrificing it to the present."

The early colonists of the old Bay State deserve to be held in high esteem and admiration ; all noble sentiments conspire to honor them. Culture and enlightenment will be derelict to their high calling if they traduce that people before they turn thought backward through two centuries, scan the imported creeds then prevalent here, observe circumstances then existing, and enter into feelings and views then bearing resistless sway. Having done that, let them calmly determine whither duty led true-hearted, clear-headed, strong, courageous, and devout men in relation to witchcraft matters. Many old beliefs may be discarded ; many mistakes and errors of the past be shunned. We are not called to grovel before our ancestors ; but shame, shame be to us if we brand them with egregious "credulity and infatuation," solely or mainly because their senses perceived and they described events which we cannot explain if we grant to them clear, sagacious, and well-balanced intellects for reporting facts which they observed. They were our peers in most good qualities and powers, and deserve our admiration.

Did we know the spot where the dust of Charlestown's gifted physician reposes, we might desire to see a modest monument there bearing the following inscription : —

TO THE MEMORY

OF

MARGARET JONES,

America's first Martyr to Spiritualism :
Who was hanged in Boston,
June 15, 1648,
Because God had given her such Organization and Receptivities
that beneficent occult Powers, using her successfully
as an Instrument in curing
Human Ills,
So excited the Consternation of a Devil-fearing People,
That, knowing not what they did,
They cried,
CRUCIFY HER! CRUCIFY HER!

ANN HIBBINS.

WE lead attention next to one who moved in the highest circle of Boston society — to an elderly lady of wit, culture, high connections socially, and of friendship with many of the most prominent and virtuous people of her day. So far as known, hers is meager as a case of witchcraft, attended by a less variety and extent of startling phenomena than most others; but it well reveals the force of the witchcraft creed, and the shifts of historians for explaining its only marvelous phenomenon which history hints at.

Hutchinson says, " The most remarkable occurrence in the colony in the year 1655 [1656 ?] was the trial and condemnation of Mrs. Ann Hibbins for witchcraft. Her husband, who died in the year 1654, was an agent for the colony in England, several years one of the assistants, and a merchant of note in the town of Boston; but losses in the latter part of his life had reduced his estate, and increased the natural crabbedness of his wife's temper, which made her turbulent and quarrelsome, and brought her under church censures, and at length rendered her so odious to her neighbors as to cause some of them to accuse her of witchcraft. The jury brought her in guilty, but the magistrates refused to accept the verdict; so the cause came to the general court, where the popular clamor prevailed against her, and the miserable old woman was condemned and executed. Search was made upon her body for teats, and her chests and boxes for puppets, images, &c.; but there is no record of anything of that sort being found. Mr. Beach, a minister in Jamaica, in a letter to Dr. Increase Mather in the year 1684, says, ' You may remember what I have sometimes told; your famous Mr. Norton once said at his own table before Mr. Wilson the pastor, elder Penn, and myself and wife, &c., who had the honor to be his guests, that one of your magistrates' wives, as I remember, was hanged for a witch only for having more wit than her neighbors. It was his very expression; she having, as he explained it, unhappily guessed that two of her persecutors, whom she saw talking in the street, were talking of her, which, proving true, cost her her life, notwithstanding all he could do to the contrary, as he himself told us.'

" It fared with her as it did with Joan of Arc in France. Some counted her a saint and some a witch, and some observed solemn marks of Providence set upon those who were very forward to condemn her, and to brand others upon the like ground with the like reproach."

The author of the above was born fifty-five years after the execution of Mrs. Hibbins, and his account of her was not published till 1764, that is, one hundred and eight years after her decease. In his youth he may have conversed with aged people who were living at the time of the trial and execution of this woman, and may have received from them their notions concerning her temper and character. But if he did, his informers, during more than half a century before he was old enough to be an intelligent listener, had been living in the midst of people who were ashamed of the treatment which they and their

fathers had bestowed upon reputed witches. Thus
ashamed and yielding to an almost universal propensity in men to make their own imputed errors and
crimes seem slight, trivial, and excusable as possible,
nothing would be more natural than a general propensity to vilify the sufferers, under a mistaken,
though common, notion that the vileness of the persecuted excuses the wrong of the persecutors.

Whether Hutchinson, in his youth, received from
any source special mental biases which inclined him
to regard all who suffered for witchcraft as quarrelsome and vicious, cannot now be ascertained ; but it
is obvious from his epithets that his disposition let
him very readily apply to such persons terms of very
decided disparagement.   He spoke of one Mary Oliver
as " a poor wretch ; " also of Mrs. Hibbins as " the
miserable old woman," and specified the " natural
crabbedness of her temper which made her turbulent
and quarrelsome."   He implies that such traits were
both the grounds and the sum of the charge and proofs
of her witchcraft, and does all this without adducing
a particle of evidence that she possessed such a temper,
or was either *turbulent* or *quarrelsome*.   His allegations
seem like the offspring of either blinding contempt or
of deluded fancy, — yes, *deluded*, — for surely clear-
eyed fancy must have foreseen that after ages could
never believe that the highest court in the colony
found natural crabbedness of temper, and consequent
turbulence, satisfactory proof of an explicit compact
with the devil, and therefore punishable by death.
The insufficiency and probable inaccuracy of his reasons for the arraignment and condemnation of this
person, will be more clearly exhibited further on, and
mainly in extracts from a later historian.

Mr. Beach's letter, quoted by Hutchinson, gives distinct indication that Mrs. Hibbins was endowed with faculties which were vastly more likely to out-work what her age deemed witchcraft, than was any amount of bad temper and crabbedness. She had "more wit than her neighbors;" she "unhappily guessed that two of her persecutors, whom she saw talking in the street, were talking of her, which, proving true, cost her her life." Here is indication of probability that this lady, as did Margaret Jones, possessed ability to comprehend the conversation of far distant parties, or to sense in the thoughts of some absent people with whom she came in rapport. Similar abilities are possessed and exercised by many persons in these days, who have constitutional endowments of a kind which were formerly believed to be diabolical acquisitions, and were then deemed proofs of witchcraft — proofs of compact with Satan.

"It fared with her," says Hutchinson, "as it did with Joan of Arc in France. Some counted her a saint and some a witch." In these words the historian himself furnishes cause for distrusting the justice of ascribing to her a crabbed temper and habitual quarrelsomeness. For who, in any community, would ever count one *a saint* who manifested such offensive qualities to any great extent as he ascribed to her? Surely no one would. And yet he states that very many persons did so count Mrs. Hibbins. Doubtless among her advocates was "your famous Mr. Norton," a very eminent, sagacious, and able minister in Boston. There was enough about her to draw out from Hutchinson the concession that the public here was divided in judgment concerning her character, as it formerly

was in France concerning Joan of Arc, that Maid of
Orleans, who heard and obeyed voices from out the
unseen.

Crabbedness of temper and quarrelsomeness were
not grounds on which any portion of the people would
count her a *saint*. The historian refutes his own
position. A more recent searcher for causes of her
fate perceived, and very clearly pointed out, the inaccuracy and obvious insufficiency of Hutchinson's
grounds and reasons why Mrs. Hibbins was arraigned
and convicted, but proceeded to assign others which
are scarcely less inadequate and improbable. He
writes as follows, vol. i. p. 422, *Hist. of Witchcraft:* —

" While it is hardly worthy of being considered a
sufficient explanation of the matter, — it being beyond
belief, that, even at that time, a person could be condemned and executed merely on account of a ' crabbed temper,' — it is not consistent with the facts as
made known to us from the record-offices. She could
not have been so reduced in circumstances as to produce such extraordinary effects upon her character,
for she left a good estate. . . . The only clew we
have to the kind of evidence bearing upon the charge
of witchcraft that brought this recently bereaved
widow to so cruel and shameful a death, is in a letter written by a clergyman in Jamaica to Increase
Mather " (as quoted above). " Nothing," Upham
adds, " was more natural than for her to suppose,
knowing the parties, witnessing their manner, considering their active co-operation in getting up the
excitement against her, which was then the all-engrossing topic, that they were talking about her.
But, in the blind infatuation of the time, it was

considered proof positive of her being possessed, *by the aid of the devil*, of supernatural insight — precisely as, forty years afterward, such evidence was brought to bear with telling effect against George Burroughs. . . . The truth is, that the tongue of slander was let loose upon her, and the calumnies circulated by reckless gossip became so magnified and exaggerated, and assumed such proportions, as enabled her vilifiers to bring her under the censure of the church, and that emboldened them to cry out against her as a witch."

Some of our quotations are introduced quite as much for the purpose of exhibiting the animus, shortcomings, and over-doings of the historians themselves, as for elucidating the general subject of witchcraft. We learn from the pages of the work from which the above extract was taken, that Mrs. Hibbins was sister of Richard Bellingham, deputy-governor of the province at the very time of her trial, and that her highly-esteemed husband had left her an estate which placed her far above poverty. It may fairly be presumed that both her social and pecuniary conditions were very respectable. Upham perceives and forcibly comments upon the inadequacy of the grounds upon which Hutchinson attempted to account for her conviction and execution. That earlier historian evinced, on very many of his pages, his persuasion, or at least a purpose to persuade his readers, that all the peculiar and disturbing phenomena of witchcraft were of exclusively mundane origin, and that temper, trick, imposture, deception, and the like, produced them all. This persuasion made him somewhat impatient of the whole matter, uncareful to scan all the facts

before him, or keep his inferences in fair and broad
harmony with them. It made him rashly severe.
Without indicating a shadow of reason why he does
so, he calls this widow of one of Boston's most
esteemed merchants and public men — this sister of
the deputy-governor of the province — this woman of
more wit than her neighbors — this woman befriended
by the eminent minister John Norton — this woman
not in poverty — this woman whom he ought to have
known, did, in her lowest condition, even when a
convict in prison and doomed to the gallows — did, in
this dire extremity, bespeak and obtain the friendly
offices of six or eight of the leading men of the city,
and therefore presumably had their respect — such a
one, Hutchinson gratuitously calls a " miserable old
woman ; " and in doing it reveals the careless and
heartless historian of those who had come under ban
for witchcraft.

Upham, going to the probate records and finding
the will of Mrs. Hibbins, which was made a few days
after her sentence of death, is able to present her in
a different aspect. His comments upon her, as she is
revealed by the will and its codicils, are as follows,
vol. i. p. 425 : —

." The whole tone and manner of these instruments
give evidence that she had a mind capable of rising
above the power of wrong, suffering, and death itself.
They show a spirit calm and serene. The disposition
of her property indicates good sense, good feeling, and
business faculties suitable to the occasion. In the
body of the will, there is not a word, a syllable, or a
turn of expression, that refers to or is in the slightest
degree colored by her peculiar situation. In the codi-

cil there is this sentence : 'My desire is that all my
overseers would be pleased to show so much respect
unto my dead corpse, as to cause it to be decently
interred, and, if it may be, near my late husband.''
Perusal and study of her will and its appendages
induced the later historian to speak of Ann Hibbins
as " this recently bereaved widow " — a phrase much
more agreeable, and seemingly vastly more just in
application to her, than " miserable old woman." In
that will she names as overseers and administrators
of her estate, Captain Thomas Clarke, Lieutenant
Edward Hutchinson, Lieutenant William Hudson,
Ensign Joshua Scottow, and Cornet Peter Oliver ;
also in a codicil, she says, " I do earnestly desire
my loving friends, Captain Johnson and Edward Raw-
son, to be added to the rest of the gentlemen mentioned as overseers of my will." Upham, having
stated the above, says, " It can hardly be doubted
that these persons — and they were all leading citizens
— were known by her to be among her friends." Yes,
the presumption is very fair, amounting to almost positive proof, that many of the prominent and best
people of the town were her friends. The appearance is, that her social walk was wide away from the
purlieus of common mundane diabolism and billings-
gate. The vulgar would see her standing off beyond
their reach, and waste no breath upon her. Only the
respectable and influential could touch her to her essential harm.

We commend and thank the later historian for
bringing this persecuted woman out into such light
as shows that she may have been equal in all good
qualities to the best of her persecutors. But his

reasons for her persecution and condemnation are scarcely more adequate or credible than those of Hutchinson. We ascribed to him the faculties of a fictionist, and he used them when he said, "The truth is, that the tongue of slander was let loose upon her." The former historian imputed certain offensive acts or traits to both Margaret Jones and Ann Hibbins severally, which he assumed to be the provoking causes of public vengeance. He deemed the sufferers themselves doers of the intolerable wrongs. But his successor makes her beneficence the crime for which Mrs. Jones suffered; and the origination and utterance of slander *by the public*, the cause of death to Mrs. Hibbins. The earlier writer was lenient toward the public and severe upon the accused women. The later was kind toward the women, but, by necessary implication, intensely aspersory upon the great body of the people; for he makes the public hang one because of her successful medical practice by the use of only simple remedies, and another because of slanders which itself had poured out upon her.

His charge of slander is fictitious. He adduces no evidence that the lady was slandered, and we have met with none anywhere. And were it true, it is quite as much "beyond belief that even at that time a person could be condemned and executed merely on account of being" *slandered*, as it is that one could have then been thus treated on account of a "crabbed temper" solely.

A much more probable cause of the persecution of Mrs. Hibbins than either of the historians drew forth and rested upon, lurks in that language of "famous Mr. Norton," which says that she "having more wit than her neighbors, unhappily guessed that two of her persecutors, whom she saw talking in the street, were talking of her, which proving true, cost her her life." Upham, commenting upon that, says, "Nothing was more natural than for her to suppose, knowing the parties, witnessing their manner, considering their active co-operation in getting up the excitement against her, which was then the all-engrossing topic, that they were talking about her." Whence and how did the accomplished rhetorician learn that those two persecutors were active co-operators, or that they were in any degree concerned "in *getting up*" the excitement against her? How *know* that their manner was expressive of any particular topic of conversation? How *know* that she or her case was the then all-engrossing topic? He put forth assumptions as though they were historic facts. No ancient record is credited with them; none contains them that we have met with. He could not well know them to be true. They are fairly reasonable fictions; but we must doubt whether they are either known or knowable as *facts*. They would be agreeable amplifications if they did not tend to mislead and blind; they would be beauties, and not blemishes, if the soundness and sufficiency of their underlying theory or assumption were conceded. But it is not. Common sense cannot concede it. Boston was neither doltish enough nor wicked enough to generate and sustain *slander* of such quantity and quality as would force one of her ladies of wit and high connections to die ignominiously on the gallows — never, never. Neither the temper of the woman herself, nor any combined baseness and malice that ever existed in the orderly and religious town

9

of Boston, is admissible as the chief cause of that woman's execution.   Her own *wit* was the historic, and,
when defined and illustrated, may appear to be the
real cause.

Whether Mrs. Hibbins received on that occasion,
and might have been accustomed to get, knowledge
by other than man's ordinary processes, and to such
extent and of such kind as implied her possession of
some faculties above or distinct from great powers at
guessing, can best be inferred by looking at the views
of her utterances which were taken by those who
heard them.   Their persecution of her unto death
tells what those views were.   Have historians made
fair and full use of the very small historic basis extant, for accounting for the state and nature of public
feeling among the neighbors of this woman?   We
think not.   Her *wit*, the true corner-stone, has not
been their basis of explanation.

When she saw two known persecutors talking, the
circumstances may or may not have been helpful to a
correct guess at the topic of their conversation *then*.
But — but these men, Upham assumes, were *already*
known to her as her persecutors.   Therefore something must have occurred before that time which had
aroused persecution of her.   These men are called
" two of her persecutors," which intimates that she
already may have had more than two, and admits the
supposition that she may have had very many such,
both prior to and at the very time when she made the
particular *guess* whose accuracy has been so plausibly
commented upon.   Something, antecedent to that
guess, had set some minds against her.   Yes, if we
may trust the conjecture of Upham, something had

already created an "excitement against her which
was then the all-engrossing topic." The cause of
antecedent and existing excitement, at the time she
made *that* guess, was seemingly unsought for by either
Hutchinson or Upham. Or, if they sought for this,
*the most important thing connected with the case, and
essential to its satisfactory elucidation*, they found nothing which they ventured to publish. Omission to
bring out the cause of public excitement, *prior to the
guess*, makes previous history very unsatisfactory.
There is some light shining now which may enable
the searcher in dark closets of the past to discover
meanings there which former explorers failed to find.
No new, positive, distinct historical statements explanatory of this case have been seen. We are confined to the same very narrow premises on which previous reasoners stood, but we find different import of
the same facts from any which prior expounders disclosed.

We join with Upham in saying that "*the only clew
we have to the kind of evidence bearing upon the
charge of witchcraft* that brought this recently bereaved
widow to so cruel and shameful a death, is in a letter
written by a clergyman in Jamaica to Increase Mather
in 1684." That letter, already quoted, imputes to her
more *wit* than others; wit, or penetration, by which
she sensed correctly the conversation going on between two of her persecutors. That is the full sum
of the direct historical evidence. And what is involved in that? Is crabbed temper there? No. Is
slander there? No; but *wit* is. Standing alone and
unexplained, this wit amounts, perhaps, to but little;
and yet when interpreted by her sad fate it may

amount to very much. It suggests forcibly the probability, bordering close upon certainty, that she was
endowed with some faculties which the sagacious Mr.
Norton called " wit " — but yet were such as could
obtain accurate knowledge so surprisingly as to suggest that it was obtained by process as occult as that
by which Jesus perceived the private reasonings of
scribes and pharisees — entrappers and persecutors
of himself.

To-day, — when observation is almost daily meeting with operations of faculties, in limited classes of
men and women, which enable them to read, at times,
the secret thoughts and hear the secret and hushed
utterances of some afar off, — that Jamaica letter intimates enough to generate presumption that Mrs.
Hibbins might have possessed like faculties, and that
her exercise of such startled, alarmed, and almost
frenzied a community in which such powers were
deemed proof positive that their possessor had made
a covenant with the Evil One, and received her surprising knowledge from him. Amid a people holding
such faith concerning the devil as the colonists here
entertained in 1656, the exercise of such powers called
upon all God-fearing and true men to rid the world
of such a devil-minion as the knowledge possessed by
Mrs. Hibbins proved her to be.

A sample of light which is now available shines
forth from the following letter, and its rays are blend-
ed in those from the lamp that guides our feet while
we move onward in tracing out the probable meaning
reachable by following up the only historic clew to
those powers of Mrs. Hibbins, her possession and exercise of which constituted a capital crime : —

"No. 1085 Washington St., Boston,
"September 23, 1873.

"Allen Putnam, Esq., Roxbury.

"Dear Friend: You solicit information in regard to hearing, from the *inner* ear, men and women speaking when miles away. I have always possessed that faculty in a remarkable degree. At one time, when building a steamboat in Southern Illinois, under peculiar circumstances, I would often hear men say, 'That man has no money to build a boat with; he's a fraud; and I pity those poor fellows who are working for him.' This was soon after I commenced her construction; and although I did not want to hear it, and tried ever so hard not to, still I could hear them seemingly more distinct than though they were close to me. One day in particular, and at a time when I could see no way out of my difficulty, I heard a Mr. Cutting, who was building some miles up river, say to his foreman, 'I wonder if Mr. Kimball realizes that his timber will be lost.' (Mr. Kimball was the man who furnished my timber and plank.) After the tide turned in my favor, and it was known about town that I paid my men regularly, I heard the remark, 'That man is the most reticent man I ever heard of,' &c."

The author of the letter does not state distinctly that in those two cases the speakers were very much too far away for his external ears to hear their voices, yet such was his statement when he gave me, previously, a verbal account of the facts; and such was his meaning, therefore, in the letter — the remainder of which here follows: —

" At one time, in Cincinnati, although three miles away, I heard my landlady say to her daughter, after I had been boarding with them a week, ' I don't like that man — he is *not* all right ; ' and went on to tell her impressions, what she thought I was, which it is not necessary to repeat. At first I felt indignant, forgetting, for the moment, I was three miles away. I finally concluded to say nothing about it when I went home at night, as I thought at first of doing, else they might think I was wrong in some way, as they were both members of the M. E. Church. But, when I got home, having a good opportunity, I told the daughter word for word what her mother had said about me, and also her response to her mother after she (the mother) had got through berating me — which was, ' What do you mean ? ' and the mother's answer to her exclamation, ' I mean just as I say.' I requested the daughter not to say anything to the mother, as it would do no good. But in the course of the following day the mother got speaking of me again in much the same strain, when the daughter could not resist the temptation, and told her to be careful what she said ; and then told her what I had said. The mother was thunderstruck, and after a moment said, ' He is a devil.' I happened to be in a condition such that I heard the mother's response. This I told to the daughter that evening. Now, if I had had a thought that the mother entertained such feelings toward me, I might have attributed it to the workings of my own mind. But as I thought they had diametrically the opposite opinion, I concluded that it was another case of the inner hearing.

" Now, if you can make use of this, or a part of it,

you are welcome to do so. Should you desire any other cases, I can furnish many.

" With high considerations I remain,
" D. C. DENSMORE."

The writer of the above, when in conversation with me in my own study, incidentally dropped a word which intimated that his inner ear was sometimes receptive of utterances put forth by embodied men and women, who, at the time, were far away from him. In response to my expressed wish to know whether such was the fact, he detailed a number of cases in which he had had such experience; I then asked him to give me one or two of them, briefly, on paper. That request shortly drew forth the foregoing letter.

Much more of the emphatically educational period of Captain Densmore's life was spent in forecastles and cabins of whaleships than in school on shore, and he perhaps expected me to reconstruct his sentences, in part at least, before presenting them in print. But such facts as his experience has encountered ought to be accompanied by the spirit of conscious knowledge and truth pervading his own vocabulary. His language is sufficiently perspicuous to convey his meaning, and possesses force which any considerable change would impair. That spirit makes rhetoric and grammar of secondary consequence in the narration of facts and experiences which show that there exist capacities in some embodied human beings for receiving intelligence-fraught impressions, in ways and under circumstances which the schoolmen and teachers of the world lack knowledge of, but ought to know and get instruction from. Therefore the reader has been permitted to see in his own words the statement of one who has at times heard with his inner or spiritual senses the exact words of speakers who were miles away from him, and thus shown that Mrs. Hibbins, through the possession of natural faculties, though of a kind but rarely developed, might have been something very different from a mere skillful guesser. An assumption that she was helped by spirits is not needful to a satisfactory explanation of a mode in which she might have learned directly and instantly what far absent ones were uttering. Her own faculties, independently of special spirit help or teaching, may have permitted her to hear with perfect distinctness what would have been utterly inaudible by mortals in their ordinary condition. Measuring the marvelousness of her knowledge by the frenzy it produced in the community, and the awful doom it drew upon herself, we look upon her manifestations of " wit " as an outflow of knowledge gained through her own inner or spiritual organs of perception — either with or without the aid of spirits.

When commenting upon what he assumed to be fact, viz., that Mrs. Hibbins made a correct guess, and only a *guess*, Upham says, that " in the blind infatuation of the time, it was considered proof positive of her being possessed, *by aid of the devil*, of supernatural insight." Thus he assumed that the mass of people in Boston were under such an infatuation as could and did cause them to believe that very successful *guessing* required the devil's help ! They may have been infatuated, but their infatuation did not act in that direction. Their senses and judgments for determining the forces needful to produce either material or mental effects, may, for aught that history states, have been as keen as any people ever possessed, and their general wisdom and thrift indicate that they did. Why, therefore, hastily brand them with the imbecility of being unequal to a fair, common-sense estimate of the adequacy of causes to produce observed effects? To do so is ungenerous, unjust, and uncalled for by their action. It may have been, and probably was, their freedom from infatuation; it may have been the very keenness and accuracy of their perceptions of the quantity and quality of cause needful to acquirement of knowledge which her utterances revealed, that generated and sustained the hostility against Mrs. Hibbins. Her accuracy in reading facts, secret and transpiring at a distance, was possibly, on many occasions, so far beyond what common experience or science was able to impute to either luck or skill at guessing, that few, if any, could avoid the conclusion that she was receiving supernal aid.

Anything supernal was then deemed devilish. After public excitement had been aroused against her, a very successful guess might possibly be evidence that the devil was its author, but not till the excitement had acquired and exercised bewildering force. Some extraordinary sayings or doings of this lady obviously must have antedated the public furore, else it would never have raged. The nature and circumstances of the case indicate an almost certainty that minds around her, while in their ordinary calmness, must have witnessed sayings or doings by her which "seemed to them more than natural" — which were startling — were out of the usual course, and readily distinguish-

able from GUESSINGS: because without something
of this kind the excitement itself could never have
commenced. What first started the public terror
of her is the most important question in the case.
The excitement did not spring up uncaused. A successful guess was no great novelty and no marvel in
times of calmness. It could not then be regarded
as diabolical. The bewilderings of antecedent causes
were needful to make a correct *guess* terrific. Excitement might metamorphose a guess into devil-imputed
knowledge, but a guess could not beget, though it
might intensify, blood-seeking excitement. Whence
the excitement itself — such excitement as could regard an accurate guess as necessarily the offspring of
diabolical insight?

Mrs. Hibbins lived among the *élite* of a province,
whose people were decidedly sagacious in matters of
both private and public business, and were also probably possessed of as high moral and religious principles, as prevailed in any other community on the
globe. As before stated, Richard Bellingham, one of
the very eminent men of the country, and at that time
deputy-governor of the province, was her brother;
she was widow of one who had been among the most
esteemed citizens of the town, and she is credited
with having possessed more wit than her neighbors.
Therefore we are hunting for a cause adequate to
excite public indignation against a woman of bright
intellect, of high position in society, and standing
under the shelter of near kinship with those in
authority. The cause must have been some strange
one. *Skill at guessing* was too common and natural,
and does not meet the requirements.

We all unite in calling the people of 1656 infatuated in relation to witchcraft. But did their infatuation so affect them as to bring obtuseness upon their external senses and their intellectual ability for discerning the nature, character, and force of testimony and evidence ? or, on the other hand, did it not show itself almost exclusively in their reception and tenacious retention of monstrous items in their witchcraft creed ? Which ? Admit an affirmative to the first part of the inquiry — admit that senses and intellects were befooled by external manifestations — and you make those noble forefathers but a band of dolts, heartless and bloodthirsty, taking life because they had not wit enough to read clearly the significance of observed external facts or to see the bearings and force of evidence. Admit the second, viz., that their creed was father of their infatuation, and you may look upon them as a band possessing clear perception of the exact meaning and logical results of all Christendom's fixed creed upon diabolism, and of unflinching purpose to fight for God and Christ against the devil. Demonologically they were infatuated, in common with the enlightened world ; while yet for keen observance of outward facts, for just estimate of the adequacy of a cause to produce an observed effect, for determining the just significance of any well-observed fact, for discriminating application of evidence under the rules of their creeds both God-ward and devil-ward, no reason appears why they were not equal to any other community anywhere. Their infatuation was not first on the practical, but on the theoretical side. It was devilward, not man-ward *directly*, though through the creed it became man-ward.

Though perceiving the meagerness and improb-
ability of Hutchinson's solution, Upham, ignoring
what he avowed to be the only historical " clew we
have " to a correct one, which led directly to the
woman's own *wit*, was pleased to find the exciting
cause of her persecution not in *her*, but in other people, and dogmatically said, " The *truth* is, the tongue
of slander was let loose against her." Such assumption — and it is bold assumption, even if it be in accordance with facts — fails — entirely fails — to meet
the fair demands of our common-sense requirements.
What started, and extended, and intensified that
tongue if it did wag? If its utterances were *slan-
derous*, they were a mixture of *falsehood* and *malice*.
What *lies* were or could be fabricated against such a
woman, the nature of which the common sagacity of
society there and then would not detect? What
lies which the truthfulness of society there and then
would not decline to repeat against her? What
malice against that lady of high connections could
so pervade society there as to generate a public sentiment that demanded and obtained , her life ? The
people of Boston were not wicked enough to let falsehood and malice triumph in their highest court of justice. Something different from *slander* was needed
to awaken and sustain the popular clamor against
this woman, and to cause the court to pass sentence
of death upon her. We granted to Upham the faculties of a fictionist, and he used them when he
declared that " the truth is, the tongue of slander
was let loose upon her." " The truth is," neither
he nor any other one among us at this day, knows
whether that woman was slandered or not. She may

have been, but it is only matter of conjecture, and should not be put forth as *truth*. Something more than slander in its utmost expandings and accretions was needful to the tragic results which ensued.

We recur again to the only historical cause of excitement against this lady, viz., Norton's hint that she possessed such marvelous wit for guessing, as Upham supposes the people around her considered "proof positive of her being possessed, *by the aid of the devil*, of supernatural insight." That hint unlocks a door behind which may be found a more adequate and philosophical cause of her arraignment and condemnation than has hitherto been assigned. Since many persons now possess, she too may have possessed constitutional faculties, which, at times, enabled her to *sense*, comprehend, and enunciate facts and truths which it was impossible for her to learn by man's ordinary processes. Admit simply that she may have possessed intuitive faculties which read the thoughts of others or sensed afar the spirit of sounds, and solution of all mysteries about her is made. Wide awake, keen-sighted, good people may have seen in her the exercise of such powers as were clearly, distinctly, and beyond all question, extraordinary, — yes, supermundane. What then? Why, by all fair logic from Christendom's faith at that time, the devil must be her teacher, and she must be his covenanted servant. Such a helper of Satan, however high in character or station, must be deprived of power to work for him. Very wonderful revelations, such as disclosures of the secret thoughts and private conversations of other and distant persons, being a few times repeated by her, what could

people, true to their God and their creed, do less
than demand her execution? Nothing — nothing less.
Their infatuated but sincere belief about the devil
plainly and with mighty force called for her blood.
And this not because of any crabbedness in her —
not because of any lies about her — not because of
malice toward her — not because of the tongue of
slander — but because of facts, unquestionable facts,
outwrought through her, which the tongue of truth
might dutifully publish and republish throughout the
town.   The trouble, the murderous impulses, sprang
from the *creed*, and especially from those parts of it
which made any and all mysterious and disturbing
outworkings devilish in their source, and which
taught that the devil could act through no human
beings but such as had made a voluntary compact
to serve him.   Those who had covenanted with him
must die.   Mrs. Hibbins was born with mediumistic
faculties, and because of her legitimate use of these,
the faith of her times conscientiously took her life.

It gladdens the heart to find a view which legitimately permits Mrs. Hibbins to have been a bright,
refined, high-toned, and most estimable lady; and
at the same time lessens the blackness of the cloud
which has long hung over her judges and executioners.   They were not so weak and wicked as to doom
one to die because of temper, nor so villainous as
to slander away a lady's life.   Stern religious adherence and application of an honest, though deluded *faith*, made them executioners of all such as
had exhibited powers which in the dim light of their
philosophy and science seemed supernatural.   Their
weakness consisted of such strong faith as could, and

in emergencies must, put in abeyance the kindlier
sentiments of their hearts. Their great, infirmity,
which was then a general one throughout Christendom, was solely infatuation *devil-ward*.

We charge our ancestors with *infatuation*. People
in all ages and nations have, no doubt, been subject
to its influence. Perhaps every individual man and
woman is more or less swayed by it. Each one
in respect to some things may act without his usual
good judgment, and contrary to the dictates of reason. The people of Boston were obviously debarred,
by their infatuation devil-ward, from perceiving that
Mrs. Hibbins might have received extraordinary gifts
from some other giver than the great evil devil. And
is it *impossible* that infatuation influenced her recent
historian first to reject the historic wit, and substitute for it fancied slander, as cause for the excitement against her, and then put his substitution forth
as the *truth;* though both common sense and sound
philosophy see at a glance, first, that it is only a conjecture, and secondly, that it is entirely inadequate
to produce the effects which it was fabricated to
account for ? In doing this *he* seemingly acted without *his* usual good judgment, and contrary to the
appropriate dictates of his enlightened reason — was
infatuated.

Both of the two historians above quoted, virtually
assumed that there never occurred here any phenomena, either mental or physical, which were not
wrought out by agents, forces, and faculties purely
mundane. Therefore the facts of history necessarily
pushed them up to make implied, and often explicit,
allegation that whole communities of resolute, wine-

awake, energetic people, were possessors of external
senses which were pitifully and superlatively deludible
— possessors of enormous general credulity — of perceptions and judgments woefully warped and benighted in matters generally, excepting only a few
of their girls and old women, who manifested cunning
and deviltry supreme in making high sport out of
the weaknesses of their elders and betters. Having
driven stakes beyond which nature and natural forces
must not go under forfeiture of historic recognition,
anything not explainable by forces recognized within
those stakes, is accounted for by the sage exclamation,
"But that was a time of great credulity;" or "in the
blind infatuation of the time," things were thus and
so. We are willing to grant the existence of much
credulity and infatuation both of old and now, but are
not willing to allow that the facts of seeing what some
other persons have not seen, and knowing the existence and partial operations of some forces in nature
which some people have not paid attention to, are
proof of either "great credulity" or "blind infatuation." Had the later historian been free from all
infatuation, he could have learned from passing developments that Mrs. Hibbins probably, at times, was
essentially a liberated spirit, hearing what Swedenborg calls "cogitatio loquens" — speaking thought
— and that her repetition of what she thus learned
took her life.

Hers was not a case of necessary spirit co-operation,
was perhaps only one of uncommon liberation of the
internal perceptive faculties. Because highly illumined, her brilliancy was judged to be diabolical, and
therefore must be extinguished.

ANN COLE.

MANIFESTATIONS differing widely from any noticed in the preceding cases, were observed in the presence of a Connecticut girl named Ann Cole. American witchcraft history has transmitted no distinct account of the use of human organs of speech by intellect that was foreign to the legitimate owner of the vocals used, prior to the instance described by Hutchinson in the following extract. The history of Ann Cole involves all that we know of the Greensmiths, husband and wife, mentioned therein, and who were executed for witchcraft.

"In 1662, at Hartford, Conn., one Ann Cole, a young woman who lived next door to a Dutch family, and, no doubt, had learned something of the language, was supposed to be possessed with demons, who sometimes spoke Dutch, and sometimes English, and sometimes a language which nobody understood, and who held a conference with one another. Several ministers, who were present, took down the conference in writing, and the names of several persons mentioned in the course of the conference as actors or bearing parts in it; particularly a woman, then in prison upon suspicion of witchcraft, one Greensmith, who, upon examination, confessed, and appeared to be surprised at the discovery. She owned that she and the others named had been familiar with a demon, who had carnal knowledge of her; and although she had not made a formal covenant, yet she had promised to be

10

ready at his call, and was to have had a high frolic at Christmas, when an agreement was to have been signed. Upon this confession she was executed, and two more of the company were condemned at the same time." Hutchinson also credits to Goffe's diary the statement that "after one of the witches was hanged, the maid was well."

Another account of this Ann's case, furnished by an eye-witness and personal hearer when she was in her trances, has been transmitted. The writer of it promptly made, but afterward lost, minutes of what he heard from her lips, and about twenty years afterward wrote his remembrances of the manifestations, and forwarded the following account to Increase Mather : —

"Anno 1662. This Ann Cole (living in her father's family) was taken with strange fits wherein she (or rather the devil, as 'tis judged, making use of her lips) held a discourse for a considerable time. The general substance of it was to this purport, that a company of familiars of the evil one (who were named in the discourse that passed from her) were contriving how to carry on their mischievous designs against some, and especially against her ; mentioning sundry ways they would take to that end, as that they would afflict her body, spoil her name, hinder her marriage, &c. . . . The conclusion was, 'Let us confound her language ; she may tell no more tales.' . . . The discourse passed into a Dutch tone, . . . and therein was given an account of some afflictions that had befallen divers, among the rest a young Dutch woman . . . that could speak but very little, had met with great sorrow, as pinchings of her arms in the dark, &c.

. . . Judicious Mr. Stone being by, when the latter discourse passed, declared it, in his thoughts, impossible that one not familiarly acquainted with the Dutch (which Ann Cole had not at all been) should so exactly imitate the Dutch tone in the pronunciation of English. . . . Extremely violent bodily motions she many times had, even to the hazard of her life, . . . and very often great disturbance was given in the public worship of God by her and two other women who had also strange fits. . . . The consequence was, that one of the persons presented as active in the forementioned discourse (a lewd, ignorant, considerably aged woman), being a prisoner upon suspicion of witchcraft, the court sent for Mr. Haynes and myself to read what we had written. . . . She forthwith and freely confessed these things to be true: (that she and other persons named in the discourse) had familiarity with the devil. Being asked whether she had made an express covenant with him, she answered, she had not, only as she promised to go with him when he called (which she had accordingly done sundry times). . . . Amongst other things, she owned that the devil had frequent use of her body with much seeming (but indeed horrible, hellish) delight to her. This, with the concurrent evidence, brought the woman and her husband to their death as the devil's familiars. . . . After this execution . . . the good woman had abatement of her sorrows, which had continued sundry years, and she yet remains maintaining her integrity.

" Ann Cole was daughter of John Cole, a godly man among us. She hath been a person esteemed pious, behaving herself with a pleasant mixture of humility and faith under very heavy sufferings, professing (as she did sundry times) that *she knew nothing* of those things that were spoken by her, but that her tongue was improved to express what never was in her mind." — *John Whiting to Increase Mather. Feb.* 1682.

The source of Hutchinson's information is not known. Rev. Mr. Whiting, of Hartford, was an eye and ear witness to what he relates, and therefore is the better authority. Some great discrepancies are obvious in the two accounts. One hundred years after her day the historian said Ann no doubt had learned something of the Dutch language. But the better authority, because it is that of one who both saw and heard the young woman when under control, and continued to obtain knowledge of her for twenty years subsequently, says she " had not at all been acquainted with " that language. The former says " the supposed demons " spoke through her sometimes in English and sometimes in Dutch ; while the latter " judged " that the devil alone was speaker, and implies that the language always was English, though the tones sometimes were very exactly Dutch. The devil was " judged " to be there divulging the malicious purposes of " a company of his familiars " toward certain human beings. Here is manifested a propensity, common to all describers of witchcraft scenes, to impute to the great devil himself whatever was projected forth from the realm of mysteries.

A careful reading of the two accounts excites conjecture that Hutchinson may have drawn his facts mainly from Whiting's letter, and yet failed to regard and adhere to opinions therein presented as to the actual speaker through Ann Cole's lips. Whiting says, that " she, or rather the *devil*, as 'tis judged, making use of her lips, held a discourse " in which sundry living persons were named as being familiars of the Evil One, and plotters of mischief against some of their neighbors, and especially against this Ann herself. This personal observer says, that " *she, or rather the devil,*" described Mrs. Greensmith and her associates, and disclosed their evil purposes toward Ann and some other mortals. But the historian greatly metamorphosed the matter ; he writes, that she " was supposed to be possessed with demons, who sometimes spoke Dutch and sometimes English," and that the persons who took notes (Mr. Whiting, Mr. Haynes, and Mr. Stone) mentioned the names of several persons " *as being actors or bearing parts in the conference, . . . particularly one Greensmith.*" Wrong — entirely wrong: these mortals were the subjects of a discourse ; were not speakers, but persons spoken of. Thus Hutchinson converted certain low-lived mortals into such demons as took possession of a human form, and through it, in varying languages, held a dialogue in which they openly told to mortal ears their own malicious purposes, and what mortals they were intending to injure. Stupid. Whiting makes the devil, in varied tones and assumed characters, speak out the names of the embodied culprits, and tell of harms they had done, and more that they intended to do. Sensible. The devil or his alias often acts well the part of a detective and informer ; in this case he managed to bring Mrs. Greensmith to confession.

Possibly, and only possibly, that devil was only an influx of auras which found entrance to Ann's inner perceptives, put in abeyance her outer consciousness

and outer senses, and let her inner ones sense and
give expression to the thoughts and purposes of some
low-lived and lewd mediumistic persons in her neighborhood, whose inner selves, she, as a relatively freed
spirit, could thoroughly read.   Occult intelligences
sometimes actuate the physical organs, while yet the
mortal's consciousness fails to perceive either the action or the will that prompts it.

The account of her life makes it apparent that Ann,
as a woman, had no affinity with the base and lewd,
but, being mediumistic, was caused, either by design
or by the out-workings of unconscious natural forces,
to disclose the baseness and lewdness of others.   She
apparently experienced entrancement to absolute un-
consciousness, so that she became, for the time being,
literally a tool — no more self-acting, and therefore
no more responsible, than a pen, a pencil, or a speak-
ing-trumpet.   Condition like hers in that respect is
experienced by many persons at the present day.

Some utterances made by her lips when she was
entranced were successfully used in court, either as
proofs, or as helps for obtaining proof, that certain
other persons in her neighborhood were in league
with Satan — were the devil's familiars.   Presentation in court of accusations that had come forth from
her vocal organs brought a woman, then on trial for
witchcraft, to prompt confession that the allegations
were true, and both she and her husband were condemned and executed.

Similar resorts for obtaining clews by which to trace
crimes to their authors are extensively resorted to
now, and frequently with success; but the statements
of the entranced and the clairvoyant are not adduced

in court, nor should they be, because our world has not yet attained to reliable skill for testing their accuracy; nor are high-minded and trustworthy spirits often willing to expose any guilty mortals to punishment by this world's tribunals and executioners.

How far the novel annunciation of their names and some of their practices contributed to the condemnation of the Greensmiths, husband and wife, or whether it did at all, is only matter for conjecture. But that either some influences went out from them and acted upon Ann, or that some went forth from Ann and acted upon them, or that there was reciprocal action back and forth, is only a fair inference from what is stated above, taken in connection with that foot-note of Hutchinson, which is credited to " Goffe the Regicide's Diary," and reads thus: " After one of the witches was hanged, the maid was well." No mention has been met with of any sickness about Ann, excepting the strangely induced *fits* in which she was used as the mouthpiece of the strange occupant or occupants of her form. Her becoming *well* may mean no more than a cessation of her fits, or obsessions. That these should cease after the execution of a person or persons with whom she had been in distressing and uncongenial rapport, was perhaps only a natural result from the action of universal laws. Drafts may have been made from her system by forces not her own, which helped invisible beings to act upon the condemned Greensmiths for good or for harm. Occasion for such use of her elements or properties may have ceased as soon as the gallows had finished its work. The fits ceased, perhaps, solely because drafts of special properties from her were discontinued.

" After one of the witches was hanged, the maid was well." The execution of one person and the restoration of health to another were viewed by Goffe as cause and effect.

The Greensmith woman's confession of the use of her form by her familiar — revolting as the isolated fact would be to us, and will be to the reader — was the controlling reason which influenced us to adduce the case of Ann Cole. We get from the old woman Greensmith an ancient indication, which is paralleled by many unproclaimed modern ones, that astounding possibilities reside within the scope and sway of forces interacting between the realms of matter and of spirit, which possibly and probably may be availed of for elevation as well as for debasement of the human race. Many whispered facts of human experience are to-day indicating that the old woman may have made true statement of her personal experiences. If degradation and fatuity permit the leaking out of some momentous facts of human experience which conscious vessels of fair soundness and delicacy will retain within themselves, and hide from a profaning world's knowledge, that world, nevertheless, may be entitled to hints at the existence of occult, though only rarely perceptibly operative forces and permissions of nature, through the only channels which have let them flow forth for the world's free observation. The Greensmith woman's fact may be regarded as representative of very many others of a like nature.

I know a man who once visited a married couple, both of whom are intelligent and refined, both estimable in character, the husband being a highly respected member of one of the learned professions.

This couple, at their own dining-table, where they and the visitor were the only occupants of the room, united in stating that once, when they had just finished taking their midday meal, and were sitting at the table opposite to each other, the lady's chair, with herself sitting in it, was moved back by some invisible power, and forthwith she, by palpable but invisible arms, was taken from her seat, laid upon the carpet, and there made to experience all the sensations of actual and pleasurable nuptial coition. While such were her positions and sensations, her husband remained on the other side of the table, and they two were the only flesh-clad persons in the room. One accomplished and truthful lady had such experience while her consciousness and all her mental faculties were fully alert. Nature enfolds astounding possibilities. The human race, in coming times, may possibly be improved rapidly and extensively, by designed infusions of supernal elements into fetal germs.

No evidence has come to us, and no apprehension is entertained, that such experiences ever eventuate in physical conception ; yet there are seen, now and then, glimmerings of evidence that supernal beings can and do inflow some of their own properties into the very marrow of some susceptible mortals of either gender, or of both simultaneously and conjointly, so as to modify physical systems in such manner and to such extent, that their offspring receive, at the very moment of conception, such properties as will ever afterward render them either better or worse because of injections through the parents by intelligences whose presence and operations elude perception by our external senses. Possibly both the most beneficent and

the most malignant of our race — both those whose
moral hues most illumine, and those whose shades
most blacken the pages of history — were conceived
while supernal beings held the parents either under
strong psychological control or in deep unconscious
trance.

The mother of the rough, lustful, and murderous
Samson was visited by a spirit being "very terrible."

The mother of Jesus was visited by the bright and
glorious Gabriel, and enwrapped in an abnormally
sound, helpful, or holy aura.

Far away from Charlestown and Boston, where the
two women noticed in the preceding pages had their
homes and met their fate, Ann Cole was the *unconscious* mouthpiece through which invisible beings
carried on dialogues, partly in languages, or, at least,
in tones, which she had never learned. The manifestations through her were no imitations of anything before known on this continent, so far as
history shows. Her reputed doings were unlike any
for which Massachusetts had hanged two of her
daughters.

From whom came the tones, if not the words, of
languages which this possessed girl had never learned?
From whom came the things put forth through her
which "she knew nothing of"? And especially
who "improved her tongue to express what was
never in her mind"? Any satisfactory explanation
of witchcraft must point out distinctly, and must admit the action of some force competent to all such
performances; a force controllable and controlled by
intelligence. The facts in the case were set forth by

a personal witness of many of them, who wrote at a time when he was not under any excitement or hallucination which their novelty might at first produce, but twenty years subsequent to their occurrence, when their recorder should have been, and no doubt was, calm and cautious, and when, too, the girl's own good character had been confirmed by good Christian deportment through twenty years succeeding the marvels manifested through her organs. If any history is worth reading, Ann Cole's lips were used by intelligences not her own "to express what never was in her mind." Either embodied intelligences — the Greensmiths and their associates whose bodies were not present with her — used her vocal organs, as Hutchinson's account implies that they did, or demons — spirits, as Whiting supposed — spoke through her form.

ELIZABETH KNAP.

At Groton, Mass., in 1671, Elizabeth Knap was more singularly beset than most others of that century who were deemed bewitched. The authority transmitting an account of her is exceptionally good, having been written by Rev. Samuel Willard, minister then at Groton, in the prime and vigor of life. He had graduated at Harvard College twelve years before, afterward became minister at the Old South Church in Boston, and was for several years at the head of Harvard College. The girl in question was his pupil, residing in his family during the earlier

portion of her affliction, and was under his watch till
its close. His opportunities for observing the case in
its rise and progress were certainly very good, and
he made a journalistic account of its phases and progress under many specific dates from October 30,
1671, to January 15, 1672, a space of eleven weeks
or more. He was an attentive observer and close
questioner of the girl, and also a cautious and intelligent chronicler.   .

   She was at first subjected to extraordinary mental
moods and violent physical actions, which came on
rather gradually, showing themselves in marked sin-
gularities of conduct, for which she, when questioned,
would give little if any account. Strange, sudden
shrieks, strange changes of countenance, appeared
first. These were soon followed by the exclamations,
" O, my leg ! " which she would rub ; " O, my
breast ! " and she would rub that, it seeming to be in
pain. Her breath would be stopped. She saw a
strange person in the cellar, when her companions
there were unable to see any such. She cried out to
him, " What cheer, old man ? " Afterward came
fits, in which she would cry out sometimes, " Money,
money ! " offered her as inducements to yield obedience ; and sometimes, " Sin and misery ! " as threats
of punishment for refusal to obey the wishes of her
strange visitant. She said the devil appeared to her,
and that she had seen him at times for three years.
He often talked with her, and urged her to make a
covenant with him, which she refused to do. November 26, six persons could hardly hold her. The physician, who for about four weeks had considered and
treated the malady as a natural one, now pronounced

it diabolical. She barked like a dog, bleated like a calf, and seemed at times to be strangled. At length distinct utterances came out. "A grum, low, audible voice" said to Mr. Willard himself, "You are a great rogue — a great rogue;" and yet "her vocal organs did not move." The voice was replied to as being that of Satan himself, and its author responded, "I am not Satan; I am a pretty black boy; this is my pretty girl; I have been here a great while." "When he said to me" (Mr. Willard), "O, you black rogue, I do not love you," I replied, "Through God's grace I hate thee." He rejoined, "You had better love me." The strength shown through the girl, the writer and witness says, "is beyond the force of dissimulation, and the actings of convulsions are quite contrary to these actings." Through all her sufferings "she did not waste in body or strength." Speech came from her without motion of the organs of speech. Also "we observed, when the voice spoke, her throat was swelled formidably, at least as big as one's fist." She said she "saw more devils than any one there ever saw men in the world."

No attendant sacrifice of life gave intensification of interest to this Groton case, and it failed to become prominently conspicuous among witchcraft events. Still it is more instructive on some points than almost any other one of them. Here first have we found in colonial history any statement that an intelligence speaking through a borrowed or usurped form disclosed *who* he was.

Mr. Willard, to whose care this girl was intrusted, and in whose family she had been a resident, was convinced that some other being than the girl herself was giving utterance through her lips, and, in harmony with a necessary inference from the general faith of his times, addressed the unknown one under supposition that he was veritably *The Devil.* The being thus accosted promptly said, " I am not *Satan;* I am a pretty black boy."

The girl said she had been accustomed to see her visitant, at times, during three preceding years, and that she saw more devils than any one there ever saw men in the world. Her notions in reference to the proper application of words were obviously just as loose as the prevalent ones in community then, which deemed any spirit visitant whatsoever a devil, or the devil. An observer of such beings as she saw would to-day call them spirits. When she perceived and called out to some personage invisible to her companions, saying, " What cheer, old man?" she plainly indicated that the being thus hailed was apparently neither more nor less than an old man, and he, judged by her address to him, was by no means austere or repulsive; and yet he doubtless was one of those whom she, or whom the reporter of her utterances, was accustomed to call *devils.* There is no indication that she ever saw one specially huge, malformed, malignant personality, or that she ever intended to indicate perception of such a one.

The purposes and moods of Mr. Willard's interlocutor seem to have been playful and kindly, rather than morose and satanic. Temporarily reincarnated spirits are often prone to smile at the long-faced and cringing thoughts which their advent evokes in persons not accustomed to interviews with them. "You are a great rogue — a great rogue," and " you had better

love me," can hardly be deemed ill-timed or inappro-
priate expressions from a lively boy, whatever his hue,
who, on being mistaken for the devil, would naturally
banter the sedate clergyman whose creed forced him
to regard such a visitant as the Prince of Evil. He
said truly, and in better spirit than the minister's, it
would be better for you to love than to " hate " me.

Common fairness asks all men to regard any speaker's account of himself as true, until some reason
appears for distrusting him. No word or deed ascribed to this pretty black boy, who said he was *not*
Satan, renders the accuracy of his statement doubtful. Distrust of him, if it spring up, will probably
be the offspring of prejudices, combined with ignorance of spirit methods of opening ways to reach
man's cognizance, and win him to seek communings
with his preceding kindred who possess more experience and consequent greater wisdom than pertains
to any dwellers in mortal forms. Our incrustations
of ignorance and prejudice withstand every gentle
appliance, and yield only to sledge-hammer blows.

Sensations, conditions, and various powers attendant
on Elizabeth Knap were emphatically extraordinary.
Detailed journalistic account of them having come
down from a sagacious, cautious, truthful, and cultured
man — from one of the eminently trustworthy men
of his generation — demands credence. He says the
strength of her body was " beyond the force of dissimulation ; " that " six persons could hardly hold
her ; " and that " the actings were contrary to those
of convulsions."

Another point is, that through the eleven weeks
of such rough exploits, " she did not waste in body

or strength." Cotton Mather speaks of some who
were so preserved through similarly tortured states,
that, "at the end of one month's wretchedness, they
were as able still to undergo another." Similar preservation of flesh and strength, amid fastings and most
excessive activity, are frequent experiences to-day
with the highly mediumistic, especially in the earlier
stages of their dominations by invisibles.

Speech came from her without motion of her vocal
organs. That much may pertain to simple ven-
triloquence; but Mr. Willard says also that " we observed, when the voice spoke, her throat was swelled
formidably, at least as big as one's fist." Ventril-
oquence has not usually such an adjunct as that.
Moreover, the minister was convinced that the utter-
ings were prompted by other will than hers.

This girl's experience abounds in evidences that
her spirit faculties of perception were so freed from
hamperings by the outer body, that she could consciously see, hear, and converse with spirits, and that
her physical system was subject to control by them
for speech in varied forms and modes, and for strange
and violent action by her limbs.

In parts of the narrative which we have not copied,
it appears that accusation came from her lips that
Mr. Willard himself and some other godly ones. in
his parish were her tormentors. This was saying to
Samuel in most startling manner, as one of old did to
David, " *Thou art the man;* " for at that day faith
was common that the devil had not power to accuse
a godly person, could not indeed accuse any others
than guilty ones of being contributors to outworkings of witchcraft. If the announcement was true,

Mr. Willard and other good ones, according to the faith of some at that day, were covenanters with the devil. It was a fearful moment when such accusation of the good clergyman fell upon his ears from the lips of his tortured pupil. His resort, and that of another accused one, was to prayer ; and we can readily fancy that petitions heavenward then rose up from the lowest depths of true and earnest souls, and went forth, in the girl's presence, with such psychologizing power as loosened the hold of any spirit possessing her form, and allowed her to regain full possession and control of all her normal powers.

This subject of spirit control retained consciousness during her entrancements, or during the times when her body was subject to a will not her own, as many mediums do at this day. Consequently she would possess more or less knowledge of whatever was said or done by her organs and limbs, whoever controlled them. Being young, she could scarcely be competent to make, and keep in remembrance, the broad severance of her individual responsibility for what was done by others and what by herself, through use of her own physical faculties. It was natural — almost necessary — that she should become self-condemnatory for having had done through her what gave distress and anguish to her friends, even though she had lent no voluntary aid to the deeds, nor had power to prevent their being enacted.

We presume her statement was true that Mr. Willard and the others then accused were, though unconsciously, made to be contributors of aid to the controllers of his pupil ; true that she felt the workings of emanations from them. Twenty years after-

11

ward an " afflicted " one in Salem Village began to
cry out upon this same man as being one of her
afflicters. And why? Because, probably, of constitutional properties in him which spirits could avail
themselves of as helps for entrancing or controlling
mediumistic persons. The laws which governed detection of tormentors of the bewitched will come
under more extended consideration in subsequent
parts of our work. Results indicate that Samuel
Willard's system possessed either material or psychic
properties, or both, which exposed him to accusation of bewitching some sensitives, whose perceptive
powers could trace back to their source any mesmer-
izing forces that entered into and acted efficiently
upon their own systems.

In his usual temper and judgment witchward,
Hutchinson pronounced the sufferings of Elizabeth
Knap " fraud, imposture, and ventriloquism "! Shade
of Samuel Willard! How look you now, and how
shall we mortals look upon the man, who, ninety
years after your day, casting a glance backward
into the darkened chambers of the long past, perceived yourself to have been a credulous dolt and
simpleton, unable, by eleven weeks' close study and
vigilant watch, to determine that the source of marvelous phenomena manifested in your own domicile,
before your own attentive eyes, was exclusively mundane? From looking at the occurrences, as they lay
dormant and half buried under the dust which ninety
full years had been throwing over them, Hutchinson
saw at a glance that they were nothing but frauds,
impostures, and ventriloquism. You, Rev. Sir, at first
doubted their supermundane source, but study of and

deliberate reflection upon them for weeks satisfied
you that your doubts were untenable ; you obviously
was devoid of such credulity as enabled Hutchinson
to very promptly obtain conviction that your Elizabeth was but an actor of fraud and imposture. Alas
for your sagacity, Samuel Willard !

Upham makes no account of either Ann Cole or
Elizabeth Knap, though these were decidedly the best
American prototypes of the magic-taught girls in
Salem Village, whose schemings and exploits he dwells
upon at great length. He claims that the witchcraft
generators and enactors there studied, schemed, and
practiced in concert at " a circle," and thus learned
how, and by what means, to originate and perform it.
All known circumstances conspire to indicate that
neither Ann Cole nor Elizabeth Knap had either visible teachers or co-operators in their marvelous operations. Therefore, had the historian adduced these
two cases — these good exemplars of the performers
at Salem — perhaps he would have been asked who
trained the isolated performers twenty and thirty
years before a necromantic seminary had been founded,
at which the arts of magic, necromancy, and Spiritualism could be taught and learned. Was there anywhere a prior institution of that kind ? If not, then
we ask, was any circle kindred to that at Salem an
essential — a *sine qua non* — to acquiring competency
for skillful practice of witchcraft ? or of acts called
witchcraft of old ? May not natural endowments
sometimes be ample qualification for admitting the
evolvement through one's form of very great marvels ? If not, the sporadic performances at Hartford
and Groton are troublesome to account for.

The advent of one spirit to Elizabeth Knap, and
his use of her organs of speech in carrying on a dialogue with the Rev. Samuel Willard, is distinctly
stated by that trustworthy chronicler. Also, according to him, the girl saw vast hosts of similar beings —
yes, more in number than any one present had ever
seen men in their lives. Here, surely, is very strong
testimony to the general fact that spirit action took
sensible effect upon and among human beings away
back in 1671-2, in the quiet inland town of Groton.

What is fit treatment of such facts and testimony
from such a source ? Should they be left unadduced
and unalluded to, as they were by one elaborate historian ? Should they be called outgrowths from
" fraud and imposture," as they were by another ?
Or should writers upon the subject, in manly way,
both let the facts come forth and speak for themselves, and leave the sagacity and veracity of their
exemplary chronicler above suspicion, till by facts,
and fair deductions from them, they render it probable that Samuel Willard was the slave of such
delusion as disqualified him for reasoning with common accuracy upon what his external senses perceived day after day and week after week ? Shrinking, by an historian of New England's witchcraft,
from distinct notice of Willard's deliberate and carefully drawn conclusions from facts transpiring in his
presence, is not only a keeping back of important
information, but possibly is an implication either
that Willard himself was an unreliable witness, or
a witness on the other side of the question, whose
testimony would be troublesome. Generous blood
boils with rebuke when boasted enlightenment either

ignores or traduces the most competent and trustworthy transmitters of marvelous facts, where so doing facilitates command of room for setting up modern
fancies in niches where ancient facts have rightful
foothold.

On the good authority of Samuel Willard we find
that Elizabeth Knap saw hosts of spirits, was roughly
handled and spoken through by some of them, and by
one who said he was *not Satan*, but a pretty black boy.
This was a case of spirit manifestation.

THE MORSE FAMILY.

LATE in the year 1679, in the part of old Newbury,
Mass., which is now Newburyport, very many startling
pranks occurred, of a kind which to-day are called physical manifestations. These clustered mostly in and
around the dwelling-place of William Morse, an aged
man, who with his wife, then sixty-five years old, and
their little grandson, John Stiles, constituted the whole
family.

Perusal of the records of this case has rendered it
probable to us that Mrs. Morse, the little boy John,
and a young mariner, Caleb Powell, who was frequently in at Morse's house, were all distinctly mediumistic, and that their systems either supplied, or
were used for holding, instrumental elements and
forces which spirits used in imparting seeming vitality, will, self-guiding and motive powers to andirons,
pots, kettles, trays, bedsteads, and many other implements and articles.

Beauty and attractiveness seldom drape the foundations of even very elegant and useful structures. Laborers digging trenches for foundations, and others. placing stones therein, are frequently rough beings, in homely garbs, from whom the refined and sensitive often turn away as soon as politeness and civility permit. Yet, though rough, coarse, and unsightly materials go into foundations, and equally rough workmen lay them, the nature and quality of materials there used, and of work there performed, deserve inspection by any one whose duty, interest, or pleasure induces him to estimate with approximate accuracy the value and prospective utility of the structure which shall rest thereon.

Palpable, audible, visible pranks, seeming to be the willed actions of lifeless wood and iron, possibly occurred in the seventeenth, because they are common in the nineteenth century. Such pranks are foundations of arguments which prove a life after death. A table, a chair. or an andiron, manifesting all the usual signs of indwelling vitality, consciousness, intelligence, self-willed action, and of possessing animal senses and capacities, testifies to its being operated upon by some unseen intelligence more convincingly than can the lips of the wisest and truest man the world contains testify to any fact whatsoever which seems supernatural. Vitalized wood or iron speaks " as never man spake ; " yes, as man, unless specially aided from outside of the visible world, can never speak ; it addresses men's external senses directly ; it confides its teachings to the most trusted and most trustworthy conveyances of facts and truths to the mind within. The oft ridiculed, slurred, contemned antics of household furni-

ture are signs put forth to human view by occult
operators, whose stand-point of vision and powers of
comprehension enable them to use some natural laws
and forces for affecting man and his interests, which
human scientists have never clearly cognized, which
schoolmen do not embrace in their philosophies, and
therefore the cultured world generally has failed to
put forth rational and satisfactory explanations of
many marvels which the ocean of mystery is often
buoying up on to its surface, where they become perceptible by human senses.

Modern mind has very extensively measured the
credibility of witnesses to witchcraft facts much as
the good woman did that of her " sailor boy." On
his return home from a voyage around the Hope, he
soon began to describe what he had seen, and gave
an account of flying fish. " Stop, stop, my son," said
the mother ; " don't talk like that; people can't believe that, because fishes haven't got no wings, and
can't fly." " Well, mother," replied Jack, " I'll pass
by the fish, and tell what happened in the Red
Sea. When we weighed anchor there, we drew up
on its flukes some spokes and felloes of Pharaoh's
chariot wheels." " That, now," rejoined the mother,
" will do to tell ; we can believe that, because *that is
in the Bible.*"

In similar manner many people are prone to measure the credibility of witnesses by the reconcilability
of the things testified to, with the general previous
knowledge, observations, and experiences of the
world. Such a course is usually very well. But the
rule it involves is not applicable in all cases. Veritable flying fish exist, notwithstanding the mother con-

ceived them to be nothing but the fictions of her wild
boy's lively fancy. The facts of witchcraft may have
been veritable ; many witnesses who testified to them
may have been both truthful and accurate describers,
notwithstanding the incredulity of some historians
whose philosophies are too narrow to enwrap many
facts which exist.

The strange manifestations at Morse's house, we
have said before, were nearly all such as to-day are
denominated *physical* ones ; that is, such as are manifested either upon, or through use of, matter that is
uncontrolled by any mortal's mind. Few if any intelligible utterances or communications imputed to invisible intelligences contributed to the consternation
which was then excited in Newbury. This case dif-
fers very widely from either of those previously noticed both as to the objects directly acted upon mysteriously, and as to the human organs employed. It
invites to extended and careful attention. We must
transfer to our pages numerous, and some long, extracts from the old records ; else we shall fail to manifest with desirable clearness and authority the multi-
plicity and character of those marvelous works, and
their probable sources and authors.

Mr. Morse himself, for aught that appears, escaped
all suspicion of complicity with, or connivance at, the
strange doings. He seemingly came forth from the
furnace with no sulphurous smell about him. Caleb
Powell, a young seaman, mate of some vessel, but
then on shore, was the first person to be legally accused in this case. He was arraigned at the instance,
and on the testimony, of Mr. Morse himself. Some
peculiar characteristics and habits ascribed to Powell

were such as would naturally cause him to be watched, if strange doings appeared where he was present. In "Annals of Witchcraft, Woodward's Historical Series," No. VIII. p. 142, it is stated that Powell " pretended to a knowledge in the occult sciences, and that by means of this knowledge he could detect the witchcraft then going on at Mr. Morse's. . . . The dancing of pots and kettles, the bowing of chairs, &c., was resumed with more vigor than ever when Powell came there ' to detect the witchcraft.' "

Upham, vol. i. p. 440, says Powell "determined to see what it all meant, and to put a stop to it, if he could, went to the house, and soon became satisfied that a roguish grandchild was the cause of all the trouble. . . . It is not unlikely, that, in foreign ports, he had witnessed exhibitions of necromancy and mesmerism, which, in various forms and under different names, have always been practiced. Possibly he may have *boasted to be a medium himself*, a scholar and adept in the mystic art, able to read and divine ' the workings of spirits.' At any rate, when it became known that, at a glance, he attributed to the boy the cause of the mischief, and that it ceased on his taking him away from the house, the opinion became settled that he was a wizard. . . . His astronomy, astrology, and *Spiritualism* brought him in peril of his life."

It is no unusual thing for even wise men to write much more wisely than they know. If Powell correctly "*at a glance* . . . found the boy to be the cause of the mischief," it becomes probably a *fact*, and not simply a *boast*, that he was " a medium himself," that he was " a wizard," or knowing one, and that his " Spiritualism," more *accurately* his mediumistic capa-

bilities, "brought him in peril of his life." One authority says the play "was resumed with more vigor
than ever" when he came into the house. For some
reason he was very soon arraigned and tried for witchcraft, but not convicted.

We have little doubt that his optics saw the boy
performing tricks, and therefore can believe that he
accused John in good faith; just as the clairvoyant
soon to be noticed accused the medium Read. Powell
probably saw the boy perpetrating the mischief. But
with what eyes? The outer or the inner — his material or his spiritual ones? And which boy did he see?
The external or the internal one — the boy material or
the boy spiritual? In evidence both that our explanations of Powell's doings will be neither sheer novelty
nor mere fancy, and for the purpose of disseminating
knowledge of highly important facts, the following
extracts are taken from an instructive and interesting pamphlet upon "Mediums and Mediumship," by
Thomas R. Hazard: Wm. White & Co., Boston, 1873.

"I once saw Read" (a well-known medium for
physical manifestations) "affected by the abrupt introduction of light at one of his circles in Boston, at
which he was, as usual, securely tied by a committee
chosen by the audience, and fastened securely to his
chair. The manifestations were after the common
order, and went on harmoniously until an Indian war-
song and dance were inaugurated. The exhibition
was very exciting, and both the song and the dance
became so uproarious and violent that, although we
were in a three-story back room, I was apprehensive
that not only the temporary platform might give way,
but that the attention of the police might be attracted

to the spot by the noise. Near by me sat Miss F., an excellent clairvoyant medium, who was earnestly describing to some of her friends the scene that was being enacted on the platform. She stated that two powerful Indians stood by Read, and that it was he who performed the wonderful dance. . . . Thus one of the 'best dark-circle mediums in the United States' was not only proved to be an 'impostor,' but taken in the very act of his trickery. : . . From all that was occurring before us, it was too evident that Read was an impostor; for 'Miss F. clairvoyantly saw him perform tricks which he palmed off on the public as spiritual.' . . . But now, . . . mark the sequel, and observe how easy it is for those who suffer their zeal to outrun their knowledge to be mistaken; and how true it is that as spiritual things can only be discerned by the spiritual eye, and material things only by the material eye, so the spiritual eye can (under ordinary circumstances) discern only spiritual things, as the material eye can discern only material things.

" It seems that a self-lighting burner had been adjusted near the platform, at which an experienced man from the gas-works was stationed, with the gas-cock in his hand, ready at a moment's notice to turn on the light. This man was within hearing distance of Miss F., and must have heard her remarks; . . . he gave the cock a sudden turn, and in an instant all was light, and of course the medium was — *exposed* — sitting fast bound in his chair, with every knot as perfect as when first tied, but in a dying condition from the effect of the tremendous shock his nervous system underwent by the sudden return of the unusual volume of elements that had been extracted from his physical body to furnish material clothing for his own *double*, or some other spiritual creation, that was performing the exhausting war-song and dance on the platform ; nor is it probable that Miss F. ever saw the *material* body of Read during the whole time she *clairvoyantly* saw him. . . . Suffice it to say, that the suffering medium was released from his bonds as soon as practicable, but not until after three or four minutes had expired, . . . after which, by the application of restoratives, Read was gradually revived, and restored to his right mind and condition."

Such statement of direct personal observations — coming from the pen of an aged, but still vigorous, gentleman of ample pecuniary means, of more than average culture, of acute perceptions, of careful and critical observations, who has spent many years in " trying the spirits " and contesting the strength and quality of testimony in their favor at every step, — who hates, with a righteous and outspoken hatred, falsehood, fraud, imposture, oppression, or hypocrisy, wherever or in whatever cause they manifest themselves — is entitled to credence, and gives important inklings of some occasional methods of spirit operations upon and around mediums. From such a witness we learn that while a medium's limbs were bound fast, and he claiming to be, and known, a few minutes before, to have been, sitting bound hand and foot on a stage in a room just made dark, a lady clairvoyant there present saw him loose, and moving about most vigorously over the stage, doing "things, as to jump up and down," as Powell saw the Morse boy acting. The clairvoyant's inner vision saw Read dancing — saw either a perfect semblance of him, formed by use of special properties drawn forth from his system, or else saw the veritable Read himself practically then a disembodied and unroped spirit. She no doubt actually saw thus, and saw the essential man Read loosed, and dancing most vigorously. A flash of light, however, let suddenly on at the time, enabled all external eyes to see the external form of Read sitting all fast bound upon the chair.

That case teaches that properties drawn forth from the little boy John Stiles, and molded into that boy's form, may have, by Powell's interior vision, been seen playing tricks with pots and kettles, while neither the boy's consciousness, will, or physical muscles had the slightest connection with the antic articles. Facts showing such susceptibilities in human organisms as were manifested in the case of Read, are too significant and important for any scientist. philosopher, or historian to ignore, so long as he claims to be, or, in fact, can be, a wise and helpful expounder of very many records of ancient marvels.

At page 392, vol. ii., of Mather's "Magnalia," New Haven ed., 1820, account is given of this case wherein it is stated that, —

"A little boy belonging to the family was a principal sufferer in these molestations ; for he was flung about at such a rate that they feared his brains would have been beaten out : nor *did they find it possible to hold him.* . . . The man took him to keep him in a chair ; but the chair fell a dancing, and both of them were very near being thrown into the fire.

"These and a thousand such vexations befalling the boy at home, they carried him to live abroad at a doctor's. There he was quiet ; but returning home, he suddenly cried out he was pricked on the back, where they found strangely sticking a *three-tined fork*, which belonged unto the doctor, and had been seen at his house after the boy's *departure*. Afterward his troublers found him out *at the doctor's also;* where, crying out again he was pricked on the back, they found an *iron spindle* stuck into him.

" He was taken out of his bed, and thrown under it ; and all the knives belonging to the house were one after another stuck into his back, which the spectators pulled out ; only one of them seemed to the spectators to come out of his mouth. The poor boy was divers times thrown into the fire, and preserved from scorching there with much ado. For a long while he barked like a dog, clucked like an hen, and could not speak rationally. His tongue would be pulled out of his mouth ; but when he could recover it so far as to speak, he complained that *a man called P——l appeared unto him as the cause of all.*

" The man and his wife taking the boy to bed with them . . . they were severely pinched and pulled out of bed. . . . But before the *devil* was chained up, the invisible hand which did all these things began to put on an astonishing *visibility*. They often thought they felt the hand that scratched them, while yet they saw it not ; but when they thought they had hold of it, it would give them the slip.

" Once the *fist* beating the man was discernible, but they could not catch hold of it. At length an apparition of a *Blackamoor child* showed itself plainly to them. . . . A voice sang *revenge ! revenge ! sweet is revenge.* At this the people, being terrified, called upon God ; whereupon there followed a mournful

note, several times uttering these expressions — *Alas!
alas! we knock no more, we knock no more!* and there
was an end of all."

In no other remembered account is that little boy
credited with saying anything whatsoever. Mather
reports that upon coming out of one of his scenes of
torture so far as to recover power of speech, "he complained that a man called P——l appeared unto him
as the cause of all." That statement discloses a fact
worth observing. There was tit for tat between little
John and Powell. Each found the other a focus of
issuing force that caused the witchery. The sensitive
boy probably saw and felt, by his interior faculties,
that properties and forces from Powell were applied
to the strangely moving objects, and also in producing
his own sufferings. Powell, too, through his inner
perceptives, could learn the same in relation to the
boy. Both were probably right in their perceptions,
and in their allegations. Mr. Morse suspected and
complained of Powell. That is something in favor of
deeming John the lesser focus of force in this case.

The mauling "fist" was once seen, but eluded
grasping, as spirit limbs generally do. At last, a
"Blackamoor child," perhaps brother to Elizabeth
Knap's "pretty black boy," was visible — and not
only that, but audible also. If it was the spirit
of either an Indian or African child, sympathizing
with his own race, and who had been taught to look
upon all whites as oppressors, *revenge* would naturally
be *sweet* to such a one, or to a band of such. Earnest,
heartfelt prayer might psychologically break their hold,
and induce them to say, "we knock no more."

Though Powell, when tried, escaped conviction,

yet, said the court, " he hath given such grounds of suspicion of working by the devil, that we cannot acquit him ; " therefore the judges charged *him* with the costs attending the prosecution of *himself*. Such was equity practice in those days.

Having failed to prove conclusively that the harum-scarum sailor boy was the devil's conduit for the startling occurrences among them, the good people of Newbury naturally proceeded to inquire what other person was the channel through which his sable majesty was pouring out malignity. Who, next to Powell, among those present at the manifestations, was most likely to have made a covenant with the Evil One ? All eyes would turn instinctively to the spot where the deviltries transpired, and to persons who were generally near by when and where the performances came off. The inmates of the house of exhibition, Mr. Morse, Mrs. Morse, and their grandson, John Stiles, would naturally be very keenly watched and thoroughly scrutinized. Their traits, habits, and antecedents would be fully discussed ; it was almost certain that one of the three must be guilty; and which of them was most likely to be the devil's tool? Result shows that Mrs. Morse was pitched upon. But why she ? Her character was good — she was religious and beneficent. *But — but —*

Mrs. Jane Sewall — Woodward's " Hist. Series," No. VIII. p. 281 — testified and said, " Wm. Morse, being at my house, . . . some years since, . . . begun of his own accord to say that his wife was accounted a *witch;* but he did wonder that she should be both a healing and a destroying witch, and gave this instance. The wife of Thomas Wells, being come to the time of her delivery, was not willing (by motion of his sister in whose house she was) to send for Goodwife Morse, though she were the next neigh-bor, and continued a long season in strong labor and could not be delivered; but when they saw the woman in such a condition, and without any hopeful appearance of delivery, determined to send for the said G. Morse, and so Tho. Wells went to her and desired her to come; who, at first, made a difficulty of it, as being unwilling, not being sent for sooner. Tho. Wells said he would have come sooner, but sister would not let him; so, at last she went, and quickly after her coming the woman was delivered."

Therefore, some years before the time of Mrs. Morse's trial, Mr. Morse, in Mrs. Sewall's own house, volunteered " to say that his wife was accounted a *witch;*" at which he wondered because of her be-neficence, and then he instanced her doings in the case of Mrs. Wells as evidence of her goodness. The accounts pertaining to her render it probable that Mrs. Morse sometimes acted as midwife, and show clearly that some people had previously called her a witch. Such reports being in circulation, it is not surprising that some women should object to admit-ting her into their houses, fearing the introduction of brimstone; while others, who had previously found her help very efficient, would seek her assistance in hours of pain or sickness. The point of most signifi-cance is, that Mrs. Morse had, some years previous to the disturbances at her house, *been suspected of witch-craft.* Why? We do not know with any certainty. But the appearance that she was a midwife, whose labors involved more or less of general medical prac-

12

tice, suggests the possibility that her "simple remedies," or her hands, had sometimes produced such
extraordinary effects, as led people to surmise that
the devil must be her helper; just as, for the same
reasons, more than thirty years before, he was believed to be co-operator with Margaret Jones. The
conjecture naturally follows that she was highly
mediumistic, and that her intuitions and magnetism,
if nothing more, enabled and caused her to be a
worker of marvelous cures. It was at the abode
of such a woman, and in apartments saturated with
her emanations, that the unseen ones frequently held
high, rude, and consternating frolic, during many
weeks; it was at the home of one *previously* reputed
a *witch*.

An indication that, even before the wonders occurred at her home, she had been suspected of exercising also perceptive faculties that were more than
human; had been suspected of manifesting "wit"
of the special kind which cost Ann Hibbins her life,
is given in the following deposition by Margaret
Mirack, who testified thus, Woodward's "Hist. Series," No. VIII. p. 287: —

"A letter came from Pispataqua by Mr. Tho.
Wiggens. We got Mr. Wiggens to read the letter,
and he went his way; and I promised to conceal the
letter after it was read to my husband and myself,
and we both did conceal it; nevertheless, in a few
days after, Goode Morse met me, and clapt me on
the back, and said, ' I commend you for sending such
an answer to the letter.' I presently asked her,
what letter? Why, said she, hadst not thee such
a letter from such a man at such a time? I came

home presently and examined my husband about it.
My husband presently said, What? Is she a witch
or a cunning woman? Whereupon we examined our
family, and they said they knew nothing of the letter."

Mrs. Morse's possession of their secret was so unaccountable that the husband in astonishment asked,
"Is she a witch or a cunning woman?" The question implies that it seemed so extraordinary to the
man that she should have knowledge of the letter
and its answer, that any process by which she could
obtain it was seemingly beyond the power of mortals to apply. Either witchcraft or supernal cunning must have helped her. When asked by the
same Mrs. Mirack afterward "how she came to
know it," the witness says, Mrs. Morse "told me
she could not tell." This indicates a mind so conditioned, as many mediumistic ones now are, that
knowledge is inflowed to them, they know not whence
or how, and, literally, they *cannot* tell whence it has
come. This gives presumption that she possessed
mediumistic receptivities, and the outworkings from
such faculties would suggest that she received supernal aid. The only imagined source of such aid at
that day was the devil. Obviously she "felt knowledge in her bones," as the acute negress did in Mrs.
Stowe's "Minister's Wooing."

Though Mrs. Morse was tried and condemned for
witchcraft, the sentence was never put in execution.
When on her way from Ipswich jail to Boston for
trial, she said, among other things, that "she was
accused about witchcraft, but that she was as clear of
it as God in heaven." When saying this she probably
spoke no more than exact truth.

She appears to have been a good woman. The candid and generally cautious Rev. Mr. Hale, of Beverly, wrote that "her husband, who was esteemed a sincere and understanding Christian by those that knew him, desired some neighbor ministers, of whom I was one, to discourse with his wife, which we did; and her discourse *was very Christian*, and still pleaded her innocence as to that which was laid to her charge." This examination occurred after her discharge from prison. The aged couple came out from their severe ordeal with characters bright enough to claim the confidence and respect of good men in their own day, and may claim as much from after ages.

There is no indication that the boy of the house, John Stiles, whom Powell accused as the great mischief-maker, was suspected of being such by any other one of the many witnesses of the strange transactions. Those witnesses were much better judges as to what persons the wonders apparently proceeded from, than any person can be to-day; and one whom they left unblamed, it is distinct injustice, as well as folly, for expounders of the case in our times to put forth and traduce as having been the contriver and performer of all that so agitated, distressed, and exposed the lives of those who sheltered, fed, and kindly cared for him. Modern historians, however, have been guilty of this great wrong.

It has recently been stated (Woodward's "Hist. Series," No. VIII. p. 141), that, "what instigated him to undertake the tormenting of his grand-parents, there is no mention as yet discovered." This begs the primal question, viz., *Did* he undertake to torment them? To this inquiry it can truly be said, there is no mention in the primitive records, as yet discovered, that he did. There is no evidence that any one but Caleb Powell (that swift witness) suspected him of undertaking any such thing. Where the records are so extensive and full as in this case, their omission to mention any other accusers of the boy is strong evidence that there was no apparent contriving or executing pranks and outrages by him. The writer above quoted says also, "How long the young scamp carried on his annoyances . . . does not appear." Neither does it appear that he ever began or was consciously concerned in any such. Only in appearance, and that only to Caleb Powell the clairvoyant, and to the eyes of modern commentators, was that boy in fault.

Upham, following the witchy Powell's lead, ignorantly regards what was done by mystical use of the boy's properties as being the boy's voluntary performances. And regarding the boy as a great rogue, and as author of all the great mischief, he says (vol. i. p. 448), "His audacious operations were persisted in to the last." We look upon that allegation as an " audacious ". defamation of an innocent youth.

In this Morse case we chose to present ostensible and reputed actors, prior to presenting descriptions of the special scenes in which history makes them prominent, because considerable knowledge of the age, character, and abilities pertaining to the chief supposed performers in the great Newbury tragedy, or semi-tragedy, will be helpful, if not essential, to any well-based conclusion as to whether any one of them was the leading intelligence that brought it upon the stage, and supervised and managed its apparent actors — and, if either was, then which *one* among them? If neither of them, then somebody else was manager there. Our instructive citation from Hazzard discloses the occasional action of agents and forces that are not recognized even to-day by the community at large, and therefore we wished it to be read in advance of facts which it greatly helps to explain. Way is now opened for introducing to those readers whose patience has sustained them through this long prologue, the facts of the case as stated by William Morse himself, and sworn to by both him and his wife.

"THE TESTIMONY OF WILLIAM MORSE: which saith, together with his wife, aged both about sixty-five years: that, Thursday night, being the twenty-seventh day of November, we heard a great noise without, round the house, of knocking of the boards of the house, and, as we conceived, throwing of stones against the house. Whereupon myself and wife looked out and saw nobody, and the boy all this time with us; but we had stones and sticks thrown at us, that we were forced to retire into the house again. Afterward we went to bed, and the boy with us; and then the like noise was upon the roof of the house.

"2. The same night, about midnight, the door being locked when we went to bed, we heard a great hog in the house grunt and make a noise, as we thought willing to get out; and that we might not be disturbed in our sleep, I rose to let him out, and I found a hog in the house and the door unlocked: the door was firmly locked when we went to bed.

" 3. The next morning, a stick of links hanging in the chimney, they were thrown out of their place, and we hanged them up again, and they were thrown down again, and some into the fire.

" 4. The night following, I had a great awl lying in the window, the which awl we saw fall down out of the chimney into the ashes by the fire.

" 5. After this, I bid the boy put the same awl into the cupboard, which we saw done, and the door shut to: this same awl came presently down the chimney again in our sight, and I took it up myself. Again, the same night, we saw a little Indian basket, that was in the loft before, come down the chimney again. And I took the same basket, and put a piece of brick into it, and the basket with the brick was gone, and came down again the third time with the brick in it, and went up again the fourth time, and came down again without the brick; and the brick came down again a little after.

" 6. The next day, being Saturday, stones, sticks, and pieces of bricks came down so that we could not quietly dress our breakfast; and sticks of fire also came down at the same time.

" 7. That day, in the afternoon, my thread four times taken away, and came down the chimney; again my awl and gimlet wanting; again my leather taken away, came down the chimney; again my nails, being in the cover of a firkin, taken away, came down the chimney. Again, the same night, the door being locked, a little before day, hearing a hog in the house, I rose and saw the hog to be mine. I let him out.

" 8. The next day, being Sabbath day, many stones,

and sticks, and pieces of bricks came down the chimney: on the Monday, Mr. Richardson and my brother
being there, the frame of my cowhouse they saw
very firm. I sent my boy out to scare the fowls
from my hog's meat : he went to the cow-house and
it fell down, my boy crying with the hurt of the fall.
In the afternoon, the pots hanging over the fire did
dash so vehemently one against the other, we set
down one, that they might not dash to pieces. I
saw the andiron leap into the pot, and dance and
leap out ; and again leap in and dance, and leap out
again, and leap on a table and there abide ; and my
wife saw the andiron on the table : also I saw the
pot turn itself over, and throw down all the water.
Again we saw a tray with wool leap up and down,
and throw the wool out, and so many times, and
saw nobody meddle with it. Again, a tub his hoop
fly off of itself, and the tub turn over, and nobody
near it. Again, the woollen wheel turned upside
down, and stood up on its end, and a spade set on
it : Step. Greenleafe saw it, and myself and my wife.
Again, my rope-tools fell down upon the ground before my boy could take them, being sent for them ;
and the same thing of nails tumbled down from the
loft into the ground, and nobody near. Again, my
wife and the boy making the bed, the chest did open
and shut ; the bed-clothes could not be made to lie
on the bed, but fly off again."

The disturbances commenced Thursday night, November 27 ; on December 3, six days only from the
commencement of the troubles (see Upham, vol. i.
p. 439), Powell was complained of before a magistrate, by William Morse, " for suspicion of working

with the devil." Powell appeared for a hearing five
days later, on the 8th, and the testimony quoted
above was, either then or at the time of the complaint on the 3d, submitted before Jo. Woodbridge,
commissioner. Therefore the facts were of such recent
occurrence as to be fresh in the memory of the de-
ponent; and his prompt suspicion of Powell gives
probability to the correctness of the statement in
Woodward's Series, that when Powell came to the
house, pots, kettles, and chairs " resumed " their
action " with more vigor than ever." Powell's presence was helpful to the performance. But the whole
of Morse's testimony is not embraced in the preceding. There is extant

" A FURTHER TESTIMONY OF WILLIAM MORSE AND
HIS WIFE," as follows : —

" We saw a keeler of bread turn over against
me, and struck me, not any being near it, and so
overturned. I saw a chair standing in the house,
and not anybody near. It did often bow toward
me, and rise up again. My wife also being in the
chamber, the chamber door did violently fly together,
not anybody being near it. My wife going to make
a bed, it did move to and fro, not anybody being
near it. I also saw an iron wedge and spade was
flying out of the chamber on my wife, and *did not
strike her.* My wife going into the cellar, a drum,
standing in the house, did roll over the door of the
cellar ; and being taken up again, the door did violently fly down again. My barn-doors four times
unpinned, I know not how. I, going to shut my
barn-door, looking for the pin — the boy being with
me — as I did judge, the pin, coming down out of
the air, did fall down near to me.

"Again: Caleb Powell. came in as aforesaid, and seeing our spirits very low by the sense of our great affliction, began to bemoan our condition, and said that he was troubled for our afflictions, and said that he had eyed this boy, and drawed near to us with great compassion: 'Poor old man, poor old woman! This boy is the occasion of your grief; for he hath done these things, and hath caused his good old grand-mother to be counted a witch.' 'Then,' said I, 'how can all these things be done by him?' Said he, 'Although he may not have done all, yet most of them; for this boy is a young rogue, a vile rogue. I have watched him and see him do things as to come up and down.' Caleb Powell also said he had understanding in Astrology and Astronomy, and knew the working of spirits, some in one country and some in another; and, looking on the boy, said, 'You young rogue to begin so soon. Goodman Morse, if you be willing to let me have this boy, I will undertake you shall be free from any trouble of this kind while he is with me.' I was very unwilling at the first, and my wife; but, by often urging me, till he told me wither and what employment and company he should go, I did consent to it, and this was before Jo. Badger came; and we have been freed from any trouble of this kind ever since that promise, made on Monday night last, to this time being Friday in the afternoon. Then we heard a great noise in the other room, oftentimes, but, looking after it, could not see anything; but, after-ward looking into the room, we saw a board hanged to the press. Then we, being by the fire, sitting in a chair, my chair often would not stand still, but ready to throw me backward oftentimes. Afterward, my

cap almost taken off my head three times. Again, a
great blow on my poll, and my cat did leap from me
into the chimney-corner. Presently after, this cat
was thrown at my wife. We saw the cat to be ours;
we_put her out of the house, and shut the door.
Presently the cat was throwed into the house. We
went to go to bed. Suddenly — my wife being with
me in bed, the lamp-light by our side — my cat again
throwed at us five times, jumping away presently into
the floor; and one of those times, a red waistcoat
throwed on the bed, and the cat wrapped up in it.
Again, the lamp standing by us on the chest, we said
it should stand and burn out; but presently was
beaten down, and all the oil shed, and we left in the
dark. Again — a great voice, a great while very
dreadful. Again — in the morning, a great stone,
being six-pound weight, did move from place to
place; we saw it. Two spoons throwed off the table,
and presently the table throwed down. And, being
minded to write, my ink-horn was hid from me, which
I found covered with a rag, and my pen quite gone.
I made a new pen; and while I was writing, one ear
of corn hit me in the face, and fire, sticks, and stones
throwed at me, and my pen brought to me. While I
was writing with my new pen, my ink-horn taken
away; and not knowing how to write any more, we
looked under the table and there found him; and so
I was able to write again. Again — my wife her hat
taken from her head, sitting by the fire by me, the
table almost thrown down. Again — my spectacles
thrown from the table, and thrown almost into the
fire by me, and my wife, and the boy. Again — my
book of all my accounts thrown into the fire, and had

been burnt presently, if I had not taken it up.
Again — boards taken off a tub, and set upright by
themselves ; and my paper, do what I could, hardly
keep it while I was writing this relation, and things
thrown at me while a-writing. Presently, before I
could dry my writing, a Mormouth hat rubbed along
it ; but I held so fast that it did blot but some of it.
My wife and I, being much afraid that I should not
preserve it for public use, did think best to lay it in
the Bible, and it lay safe that night. Again — the
next day I would lay it there again ; but in the morning, it was not there to be found, the bag hanged
down empty ; but after was found in a box alone.
Again — while I was writing this morning, I was
forced to forbear writing any more, I was so disturbed
with so many things constantly thrown at me."

Such is the account given by an eye and ear witness, who had as good opportunities to receive sensible demonstration of acts performed as can well be
imagined. Did he see, hear, and feel all that he testifies to ? Has he left record of a series of facts, or
only of fictions which he set forth as facts ? Was he
a faithful and true witness, or not ? Who and what
was he ? An aged shoemaker, who ran the gantlet
of a fierce witchcraft ordeal and came out with character sound and untarnished ; a man who " was esteemed a sincere and understanding Christian by
those that knew him." The strong words in his favor, which came from such a trustworthy scribe as the
Rev. Mr. Hale, on an occasion when circumstances
would influence him to be careful and exact in expression, are clearly indicative that Morse's testimony was
probably true and discriminative. " A sincere and

understanding Christian." What qualities give better
a *priori* promise of correct testimony than do sincerity
and a sound understanding? Where these combine,
their utterances imperatively claim very respectful
hearing by any one who is in pursuit of positive facts
pertaining to human experience. The history of him
and his family, during those ten or eleven days and
nights through which they were enveloped in the
waters of mystery, trouble, and consternation, gives no
indication that Mr. Morse's reason ever yielded its
normal and just sway over his actions or his words —
no indication of his being blinded by any excessive or
bewildering excitement or enthusiasm. The fact that
he himself wrote out with his own hand, and in the
very midst of the startling and hair-lifting phenomena, a narrative of events which gives dates, occurrences, and experiences clearly, in perspicuous and
often terse language, accompanied by appropriate specifications of circumstances which elucidate the character of the whole scene, bespeaks a straightforward,
truthful, unexaggerating mind, self-controlled, and
moving straight forward in an honest statement of
events actually witnessed. Our ancient records contain few testimonies that exhibit clearer or stronger
internal evidences of exactitude and reliability than
that of William Morse. The form, language, and tone
of his account are all in favor of his intelligence, discrimination, and credibility; so much so, that, taken
in connection with his whole character, we can conceive of no objection to crediting his narration, excepting what shall be wrung out from the nature and
kind of facts he swore to. But neither their nature
nor source was concern of his, *as a witness;* and his

own sound *understanding* perceiving this, kept him back from expressing any surmises or innuendoes as to who were the actual authors of his great annoyances. The man understood his position as a witness, kept his reason at the helm throughout the fearful storm, and suspected and accused, not the little boy, but Powell. Obviously his own senses, unbeclouded by the mists of unreasoning excitement, had witnessed the facts he stated, and he knew that they had occurred. His testimony is true.

How can the occurrence of such facts be explained, or rather *who* produced them? Historians say that the little boy, John, did. How could he? Had history-weaving heads, when at work in the quiet study, been as clear and as free from the blinding action of foregone conclusions, as was that of Mr. Morse amid the flying missiles about his head while he was writing, their reason, as his did, would have asked their witness Powell, " How *could* all these things be done. by him," the boy? And the cowed witness would have replied to them in the nineteenth century as he did to Morse in the seventeenth, " Although he may not have done *all*, yet most of them." He would have backed down before the historians as he did before the better " understanding " of Mr. Morse. Obviously to common sense, the boy was incompetent to perform a tithe of what was ascribed to him. No one but Powell accused him. The age of that boy is not given. He is not known to have been called upon as a witness, and Powell says to him, " You young rogue, to begin so soon." These facts, together with the absence of any words spoken by him to any one, excepting on a single occasion, lead naturally to the inference that he was quite young, and perhaps also that he was apparently inactive. At no age in boyhood, nor yet in manhood, could a single performer, or a host of men, have accomplished by unobservable processes and forces all that is distinctly stated to have been performed in and around the house of William Morse.

Any designation of its source which avows the mischief to have come primarily from the mind of little John Stiles, by necessary implication impeaches Mr. Morse's powers of perception and observation, and the worth of his testimony. It indirectly, at least, accuses him of a great blunder when he suspected Powell rather than little John. On the hypothesis of modern historians, the sedate old man — the " understanding Christian " — was but making much ado about nothing, or next to that ; for the little boy was not competent to much. So little could he do alone, that, were he the chief deviser and performer, Mr. Morse was incompetent to distinguish with common acuteness between the ordinary and the marvelous, or else he was an egregious fictionist and impostor. Far, far better would it be both for himself and his readers if the historic instructor recognized, and based his inferences upon, facts well attested, and sought for agents and forces adequate to manifest such results as were evolved. Vastly better would be history when founded upon broad comprehension of existing agents and forces, and a firm basis in the nature of things spreading out wide enough to underlie each and all of the ancient marvels, and admitting an imputation of them to authors whose inherent powers could bring them out to distinct cognition by human senses, than it can be when it ruthlessly pares down the dimensions of facts, dwarfs their fair import, and impeaches the trustworthiness of those who solemnly attested to the truth of descriptions which have come down from former generations! Better, much better would it be to honor the fathers by omitting to undermine and topple over their strong powers and good traits of character, and perversely bring their positive knowledge, gained through the senses, down to the lower level on which modern speculation obtains convictions! Descent to free and reiterated insinuations and allegations that the best individuals and communities of old were infatuated, credulous, deluded, stultified, because some of their statements and actions are unexplainable by our theories and philosophies, is unbecoming any generous and philanthropic spirit. Fair play calls for frank admission that giant facts occurred of old, — facts so huge that they cannot be stretched at full length upon the beds of modern science and philosophy, nor be wrapped up in the narrow blankets now in fashion, — facts so huge that they cannot squeeze themselves through, nor be forced through, the narrow entrance doors of some modern mental chambers. Does the hugeness which debars them from entering contracted domiciles to-day prove their existence to be but fabulous? Surely not. The sagacity and truthfulness of our predecessors were sound and good. They recorded facts. Shame be to those who are ashamed to admit that their equals in mental acuteness and accuracy of statement may, of old, actually have witnessed genuine phenomena which justified their descriptions. To brand the events as being the products of fraud, credulity, and infatuation, because only modern limitations to nature's permissions and powers render them unexplainable as facts, is shameful.

Newbury, in 1679–80, was obviously visited and disturbed by giants. To deem that the biggest of these were children of little John Stiles, is not only farcical in the extreme, but it necessarily, however indirectly, asperses good William Morse, that "sincere and understanding Christian," and also his equally good wife, who passed through the severe ordeals of witchcraft scenes and persecutions, and came forth untarnished, — asperses them by an imputation of incompetency to observe and describe with average clearness and accuracy events that passed before their eyes, — incompetency to give a truthful and unexaggerated account of what they saw.

Every sentiment of justice begs for a tongue with which to rebuke the sneers that overweeningly wise witchcraft historians have cast upon the senses and the mental and moral states of the observers and describers of the great marvels of former days. The foul broods of harpy adjectives which history has sent forth to prey upon the vitals of good characters for truthfulness and discrimination, should be forced to unloose their talons, and hie themselves back to roost where they were hatched.

Assuming, as the histories of all nations in all ages and lands indicate, and as many tested modern workers demonstrate, that some disembodied, unseen intelligences can at times either banish from the human body, or put in abeyance, or irresistibly control, the mental, affectional, and moral powers of some impressible human beings, and also use their whole physical

13

structures and nerve elements as instruments ; assuming, further, both that such unseen workers may
have been the actual authors of many startling phenomena which the preceding pages have brought up
before the reader's mind, and that Mrs. Morse, Caleb
Powell, and the boy were each of them mediumis-
tical, contributing to the performance of the wonders
— assuming this, the proximity of those several persons to the spots where the marvels appeared, would
subject them all to rigid scrutiny, and their movements or their positions would probably, at times,
indicate to external senses that they were somehow
actors in the *mêlée*. They were obviously unconscious reservoirs of the forces there used, and as
such were all involved in the production of the great
mischief. It is credible, yes, quite probable, that
the little boy was actually seen by Powell enacting
a prominent part; but that Powell, who then saw,
was practically a spirit, beholding a spirit form like
in all things to the boy, but moved, energized, and
controlled, all imperceptibly to external vision, by
disembodied spirits. At the very time when all
merely external beholders saw the external boy
standing about the room in quiet and repose, or
sitting still in the corner, spirit vision might have
seen his semblance being used for infiltrating seeming life, motive powers, and longings for a lively jig
and a merry time generally into the whole group of
household utensils and supplies. When dead wood
and iron, when leather and wool, when sausages and
bread, when an iron wedge and a spade, find legs, and
arms, and wings, — when such become things of
seeming life, of forceful life, too, and of self-guiding

actions, — they preach with power which no mere
human tongue can command. No eloquence from its
common sources can equal theirs in forcing conviction. They say "unseen intelligences move us" —
" unseen intelligences move us," and every self-possessed and logical hearer responds, Amen.

All things have their use. This case of seemingly
low as well as rough manifestations, where spirits
exhibited the effects of their force mainly upon
gross, lifeless matter and brute animals, shows more
forcibly and convincingly, if possible, the fact of
supermundane agents, than did the effective hands,
and simples, and clear visions of Margaret Jones;
the " wit" or clairaudience of Ann Hibbins; the
Dutch tones and unconscious utterances of Ann
Cole, or the contortions of Elizabeth Knap, and the
words of the pretty black boy. Life and self-action
in dead wood and iron are phenomena too striking
and pregnant with meaning to be wisely slurred or
ignored.

Essex County has been the theater of several exhibitions of astounding marvels. The performances
detailed in this chapter beyond question excited
fears and disturbed peace throughout Newbury and
its surrounding towns. Also an apparitional boy has
recently shown himself to a teacher and her pupils
in Newburyport, to the no small disturbance of that
place. During the first decade of the present century, famous Moll Pitcher, who, as Upham says,
" *derived her mysterious gifts by inheritance*, her grandfather having practiced them before in Marblehead,"
practiced fortune-telling and kindred arts at the base
of High Rock, in Lynn, where " she read the future,

and traced what to mere mortals were the mysteries of the present or the past . . ." so successfully, or at least so notoriously, that "her name has everywhere become the generic title of fortune-tellers." In that county, too, the mysteries and horrors of Salem witchcraft were encountered. But scarcely any other event in that territory seems more highly charged with the elements of incredibility than the Salem historian's perception that little John Stiles was the *bona fide* author of the pranks played at William Morse's house. No cotemporary of the boy, excepting impressible, wayward Powell, seems ever to have suspected the little one as being the giant rogue. How blind, therefore, were the eyes of all others of that generation! For now an historic eye, looking back through the darkening mists of eight score years and twenty miles north, absolutely sees *audacity* and action, which all living eyes, alert and vigilant on the spot and at the time, were incompetent to detect. The world progresses; new clairvoyance has been developed — clairvoyance which sees what never existed — to wit, little John Stiles as the designing and conscious enactor of superhuman works.

Very many modern scenes rival this ancient one at Newbury in the roughnesses of manifestations and the difficulty of fathoming the purposes and characters of the performers. Perhaps no other one of them is more worthy of attention or more instructive than the prolonged one which occurred at the residence of Rev. Eliakim Phelps, D. D., at Stratford, Conn., 1850. In "Modern Spiritualism, its Facts and Fanaticisms,"- by E. W. CAPRON (Bela Marsh, Boston, 1855), page 132, commences a very lucid and authentic account of this case, covering nearly forty pages. The character and position of Dr. Phelps, who furnished Capron with his facts, and whose permission was obtained for their publication, make the account referred to well worthy of careful perusal. On several different occasions, years ago, it was our privilege to hold familiar conversations with Dr. Phelps upon the subject of Spiritualism, and his details of spirit performances in his presence prepared us to view him as having transmitted to his offspring properties which were very helpful in setting THE GATES AJAR.

THE GOODWIN FAMILY.

IN the family of John Goodwin, of Boston, in 1688, four children, all young, were simultaneously either sorely afflicted or set themselves to playing pranks and tricks with diabolical furore. Which? An elaborate account of what was either imposed upon them by other beings, or of what themselves devised and enacted, was promptly written out by Cotton Mather, who was an observer of many of the marvels while they were transpiring.

Poole, in "Genealogical and Antiquarian Register," October, 1870, says those children were "Martha, aged 13; John, 11; Mercy, 7; Benjamin 5." Drake, in "Annals of Witchcraft," says they were "Nathaniel, born 1672; Martha, 1674; John, 1677; and Mercy,

1681." According to him, their ages in 1688 were about 16, 14, 11, and 7, respectively. The two statements agree as to Martha, John, and Mercy; but one makes the fourth, a boy of 5, named Benjamin, while the other's fourth is a boy of 16, named Nathaniel. We have not sought for data on which to either confirm or correct the statement of either author. To show that they were young, is all that our present purpose requires.

More than seventy years subsequent to the occurrences in the Goodwin family and to the manifestations at Salem, Hutchinson said, " It seems at this day with some people, perhaps but few, to be the question whether the *accused* or the *afflicted* were under a preternatural or diabolical possession, rather than whether the afflicted were under bodily distempers, or altogether guilty of fraud and imposture." Poole, having quoted the above, makes the following sensible query and comment. " Why make an alternative ? Both accusers and accused were generally possessors of NOT *bodily distemper*, but of *peculiar susceptibilities growing naturally from their special organisms and temperaments*, and were probably as free from and as much addicted to fraud and imposture, as the average of the community in which they lived."

If we read Hutchinson aright, he stated that a few people, even at his day, were believers that there had formerly been some " preternatural or diabolical " inflictions, but were in doubt whether such inflictions came upon the accusers or upon the accused ; while, in his opinion, all ought to drop belief in anything preternatural or diabolical in the case, and seek only to determine whether the strange phenomena resulted partly from *bodily distempers*, or were exclusively frauds and impostures. We think he made no alternative himself between accusers and accused, but exempted both classes from supermundane influences, and queried only whether witchcraft resulted partly from ill health or wholly from fraud. Be it so or not, Poole's comment is appropriate, instructive, and valuable. It is in harmony with the view which the present work is specially designed to illustrate. We repeat and adopt his words, and say that "both accusers and accused were generally possessors of *not* bodily distemper, but of peculiar susceptibilities growing naturally from their organisms and temperaments," and in general character were on a par with their neighbors.

Hutchinson's account of the family now under consideration is as follows: —

"In 1687 or 1688 began a more alarming instance than any which preceded it. Four children of John Goodwin, a grave man, a good liver, at the north part of Boston, were generally believed to be bewitched. I have often heard persons who were of the neighborhood speak of the great consternation it occasioned. The children were all remarkable for ingenuity of temper, had been religiously educated, and were thought to be without guile. The eldest was a girl of thirteen or fourteen years. She had charged a laundress with taking away some of the family linen. The mother of the laundress was one of the wild Irish, of bad character, and gave the girl harsh language ; soon after which she fell into fits, which were said to have something diabolical in them. One of her sisters and two brothers

followed her example, and it is said were tormented
in the same parts of their bodies at the same time,
although kept in separate apartments and ignorant
of one another's complaints. One or two things
were said to be very remarkable: all their complaints were in the daytime, and they slept comfortably all night: they were struck dead at the
sight of the Assembly's Catechism, Cotton's Milk
for Babes, and some other good books, but could
read in Oxford's Jests, Popish and Quaker books,
and the Common Prayer without any difficulty. Is
it possible that the mind of man should be capable
of such strong prejudices as that a suspicion of fraud
should not immediately arise? But attachments to
modes and forms in religion had such force that
some of these circumstances seem rather to have
confirmed the credit of the children. Sometimes
they would be deaf, then dumb, then blind; and
sometimes all these disorders together would come
upon them. Their tongues would be drawn down
their throats, then pulled out upon their chins.
Their jaws, necks, shoulders, elbows, and all their
joints would appear to be dislocated, and they would
make most piteous outcries of burnings, of being cut
with knives, beat, &c., and the marks of wounds
were afterward to be seen. The ministers of Boston
and Charlestown kept a day of fasting and prayer
at the troubled house; after which the youngest
child made no more complaints. The others per-
severed, and the magistrates then interposed, and
the old woman was apprehended; but upon examination would neither confess nor deny, and appeared
to be disordered in her senses. Upon the report

of physicians that she was *compos mentis* she was executed, declaring at her death the children should not be relieved. The eldest, after this, was taken into a minister's family, where at first she behaved orderly, but after a time suddenly fell into her fits. The account of her affliction is in print; some things are mentioned as extraordinary which tumblers are every day taught to perform, others seem more than natural; but it was a time of great credulity. The children returned to their ordinary behavior, lived to adult age, made profession of religion, and the · affliction they had been under they publicly declared to be one motive to it. One of them I knew many years after. She had the character of a very virtuous woman, and never made any acknowledgment of fraud in the transaction."

This historian was born more than twenty years after the " great consternation " which the Goodwin case occasioned, and therefore those must have been elderly people who gave him accounts of personal remembrance of it, and rehearsed to him their mellowed recollections of the past. From such people he had probably heard many particulars, and received general impressions which were one source from whence he drew materials for his history, at least for his comments; also opinions then prevalent around him were aids to his judgment when reading Mather's account. He omitted to express directly any doubt as to the occurrence of such facts as the records presented, but innuendoed, all through his account, that fraud, acting upon credulity, begat and brought forth that entire brood of marvels. He left us the facts, and stated that the children were

" all remarkable for ingenuity of temper." Probably
his meaning is, that they were remarkably bright or
quick-witted. The historian adds, that they " had
been religiously educated, and were thought to be
without guile." These are points of interest both as
items on which public judgment concerning the facts
was based at the time of their occurrence, and also
as things to be regarded by moderns when attempting
to determine the probability whether such marvels
were produced voluntarily by embodied actors alone,
or by force exerted upon and through mortal forms
by wills putting forth power from imperceptible
sources.

What do the quoted statements indicate as to the
constitutional endowments and acquired skill of those
children for purposely acting out the feats ascribed
to them? Ready wit, sprightliness, or whatever is
meant by " ingenuity of temper," was a very good
basis for any kind of performances; but the character of the doings likely to proceed from that basis
in a given case, will be indicated by other possessions. Religious education and freedom from guile
are not very probable prompters of either egregious
trickery, or prolonged and mischievous imposture.
Hutchinson's remark that " some things are mentioned as extraordinary which tumblers are every
day taught to perform," is doubtless true; but he
adds that " others seem more than natural." Yes,
they do. And it is these especially that the world
desires to see traced to competent performers. How
did the historian account for such — for those seeming " more than natural "? Solely by the dogmatic
remark that " it was a time of great credulity."

What if it was ? Could credulity in the public mind enable untrained children to outact jugglers, tumblers, and most efficient dissemblers and tricksters of various kinds in their special vocations ? What did the historian mean by alleging *credulity* in way of accounting for facts which he adduced, and left without direct controversion, or any attempt at such ? Was he intimating that belief of the actual occurrence of such facts, though witnessed through many months by the physical senses of multitudes, argued credulity ? If so, he put upon the word *credulity* an inadmissible meaning.

Did he intend to say that credulity caused the senses of our fathers to see, hear, and feel erroneously, so that they would testify less accurately than those of the generation in which he was living ? Perhaps he did ; and yet on what rational grounds could he ? None that we perceive. Was the former generation less truthful than his own ? Probably not. Had it less sagacity than his own ? We can think of no evidence that it had. Were its senses less reliable ? Probably not. Was its belief in the testimony of its own senses a proof of its *credulity ?* No. Was clear statement of what its senses had witnessed evidence of its credulity ? It seems to have been so to the historian, but is not to us. The fathers told of witnessing things, which, if they occurred, were seemingly " more than natural." What then ? Does that prove that the things they described did not occur, and thus prove a generation of the fathers to have been, as a whole, either dolts or liars ? No. The appearance is, that the historian was obliged to admit that valid testimony to occurrence of facts around the Goodwin children, which seemed more than natural, must be conceded; and yet he could not account for the facts; he was mentally baffled, non-plussed, and could only say, " It was a time of great credulity." That explains nothing, while it tempts us to suspect its author of such credulity in his own penetration, that he apprehended that a whole line of ancestry through successive generations had been fatuous and exaggerative, since it continuously described and swore to occurrences which conflicted with his own theoretical limits to things credible. A credulity which caused him to regard himself a better knower and judge of what actually transpired in preceding ages, than were the very persons who lived in that past, and were eye and ear witnesses of what then occurred, impelled the pen of this witchcraft historian to ascribe the marvels of other days to causes or to conditions absolutely incompetent to produce them.

We can extend much leniency to Hutchinson, because he lived and wrote when the pendulum of belief, recently wrenched from the disturbing grasp of witchcraft, and allowed to swing back toward extreme Sadduceeism, had not acquired its legitimate movements under the action of mesmerism, Spiritualism, psychology, and other regulating forces. Witchcraft's unnatural devil had died from the blow he received at Salem Village in 1692, and for a long time afterward there was seeming non-intercourse between men and dwellers in spirit realms; partially man was forgetting that there are spirits, and doubting whether they had ever acted overtly among men. Probably Hutchinson's thoughts were never led to inquire

whether the forces and realms of nature may not extend far above, below, and around the confines of
palpable matter, — extend beyond where man's external senses take cognizance, — or where his natural
science has penetrated. His thoughts, perhaps, were
never led to inquire whether there exists natural provision for mesmeric and varied psychological operations, nor to inquire whether, under possible fitting
conditions, unseen intelligences could possess and control certain peculiar physical human forms. Lacking
not only knowledge, but also circumstances which
would naturally generate any conjecture that both
good spirits and bad alike might sometimes come to
earth in freedom, and work wonders on its external
surface and among its living inhabitants, Hutchinson, cornered and baffled in search for an adequate
cause for facts which he felt called upon to state,
could only credulously say, in *quasi* explanation of
them, "*It was a time of great credulity*"!

His implied position that all the works were nothing more than natural acts and sufferings of children,
magnified and made formidable by popular credulity,
fails to yield satisfactory revealment of the nature
and origin of such facts as he himself presents and
leaves uncontroverted.

What was the character of the Goodwin children
themselves? They were bright, religiously educated,
and free from guile. The account shows that four
such children, of a sudden, without previous training
for it, all join at first, and three of them long unitedly
continue, in a course of most distressing imposition
upon their own family, upon physicians, clergymen,
magistrates, and the neighborhood; also that the im-

position is manifested by astounding physical feats, and simultaneous, identical· signs and complaints of suffering, even though the sufferers are in separate apartments. If, possibly,· by their own wills and powers they could perform the tricks, how incongruous it would be with their alleged traits and ages! How inconceivable that four such children, from the boy of sixteen down to the girl of seven, or from the girl of thirteen down to the boy of five, should conspire, and three of them co-operate thoroughly, effectively, and long, in voluntarily and purposely producing such mischief and misery as were there experienced! *Suspicion* of fraud no doubt arose. But the appearance is, that facts soon put the case beyond any powers of fraud which such children, or any embodied human beings, could put forth. Without previous practice and training in concert, a successful attempt by themselves at what was done through and upon them is incredible. No hint is given that they ever practiced in preparation. Had they have done so, seemingly their father, the "grave man and good liver," must have known it, and would have been governed by his knowledge of it in judging and treating his children. Who doubts that it would be shameful to charge or suspect that man, and his friends and physicians, with such credulity, *at the first coming on of the fits*, that they could not judge fairly and sensibly of what nature of cause the actions and sufferings indicated?

> " O, star-eyed " Fancy, " hast thou wandered there,
> To waft us back the message of " — *credulity !*

Look still more closely at the circumstances of this case. The bright girl of " great ingenuity of temper,

of religious education, and without guile," *was just
out from under the infuriated lashings of a wild Irish
tongue*, when she commenced her — what? her frolic?
her course of fraud and imposture? Was that a *playful* moment? Was that the time for a general mood
which would start a whole family of guileless little
children to unite spontaneously and instantly for a
guileful and distressing imposition upon relatives and
friends? When she fell in fits, *from such a cause*, was
it a credible time for her bright brother to recklessly
increase the family excitement by imitating the sufferer's movements and tones of distress? Was that a ·
condition of things in which the younger two would
join the elder in sly additions to the distress around
them? No; most surely, No.

" Is it possible," asks the historian, " that the mind
of man should be capable of such strong prejudices
as that suspicion of fraud should not immediately
arise?" We answer for him and say, No; emphatically, No. Such suspicion must have been felt. And
we ask in turn, is it possible that an historian's mind
can be capable of such strong prejudices as that suspicion that such a family as he described, circumstanced as he made it, was absolutely incapable of
practicing fraud and imposition competent to the results which he indicates were wrought out? Yes, his
mind failed to receive such a suspicion, and therefore
reveals its own blinding prejudices. Skepticism in
one direction generated credulity in another with him,
as it does with many to-day.

Four children of the " grave man " were simultaneously and excruciatingly racked and tortured precisely alike, and in the same parts of their bodies,

although being, some of them, in separate apartments, and ignorant of one another's complaints. Such are the alleged and uncontested facts. The citizens of Boston, two or three years ago, were permitted to see, and we saw, even more than four, yes, eight or ten boys, strangers to the operator, and mostly to each other, volunteer to go upon a stage, where, in a few minutes, after two or three out of a dozen had been requested to leave the stage, all the others were made to move, and act, and suffer precisely and simultaneously alike, many of them standing often back to back, and no one among them perceptibly looking at any other. This was all occasioned by the mental, magnetic or psychological force of Professor Cadwell.

If we presume (and why may we not?) that the wild Irish woman possessed strong psychological powers; that Martha Goodwin was easily subjectible to psychological control; that her brothers and sister were so too, and that they were all naturally sympathetic, then we can see that nothing more occurred, even if the whole that is told be literally true, than falls within the scope of such psychological forces as have in recent years been manifested by embodied, and, we may add, by disembodied minds. If in her anger the old woman forced or found rapport between her own sphere or aura and that of Martha Goodwin, way was opened for injection of germs of suffering to the girl's system, and the systems of others in rapport with her. Way was opened through which the tormentor could, though absent, send upon the child ugly wishes that would keep torturing her so long as the old woman kept the wishes active; as perhaps she did in many of her waking hours. The account says, " One

or two things were *very remarkable*. All their complaints were *in the daytime*, and they slept comfortably *all night*." When the old woman was asleep, and
her resentful feelings were dormant, the children also
slept.

A passage-way so opened as to admit the entrance
of one, usually admits others of the same kind to follow. Where the old woman's subduing will-force had
entered and gained sway, that of her sympathetic, and
many other spirits, might do the same; and could
make the children's outer forms either accept or reject, at the controller's pleasure, any books or class
of literature which should be offered for perusal.
Catholic spirits, or any spirit, liking a little fun, might
keenly relish the work of astonishing Cotton Mather
and his ilk, by showing preferences antagonistic to
his own righteous ones.

The case of Philip Smith, a very intelligent, efficient,
and highly respected citizen of Hadley, Mass., exhibits analogous phenomena. We shall not go into that
case in detail. It occurred 1685, and is very instructive. Being sick, sensitive, clairvoyant, and pining
away, " he uttered a hard suspicion " that one old
Mrs. Webster, *who had once been tried for witchcraft*,
and also had taken offense at some of Smith's official
acts, " had made impressions with enchantments upon
him." His " suspicion " and sufferings fired the minds
of young men in the town to go " three or four times "
and give that old woman disturbance. Drake, in Woodward's " Hist. Series," No. VIII. p. 179, presents the
following account : " It is said by a reliable historian
that the young miscreants went to her house, dragged
her out, and hung her up till she was almost dead.

14

They then cut her down, rolled her some time in the snow, and then buried her up in it, leaving her, as they supposed, for dead. But by a miracle, as it were, she survived this barbarity. Still more miraculous it was, that the sick man was greatly relieved during the time the helpless old woman was being so beastly abused." Mather, in his account (ib. p. 177) says, "All the while they were disturbing her, he was at ease, and slept as a weary man." This is all possible, and not improbable. The man was obviously very susceptible to psychological influences, and could trace felt malignant forces to their source. She, no doubt, was a turbulent and odd old woman, for she had been tried for witchcraft, and was probably a natural psychologist. As long as rough handling caused her to call in, and keep at home, and concentrate all her thoughts and forces for self-defence and protection, no emanations from her went out to the sick man, who then consequently dropped into quiet sleep.

One of these Goodwins, says Hutchinson, "I knew many years after. She had the character of a very sober, virtuous woman, and never made any acknowledgment of fraud in the transaction." Probably, therefore, there was no fraud. This sober, virtuous woman, a party concerned, years subsequently made profession of religion, continued long to live a useful and respected life, and never made acknowledgment of fraud. The probability is near to certainty that she never acted any.

And how was it with the others? " They returned to their ordinary behavior, lived to adult age, and made profession of religion." Look at the case. Four guileless, bright little sisters and brothers, residing together under their father's watch, in the twinkling of an eye, flash upon the gaze of the town in which they lived, seemingly as adroit and proficient tricksters as were ever known, and all of them alike competent to their several parts. They remain the town's wonder for months, and then all return to their former behavior, grow up and live Christian lives among the witnesses of their strange doings, and never make confession of fraud. Was there any *fraud?* Only the over-credulous in self-powers of divination backward will believe that there was.

In the process of watching these children, and the annoyances and sufferings they endured, it was discovered that when absent from home they were in great measure exempt from the special evils; therefore arrangements were made for their abode elsewhere; and probably not for all of them together in any one family. We find that the girl Martha became a resident in Cotton Mather's family not many weeks after the commencement of the great consternation. And it is stated that for a time none of her extraordinary demeanor was manifested there; yet subsequently the fits and antics revealed themselves abundantly, even under the roof of the devil-fighting clergyman. Some sayings and doings while she was residing there, manifested more frolicsome and quizzical motives than prompted the manifestations described by Hutchinson.

Turning to a much later historian, we quote from Upham as follows: —

" One of the children seems to have had a genius scarcely inferior to that of Master Burke himself; there was no part nor passion she could not enact.

She would complain that the old Irish woman had tied
an invisible noose round her neck, and was choking
her; and her complexion and features would instantly
assume the various hues and violent distortions natural
to a person in such a predicament. She would declare
that an invisible chain was fastened to one of her limbs,
and would limp about precisely as though it were really the case. She would say that she was in an oven;
the perspiration would drop from her face, and she
would produce every appearance of being roasted;
then she would cry out that cold water was being
thrown upon her, and her whole frame would shiver
and shake. She pretended that the evil spirit came
to her in the shape of an invisible horse; and she
would canter, gallop, trot, and amble round the rooms
and entries in such admirable imitation, that an observer could hardly believe that a horse was not beneath her, and bearing her about. She would go up
stairs with exactly such a toss and bound as a person
on horseback would exhibit."

Such is a general summary of her feats as presented
by this historian. Does he believe that such things
were actually performed either by or through her?
Does he believe that such were the literal facts even
in appearance? He nowhere, so far as we notice, till
he sums up the case, *distinctly* charges fraud on the
one side, or such credulity on the other, as made witnesses falsify as to appearances. He seems to admit
the facts as *appearances*, and charge them all to the
girl's extra cunning and skillful acting. " She *pretended* that the evil [?] spirit came to her." Was it
only her *pretense?* Who knows? Why say *pretended?* Was she so generous as to give credit to

another, and that other an "evil spirit," for help
which she did not receive? Are expert tricksters
accustomed to disown their own powers to astonish?
Especially do they ever spontaneously avow that the
devil or any *evil spirit* is helping them? We think
not. And yet it is stated that Martha Goodwin's
own lips declared that some invisible spirit was acting through her, or was helping her perform her marvelous feats. Why call that a *pretense*, and make her
a liar? Why not put some confidence in the words
of this religiously educated girl?

The historian says that while she was residing with
Mather, " the cunning and ingenious child " — please
mark the adjectives of the modern expounder, applied
by him to one whom the earlier records put among
those who " had been religiously educated and thought
to be without guile " — " the cunning and ingenious
child," he says, " seems to have taken great delight
in perplexing and playing off her tricks upon the
learned man. Once he wished to say something in
her presence to a third person, which he did not
intend she should understand. She had penetration
enough to *conjecture* " (why say *conjecture?*) " what
he had said. He was amazed. He then tried Greek;
she was equally successful. He next spoke in He-
brew; she instantly detected his meaning. He resorted to the Indian language, and that she pretended
not to know." Such are facts as deduced from
Mather's account by Upham and put forth by the
latter, and which he attempts to account for by
supposition that the girl's own *conjectures* enabled
her to get at the meaning of sentences put forth in
languages of which she had no knowledge. No

doubt she was bright, but not competent to all that.
Fancy and imagination ply their wings needlessly
when they rise from the ground of fact and fly off
to the lands of conjecture and pretense, thinking to
bring thence true solution of such a marvel. The
girl avowed the presence of a spirit with herself, and
that he helped her. That explains the whole transaction. Upon full separation from the body, each
human mind loses all knowledge of earth language,
having no further use for it, because the mind then
enters conditions in which the thoughts of any other
spirit, whatsoever its native language, may be read
at a glance. Whatever language Mather might have
spoken in, he would have been intelligible by any
disembodied spirit. For not words, but the thought,
irrespective of its dress, could be read. The Indian
language she *pretended* not to know. Perhaps so;
but probably that was no *pretense.* It is not probable
that the girl herself, as such, had much acquaintance
with any other language than English; any departed
spirit who controlled her would have no knowledge
of any earth language whatsoever, nor need he have,
for unclothed thought was perceptible by him. A
roguish mind behind the scenes — and such a one may
have played many a trick at the parsonage — would
be likely, at his own pleasure, to bother, astonish, or
confound the Rev. Polyglot by seeming either to comprehend or not, just according to his own whims or
varying moods as the play went on from step to step.
Mather's attempt to conceal his meaning from the
girl might very naturally be amusing to the thought-
reading intellect then lurking in and controlling the
girl's organs, and quite as naturally would incite him

to play the wag a while. Martha neither *conjectured* nor *pretended* at all; she was then quiescent, while other eyes looked through hers and saw what was inside the mill-stone.

We have stated essentially that each mortal upon departing from this life enters into conditions where human language is not only not needed, but is unusable; therefore we may be asked how returning spirits can possibly speak to us in our language, which is no longer at their command. They measurably re-change or change back their conditions when they reconnect themselves with a mortal form; they then come back to where earth language is needful, and where fitting instrumentality for revival of knowledge and use of such language exist. They, however, do not reconnect themselves with their own former forms, nor often with forms which they can use as well as they formerly did their own; in many, very many instances, those who, in their own forms, were eminent for polished diction and fervid eloquence, either get such slight control or get hold of such rickety or such rigid vocal apparatus, that they can make no perceptible approximation to their former productions. The reincarnated spirit is a somewhat mystical being, half spirit, half man, and as a spirit can read the thoughts of man, and as man can use human language.

Flattery was sometimes poured over the minister through the lips of Martha, with a lavishness indicative of its flowing from some ensconsed waggish spirit, amusing himself by tickling the vanity of the egotistical black coat, much more than from a guileless miss speaking to her consequential minister.

A special scene is thus described by Mather : —

" There stood open the study of one belonging to the family, into which entering, she stood immediately on her feet, and cried out, ' They are gone ! They are gone ! They say they cannot. God won't let 'em come here ! ' adding a reason for it which the owner of the study thought more kind than true ; and she presently and perfectly came to herself, so that her whole discourse and carriage was altered into the greatest measure of sobriety."

Very likely Mather was then egregiously cajoled by *some* one. Observation, together with information otherwise obtained, renders it obvious that one essential condition of psychological control is, that the magnetisms or auras of the controlling mind shall, at the time, be, in the mass of its operative qualities and powers, stronger than, or positive to, any other person's spheres, auras, or emanations amid which the control is either to be taken or held on to. Suppose, then, what would be necessary under the circumstances, that the atmosphere, walls, and furniture of that study were highly charged with emanations from the vigorous minded Mather, who was then present, and consequently his own halo was radiating there and keeping his surroundings fully charged with himself. Physical and also external mental and emotional effluvia from him might then be so repulsive to magnetisms pertaining to spirits of any moral quality whatsoever, that no visitant from unseen realms would try to withstand the repulsion. If such was the condition of things, the parting exclamation of the last to remain, might well be, " They are gone ; God won't let 'em come here ! " Such statement would be in full harmony with the most common use of language to-day by spirits, for they are accustomed to say that God won't let them do this or that, when, accórding to their own oft-repeated explanation, they mean only that the forces of nature oppose or control them. God and natural forces with them generally mean one and the same all-dominating power — God's forces as well as himself are called by his name by visitants who read his operations with more than mortal accuracy.

" She presently and perfectly came to herself, so that her whole discourse and carriage was altered into the greatest measure of sobriety." Yes, naturally so ; for Martha Goodwin herself resumed control of her own body, and re-exhibited the religiously educated and guileless girl which she in fact was, just as soon as usurping visitants vacated her legitimate premises. So long as her form was dominated by another's mind, her existence was either a blank to herself, or, if conscious, she was powerless.

Upham teaches that once, according to Mather, when people attempted to drag this girl up stairs, " the demons would pull her out of the people's hands, and *make her heavier* than perhaps three times herself." Did the historian himself who quoted those words and let them appear to be accurately descriptive of facts, believe that they were such ? Did he believe that *demons* acted within her, held her back, and made her something like three times heavier than she normally was ? Such things were adduced by him as being *facts*, and it would be pleasant to know whether he believed that the girl herself was those demons, and by her own action made

her own body three times heavier than common gravitation would make it. Did such observable effects
occur as Mather described? Probably they did, and
the historian's process of accounting for them implies
that by her own cunning, ingenuity, and histrionic
skill, the child made herself three times heavier than
she actually was. If the allegations were not in his
estimation facts, why did he let them stand unaccounted for in his summary of things accomplished by
his " cunning and ingenious child"? Perhaps he presumed that readers to-day are generally as ignorant
as himself of the vast many cases in which the present generation has tested and proved by the best of
Fairbanks's scales, that spirits augment or diminish
the weight of material substances at pleasure, and
to as great and sometimes greater extent than either
demons or Martha Goodwin are alleged to have
done in the case above cited. He perhaps presumed
that the reading world at large was as ignorant and
prejudiced as himself on this subject, and that the
world's clearing and opening eyes will continue to
see, as his glamoured ones did, only fibs in Mather's
facts. This was a sad oversight. Light from Spiritualism (see Dr. Hare, Dr. Luther V. Bell, William
Crookes, Alfred R. Wallace, and many others) has
already substantiated facts which prove that nature
infolds forces by which agents unseen can at their
pleasure produce either levitation or increase of the
weight of material objects. Therefore such action
may have been put forth upon the body of Martha
Goodwin. Yes, we now may *rationally* believe that
there existed too much sagacity and truth among the
men of witchcraft times, and too little deviltry among

the guileless children of that day, to permit that fictions and rhetoric shall long be suffered to malign our
forefathers because they recorded true accounts of
what transpired among them.

Mather states that this girl, at times, by whistling,
yelling, and in other ways, disturbed him when at ·
family prayers. Upham says, " She would strike him,"
Mather, " with her fist and try to kick him " — probably meaning, try both to strike and kick him, for he
adds, " her hand or foot· would always recoil when
within an inch or two of his body; thus giving the
idea that there was an invisible coat of mail, of heavenly temper, and proof against the assaults of the
devil around his sacred person." That " idea " looks
much more like a child born within the historian's
own mind than a gift to him by Mather. A statement by the latter that her hand or foot would always
recoil when within an inch or two of his body, hardly
justifies the slurring innuendo which seems to be appended to it. But ignorance of many operating laws,
forces, and agents pertaining to the subject discussed
by the modern historian, let him sometimes become as
tempting a target for the shafts of ridicule as he found
Mather to be. Without presuming that Mather perceived that natural laws generated repulsion between
matter animated and moved by a disembodied spirit
and matter in its normal conditions, we can state that
extensive observation has generated the conclusion
that unless there exists rapport with, or at least an
absence of repulsion between, the sphere of the spirit
using the borrowed hand or foot, and the sphere of the
normal person aimed at, natural law forbids their contact. William Morse made such observation as caused

him to say in his deposition that "the wedge and
spade flying on his wife *did not touch her.*" Forceful
and rapid approximations of hands and feet under
control of invisibles, toward the bodies of surrounding witnesses, and marvelous arrestings of those mov-
.ing limbs so that no contact ensues, are of very frequent occurrence. Very many parlor ornaments and
household utensils, hard and soft, light and heavy,
are, by spirits, not unfrequently set in rapid motion
back and forth, and crosswise, promiscuously over and
amid a crowd of people in a room, and yet but few
persons are ever hit, and the few sensitives in rapport
with the performers, and contributors to their apparatus, if hit, are never hurt. The temper of Mather's
shielding coat of mail was just as heavenly as that of
each other human being's coat which the Master Ar-
morer in nature's boundless shop forges and furnishes
for the protection of each human child who is sent forth
to fight the battles of life in gross flesh and bones.
Not his own holiness, but either nature's antipathies
or spirit forbearance saved Mather from the blows,
and the historian wronged him perhaps when he intimated that the divine thought otherwise; for that
man, halting as his steps were, and small as his advance
was, made nearer approach toward a fair comprehension and exposition of our witchcraft than any other
American who wrote upon that subject, till since the
publication of "History of Witchcraft."

Many other pranks, not less marvelous than the
ones already presented, are ascribed to this girl; but
notice of them may be omitted here, because the general character of the operations around her are all
that this work proposes to exhibit. We must, how-

ever, give the reader opportunity to peruse the historian's concluding comments upon this case. He says, —
" There is nothing in the annals of the histrionic
art more illustrative of the infinite versatility of the
human faculties, both physical and mental, and of the
amazing extent to which cunning, ingenuity, contri-
vance, quickness of invention, and presence of mind
can be cultivated, even in very young persons, than
such cases as just related. It seems, at first, incredible that a mere child could carry on such a complex
piece of fraud and imposture as that enacted by the
little girl whose achievements have been immortalized
by the famous author of the ' Magnalia.' "

We are glad to note the author's frank and distinct
confession that his own solution seems *at first* incredible. Why he put in the phrase "at first" needs explanation, which he fails to furnish. He makes no
attempt to show why the *first* seeming should not be
the permanent one. It is permanent. It will continue
permanent to the end of time. It is and forever will be
incredible that the Goodwin girl herself performed all
the feats which the evidence proves were performed
through her organism. If her body was the organ
of all the performances which are distinctly ascribed
to her, she was not the author of them all, but only
a channel for the occurrence of many of them. Can
reflection find her competent to all that was ascribed
to her ? Incredible. Incredible not only *at first*, but
also on and on to the latest last.

Ingenious fancy, while weaving over this case a
dazzling web of rhetoric, may have deluded the eyes
that overlooked the loom, and caused them to discern
other seemings than the first ones ; but such delusion
will never become epidemic.

Hutchinson, usually a scornful handler of aught
that emitted any odor of witchcraft, we now requote
where he said, concerning the family which included
this Martha, that "they all had been religiously educated, and were thought to be without guile; . . .
they returned to their ordinary behavior, lived to
adult age, made profession of religion. . . . One of
them I knew many years after. She had the character of a very sober, virtuous woman, and never
made any acknowledgment of fraud in this transaction." Such is the testimony of one whose views and
feelings obviously inclined him, as far as possible, to
consider all witchcraft works the products of imposture and fraud; and who, therefore, was not likely to
assign to this family any good qualities which they
were not widely and well known to possess. He
spoke of them as above, and refrained from any direct
imputation of fraud to them. He hinted at fraud, it
is true, but probably both lacked any historical or tra-
ditionary evidence of it, and was conscious that if
fraud were alleged, and even proved, it would fail to
meet the case in all its parts — in those especially that
" seemed more than natural." Nonplussed in the way
of solution, he could only say " it was a time of great
credulity "! In one important respect he had better
facilities for judging this case correctly than can be
obtained to-day. He had listened to conversations
of many persons who were living at the time of its
occurrence, and yet refrained from direct charge of
fraud or imposture. Also he intimated that such
causes, even if alleged, would be inadequate, because
some of the transactions "seemed more than natural."

The later historian, unhampered by need to move

in harmony with the knowledge and beliefs of any
cotemporaries of those Goodwins, and abandoning historic grounds which furnish supermundane agencies
for solving the occurrence of acts which filled the
town and colony with consternation, delved into the
composition of man, and fancied that he found therein enormous capabilities for credulity, fraud, imposture, infatuation, spontaneous out-flashings of highest,
and more than highest, feats of histrionic art, for self-
generated triplication of personal weight, for aviarial
flittings, for equine antics, for self-induced roastings,
self-induced showerings, for comprehension of languages never learned, &c. ; fancied that he had found
how one little girl, " religiously educated, and thought
to be without guile," could execute to admiration each
of those many things " seeming to be more than natural," and could mimic with admirable exactness most
astounding feats, and such as always before had been
supposed to require the powers of disembodied intelligences.　That was an astounding discovery.　But the
present are times of great credulity, and in the infatuation of these days mental optics have been molded,
which, looking back nearly two hundred years, see
the brightest, most vigorous, and keen-sighted men
of Boston — the " solid men of Boston " — see them
stolid and gullible, and see, too, among the people
there three or four little children, bright and religiously educated, and yet malignant and agile as the
very devil.　What a contrast between the old and the
young then !　Was there ever a day when Boston's
wisest adults were prevailingly blockheads easily befooled, and when those of her children who had " great
ingenuity of temper " metamorphosed themselves into

devil-like incendiaries, and set the town ablaze with sulphurous fires? Alas! one modern eye has penetration enough to convince its owner that such a day once was. That eye, "by the aid of" — something, seems "gifted with supernatural insight;" certainly with very uncommon back-sight.

Grant to the Goodwin children all the natural human endowments which imagination can conjure up and embody, also grant to them skillful training and long-continued practice, which there is no probability they had, and even then it was impossible for them, when in separate rooms, to have voluntarily and designedly acted, and seemingly suffered, precisely and simultaneously alike, as they are alleged to have done, and as they would have naturally been made to do if all of them were under and controlled by the psychologic influence of the single mind of the resentful wild Irish woman, because then the same mental impulses would move them all like machines, and simultaneously.

After their separation, the girl at Mr. Mather's house could never have accomplished single-handed what is ascribed to her. The internal evidence of the narrative of events which transpired there combines with common sense in pronouncing it farcical — distinctly *farcical* — to regard that young girl as the contriver and performer of all the works and pranks which history says transpired through her physical organism, and, therefore, to. external eyes, seemed to be products of her own volitions. The nature, quality, and extent of those performances bespeak producing powers both different from and greater than such a girl possessed; bespeak just such powers as departed spirits are now putting forth all around us through living human forms.

It is not only at first, but *permanently* incredible, " that a mere child could carry on such a complex piece of fraud and imposture as that enacted " through " the little girl whose achievements have been immortalized by the famous author of the Magnalia ; " and therefore the world demands, and will yet obtain, a simpler, more rational, and more satisfactory solution of this and kindred cases ; solution that will admit all the amazing feats of witchcraft to be embraced within the scope of forces that finite human beings, the seen and the unseen in conjunction, could in the past and can now so apply as to execute all the world's marvels without aid from either the One Great Devil, from fraud, or from imposture. Neither of these need ever have any connection whatever with, or complicity in, such matters. The records teach, and man's recent experience divines, that other, more befitting, and more competent actors than mere children were on hand and at work in Cotton Mather's presence.

Though justice would have us assign to any Great Devil his honest dues, it also permits us to pull off from his sable brows any unearned wreaths which Cotton Mather and others credulously placed upon them. It also and especially requires us to tear off from the fair head of guileless Martha Goodwin that badge labeled *Fraud and Imposture* — that emblem of deviltry — which *modern delusion* has most cruelly, and yet most artistically, wreathed around temples that seem worthy of a pure *martyr's honoring crown.*

15

RETROSPECTION.

From among the works of witchcraft that occurred from 1648 to 1688, we have now presented six cases, which bring into view some phenomena that are very like many which are now called spirit manifestations. The efficient touch of Margaret Jones, of Charlestown, the extraordinary efficacy of her hands and simple medicines, her prophetic powers, the keenness of her hearing, and the materialization of a spirit-child in her arms, brought her to the gallows in 1648. Ann Hibbins, of Boston, seemingly because of the wit-sharpening acuteness of her hearing, was hanged in 1656. Ann Cole, of Hartford, Conn., in 1662, had her vocal organs " improved " by some intelligence not her own for the utterance of thoughts which were never in her mind, and some of the utterances through her contributed to the conviction and consequent execution of the two Greensmiths, husband and wife. At Groton, a spirit controlling the form of Elizabeth Knap, in 1671, made avowal that he was " a pretty black boy, and not Satan." At Newbury, in 1679, the wild dance of pots, kettles, andirons, and things in general, came off on the premises of William Morse. And at Boston, in 1688, inflictions upon the Goodwin children led to the execution of Mrs. Glover, " one of the wild Irish."

Cases thus scattered in both time and space, half of them limited each to a single actor or sufferer, and each differing widely from any other in many of its prominent features, cannot satisfactorily be ascribed to acquired skill in legerdemain, histrionic art, magic, or necromancy, unattended by help from the living dead.

The name of the wild Irish woman, whose harsh language was speedily followed by the distortions and sufferings of the Goodwin children, was Glover. Calef calls her "a despised, crazy, ill-conditioned old woman — an Irish Roman Catholic." The public believed that she put forth criminal action upon that family, arrested her therefor, received at her trial some indications that she had dealings with invisible beings, pronounced her guilty of witchcraft, and hanged her. She doubtless forsensed retention of power to act either directly or through others upon the objects of her resentment, even after the gallows should have done its utmost work upon herself. For it is stated that "at her execution she said the children would not be relieved by her death . . . and . . . the three children continued in their furnace as before, and it grew rather seven times hotter than it was, and their calamities went on till they barked at one another like dogs, and then purred like so many cats; would complain that they were in a red-hot oven, and sweat and pant as if they had been really so. Anon they would say cold water was thrown on them, at which they would shiver very much. They would complain of being roasted on an invisible spit; and then that their heads were nailed to the floor, and it was beyond an ordinary strength to pull them from it." — *Annals of Witchcraft*," p. 185.

Such facts were gathered from Cotton Mather's account; they come to us from one whose influences and writings are alleged to have been most strongly provocative of executions for witchcraft. Perhaps some of them became so. But his presentation of both the momentous fact and its confirmation by observed experiences, that the spirit of an executed psychologist could act back from beyond the gallows, involved a crushing argument against the wisdom of suspending her or any one else with a view to stop bewitchment. The liberation of one's spirit increases its powers for action upon surviving mortals. Mather's facts argued that.

SALEM WITCHCRAFT.

THE world-renowned and momentous display of extraordinary manifestations, known the world over as *Salem Witchcraft*,. originated and was mainly manifested in what was then called Salem Village — territory distinct from Salem *proper* — embracing the present town of Danvers, together with parts of Beverly, Wenham, Topsfield, and Middleton, in the County of Essex and State of Massachusetts.

There, in the family of the Rev. Samuel Parris, minister at the Village, on the 29th of February, 1692, mysterious causes had wrought strange maladies upon two young girls during the six preceding weeks, which excited great public alarm, and produced such mental agitation that the civil authorities were called upon to give the matter official attention.

The true origin and the actual authors and enactors of that tragedy are among the prime objects of our present researches. It is not our purpose to furnish a *full* history, but to scrutinize and test the hypotheses of other writers; and give a solution of the origin and specification of the actors and effects of that tragedy different — widely different — from the prevalent modern ones. Upham, Drake, and Fowler all agree in fundamentals. All of them have assumed that the agents and forces which evolved those marvelous operations were scarcely, if anything, other than ten or twelve respectable girls, from nine to

twenty years of age, together with a few married
women and a few men, voluntarily exercising and
manifesting only their own wayward constitutional
faculties and forces, in the performance of tricks, impositions, and malignancies ; and with none other than
lamentable results. Their positions we deem open to
deserved attack, and we expect to overthrow much
that has been reared upon them, by using facts
abounding in the primitive records of testimony given
in at trials for witchcraft as our chief instrumentalities. The three expounders just named have rested
much upon allegations that the girls and women
alluded to above had, just previous to the strange
outburst of terrors at the Village, been accustomed to
meet as *a circle*, and at their meetings put themselves
in training for the efficient and successful performance of what soon after transpired through them.
Our readings of the records pertaining to Salem
witchcraft have, as we know and freely confess, fallen
short of complete exhaustion ; and yet we have read
much, and also have failed to find any remembered
allusion to such a circle prior to its mention in the
present century.

Upham states (vol. ii. pp. 2 and 386) that " for a
period embracing about two months they" (certain
girls and women) " had been in the habit of meeting
together, and spending the long winter evenings, *at
Mr. Parris's house*, practicing the arts of fortune-
telling, jugglery, and magic."

Drake says ("Annals of Witchcraft," p. 189) that
"these females instituted frequent meetings, or got
up, as it would now be styled, a club, which was
called a circle. *How frequent they had these meetings*

is not stated; but it was soon ascertained that they met to try projects, or to do or produce superhuman acts."

Fowler remarks, in Woodward's Series (vol. iii. pp. 204 and 205), that "Mary Warren, one of the most violent of the accusing girls, lived with John Proctor," who, "out of patience with the meetings of the girls composing this circle," &c. "It is at the meeting of this circle of eight girls, *for the purpose of practicing palmistry and fortune-telling*, that we discover the germ or the first origin of the delusion."

The position of each of these writers substantially is, that the accusing girls, at circle meetings which they held, qualified themselves for the parts they subsequently performed, wherein, Fowler says, "their whole course, as seen by their depositions, discloses much malignancy."

Upham has told us that these meetings were held "at Mr. Parris's house," and that they occurred within the space of "about two months . . . during the winter of 1691 and 1692." Drake found no statement as to "how frequent they had these meetings," and Fowler finds in them "the germ . . . of the delusion." We have found no mention at all of this circle in the more ancient records and accounts, and not one of the authors named makes mention of the source of his information. Those men, two of whom are our personal acquaintances and friends, would not state anything which they did not believe to be true. We therefore shall not gainsay their allegations. Still, we feel privileged to doubt whether their uncertain number of meetings during the short space of two winter months, held *at the minister's own house*, and under an eye as vigilant as that of Mr. Parris, could have furnished those girls with opportunity to learn very much in any arts whose practice would not receive the approbation of the Rev. Master of the house — not much could they there of themselves learn, at their few meetings in two months, of the anti-Christian arts of " palmistry . . . and fortune-telling ; " not much could they then and there accomplish in the way " of becoming," by their voluntary efforts, " experts in the wonders of necromancy, magic, and Spiritualism."

The general purpose of any stated meetings " at Mr. Parris's house," naturally and almost necessarily had his approbation ; and the presumption from his general character is, that he was neither the good-natured indolent man who let others take their own course, however wayward, nor the absent-minded one whom children or even bright adults could easily and repeatedly deceive and hoodwink. The probability seems excessively small that such a one as he would permit repeated gatherings under his own roof for the special purpose of acquiring knowledge of and skill in practicing tabooed arts. Whatever their authority for it, the writers referred to imply that the members of a circle of girls and misses, meeting statedly " *at Mr. Parris's house*," there very expeditiously qualified *themselves* to become not only most efficient actors of long-continued dissimulation, imposture, cunning, devilish trickery, and fiendish malice, but also to be *bona fide* concoctors and successful executors of vastly complicated, deep, and broad schemes of hellish outrages upon parents, neighbors, and the country.

Wiser heads and greater powers than those girls possessed were manifested by the acts they *seemed* to perform. In a literary sense they were uncultured; but they, doubtless, had been subject to as good domestic, social, moral, and religious teachings and example as existed in any community. The literary deficiencies of the girls are indicated in the following extracts : —

Drake says, "They were generally very ignorant, for out of the eight but two could write their names. Such were the characters which set in motion that stupendous tragedy which ended in blood and ruin." In vol. i. p. 486, Upham says, "How those young country girls, some of them mere children, most of them wholly illiterate, could have become familiar with such fancies to such an extent, is truly surprising. . . . In the Salem witchcraft proceedings, the superstition of the middle ages was embodied in real action. All its extravagances, absurdities, and monstrosities appear in their application to human experience."

Such, according to their own concessions, was the feebleness of the agents whom the historians credited with performances which seem superhuman, and required for their production intellect and forces above what any community has often witnessed. Notwithstanding the inherent and insuperable incompetency of such persons to voluntarily devise and perform what has been ascribed to them, those females have been earnestly set forth as the actual and almost impromptu devisers and enactors of as intricate and effective a scheme for inflicting tortures and misery upon a vast multitude of human beings as has rarely been found in the annals of the race. If it be admitted that they, through frequent meetings at the parsonage, became fitted to conjure up and control the devastating monster that had his lair and foraging-grounds at Salem Village, the presumption amounts closely to certainty that those gatherings were ostensibly held for some laudable object. Meetings for some purpose may possibly have been held when and where the historians assume them to have occurred. But if so, it is our privilege to assume the possibility that the meetings were availed of by unseen intelligences of some grade, for developing into facile mediums such members of the circle as were constitutionally impressible and controllable by spirits; and, if so, the meetings may have become productive of results widely different from any contemplated by either the members themselves or the master of the house in which they met.

In his general history of Salem Village, introductory to that of its witchcraft, Upham, giving us the geographical positions of their several residences, and also their relations and positions in domestic life, furnishes ample grounds for very strong presumption that frequent attendance upon sportive meetings at the parsonage must have been so inconvenient and onerous to several of those girls, that they would not have been present many times in the sort space of two months. Ann Putnam, a sensitive girl only twelve years old, and Mercy Lewis, a servant girl, or "the maid," in the family of Ann's father, two of the most efficient pupils in that necromantic school, resided together in a home situated not less than two and a half miles distant, in a north-westerly direction from the specified place of the meetings. Elizabeth Hubbard, an important member, lived about the same distance off, on a different road at the east. On a still different road, and equally as far away at the south-east, resided Sarah Churchill; and quite as remote, at the south, was the home of Mary Warren; and the last two must take divergent roads when they had gone only a little more than half way home. Each one of these five was very conspicuous amid the ostensible accusers, and the genuinely " afflicted ones." Excepting Ann Putnam, each was old enough to be an efficient helper in household labors, and each, unless we except Elizabeth Hubbard, — and such exception is hardly needful, because, though a niece of his wife, she is mentioned as Dr. Griggs's " maid," which probably implies that she was compensated for services she rendered, — excepting Ann Putnam, each of them was " out at service."

What, therefore, is the probability that these five girls, with any great frequency or regularity, went to and returned home from avowedly sportive or necromantic meetings *at the parsonage?* Each of them would have to travel, in going and returning, not less than five or six miles, mostly along separate routes, in winter's shortest days, by lonely and crooked roads, through miles of dark forests, over winter's snows, and amid its freezing airs. What is the probability that such persons, so circumstanced, would either desire to go, or be permitted by parents and employers to go, frequently and regularly to such meetings? Slight — very slight — because both natural and domestic obstacles must have been great. Were horses, vehicles, and drivers, or were even saddle-horses, regularly at the command of such girls for conveyance to and from such meetings? Would such persons, if physically strong and courageous enough to go on foot, be often spared by their employers to spend long winter evenings, and two hours more for travel, in practicing "fortune-telling, necromancy, and magic"? Such questions of themselves put forth a negative answer. Frequent attendance by such members of the circle was next to an impossibility. If they learned much upon any subject at the very few meetings which circumstances would permit them to attend in the short space of two months, they were very apt pupils indeed. That they became very considerably modified and unfolded in certain directions in consequence of meeting together occasionally is very credible.

We should concede its probable correctness, were an historian to make the supposition that the two Indian slaves in Mr. Parris's kitchen, John Indian and his wife Tituba, often amused themselves and any young folks or other visitors, who there basked in genial light and warmth from blazing logs in a huge New England fireplace on a cold winter's evening, by rehearsing ghost stories and magic lore, and performing any such feats in fortune-telling or other mystical doings as they might be able to exhibit, or as might transpire through them. That the little girls, Elizabeth, daughter of Mr. Parris, and Abigail Williams, his niece, were accustomed to spend many cold winter evenings in the warm kitchen of their own home is very credible. Mary Walcut and Susanna Sheldon, who lived in the near neighborhood, perhaps dropped in frequently. But the

majority of those whose astonishing proficiency in performing what Drake said the circle met for, viz., "to
do or produce superhuman acts," and for *learning*, as
Upham would say, how to manifest "the superstition
of the middle ages . . . embodied in real action," — the
majority of those girls obviously must have had only
very restricted opportunities for study and practice at
the parsonage. It is not at all improbable that each
of them was present in that kitchen occasionally during two months of that winter; nor that each of them
was impregnated by the auras of that place and of its
occupants both visible and invisible; nor that the
physical and psychic soils in each were there mellowed, and also sown with some seed which produced
unlooked-for fruits during the following spring and
summer.

Mediumistic capabilities are innate peculiarities,
measurably hereditary, and nearly always amenable
to special conditions and surroundings for conspicuous
development. King Saul became a prophet, i. e., a
medium, only when he met, mingled with, and imbibed emanations from prophets or mediums. Messengers whom he sent to the prophets succumbed to
new and developing influences upon arriving at their
destination, and became suddenly prophets themselves.
Latent germs of spiritualistic capabilities, if permeated
by quickening auras, which often emanate from positive mediums, frequently unfold into mediumship, as
naturally as specific elements, reaching latent germs in
many human systems, expand those germs into measles,
or into whooping-cough; or as naturally as listening
to soul-stirring music energizes latent capabilities in
many who are acted upon by its strains, and helps

such to become themselves better musicians than before.

The parsonage kitchen — that nestling-place of John Indian and his wife Tituba — may have been that winter a little Delphos, or a little Mount Horeb, that is, a spot where developing nourishments of mediumistic germs were collected in unusual abundance, and were unwontedly operative. We are not only ready to admit, but deem it probable, that any susceptible persons who came into the presence of John and Tituba, in their special room, may have there imbibed properties unsought and unperceived which fostered the development of such visitors into tools or instruments, by the use of which the genuine authors of Salem witchcraft brought out their work upon a public stage, and prosecuted its terrific enactment. Smothering our serious doubts whether any regular meetings at stated times were arranged for or held, we are entirely ready to let the supposition stand that gatherings, more or less extensive, occasionally occurred, at which fortune-telling, necromancy, magic, or Spiritualism, was made the subject of either sportive or serious attention, and we will let results indicate who managed the visible performers during the exercises or entertainments there.

Upham's beautifully rhetorical and eloquent efforts to show that because they, as he states, held a number of meetings for learning and practicing mystic arts, those rustic, illiterate girls thereby and thereat qualified themselves to concoct and accomplish of their own accord, and by their histrionic and malicious capabilities, all that mighty scheme or plan which his predecessor and himself lay to their charge, fail, entirely fail, to meet the fair demands of that common sense which rigidly requires forces and agents adequate in their nature and conditions to produce all effects which are ascribed to them.

Fowler seems to have inferred from some statements ascribed to Proctor, that the latter threatened to go and force Mary Warren to leave the *circle*. We do not so read the account.

The morning of March 25, — that is, the next morning after the examination of Rebecca Nurse, — John Proctor said "he was going to fetch home his jade" (Mary Warren); "he left her there" (at the village) "last night, and had rather given 40 c than let her come up." That is, apparently, he had rather have given that sum than to have had her be present at the examination of Mrs. Nurse ; for, continued he, "if they were let alone, Sr., we should all be devils and witches quickly ; they should rather be had to the whipping post; but he would fetch his jade home and thrust the devil out of her, . . . crying, hang them — hang them. And also added, that when she was first taken with fits he kept her close to the wheel, and threatened to thrash her, and then she had no more fits till the next day" (when) "he was gone forth, and then she must have her fits again forsooth," &c. — *Woodward's Series*, vol. i. p. 63.

It is obvious from the above that Proctor's objection was to his jade's attendance upon the examination of the accused — to her attendance at court — and not at the circle, which, according to Upham, should have closed its meetings a month at least before the 25th of March. And yet S. P. Fowler says (Woodward's Series, vol. iii. p. 204), that "Proctor, out of all patience

with the *meetings of the girls composing this circle*, one
day said he was going to the village to bring Mary
Warren, the jade, home." Most readers will infer
from such a statement that Proctor proposed to take
the girl away from the "circle;" but the statement
from which the annotator drew his information, when
taken in connection with its date, clearly shows that
the threats to bring home the jade and thrash her
were subsequent to the assemblages of the circle, and
were made at a time when the girls were being used
as witnesses before the examining magistrates. That
which tried the resolute man's patience, was not the
meetings of the *circle*, but the testimony of the girls
in court, which threatened to make all the people
"devils and witches quickly."

Proctor's stopping the *fits*, by threats to thrash the
girl, intimates that the fits were measurably controllable by the will of some one. That much may be
true in relation to almost all diseases and maladies of
the body, but probably not as much so in most other
kinds as in those which are imposed by a will that has
no natural alliance with the agitated body. Under
the influence of threats, the girl would naturally
struggle to get full possession of all her own powers
and faculties, and the effort would put her own
elements in such commotion that for a time no foreign will could get control over her form. Threats,
medicines of certain kinds, and many other applications, may temporarily render almost any medium's
system uncontrollable by spirits. Calmness, both of
mind and body, and darkness, too, which is less positive and disintegrating than light, in action upon instruments made and used by spirits, are very helpful
to control of borrowed forms.

In some of his comments (vol. ii. p. 434) Upham wrote more wisely than himself seems to have known. Words from his pen state that "one of the sources of the delusion of 1692, was ignorance of many natural laws that have been revealed by modern science. A vast amount of knowledge on these subjects has been attained since that time." True, true indeed. And had the author of that statement been familiar with important portions of that "vast amount of" new "knowledge," he himself, as readily as those who are better versed in a certain class of modern revealments, would have seen and felt the perfect childishness of his attempt to make those rustic girls the conscious contrivers and perverse and malignant actors of the whole of the vast, complicated, and terrific tragedy of Salem witchcraft.

He might have known when he wrote, he ought to have known then, that Dr. Robert Hare, of Philadelphia, who was eminent, distinctly and broadly eminent, as a scientist, had in 1855 published to the world a rigidly scientific *demonstration* that some unseen agent, intelligent enough to understand and comply with verbal requests, repeatedly moved the arms of scale-beams contrary to the normal action of gravitation. Science, there and then, revealed the existence of some natural law or laws which permit unseen and impalpable intelligences, under some conditions, to put forth action upon matter, with force and to extent, which man can measure in pounds avoirdupois. That single achievement of modern science teaches the wisdom of exempting seemingly diabolized and mischievous children from charge of being devils incarnate, until we have determined whether some

16

beings of greater powers and different dispositions may not have usurped control of youthful and pliant human forms, and through them manifested schemes and pranks that originated in supernal brains, and were enacted by use of such forces as can be manipulated by none below disembodied intelligences.

Obviously he who was cognizant that science had made recent discoveries, suffered himself to remain in ignorance of what to him, as witchcraft historian, were the most pertinent and important parts of the knowledge recently gained ; ignorant of those parts which were most closely connected with philosophical solution of the mysteries which pervaded the history he was elaborating.   His blindness to what science — yes, to what exact physical science — by her rigid processes of weighing and measuring had positively *demonstrated*, bespeaks his short-comings, and would bespeak the unphilosophical stand-point of any historian of, or critic upon, the world's marvels, who, since the day of Hare, ignores the light radiating from his demonstration, and continues to grope on in darkness which use of that light would dispel.   Take into the catalogue of natural agents and forces all those whose existence and action, science, as applied by Dr. Hare twenty years ago, and again by Mr. Crookes and others in England more recently, backed, too, by the observations and tests of thousands less erudite, has *demonstrated*, and then all occasion to look upon our fathers as numskulls, and their daughters as proficient devils, at once disappears.   New England soil, two centuries ago, was not populated mainly by jackasses ; and even had it been, their offspring would have been neither monkeys nor hyenas.

Since the work by Dr. Hare, entitled "Spiritualism Scientifically Demonstrated," may not be readily accessible by many readers, his description of one demonstrative process is quoted from page 49, as follows : —

"A board, being about four feet in length, is supported by a rod, as a fulcrum, at about one foot from one end, and, of coure, three feet from the other, which is suspended on a spring balance. A glass vase, about nine inches in diameter and five inches in hight, having a knob to hold it by, when inverted had this knob inserted in a hole made in the board six inches, nearly, from the fulcrum. Thus the vase rested on the board mouth upward. A wire-gauze cage, such as is used to keep flies from sugar, was so arranged by a well-known means as to slide up or down on two iron rods, one on each side of the trestle supporting the fulcrum. By these arrangements it was so adjusted as to descend into the vase until within an inch and a half of the bottom, while the inferiority of its dimensions prevented it from coming elsewhere within an inch of the parietes of the vase. Water was poured into the vase so as to rise into the cage till within about an inch and an half of the brim. A well-known medium (Gordon) was induced to plunge his hands, clasped together, to the bottom of the cage, holding them perfectly still. As soon as those conditions were attained, the apparatus being untouched by any one excepting the medium as described, I invoked the aid of my spirit friends. A downward force was repeatedly exerted upon the end of the board appended to the balance, equal to three pounds' weight nearly; . . . the distance of the hook of the balance from the fulcrum on which the board turned was six times as great as the cage in which the hands were situated. Consequently a force of $3 \times 6 = 18$ pounds must have been exerted."

The above experiment was performed in Dr. Hare's own laboratory, in the presence and under the watchful scrutiny of John M. Kennedy, Esq., and was made with extraordinary care, because Professor Henry had just treated a similar result formerly obtained as incredible. Plate III. in the book furnishes a diagram illustrating Dr. Hare's apparatus. This experimenter, whom Alfred R. Wallace calls America's foremost chemist, had spent very many years in both constructing and in using, as a scientist, varied kinds of apparatus for testing the presence and action of subtile forces in nature, and he was competent to know, and did know as well as any other man whatsoever in the world's great body of scientists, when results were obtained to positive certainty. He *proved* that some invisible and intelligent power moved his scale-beam contrary to the action of gravitation. The above demonstration, accompanied by many other evidences of spirit-action upon matter through mediums, had been published twelve years when Upham put forth his work. Therefore he was either ignorant of or he ignored late discoveries of science which had revolutionizing applicability to the very theories which he was putting forth.

After having eloquently depicted the sad results of witchcraft, that author says (vol. ii. p. 427), " Let those results for ever stand conspicuous, beacon-monuments, warning us and coming generations against superstition in every form, and all credulous and vain attempts to penetrate beyond the legitimate boundaries of human knowledge." If there ever was "a *credu-lous and vain attempt* to penetrate beyond the legiti-mate boundaries of human knowledge," one was made by him who sought to find that the keen-eyed, energetic, common-sense, virtuous, religious men of Massachusetts in the seventeenth century lacked common sagacity, and that their little girls rivaled Satan himself in malignity. Most seriously we ask whether forces which can be and have been meas-ured by palpable scales, are "beyond the legitimate boundaries of human knowledge?" We ask whether, anywhere in the universe, there exist boundaries be-yond which it is, or can be, illegitimate for man to go in search after agents and forces which either habit-ually or occasionally act legitimately upon him in this mortal life?

Another question is suggested by the foregoing quotation. Would not positive knowledge that there are unseen agents and forces within the realms of nature that can legitimately exhibit the phenomena once deemed witchcrafts, transfer such phenomena from the domain of either superstition or crime into that of science or that of beneficence? Surely it would. And, therefore, how can one possibly work more efficiently for depopulating the domain of super-stition, than by bringing its inhabitants forth and colo-nizing them on the lands of knowledge and science? Shall we comply with the historian's advice, and still continue to leave what ignorance denominates hob-goblins and ghosts to remain shrouded in appalling mists, and thus aid them to continue to be to coming generations the same awful beings they were to the generations past? Or shall we, on the other hand, now, while experience and science are showing that such work is practicable, push discovery onward till we both find laws and learn conditions which permit closer access of disembodied beings to us, and which also permit most beneficent reciprocal action between them and us, just as soon as familiariry, confidence, calmness, and mutual trust make their access easy? Which shall we do? Which is most scientific? Which is most dutiful to God and friendly to man? Which? Is ignorance of, or is knowledge of, nature's forces and inhabitants the greater blessing? Which? Away with ignorance where knowledge is attainable.

We choose to learn as much concerning the universe and its inhabitants as God gives us power and opportunities to acquire; not fearing his censure, but trusting to win his approbation, by so doing. When one learns that issuers from the vailed realms of spirit-land are only earth's emancipated children revisiting their former homes, the cry that devils are coming lacks any startling power. Faith, and even knowledge, sometimes says, "It is my friends and loved ones and those who love me, who are in the circumambient hosts, and I will do what I may to facilitate their more sensible approach; will extend toward them a friendly and helping hand."

Only superstition and ignorance quail and skulk before visitants that come from unseen realms; knowledge stands fast and meets them with welcome and joy.

The "legitimate boundaries of knowledge"! Where are they? Surely not within any domain where knowledge can supersede ignorance and its consequent superstitions.

Perhaps only few persons who give credence to the substantial accuracy of the transmitted statements of witchcraft facts, will dissent from Hutchinson's obvious meaning when he said that "some of them seem to be more than natural;" that is, as we suppose him to have meant, they seem to have required for their production something beyond the recognized powers of embodied human beings. He, however, in spite of such seeming, sought to lead other minds to fancy that fraud and malice acting upon credulity — in other words, that cunning and malicious embodied human beings, and none other — were concerned in their manifestation. Upham and Drake have not only followed Hutchinson's lead in excluding invisible agents, but have omitted to admit that some of the facts *seem* to be more than natural. They blindly fancy that they find resident in human minds and hearts of seeming brilliancy and goodness, capabilities of artfulness, malice, and might which wrest from Satan's brow all laurels which the world has meeded to him for his imputed prowess on witchcraft's battle-fields. As one of the human race, we protest against such slander of our kindred humans while embodied, none of whom, while dwellers here below, were ever smelted in fires hot enough to elicit from their own interiors some forces which were put in action through their forms — forces which, in common parlance, though not in absolute fact, were "more than natural." Events fearfully mysterious have long been, and now often are, spoken of as the productions of beings, or at least of One Special being, lurking some-where away off beyond the outmost limits of nature. But each and every hiding-place of even Old Nick is somewhere within those limits, and even he can never and nowhere act otherwise than in obedience to nature's laws. How far up, down, around, do natural forces and agents extend and operate? If there be a fixed limit to nature's domain, where is it? When life departs from man's body, are the forces which continue to act upon his invisible spirit, whether that continues to be or ceases to be a conscious individuality, — are the forces which then act upon it and which bear it to its appropriate position in spirit spheres, *natural* forces, or are they other?

When man escapes from his gross and sluggish encasement, and becomes — as the reappearance of many of the race teaches that he does — a freed spirit, he does not escape from within the realm of nature, nor pass to where natural substances and forces cease to sustain and act upon him. The word "supernatural" as well as its equivalent phrase, "more than natural," is often misleading; it tends to generate supposition that nature *terminates* where man's external senses cease to take cognizance. Absolutely, however, as we believe, all beings, including even God, and all things whatsoever, are parts of nature; so that the word "supernatural" can scarcely find place for rigid, unqualified application. No objection to its usual application is here intended, provided it is not used to convey the idea that things to which it is applied are the work of intelligence above and beyond the control and restrictions of universal laws or forces; provided it does not intimate that the works are what theology has called miracles, i. e., acts " contrary to the established course of things."

Such works probably never did and never can occur. Higher and unrecognized laws are availed of whenever known laws are thwarted in their results, as when the magnet takes the steel upward in spite of gravitation: gravitation works on with as much steadiness and force as ever, while the magnet overpoweringly pulls against it. The overbalancing magnetic force does not act " contrary to the established course of things," but simply performs its own functions in full harmony with that course ; so of all mysterious events in the vast universe. All move on in obedience to law ; all events are outworkings of universal forces, none of which are ever broken or suspended, though sometimes some of them are restrained by other and counteracting forces from manifesting their usual results.

All the marvelous works of both ancient and modern Spiritualism may have occurred, and yet none of them have been, in fact, " more than natural," however much so some minds may be accustomed to ·deem them. Take psychic forces as natural instrumentalities, take both embodied and disembodied intelligences who had skill and power for the control of such forces, and with these take also others who had special susceptibilities for yielding to psychic action, and you will then have in your conceptions ample natural means for the production of each and every marvel that was ever described in human history, and all such may have been produced without any more help or hindrance in kind from either God or the devil, than we all receive in the ordinary acts of daily life. Bring in what is meant by either magnetism, or mesmerism, or psychology, or psy-

chism, or by any other term expressive of that
action upon and within a human being, which lets
either his own spirit-senses or the forces of some
outside intelligence get play therein independent of
and superior to the owner's outer or physical senses,
and we then may have fitting and adequate instrumentality through which finite intelligence can legitimately produce all the marvels that human eyes have
ever witnessed. Professor Cromwell F. Varley, one
of England's most eminent electricians, said, when
addressing a committee of the London Dialectical Society, " I believe the mesmeric trance and the spiritual trance are produced by similar means, and I
believe the mesmeric and the spiritual forces are the
same. They are both the action of a spirit, and the
difference between the spiritual trance and the mesmeric trance I believe is this: in the mesmeric
trance, the will that overpowers or entrances the
patient is in a human body; in the spiritual trance,
that will which overpowers the patient is not in a
human body."

The position taken by Mr. Varley, whose observations were made mostly within his own domestic
circle, and whose professional pursuits led him to
be a constant and careful observer of the nature,
properties, and actions of delicate forces, is worthy
of much regard. His view is probably in harmony
with the conclusion of most minds which have studied
carefully the outworkings of mesmerism and Spiritualism. The two isms, in some views of them, are essentially one in nature, the latter being the butterfly
or moth that came from out the former. The grub
and its moth are the same being in different stages

of development. Multitudes of human beings raised, and to be raised, from lower to higher development have their habitats along the line where the material and spiritual interblend, and some are measurably amphibious there — can move and act in either of two auras. The younger, or less advanced, flesh-clad mesmerists, prevailingly abide in the material, while spirits have their most congenial residence generally beyond where the palpably material extends; but either class can at times bring under their control the physical systems of many human beings.

By means of this psychism, or this outworking of soul power, there may be kept up reciprocal action or intercommunion between what are usually called the material and spiritual worlds, both of which absolutely are natural, and are pervaded by inter-acting natural forces which are at the service of peculiarly endowed, or constituted, or unfolded persons, who are, or may become, competent and disposed to use them. A disembodied spirit no more needs special permission or aid from Omnipotence for acting upon men and matter, than the diver needs such for deep descents beneath the water's surface. Natural permission for spirits to reincase themselves in, or to act upon, palpable matter, is as free and full as man's is to put on submarine armor.

This much we have said for the purpose of disclosing our stand-points of observations and reasonings pertaining to Salem witchcraft, and now come to more direct consideration of that special topic.

At Salem Village about a dozen people, mostly the girls previously named, were strangely and grievously tormented, at short intervals, during several months.

They often endured contortions, convulsions, and very acute sufferings. At times many of them became deaf, dumb, blind, &c. Seemingly to beholders they personally performed most strange and incredible feats of strength and simulations, and made astounding utterances. Because of these doings and sufferings they were, after some weeks of observation, deemed to be "under an evil hand"—were pronounced *bewitched*, and were termed, in the parlance of that day, "the afflicted."

According to the faith of those times, no person could be bewitched in any other way than through some other embodied person who had entered into a covenant with the *Devil*, and voluntarily become his instrument or his agent. It was then assumed, also, that the afflicted ones could perceive who the person or persons were through whom the devil tormented them. Consequently the sufferers were teased, coaxed, or driven to name some one or more who was causing their sufferings. Those named by the sufferers as producers of their maladies were called the accused, or were said to be "cried out upon."

Belief in the ability of the afflicted to designate accurately their afflicters, was then prevalent; but though probably born of facts in human experience, and in itself fundamentally correct, it was indiscreetly and harmfully applied. The mediumistic or psychologized condition often renders its subjects practically independent of time, space, and gross matter, and makes them possessors of ability to feel, or rather to *sense*, contact with the properties of some peculiarly constituted mortals, even though such persons at the time be physically many miles away. The persons from whom such agitating emanations would proceed would generally themselves be highly mediumistic.

If the inner or spiritual perceptive organs of Mr. Parris, Dr. Griggs, Thomas Putnam, and their consulting associates, of whom we shall speak hereafter, were inextricably interblended with their outer bodies, so that they were, par excellence, non-mediumistic, their presence near the bodies of persons infilled with abnormal properties by spirits might be imperceptible by the entranced, while either the poor, " melancholy, distracted " (?) Sarah Good, or " bedrid " Mrs. Osburn (who will come into notice on a future page), if highly mediumistic, might, though being then in their distant homes bodily, be present as spirits, and their emanations might be distinctly felt by the suffering girls, and be by them visibly traced to their sources. Mediumistic states or entrancements, however induced, often bring their subjects into rapport with other mediumistic persons afar off, while they as often shut off sensibility to the presence of the physically imprisoned or very slightly impressible ones who are near by. The saying that " birds of a feather flock together " apparently has more constant application outside of gravitation's dominating reach than within it — more among relatively freed spirits than among rigidly body-hampered ones.

That there exist special occult forces, whose action frequently enables mediumistic persons, while under spirit manipulations, to know assuredly that emanations from special human organisms act upon them to

either their pleasure or their annoyance is very clearly
indicated by the experiences of some modern mediums ; for these are often heard to speak of influences
coming to their help or their harm from particular
persons, who, at the time, are known to be miles away.
Mediumistic intuitions often very accurately trace influences to some definite mundane source ; that source
frequently is where the disembodied operating spirit
gets such an equivalent to a nervous fluid as is needful to give him or her contact with and control over
matter. Some mediumistic systems may at times contain enough of such quasi nerve-producing elements
to meet all the needs of the controlling spirit, while
others usually lack them to such extent that drafts to
supply the deficiency are made from the systems of
others more or less remote from the point of application. If the harassed and tortured children in the
family of Mr. Parris were acted upon by spirits, they
might be, at times, able to *sense* the fact that forceful
action upon them came perceptibly forth from the
bodily forms of particular living persons. Broad human observation and experience through the ages had
generated conclusion that bewitched persons could
designate those from whom their inflictions came.
Therefore our fathers would with conscious propriety
ask any one whom they supposed to be under "an
evil hand," "Who hurts you ?" They would look for
an answer, and, if one came, would deem it correct.
It was, then, logically necessary for them to confide
in the accuracy of any responses which might issue
from the lips of the sufferers, so long as their creed
was made chief premise. Sneers at belief that psychologized persons know from whom the force comes

which generates their condition, may argue less knowledge in the sneerer's brain, of forces and agents that
sometimes act upon men, than in the heads of those
who in former days sought to learn from bewitched
girls what particular persons afflicted them. The
world, while learning much, may have been forgetting some important knowledge.

The belief held by many of our forefathers, that
the afflicted would generally know that afflicting
forces came to them from the persons whom they
named, though measurably correct in itself, was rendered most woefully disastrous in its application, because of its concomitant erroneous belief that such
afflicting forces could go forth from none but such
as were in covenant with witchcraft's awful devil.
The fact of one's being a channel through which occult wonder-working forces could flow, was, in those
days, proof positive that he or she had tendered alle-
giance to and made a compact with the Evil One.
That was the specially great and disastrous error
which engendered witchcraft. Susceptibilities which
were in fact only nature's boons, were looked upon
as acquisitions obtained through a diabolical compact.
Some laws of psychology partially revealed and comprehended now, were then not dreamed of; and deductions from false premises or from an erroneous belief,
being then applied by clear-headed and good men for
noble ends, yes, for God's glory and man's protection,
caused out-workings of unspeakable woes.

The persons most *afflicted* at Salem Village were
Elizabeth, daughter of Mr. Parris, nine years old;
Abigail Williams, his niece, eleven; Ann Putnam,
twelve; Mercy Lewis, seventeen; Mary Walcut, sev-

enteen ; Elizabeth Hubbard, seventeen ; Elizabeth Booth, eighteen ; Sarah Churchill, twenty ; Mary Warren, twenty : to these girls may be added Mrs. Ann Putnam, mother of the girl of the same name ; also a Mrs. Pope and a Mrs. Bibber. Nearly all of these occupied very good social positions, and many of them were surrounded and cared for by as intelligent, moral, and religious people as that or any other parish in the neighborhood contained. Yes, from amidst the very breath of prayer, the light of intelligence, the sway of strong authority, and the restraining influences of religion, these reputable, and no doubt generally amiable, conscientious, and kind-hearted girls and women during all their previous years, suddenly became utterers of what were then regarded most damning accusations against their neighbors and acquaintances first, and subsequently against strangers living remote from them ; against the low and the high, the vicious and the virtuous, the feeble-minded and the strong in intellect alike. And in their strange and desolating work these people, of exemplary deportment previously, moved on harmoniously, encouraging and strengthening each other, and without manifesting the slightest regret. A marked and startling specimen this of what mortal tongues may be used to accomplish ! And yet those tongues generally may have only described what senses perceived.

History has said — no, not history — but invalid supposition has said that sportiveness, malice, love of notoriety, and the like, inherent in the minds and hearts of those young girls and women, were the chief incentives to and producers of the woeful, the murderous accusations and statements which came forth from their youthful lips. It was not so. One may as well call a pencil or a pen a malicious accuser when it is made to record malicious accusations, as to call those girls the contrivers and enactors of many scenes which were presented by use of their bodies.

We quote as follows from church records, penned by the Rev. Mr. Parris himself, in whose house the great and awful commotion originated : —

" It is altogether undeniable that our Great and Blessed God, for wise and holy ends, hath suffered many persons in several families of this little Village to be grievously vexed and tortured in body, and to be deeply tempted to the endangering of the destruction of their souls, and all these amazing feats (well known to many of us) to be done by witchcraft and diabolical operations.

" It is well known that when these calamities first began, which was in my own family, the affliction was " (had existed) " several weeks, before such hellish operations as witchcraft was suspected ; Nay, it never broke forth to any considerable light, until diabolical means was used, by the making of a cake by my Indian man, who had his directions from our sister Mary Sibly. Since which time apparitions have been plenty, and exceeding much mischief hath followed. But by this means (it seems) the devil hath been raised amongst us, and his rage is vehement and terrible, and when he shall be silenced, the Lord only knows."

The statements just presented have come down from one whose position and whose mental powers qualified him to be as important a witness as any other person whatsoever could be ; they come from

17

one of keen intellect and ready perceptions, who saw the scenes of *Salem* witchcraft in their first externally observable stages of development, and also throughout most of their subsequent unfoldments and disastrous workings. These statements were semi-private; were made in the *church* and not the parish records; were made to be read by those who should come after him, rather than by those of his own times. And in such records he states that "amazing feats" were performed "*by witchcraft and diabolical operations.*" What were those feats? It has been said generally concerning the whole Salem circle of proficients in "necromancy, magic, and Spiritualism," that "they would creep into holes, and under benches and chairs, put themselves into odd and unnatural postures, make wild and antic gestures, and utter incoherent and unintelligible sounds. They would be seized with spasms, drop insensible to the floor, or writhe in agony, suffering dreadful tortures, and uttering loud and fearful cries." — *History of Witchcraft and Salem Village,* vol. ii. p. 6.

An acute observer, who was also a definite and methodical describer of a portion of the actions referred to, says the sufferers were "in vain" treated medicinally; that "they were oftentimes very stupid in their fits, and could neither hear nor understand, in the apprehension of the standers-by;" that "when they were discoursed with about God or Christ . . . they were presently afflicted at a dreadful rate;" that "they sometimes told at a considerable distance, yea, several miles off, that such and such persons were afflicted, which hath been found to be done according to the time and manner they related it; and they said the specters of the suspected persons told them of it ; " that " they affirmed that they saw the ghosts of several departed persons ; " that " one, in time of examination of a suspected person, had a pin run through both her lower and her upper lip when she was called to speak, yet no apparent festering followed thereupon after it was taken out ; " that " some of the afflicted . . . in open court . . . had their wrists bound fast together with a real cord by invisible means ; " that " some afflicted ones have been drawn under tables and beds by undiscerned force ; " that " when they were most grievously afflicted, if they were brought to the accused, and the suspected person's hand laid upon them, they were immediately relieved out of their tortures ; " that " sometimes, in their fits, they have had their tongues drawn out of their mouths to a fearful length, . . . and had their arms and legs . . . wrested as if they were quite dislocated, and the blood hath gushed plentifully out of their mouths for a considerable time together ; I saw several violently strained and bleeding, . . . certainly all considerate persons who beheld those things must needs be convinced that their motions in their fits were preternatural and involuntary, . . . they were much beyond the ordinary force of the same persons when they were in their right minds ; " that " their eyes were, for the most part, fast closed in their trance-fits, and when they were asked a question, they could give no answer ; and I do verily believe they did not hear at that time ; yet did they discourse with the specters as with real persons." — *Deodat Lawson.*

They affirmed that " *they saw the ghosts of several departed persons,*" and they did " *discourse with the specters as with real persons.*" This looks like Spir·itualism.

The above extracts describe a part only of the amazing feats.

Mr. Parris apprehended that this extensive diabolism was inaugurated through the making of a peculiar cake by his Indian man John. Either a sneer or a smile will probably drape the reader's face when he perceives that a clergyman in a former age deemed it probable that a compound offensive to refined taste (a cake made of meal mixed with urine from the suffering children) was so appetizing to the devil that it drew him from his wonted distance into close affinity with mortal forms, and increased his power to afflict them. Perhaps that clergyman had read what the reader may peruse by turning to the concluding portion of chap. iv. of Ezekiel, where preparation of food was prescribed for that prophet's use while he was in process of being trained for pliancy under manipulations by some unseen intelligence — such preparation of food as was not less offensive than such a cake as John Indian furnished.

We do not find a great producing cause of the *amazing feats* where Mr. Parris did, and are not prepared to regard Mary Sibley's prescription as having been very efficacious. Still we might admit the possibility that the real author of the feats was present when John kneaded that cake, leavened it with supermundane yeast, and made use of it as an instrumentality for coming into closer contact than before with the human bodies from which part of the ingredients of the cake had been derived.

Both spirits and unfolded mediums often either prescribe or apply — as Jesus did when he treated a blind patient by application of a plaster composed of his own spittle and street dust — things which mankind at large would regard as either offensive or inert. Human mediums may be, and the observations of thousands now living indicate that they often are, made to prepare strange compounds, and prescribe them for the sick, the suffering, and for unpliant mediums.

Who was " my Indian man " ? Yes ; who that baker whose cake raised the devil, and caused apparitions to become exceeding plenty ? Mr. Parris, prior to being a minister of the gospel, had been a merchant in Barbadoes, and at the commencement of the strange feats alluded to, had in his family some servants, whom he called Indians ; but they probably were natives either of some one of the West India islands or of the neighboring coast of South America, whom he had brought thence, and who were, doubtless, by nature less firm and self-reliant than our northern Indians usually are. Two of these servants, or slaves, viz., John Indian, the cake-baker, and his wife, Tituba, were among the first, if they were not the very first, persons there to succumb, and yield subjection to the peculiar influences which developed the terrible events we are considering. Those two humble, ignorant, weak-minded slaves may have been, and we regard them as having been, though unintentionally and unconscious of it, very efficient aids in the outward manifestation of what their master properly termed " amazing feats."

John seems, so far as records depict him, to have been only about as much of a medium as King Saul was ; that is, one that could be made to tumble down and roll about in unseemly ways. There may, and there may not, have been properties in his composition which were very helpful to spirits in gaining control over other persons. However that may have been, he was not perceptibly much of a medium, and had but little connection with the events which so harassed his master and neighbors, as far as can now be shown. But his wife, Tituba, deserves extended notice and careful study. Before the observable works were commenced, she was clairvoyant and clairaudient, and her aid in the amazing feats which transpired was solicited in advance by a nocturnal visitant needing no opened door for entrance. She entered behind the scene, — behind the vail of flesh, — and her spirit eyes saw the chief manager. She is the great eye-witness in the case. She was a medium easy of control, and, Agassiz-like, retained her consciousness and her memory of experiences while her form was subjected to control by another's will. Obviously, also, she was an uncommonly good developing medium, or, in other words, her constitutional properties were such as greatly aided spirits to develop the mediumistic susceptibilities of other persons.

This humble, illiterate slave, besides being apparently the chief focus or reservoir of supermundane forces that evolved the Salem wonders, was one among the first three persons who were arrested and brought before the civil tribunals under charges of practicing witchcraft. Her statements at her examination were recorded very fully by one of the two magistrates who conducted the proceedings. And the transmitted words of this simple-minded creature, whose intellect was incompetent to foresee the conse-

quences of her answers and statements, throw more
light upon the origin and growth, and upon the nature
and true character, of Salem witchcraft, than does all
that came from other lips, or any pens of her cotemporaries, or than has come from subsequent historians.
Her mediumistic susceptibilities gave her admittance
where she was an actual observer of the real author
of and actors in that memorable drama. Her knowledge was derived directly through one set of her
own senses, and therefore she was able to speak of,
and apparently did speak simply and truthfully of,
persons and scenes which her inner organs of sense
had cognized. She *knew* more than did all her prosecutors and judges combined concerning the matters
under investigation at her trial ; and could those who
then presided have been nobly humble enough to
learn from such a witness, and single-eyed enough to
admit into their own minds the literal import of her
simple statements, the horrors which were subsequently experienced would never have transpired.
But the faith of those times forbade such elevation.

Tituba's general, if not uniform frankness, and the
extreme simplicity of her answers, tend strongly to
beget confidence in the intentional and substantial
truthfulness of her statements. We deem it unjust
to doubt her truthfulness. And the general accuracy
of her testimony is now rendered credible by its
harmony with a mass of facts pertaining to Spiritualism. If the truth and accuracy of her words be conceded, — and they ought to be, — we learn distinctly
that during the " several weeks " through which Mr.
Parris's afflicted daughter and niece were treated
by their physician and cared for by the family and

friends without suspicion of witchcraft, Tituba was positively *knowing* that something like a man, invisible to outward sense, visited herself, and sought and sometimes forced her co-operation in pinching the two little girls and in producing their seeming sicknesses. Her experience proved to her that the sufferings of the children were purposely inflicted by an intelligent being something like a man. Her statements prove the same to us.

Such testimony as hers, by such a lowly person as she was, when given before a tribunal whose members were firm believers in such a devil and in such a creed as have been described in our Appendix, even if fairly comprehended by them, would cause her judges to believe that she was virtually confessing that she had made a covenant with the Evil One. From their premises they could not logically draw any other conclusion. Perhaps, unfortunately for her, but not for us at this day, her intellect was too feeble to perceive the inferences which would be drawn from her words. Fearing not consequences, she could frankly tell her experiences and observations; she let out the exact facts of the case, and furnished for us a sound historic basis for the assertion that the strange maladies which came upon the little girls in Mr. Parris's house were designedly and deliberately imposed by a disembodied spirit or a band of spirits.

The mouths of not only babes and sucklings, but of adults of feeble intellect, present facts, sometimes, better than those whose intellects are swayed by fears of dreaded consequences which might ensue from frank and full avowal of their knowledge. From

Tituba came statements of facts to which we must give prolonged attention.. A perusal of the fullest minutes of her testimony may be wearisome, but her account of what she saw, heard, and was made to do, is so instructive that we shall present it without abridgment, because it was first printed in full only a few years ago, was probably never seen or known to exist by Hutchinson, was not availed of by Upham, and not very carefully analyzed by Drake. Only a very limited portion of the reading public has ever had opportunity to learn more than a small fraction of the disclosures made by this important witness.

Upham, though he had perused the minutes of testimony to which we allude, elected to use a briefer report of Tituba's statements, which was made by Ezekiel Cheever. The more extended one he noticed thus : " Another report of Tituba's examination has been preserved in the second volume " (we find it in vol. iii., appendix, p. 185) " of the collection edited by Samuel G. Drake, entitled the ' Witchcraft Delusion in New England.' It is in the handwriting of Jonathan Corwin, very full and minute." It is " full, minute," and abounding in facts which the faithful historian should adduce and comment upon. It was written out by one of the magistrates before whom Tituba was examined, and therefore its authority is good. It surprises us that the historian who noticed it as above failed to use much important matter contained in it which was lacking in the report that he preferred to this.

Drake, under whose supervision this ampler report was first printed, says, in Woodward's " Historical Series," No. I. Vol. III. Appendix p. 186, that " it

is valuable on several accounts, the chief of which
is the light it throws on the commencement of the
delusion. . . . This examination, more, perhaps, than
any of the rest, exhibits the atrocious method employed by the examinant of causing the poor ignorant accused to own and acknowledge things put
into their mouths by a manner of questioning as
much to be condemned as perjury itself, inasmuch as
it was sure to produce that crime. In this case the
examined was taken from jail and placed upon the
stand, and was soon so confused that she could
scarcely know what to say. While it is evident that
all her answers were at first true, because direct,
straightforward, and reasonable. The strangeness of
the questions and the long persistence of the ques-
tioners could lead to no other result but confounding
what little understanding the accused was at best
possessed of. . . . The examination was before Messrs.
Hathorne and Corwin. The former took down the
result, which is all in his peculiar chirography." Upham, it will be noticed, says the report was written
by Corwin, while Drake here ascribes it to Hathorne.
But since those two men were both present as joint
holders of the examining court, the authority of
either gives great value to the document; we regard
the record as having been made by Corwin.

While Drake says this record of "the examination is valuable" for "the light it throws on the
commencement of the delusion," he also calls it a
"record of incoherent nonsense." The public very
narrowly escaped loss of opportunity to get at the
important and luminous facts contained in this document. Drake, in 1866, says, "The original (now

for the first time printed) came into the editor's
hands some five and twenty years since," at which
time, "on a first and cursory perusal of the examination of the Indian woman belonging to Mr. Parris's family, it was concluded not to print it, and
only refer to it; that is, only refer to the *extract* from
it contained in the HISTORY AND ANTIQUITIES OF
BOSTON. But when editorial labors upon these vol-
umes were nearly completed, a re-perusal of that examination was made, and the result determined the
editor to give it a place in this Appendix." We are
constrained to doubt whether this editor attained to
anything like either fair comprehension of the value
of this document even upon its re-perusal, or that he
perceived one half the import which facts fairly give
to the following words from his pen: "The record
of this examination *throws light on the commencement
of the delusion.*" Yes, light upon the time, place,
source, and nature of that commencement, and which
also discloses who was the originating, and probably
the guiding agent of all that witchcraft's subsequent
process up to its culmination — light which, to great
extent, exculpates both the fathers and their children
— light which reveals the true actors and exoner-
ates their *unconscious* instruments. That document,
read, as it now can be, with help from modern revealments, proves that some spirit, or a band of spirits,
was witchcraft's generator and enactor at Salem, and
indicates that simple Tituba comprehended the genuine source of the disturbance more clearly than did
any other known person of that generation. She
furnished for transmission a key that now unlocks the
door of the chamber of mystery, in which she and

her associates were made to enact thrilling and bloody scenes one hundred and eighty years ago.

That such as desire to do so may be enabled to peruse the whole of her testimony, which probably can now be found printed only in Woodward's very valuable Series of original documents pertaining to witchcraft, — a work too voluminous and costly to obtain general circulation, — we shall do what we can to further public accessibility to Tituba's state- ment, ungarbled and unabridged. Still, to both re- lieve and enlighten the reader, we shall break up its continuity by interjecting comments upon many parts as we go on, but do this in such form, that, if the reader chooses to peruse the whole unbiased by com- ment, he can ; for this will require only an observance of our quotation marks. By skipping our comments he can read in their original collocations all parts of what Drake calls " incoherent nonsense," but which to us, notwithstanding some perplexing incoherence of both questions and answers, is rich in instructive *facts.*

Prior to March 1, the malady seems to have spread out beyond the parsonage and seized upon other persons, for on that day several afflicted ones were convened as witnesses, or accusers, or both, at the place where the magistrates then appeared for attend- ing to the cases of three women who had been accused of witchcraft, arrested, and held for examination. Here was the commencement of reputed folly and barbarity so exercised as soon to redden that region with the blood of the innocent, the manly, the virtu- ous, and the devout.

Sarah Good, Sarah Osburn, and Tituba were brought

into the meeting-house as suspected witches and as producers of the sufferings of the several afflicted ones, to be examined in the presence of their accusers and the public. What course the magistrates either elected or were constrained to pursue in order to educe such facts as would sustain a charge for witch-craft, will reveal itself as we proceed, through the questions which they put to the accused, and the kinds of evidence which they admitted.

TITUBA.

" *Tituba, the Indian woman, examined March* 1, 1692.

" *Q.* Why do you hurt these poor children ? What harm have they done unto you ?

" *A.* They do no harm to me. I no hurt them at all."

The first question by the magistrates implies the presence there of the afflicted children, and of their then seeming to be invisibly hurt. It also implies the magistrate's assumption that Tituba was hurting them. Her denial that either they had harmed her or that she was hurting them was distinct. But the magistrate seemingly doubted its truth or its suffi-ciency, for he next asked, —

" *Q.* Why have you done it ?

" *A.* I have done nothing. I can't tell when the devil works.

" *Q.* What ? Doth the devil tell you that he hurts them ?

" *A.* No. He tells me nothing."

She conceded here that the *Devil* might be, and probably was, at work upon the children ; but *his*

doings were beyond the reach of her perceptive faculties. *He* made no communication to her. Thus early
her words indicate that her knowledge of spiritual
matters caused her to draw and adhere to a distinction
between *The Devil* and either *a Spirit*, or bands of
spirits, which distinction she and other mediumistic
ones of her times adhered to, while the public lacked
knowledge that facts required it, and ignorantly called
all visitants from spirit realms *The Devil*.

When glancing at Cotton Mather's unpublished
account of Mercy Short, we copied from it the following statement : "As the bewitched in other parts
of the world have commonly had no other style for
their tormentors but only THEY and THEM, so had
Mercy Short." Clairvoyants and all who obtained
knowledge of spirits through perceptions by their
own interior organs seldom, if ever, have seriously
spoken of either seeing, hearing, or feeling the
Devil. Possibly, at times, some may have done so
by way of accommodation to the unillumined world's
modes of speech. But, as Mather says, they have,
the world over, *generally* called the personages perceived, " *They* " and " *Them*." Such a fact demands
regard. The personal observers of spiritual beings
have never been accustomed to designate them by
bad names. Fair inference from this is, that such
beings have not generally worn forbidding aspects.
It has been the reporters, and not the utterers, of descriptive accounts of spiritual beings who have made
use of the terms "devil," "satan," and the like.
Mather perceived the common "style" of the bewitched, and yet the warping habit of Christendom
made him preserve continuance of inaccurate report-

ing; for he, like most others in his day, persistently
wrote "devil," where that name was not announced,
and ought not to have been foisted in. Tituba saw no
one whom she ever called *The Devil*, though history
has taught that she did.

" *Q.* Do you never see something appear in some
shape? *A.* No. Never see anything."

This answer is not true if construed literally in
connection with its question. She did, as will soon
appear, sometimes see many things clairvoyantly, but
never *The Devil*, who had just before been mentioned.

" *Q.* What familiarity have you with the devil,
or what is it that you converse withal? Tell the
truth, who it is that hurts them. *A.* The devil, for
aught I know."

She persistently admits that the devil *may* be then
and there at work, but asserts that she does not
know anything about *him*.

" *Q.* What appearance, or how doth he appear
when he hurts them?"

She makes no reply when asked how the *Devil*
hurts. She ignores *him*.

" *Q.* With what shape, or what is *he* like that hurts
them? *A.* Like a man, I think. Yesterday, I being
in the lean-to chamber, I saw a thing *like a man*, that
told me serve him. I told him no, I would not do
such thing."

Devil had now been dropped from the question, and
he substituted. What is *he* like? Then she promptly mentioned an apparition not only visible, but audible, who, if carefully scanned, may prove to have
been chief author and enactor of Salem witchcraft.
She who saw and heard him says he was "like a man,

I think," — was "a thing like a man." According
to her perceptions he was not the devil. She did
not know the devil. Others at that time and ever
since have called her visitant the devil. But Tituba,
who saw, heard, and thus knew him, did not and
would not.

Next comes in, parenthetically, a summary of her
sayings and doings, as follows : —

("She charges Goody Osburn and Sarah Good,
as those that hurt them children, and would have
had her done it ; she saith she hath seen four, two
which she knew not ; she saw them last night as she
was washing the room. They told me hurt the children, and would have had me gone to Boston. There
was five of them with the man. They told me if I
would not go and hurt them, they would do so to
me. At first I did agree with them, but afterward, I
told them I would do so no more.")

According to this summary, apparitions multiplied ;
for, besides the man, she saw four women around
herself : that company threatened to hurt her if she
would not unite with them in hurting the children.
Two of these were apparitions of her living neighbors, Good and Osburn, then under arrest ; the other
three were strangers. We shall soon see that she
believed, what is probably true, that apparitions of
particular persons can be not only presented by
occult intelligences to the inner vision, but put into
apparent vigorous action, while the genuine persons
thus presented in counterfeit have no consciousness
either of being present at the exhibition, or of performing, either then or at any other time, the acts
which they seem to put forth.

The conceptions which this simple mind held concerning the nature, powers, and purposes of those
who came to her in manner strange to most mortals,
are pretty clearly indicated. By her likening them to
men and women, and by her protests against their
forcing her to act cruelly, she justifies the inference
that she failed to see in or about them anything very
forbidding, awful, or satanic. She admitted the possibility that the devil might have hurt the children,
but also asserted that, if so, *his* action was unbeknown
to her. The "something like a man," together with
these women and herself under compulsion, were
the afflicting ones, so far as her vision or other senses
could determine. *She* nowhere applies the term
"devil" to her male apparition. No hoofs, horns, or
tail, no sable hues or frightful form, are brought to
view by this clairvoyant's description of her occult
companions. They wore, in her sight, the semblances
of a man and of women — not of devils.

How different would have been results had her
simple words and instructive facts been credited and
made the basis of judicial decisions! Could she have
been calmly and rationally listened to by minds
freed from a blinding and irritating faith that Christendom's witchcraft devil was her companion and
prompter, her plain and definite exposition of the
actors who generated troubles which were profound
mysteries to her superiors in external knowledge and
penetration, would have brought all the marvels of
that day within the domain of natural· things, and
warded off the horrors which ensued.

" *Q.* Would they have had you hurt the children
last night? *A.* Yes, but I was sorry, and I said I
18

would do so no more, but told I would fear God. *Q.* But why did not you do so before? *A.* Why, they tell me I had done so before, and therefore I must go on. (These were the four women and the man, but she knew none but Osburn and Good only; the others were of Boston.")

If we get at what Tituba meant by the words just quoted, it was substantially this: "They wanted me, and forced me against my will, to join with them in hurting the children last night. I was sorry that I was forced to act cruelly, and told them that I would not be forced to it again, but would serve God. I did not take that stand before, because they told me I had already worked with them, and therefore must go on.

"*Q.* At first beginning with them, what then appeared to you? What was it like that got you to do it? *A.* One like a man, just as I was going to sleep, came to me. This was when the children was first hurt. He said he would kill the children and she would never be well; and he said if I would not serve him he would do so to me."

The witness was here apparently brought to describe her *first* interview with the author of Salem witchcraft. We see her now standing at the fountain-head of the devastating torrent which soon deluged the region far around with terror, anguish, and blood. Who first appeared to her? Who was the prime mover? And when was he first seen? Subsequent statements are soon to show that on Friday, January 15, 1692, six weeks and four days before the time when she gave in this testimony, *one like a man, just as she was going to sleep*, came to her and demanded her aid in hurting the children. The fact is clearly stated that five days before the Wednesday evening when the children were first hurt by spirit appliances, and supposed to be taken sick, "*one like a man*," when Tituba was about going to sleep, came to her and avowed his purpose, in advance, to torture and even kill the children. From that time forth she knew the source of the strange operations in her master's family.

" *Q.* Is that the same man that appeared before to you, that appeared last night and told you this? *A.* Yes."

Her visitor was the same person on these two different occasions, which were more than six weeks apart, and in her various clairvoyant excursions and feats he was frequently, if not always, her attendant.

" *Q.* What other likenesses besides a man hath appeared unto you? *A.* Sometimes like a hog — sometimes like a great black dog — four times."

" The man " probably assumed or presented those brutish forms. A frequent teaching of spirit visitants is, that they " can assume any *form* which the occasion requires ; " they also have often given the impression that they cannot assume *hues* brighter than inherently pertain to their own intellectual and moral conditions, but of this we have yet no conclusive information.

" *Q.* But what did they say unto you? *A.* They told me serve him, and that was a good way. That was the black dog. I told him I was afraid. He told me he would be worse then to me."

Her dog could talk. She and the court obviously understood the dog to be the same being, essentially, as the " one like a man." For, —

" *Q.* What did you say to him, then, after that? *A.* I answer I will serve you no longer. He told me he would do me hurt then."

Can any one doubt that she conceived herself to be speaking to the same being, though in dog form, that she had yielded to before in form like a man? There is no indication that she had *previously* served a dog, and yet she says to this one, I will serve you *no longer.*

" *Q.* What other creatures have you seen? *A.* A bird. *Q.* What bird? *A.* A little yellow bird. *Q.* Where does it keep? *A.* With the man, who hath pretty things more besides. *Q.* What other pretty things? *A.* He hath not showed them unto me, but he said he would show them to me to-morrow, and told me if I would serve him, I should have the bird. *Q.* What other creatures did you see? *A.* I saw two cats, one red, another black, as big as a little dog. *Q.* What did these cats do? *A.* I don't know. I have seen them two times. *Q.* What did they say? *A.* They say serve them. *Q.* When did you see them? *A.* I saw them last night. *Q.* Did they do any hurt to you or threaten you? *A.* They did scratch me. *Q.* When? *A.* After prayer; and scratched me because I would not serve her. And when they went away *I could not see,* but they stood by the fire. *Q.* What service do they expect from you? *A.* They say more hurt to the children. *Q.* How did you pinch them when you hurt them? *A.* The other pull me and haul me to pinch the child, and I am very sorry for it."

The cats also as well as the dog spoke and commanded her obedience. She saw these the night before her examination. "When they went away," she says, "I could not see." Those words may admit of two distinct and different meanings. First, that the cats disappeared without her being able to notice their exit; or, second, that before they went she became spiritually blind — " could not longer see " clairvoyantly. In a subsequent statement she pleads a sudden obscuration of her internal vision. All clairvoyants are subject to sudden interruptions of their spiritual power to see.

She was pulled and hauled by "the other " with a view to force her to "pinch the child." Here again her obvious conviction was that the "other " was essentially more than mere brute. She did not think a cat pulled and hauled her, but meant that when the cats visited her, the "something like a man "— "the other "— was also present, and urged her on to mischief.

"*Q.* What made you hold your arm when you were searched? What had you there? *A.* I had nothing. *Q.* Do not those cats suck you? *A.* No, never yet. I would not let them. But they had almost thrust me into the fire. *Q.* How do you hurt those that you pinch? Do you get those cats, or other things, to do it for you? Tell us how it is done. *A. The man sends the cats to me, and bids me pinch them;* and I think I went once to Mr. Griggs's, and have pinched her this day in the morning: The man brought Mr. Griggs's maid to me, and made me pinch her."

By "the man " she obviously meant her frequent spirit visitor. He it was who brought the cats to her, and made her pinch them, and by so doing pinch the "maid," who physically was miles distant. Such is her statement. An inference from it is, that properties from Elizabeth Hubbard,—the maid in question, — who was among the afflicted ones, and was a member of *the circle*, were drawn out from her by "the man," and made component parts of apparitional cats formed by the man's thought and will powers, which seeming cats, being pinched by Tituba's spirit fingers, the Hubbard girl, some of whose properties were used for constructing those apparitional cats, felt the pinchings, first in her spirit, and thence in her flesh, though her body was two or three miles distant from the pincher. In that mode "the man" commanded the use of some properties in Tituba, by which he produced torture in a mediumistic physical organism then being far away. Another mode of spirit operation is indicated. Tituba confessed to a dim consciousness that once, by some process, her spirit-self had been got over to Dr. Griggs's, and pinched the maid at her home. Again, she believed that the same maid had been brought to her (Tituba's) abode and pinched there. Also it will be seen a little further on, that, Tituba being charged with having been over at the maid's home on a specified day, denied having been there at that particular time, but admitted that her apparition might, unconsciously to herself, have been seen there then, for she says, "may be send something like me."

We enter a distinct protest against stigmatizing such testimony as "incoherent nonsense." In response to a command to tell *how* the mysterious inflictions were brought about, this untaught, ignorant woman, calmly and with much distinctness, indicated four or five modes by which psychologic forces were brought to bear upon mediumistic subjects. She had seen the processes, and, in her simple way, told what she had learned by personal observation and experience; and thus she helps us, at this day, to fathom and expound the mysteries of witchcraft more effectually than do all her cotemporaries. Notwithstanding her limited command of language, her statements were about as distinct and instructive as any one then could have made upon such a topic; but the devil-warped public mind of that day was unable to see the literal import of her testimony, or to turn her knowledge to good account.

Two other women, Sarah Good and Sarah Osburn, names previously mentioned, were, on the same March 1, 1692, under examination as co-operators with Tituba in practicing witchcraft. "*Q.* Did you ever go with these women? *A.* They are very strong, and pull me, and make me go with them. *Q.* Where did you go? *A.* Up to Mr. Putnam's, and make me hurt the child. *Q.* Who did make you go? *A.* A man that is very strong, and these two women, Good and Osburn; but I am sorry. *Q.* How did you go? What do you ride upon? *A.* I ride upon a stick or pole, and Good and Osburn behind me; we ride taking hold of one another; don't know *how* we go, for I saw no trees nor path, but was presently there when we were up."

The child above referred to was Ann Putnam, daughter, twelve years old, of Thomas and Ann Putnam, who resided from two to three miles north-west from the parsonage. This girl, Ann, was one of the excessively bewitched; that is, was one of the most impressible and mediumistic members of *The Circle.*

Tituba and her two fellow-prisoners had, either all as
spirits, or she as a conscious spirit and the other two
as apparitions, visited that child at her home; and,
according to her own apprehension, the three women
all mounted one pole, rose up into the air, and were
forthwith at Mr. Putnam's, having noticed neither
path nor trees on the way. No reader will apprehend
that Tituba's physical body then left the house of Mr.
Parris and went off two miles or more, on a winter's
night, to Mr. (Thomas) Putnam's house. She says
that they were "presently [instantly] there." It was
only her spirit form — *thought* form — that went riding
upon a pole above all woods and paths. But why to
Thomas Putnam's? Probably because his wife and
his daughter, as subsequent events showed, were both
intensely mediumistic or susceptible to influence by
thought beings; they were persons upon whom such
beings could work efficiently; and that was the special
reason, probably, for a visit to them. "The man"
may well be presumed to have possessed perceptive
powers that could determine with much accuracy
what persons in all the region round about possessed
the constitutional properties and the surroundings
which would permit them to become pliable and serviceable implements in executing any scheme he had
devised. Subsequent events proved that he selected
and used such as enabled him, through intense human
agony and bloodshed, to break in pieces and abolish a
most cramping and enslaving creed devil-ward, which,
like a horrid and disabling nightmare, had for centuries been depressing and agonizing all Christendom.
Whatever was his design, his selection of instrumentalities facilitated the out-working of a broad and hap-

py emancipation from vast mental evil. It abolished
prosecutions for witchcraft throughout both America
and Europe.

The ostensible object of that mental journey was to
hurt the child. Such was the man's apparent intention. That man was "very strong," and he accomplished his purpose. Ann was hurt. His will-power
was such, that, having once got hold of the elements
of three susceptible and ignorant women, they were
completely under his control. Tituba, who seems to
have been always a *conscious* medium, yielded perforce
to him. Her own selfhood fought against his cruelties, and she felt sorry for what she was forced to do.
When under examination she made free confession of
her involuntary participation in the tormenting inva-
sions upon innocent girls, thus unwittingly jeopardiz-
ing her own life. She seems to have been frank and
truthful.

" *Q.* How long since you began to pinch Mr. Parris's
children? *A.* I did not pinch them at first, but they
made me afterward. *Q.* Have you seen Good and
Osburn ride upon a pole? *A.* Yes; and have held
fast by me; I was not at Mr. Griggs's but once; but
it may be send something like me; neither would I
have gone, but they tell me they will hurt me."

Her statement that " it may be send something like
me," shows her belief, and probably her knowledge,
that her " very strong " " something like a man " was
able to produce the apparition of a mediumistic person even where such person had no consciousness of
being present. Spirits, in modern times, often produce such effects, and show thereby that Tituba's
comprehension of the case may have been in harmony

with the nature of things, and strictly correct. She repeats again that her participation in the affairs was forced — that others made her pinch.

" *Tituba*. Last night they tell me I must kill somebody with a knife. *Q.* Who were they that told you so? *A.* Sarah Good and Osburn, and they would have had me kill Thomas Putnam's child last night. (The child also affirmed that at the same time they would have had her cut off her own head; for if she would not, they told her Tituba would cut it off. And then she complained at the same time of a knife cutting her. When her master hath asked her (Tituba?) about these things, she saith they will not let her tell, but tell her if she tells, her head shall be cut off.) *Q.* Who tells you so? *A.* The man, Good, and Osburn's wife. (Goody Good came to her last night when her master was at prayer, and would not let her hear, and she could not hear a good while.) Good hath one of those birds, the yellow-bird, and would have given me it, but I would not have it. And in prayer-time she stopped my ears, and would not let me hear. *Q.* What should you have done with it? *A.* Give it to the children, which yellow-bird hath been several times seen by the children. I saw Sarah Good have it on her hand when she came to her when Mr. Parris was at prayer. I saw the bird suck Good between the fore-finger and long-finger upon the right hand."

Those statements relating to the use of the knife, apparently *volunteered* by Tituba and confirmed by the child, are quite suggestive. Assuming that there was present with them some powerful male spirit bent upon forceful action, and who, through Tituba and other impressibles, had obtained some palpable hold upon certain human forms and the affairs of external life, it was in his power to excite in the minds of any and all who had then been brought into rapport with himself, such ideas as those relating to the knife, and also to make the psychologized girl experience the sensation of being actually cut by it. Such would now be deemed an easy feat by any fair psychologist, either in the gross form or out of it, provided he had a favorable subject on whom to operate.

The same spirit, too, drawing elements from Mrs. Good, and using them, could make Tituba feel as though Mrs. Good was by her side and making her suddenly deaf in prayer-time, even though it was the male spirit himself who then closed her ears.

Evidences of mediumistic capabilities in either the afflicted or the afflicters are worthy of distinct observation, and therefore we draw attention to the statement that the yellow-bird " hath been several times seen *by the children.*" Therefore the sufferers were clairvoyants, as well as the accused.

" *Q.* Did you never practice witchcraft in your own country ? *A.* No ; never before now."

That answer renders it probable that previous to the winter then passing she had never been conscious of the presence of spirits, or of conversations with or subjection to them. She, perhaps, reveals a lurking suspicion that her experiences of late might be witchcrafts. But her notions as to what constituted that might well, if not necessarily, be very different from those existing in the more unfolded and logical minds of her master and her examiners, who made the chief essence of it consist in a compact made with a Majes

tic and Malignant Devil — such a devil as would differ
very widely in appearance from Tituba's "*man*." She
freely described the unsought presence of a spirit-man
with her on sundry occasions; also her talks with him,
and forced service under him. This essentially was
only disclosure of the fact that her own organism and
temperaments were such and so conditioned that disembodied intelligences could sometimes be seen and
heard by her, and could force her to be their tool.
Her witchcraft was devoid of voluntary compact to
serve an evil one ; devoid of evil intent in its practice. If she confessed herself to be a witch, it was
only a kindly and loving one, desiring to be truthful
and good, and inflicting hurt only when forced to it.
She confessed only to clairvoyance, clairaudience, and
weakness of her own will-powers.

" *Q.* Did you see them do it now while you are examining (being examined) ? *A.* No, I did not see
them. But I saw them hurt at other times. I saw
Good have a cat beside the yellow-bird which was
with her."

Obviously some contortions, antics, or sufferings
which the afflicted girls, who were present at the examination, had just experienced or were then manifesting, led to the question, " Did you see them do it
now ? " Here again appears the assumption of the
court that Tituba might be gifted with powers or faculties which would enable her to discern animate and
designing workers who were invisible by external optics. Her inner sight was closed then, but at some
other times had been open.

" *Q.* What hath Osburn got to go·with her? *A.* A
thing; I don't know what it is. I can't name it. I

don't know how it looks. She hath two of them. One of them hath wings, and two legs, and a head like a woman. The children saw the same but yesterday, which afterward turned into a woman. *Q.* What is the other thing that Goody Osburn hath? *A.* A thing all over hairy; all the face hairy, and a long nose, and I don't know how to tell how the face looks; with two legs; it goeth upright, and is about two or three foot high, and goeth upright like a man; and last night it stood before the fire, in Mr. Parris's hall."

The obscurity of this description is fully paralleled by the prophet Ezekiel, who, in presenting the beings seen in the first of his " visions of God," uses the following language, in chap. i. : " They had the likeness of a man, and every one had four faces, and every one had four wings; and their feet were straight feet; and the sole of their feet was like the sole of a calf's foot; and they sparkled like the color of burnished brass. And they had the hands of a man under their wings on their four sides; and they four had their faces and their wings; and their wings were joined one to another; and they turned not when they went; they went every one straight forward; as for the likeness of their faces, they four had the face of a man, and the face of a lion, on the right side; and they four had the face of an ox on the left side; they four also had the face of an eagle." This quotation from the Bible hints with much distinctness that inherent difficulties may beset any clairvoyant who undertakes to set forth in our language, which was formed for description of material objects, some things which are occasionally perceived by the spiritual senses. Where the prophet was so vague and mystical we may pardon the ignorant slave if she failed to be very lucid, and if one suspects her of attempting to put forth nothing but fiction, because she was so obscure, how can he consistently withhold similar suspicions in relation to the prophet?

We will pass to the children's credit the fact that they also saw Osburn's ungainly and hairy attendant.

" *Q.* Who was that appeared to Hubbard as she was going from Proctor's? *A.* It was Sarah Good, and I saw her send the wolf to her."

Facts are transpiring in the present age which indicate with much distinctness that a spirit can present the semblance of a spirit-beast or other spirit-object to the vision of many clairvoyants at the same time, and also that he can, if he so elect, psychologize simultaneously all clairvoyants with whom he is in rapport, and cause them all to believe that they see any beast or object which his mind merely conceives of with distinctness. Therefore sight of a wolf by the mediumistic Hubbard girl, and Tituba's perception of the same proceeding from mediumistic Sarah Good, could all be produced by the mere volition of that " something like a man," provided only that he was then in rapport with all of those three sensitive ones.

" *Q.* What clothes doth the man appear unto you in? *A.* Black clothes sometimes; sometimes serge coat of other color; a tall man with white hair, I think. *Q.* What apparel do the women wear? *A.* I don't know what color. *Q.* What kind of clothes hath she? *A.* Black silk hood with white silk hood under it, with top-knots; which woman I know not, but have seen her in Boston when I lived there. *Q.* What clothes the little woman ? *A.* Serge coat, with a white cap, as I think. (The children having fits at this very time, she was asked who hurt them. She answers, Goody Good ; and the children affirmed the same. But Hubbard being taken in an extreme fit, after [ward] she (Tituba) was asked who hurt her (Hubbard), and she said she could not tell, but said they blinded her and would not let her see ; and after that was once or twice taken dumb herself.")

That account of the clothes described the usual costumes of the time. We are glad to hear her say, "A tall man, with white hair, I think." That is her description of the "something like a man," and "the man" who has been so demonstrative. A tall man with white hair, need not be a very frightful object, and we can readily conceive that such a mind as Tituba's might be perfectly calm and self-possessed in his presence, and never imagine that abler minds might confound such a one with the devil. She never calls him the devil. The fact that she was made dumb two or three times, gives her case some resemblance to those of Ezekiel and Zacharias. Her ears, as before stated, had been stopped by Good, as she supposed, one evening during prayer-time. Thus we find her organs of sense subject to just such control as invisible intelligent operators exercised over prophetic or mediumistic ones of old, and such as spirits exercise over many mortal forms to-day. Her clairvoyance was obscured, perhaps, by "the man" when she was asked who was hurting the Hubbard girl, and replied that they blinded her now.

Second Examination, March 2, 1692.

" *Q.* What covenant did you make with that man that came to you ? What did he tell you ? "

The first of those two questions was the crucial one at a trial for witchcraft. Had she made a *covenant* with the devil, or any devotee of his ? That was the main point to be determined. If she had, she was a witch, according to the prevalent creed ; if she had not, she might be innocent of witchcraft. But seemingly the court could not wait for an answer, because, in the same breath, it asked, What did your visitant tell you ?

" *A.* He tell me he God, and I must believe him and serve him six years, and he would give me many fine things. *Q.* How long ago was this ? *A.* About six weeks and a little more ; Friday night before Abigail was ill."

That last answer is very instructive. It fixes the exact time when one of the children in Mr. Parris's family was first attacked. For this second day's examination was held on Wednesday, March 2. It will appear from the above and future answers that the specters first attacked the children on a Wednesday evening, just six weeks before this 2d of March. The man appeared to and talked with Tituba on the Friday evening before that Wednesday in January.

The testimony, therefore, takes us back to January 20th as the commencement of overt manifestation of spirit infliction of sufferings there. Five days further back, i. e., the evening of January 15, is apparently the date of " the man's " first recognized appearance.

Therefore, until better information is obtained, we shall regard that as the date of the primal advent of the genuine author of witchcraft at Salem Village, whom we deem to have been also its regulator through its heart-rending unfoldings.

" *Q.* What did he say you must do more ? Did he say you must write anything ? Did he offer you any paper? *A.* Yes, the next time he come to me ; and showed me some fine things, something like creatures, a little bird something like green and white. *Q.* Did you promise him this when he first spake to you ? Then what did you answer him? *A.* I then said this : I told him I could not believe him God. I told him I ask my master, and would have gone up, but he stopt me and would not let me. *Q.* What did you promise him? *A.* The first time I believe him God, and then he was glad. *Q.* What did he say to you then? What did he say you must do? *A.* Then he tell me they must meet together."

There is some obscurity in this quotation, which raises the question whether the witness contradicts herself by stating that at her first interview she believed that her visitant was God himself (as John the Revelator did that a prophet returning from the spirit spheres and appearing to him was God), and her stating again that at the first interview she told him she could not believe that he was God, and proposed to go up and ask her master, Mr. Parris, what he thought about it, but was held back by her spirit-attendants from doing so. There is, we say, obscurity as to whether the account makes her apply both of these opposing statements to her conceptions of her visitor at the first interview with him, or whether it

19

was not till a subsequent meeting that she doubted
his Godship. As reported, her examiners are made
quite as hard to understand and track as she is in
her answers. But, upon a careful reading, we judge
it fair and proper to conclude that her doubts concerning the character of her acquaintance were expressed as late as at the meeting on Wednesday, January 20, and not on the previous Friday.

" *Q.* When did he say you must meet together?
A. He tell me Wednesday next, at my master's
house; and then we all [did] meet together, and
that night I saw them all stand in the corner —
all four of them — and the man stand behind me,
and take hold of me, and make me stand still in the
hall."   .

. We now must relinquish doubt as to the meetings
at the parsonage, for here we have distinct historical
mention of *a circle*, which met "at Mr. Parris's
house" for the purpose of practically manifesting
the skill and powers, not of learners, but of an expert in the wonders of "necromancy, magic, and
especially of *Spiritualism*." This circle met, at five
days' notice, on the evening of January 20, 1692. A
man, or "something like a man," was at the head
of it, and five females, three of them at least embodied ones, were his assistants, or rather were reservoirs from whence he drew forces with which to
experiment upon two little mediumistic girls. If
a club of women and girls sometimes met for such
purposes as are alleged in foregoing citations, — and
perhaps it did in a loose, irregular way, — we fancy
that Tituba's tutor was ever among them taking
notes, scrutinizing their several properties, capabili-

ties, and circumstances, and planning when and how
to use them for most efficient accomplishment of his
purposes. The fact that he was present as author
and master spirit when the first act of the Salem
Village tragedy was visibly manifested through the
twitchings and contortions of two little girls, is distinctly shown by Tituba's testimony. Therefore
henceforth there can be neither historical nor philanthropic justice in imputing to the brains and wills
of the little girls what a present and conscious clairvoyant witness imputes distinctly to one who looked
"something like a man." Give to him — whoever
he was — give to him his just dues; also bestow
upon the girls neither censure nor praise for the help
which their organisms and temperaments necessarily
afforded him. This meeting of apparitions, be it
noted and remembered, took place immediately *before* the sickness of the children came on, and during its session, the children were pinched, and thus
first became "afflicted ones." On that Wednesday
night "Abigail first became ill."

"*Q.* Where was your master then? *A.* In *the
other room. Q.* What time of night? *A.* A little
before prayer-time. *Q.* What did this man say to
you when he took hold of you? *A.* He say, Go into
the other room and see the children, and do hurt to
them and pinch them. And then I went in and
would not hurt them a good while; I would not
hurt Betty; I loved Betty; but they haul me, and
make me pinch Betty, and the next Abigail; and
then quickly went away altogether a[fter] I had
pinch them. *Q.* Did you go into that room in your
own person, and all the rest? *A.* Yes; and my

master did not see us, for they would not let my master see."

Mr. Parris and the children seem from the above to have been in the same apartment that evening, for Tituba states that he was "in the other room," and her dictator said to her, "Go into the other room," and hurt the children. That the master of the house was present with his daughter and niece then, may be indicated also in the statement that "they would not let my master see;" for this implies that they were in his presence, though invisible. If she went to the room in her physical form — which is not stated, and is not probable — though she did go there in her "own *person*," the others went only as spirits or as apparitions; and they did not so enrobe or materialize themselves as to be visible by outward eyes, and therefore did not become visible to Mr. Parris — they "would not let" him see. The first infliction upon the children, therefore, was made in his very presence, but by invisible hands — spirit hands or apparitional hands — touching the spirit forms of the mediumistic little girls, and through their own inner forms reaching, paining, and convulsing their physical bodies. It is interesting to note that because Tituba "loved Betty," she was able to resist the pressure upon her "a good while;" but her feeble powers were incompetent to oppose unyielding and effectual resistance to the strong will of the producer of painful experiences.

"*Q.* Did you go with the company? *A.* No. I staid, and the man staid with me. *Q.* What did he then to you? *A:* He tell me my master go to prayer, and he read in book, and he ask me what I remember: but don't you remember anything."

This account fails to furnish any very conclusive evidence that either of the four other women was on that occasion consciously present with Tituba and the man; it need only indicate the probability that he drew properties from each of them, wherever located, whether in the Village, in Boston, or elsewhere, which enabled him to present their apparitions to Tituba as helpers, and to effect rapport with and get power over the children. When his immediate purpose had been accomplished, no one but the man could be seen by her. He perhaps left the female apparitions to dissolve when his further need of their properties ceased. There is no evidence that Good and Osburn were conscious of being present where Tituba saw them, and therefore the other two female forms may have been purely apparitional — mental fabrics of "the man." But important points are clear. The man's controlling will, and subjugated Tituba's conscious self, were there.

"Q. Did he ask you no more but the first time to serve him? Or the second time? A. Yes, he ask me again if I serve him six years; and he come the next time and show me a book. Q. And when would he come then? A. The next Friday, and showed me a book in the daytime, betimes in the morning. Q. And what book did he bring, a great or little book? A. He did not show it me, nor would not, but had it in his pocket. Q. Did he not make you write your name? A. No, not yet, for my mistress called me into the other room. Q. What did he say you must do in that book? A. He said write and put my name to it. Q. Did you write? A. Yes, once, I made a mark in the book, and made it

with red like blood. Q. Did he get it out of your
body? A. He said he must get it out. The next
time he come again, he gave me a pin tied in a stick
to do it with ; but he no let me blood with·it as yet,
but intended another.time when he came again. Q. Did
you see any other marks in his book ? A. Yes, a great
many ; some marks red, some yellow ; he opened his
book, and a great many marks in it. Q. Did he tell
you the names of them ? A. Yes, of two ; no more:
Good and Osburn ; and he say they made them marks
in that book, and he showed them me. Q. How many
marks do you think there was? A. Nine. Q. Did
they write their names? A. They made marks.
Goody Good said she made her mark, but Goody Osburn would not tell. She was cross to me. Q. When
did Good tell you she set her hand to the book? A. The
same day I came hither to prison. Q. Did you see the
man that morning ? A. Yes, a little in the morning,
and he tell me the magistrates come up to examine
me. Q. What did he say you must say? A. He tell
me tell nothing ; if I did, he would cut my head off."

The questions relating to the book and signatures
were based on, and made important by, then prevalent belief that one's signature in the devil's book
proved the signing of a covenant to be henceforth his
servant. Tituba's statement that she had seen therein Sarah Good's signature in her own blood, well might
be then deemed strong evidence that Mrs. Good was
a witch, and was guilty of witchcraft. But we doubt
whether the witness had any conception of the fatal
import of her statement. Her testimony that Goody
Osburn was cross to her, while amusing, is also suggestive of the deep question whether even an apparition,

produced by use of unconscious elements drawn from
a human system, could or would be so permeated with
the existing mentàl and emotional moods of the person from whom they were drawn as to cause those
moods to be perceived and felt by those who might
see, and receive influences from, the apparition. " The
man " told her that the magistrates had come or were
coming to examine her. She might have known this
already, and might not. Be that as it may, on the
morning of her examination A SPIRIT spoke to her.
His counsel was, that she should say nothing. This
advice seems wise. But it was not very " cunning "
in her to repeat it, and make known its source " in
presence of Authority." Willing or not she was there
constrained to speak out. Robert Calef, in " More
Wonders of the Invisible World," reports her as saying, " that her master did beat her and otherwise
abuse her to make her confess and accuse (such as he
called) her sister witches, and that whatsoever she
said by way of confessing, or accusing others, was the
effect of such usage."

" Q. Tell us true ; how many women do you use to
come when you ride abroad ? A. Four of them ; these
two, Osburn and Good, and those two strangers.
Q. You say there was nine. Did he tell you who
they were ? A. No, he no let me see, but he tell me
I should see them the next time. Q. What sights did
you see ? A. I see a man, a dog, a hog, and two cats,
a black and red, and the strange monster was Osburn's that I mentioned before ; this was the hairy
imp. The man would give it to me, but I would not
have it. Q. Did he show you in the book which was
Osburn's and which was Good's mark ? A. Yes, I see

their marks. *Q.* But did he tell you the names of the other? *A.* No, sir. *Q.* And what did he say to you when you made your mark? *A.* He said, Serve me; and always serve me. The man with the two women came from Boston. *Q.* How many times did you go to Boston? *A.* I was going and then came back again. I never was at Boston. *Q.* Who came back with you again? *A.* The man came back with me, and the women go away; I was not willing to go. *Q.* How far did you go — to what town? *A.* I never went to any town. I see no trees, no town. *Q.* Did he tell you where the nine lived? *A.* Yes; some in Boston and some here in this town, but he would not tell me who they were."

We have now presented the full text of Tituba's testimony as recorded by Corwin and printed by Drake. Severed from the leading and jumbled questions which drew it forth, and reduced to a simple narrative, her statement would in substance be nearly as follows: —

Something like a man came to me just as I was going to sleep the Friday night before Abigail was taken ill, six weeks and a little more ago, who then told me that he was God, that I must believe him, and that if I would serve him six years he would give me many fine things. He said there must be a meeting at my master's house the next Wednesday, and on the evening of that day he and four women came there. Then I told him I could not believe that he was God, and proposed to go and ask Mr. Parris what he thought on that point; but the man held me back. They forced me against my will and my love for Betty to pinch the children; we did pinch them. That was

the first night that Abigail was sick. Sometimes I
saw the appearances of dogs, cats, birds, hogs, wolves,
and a nondescript animal, some of whom spoke to me,
and talked like the man. Yesterday, when I was in
the lean-to chamber, I saw a thing like a man, — the
same that I had seen before, — who asked me to serve
him ; and last night, when I was washing the room,
the man and the four women all came again, and
wanted me to hurt the children ; and we all went up
to Mr. Thomas Putnam's, and hurt Ann, and cut her
with a knife. I went to the Hubbard girl once, and
pinched her, and once the man brought her over to
me, and I pinched her ; but I was not there when
they say I was, though it may be that the man sent
my apparition over there then without my knowing it.
I once saw what looked like a wolf go out from Mrs.
Good and run to the Hubbard girl. How we travel I
don't know ; we go up in the air, and we are instantly
at the place we intend to go to ; we see no trees, no
roads. The man brings cats or other things to me, and
I pinch them ; and by doing so the girls are pinched.
Sometimes I can see these things for a while, and then
instantly become blind to them. This morning the
man came and told me the magistrates had come to
examine me.

Such are the principal points in Tituba's account of
the origin and author of the disturbance or "amazing
feats" at Mr. Parris's house. In the main, they are
plain, direct, and seemingly true. They teach as
clearly as words ever taught anything, that "something like a man" — "a tall man with white hair,"
dressed in "serge coat" — came and forced Tituba to
pinch the children at the very time when one of them

was first taken sick. They teach also that the same man appeared to Tituba several times, and was with her on the day of her examination. The spiritual source of the first physical manifestations which generated the great troubles at Salem Village is thus set forth with such clearness as will command credence in future ages, even if it shall fail to do so in this Sadducean generation.

As before stated, another record of Tituba's testimony was made by Ezekiel Cheever, which is much less ample and particular than the one above presented. It omits entirely several very instructive and important parts — especially those which make known Tituba's earlier interviews with "the man;" those which fix the exact time when he first came to her; the exact time when Abigail was taken ill; and, more important still, those parts which describe the assemblage of spirits at Mr. Parris's house, and their deliberate inflictions of pains upon the children at the very time when their disordered conditions came upon them.

Upham, by using Cheever's instead of the other account, failed to adduce several vastly important historic facts; the special facts which are essential to a fair presentation of the origin and nature of *Salem* witchcraft. He nowhere recognizes the probably acute intellect, strong powers, persistent action, and inspiring presence of the *tall man with white hair and in serge coat.* Omitting these, he has but given us Hamlet with Hamlet left out. And this, too, not in ignorance, for he had seen Corwin's manuscript, which made clearly manifest the presence and doings of one spirit-personage especially, and taught many other facts that were not reconcilable with his theory.

The tall man with white hair who visited Tituba on the evening of January 15, 1692, has such obvious and important connection with, and influence over, all the ostensible actors in the scenes which former witch-craft historians have depicted, as may revolutionize their theories, and teach the world that those expound-ers never traced their subject down to its genuine base; that they built, partly at least, upon the sands of either ignorance or misconception of the nature and actual source of what they discussed.

There are some important differences in the two records of Tituba's testimony, even where the words and facts must have been the same. The following parallel passages present quite differing reports of what she said concerning her own knowledge of the devil:—

Cheever.	*Corwin.*
"Why do you hurt these children?" "I do not hurt them." "Who is it then?" "The devil, for aught I know." "Did you ever see the devil?" "The devil come to me, and bid me serve him."	"Why do you hurt these poor children? what harm have they done unto you?" "They do no harm to me. I no hurt them at all." "Why have you done it?" "I have done nothing. I can't tell when the devil works." "What! Doth the devil tell you that he hurts them?" "No, he tells me nothing."

Thus Cheever makes her say that "*the devil*" came to her and bade her serve him, while Corwin, reporting the same part of the examination, makes her say that "*the devil*" never told her anything. Further on, Corwin makes her say, "A thing like a man told me serve him." Cheever says the *devil* told her thus. Tituba herself, and all the clairvoyants of that age, preserved a distinction between the devil and the personages they saw, heard, and talked with. But the recorders of their testimony, failing to observe this distinction, often perverted the evidence. A comparison of the two records throughout suggests the probability that Corwin, who is most minute, gives the questions and answers in their original order and sequences much more nearly than does Cheever, whose record, when compared with the other, appears in some parts to be summings-up of several minutes' talks into a brief sentence or two, and also gives evidence of his taking it as obvious fact, that Tituba's "thing like a man" was the veritable devil. This is probable, because his minutes make her say "*the devil* come to me, and bid me serve him," at a point in the examination where, according to Corwin, she said *the devil* "tells me nothing." Thus the appearance is, that Cheever carried back in time words which *she* subsequently applied to her "thing like a man," and on his own authority— not hers—applied them to "the devil." In Corwin's account, her conception of the separate individualities of "the devil" and her "thing like a man" reveals itself clearly, and is nowhere contravened. But Cheever, almost at the commencement of his record, and at a point where she, according to Corwin, said the devil told her *nothing*, reports her as then applying to *the devil* what she a few minutes or hours afterward applied to her "thing like a man." According to the more full and the more trustworthy record, she at no time confessed to any interview with " *The Devil*," though she did freely to many conversations with " the man." These facts are important, very interesting, and instructive. As we interpret them now, they indicate that Tituba never confessed to any intercommunings with the devil, never charged Mrs. Good, Mrs. Osburn, or any one else with being familiar with his Sable Majesty, but only with " a tall man, with white hair," wearing a " serge coat."

The court before whom she was questioned, and the people around, generally, no doubt, deemed her " thing like a man " to be the veritable devil, as Cheever did. But the more exact recorder of her words furnishes good grounds for belief that Tituba herself conceived otherwise. She who was gifted with faculties which let her see, hear, and feel the actors, apprehended that one of them at least was a disembodied human spirit; while the spiritually blind, but physically and logically keen-eyed ones around her, wrongfully inferred the presence of their Malignant and Mighty Devil with her.

Some dates fixed by this witness in Corwin's account, and entirely omitted in Cheever's, are interesting and somewhat important. We learn what, so far as we know, escaped the notice of all former searchers, that it was on Friday, January 15, just as she was going to sleep, that " one like a man " came to her and appointed a meeting there at Mr. Parris's house, to take place on the next Wednesday evening. Accordingly, on Wednesday evening, January 20, "the man " and four women came, and then designedly and deliberately pushed Tituba on, and made her pinch the daughter and niece of Mr. Par-

ris ; and *on that very evening*, Abigail, at least, if not
Betty also, *"was first taken ill."* Here is an important and significant coincidence. Just at the
time when the illness was developed, spirits, in compliance with a previous arrangement, were there present at work seeking to produce just such a result as
was manifested.   Did they, or did other agencies,
produce the mysterious disorders which seemed to
devil-dreading beholders like diabolical obsessions ?
In view of all the facts, it is plain that a spirit or
spirits caused the children to suffer.

By failing to present the above points, which,
though lacking in the account that he copied and
followed, yet came under his eye, Upham clearly
failed to use some very important historic facts which
are essential to a fair presentation of both the time
at which, and the agents through whom, Salem witchcraft had its origin, and consequently to a fair presentation of its nature.   But those facts strenuously
conflict with his theory that embodied girls and
women were the designers and perpetrators of that
great and terrific manifestation of destructive forces.
How strong the chains of a pet theory ! How blinding the cataracts of long-cherished conclusions !

If there exists in the world's annals more distinct
testimony that a particular individual was the deliberate and intentional producer of acts which generated suffering, than Tituba gave that the " thing
like a man," which came to her once " when she was
about going to sleep," once " in the lean-to chamber,"
once " when she was washing the room," and who,
on Friday night, appointed a place for meeting the
next Wednesday night, and, with assistants, kept

his appointment, and then and there, as he had previously announced his purpose to do, severely "hurt
the children " — if there ever was recorded testimony
which more distinctly designated a particular being as
the principal in planning and enacting any scheme
than is this from Tituba, by which she designates
over and over again "a tall man with white hair,"
wearing "black clothes sometimes, and sometimes
serge coat of other color," as the chief executor of
the strange and momentous development of illnesses
in the family of Mr. Parris, I know not where
that clearer testimony is recorded. He who ignored
several very significant parts of what Tituba said,
rejected corner-stones which are essential to the foundation of a genuinely philosophical disclosure of the
source and consequent nature of the mysteries he
attempted to explain. Tituba has been described by
Upham as "indicating, in most respects, a mind at
the lowest level of general intelligence," so that any
one must be more rash than prudent who will impute
to her ability to fabricate a series of facts, all of
which seem to be natural and probable in the province
of psychology.

Mr. Parris informs us that the strange sicknesses
existed in his family during several weeks before he
or others had any suspicion that they might be of
diabolical origin. Tituba dates their commencement
on the evening of January 20, just six weeks before
her examination. Therefore Mr. Parris's "several
weeks " may have been five at least, during which
he and his wife and their physician and friends probably studied symptoms, administered and watched
the action of medicines, and cared for the children

in every way, with as much freedom from delusion
or bewildering excitement, as they could have done
in any other equal portion of their lives. Such
medical skill as then existed there, obviously had
and used a very considerable period of time, not
less than four or five weeks, in which to do its
best, and yet was baffled. Its best was unavailing.
We to-day perceive sufficient cause of its failure. It
was contending against a special spirit infliction, the
authors of which could either counteract, intensify,
or nullify at their pleasure, the normal action of any
common medicines or nursings. Parents, physician,
and nurses no doubt witnessed from day to day
such anomalous and changeful manifestations, sequent upon the administration of " physic," as confounded their judgments, and made them at last
suspect " an evil hand." Tituba knew the cause
of the illnesses, but probably lacked power to see
and appreciate the continuous connection of that
cause with the long series of its effects. Had she
divulged her knowledge, what heed would have been
given to the word of the ignorant slave? What
beatings might she not well fear if she confessed to
any dealings with invisible beings? No wonder that
she kept her knowledge to herself, till fear of her
master's cane influenced her to disclose the facts to
the magistrates.

Small as Tituba's mental capacities were, she had
some unusual susceptibilities, which permitted, or
rather obliged, her to possess more knowledge of the
origin and progress, and also of the nature and of
the active producer, of the distressing ailments and
" amazing feats " in her master's family, than did

master, mistress, physician, and magistrates combined. They saw — if it can be said that they saw
at all — they saw only through thick, coarse, and
blurred glasses, very dimly; while she, at times,
clearly saw living actors face to face. From her we
get the testimony of a witness who learned directly
through her own senses what she stated ; her testimony gives forth the ring of unflawed truth, and
lifts a vail off from long-hidden mysteries.

Hutchinson, Upham, and Drake each sought to
make it apparent that mundane roguishness, trickery,
and malice, operating amid public credulity and
infatuation, prompted and enabled frail girls and
women to produce the "amazing feats," marvelous
convulsions, and all the many other woeful outworkings of witchcraft. Having been either unobservant
of, or having ignored, the plain historic fact seen
over and over again in Tituba's testimony, that
certain other intelligences than girls, that minds
which were freed more or less fully and permanently
from the hamperings of flesh, actually started the
first display of witchcraft pinchings, fits, and convulsions at Salem Village, those historians wrongfully charged girls and women, whose bodies were
then the subjects and tools of other intelligences,
with being the feigners of maladies and the producers
of acts which an eye-witness and reluctant participator distinctly declares were manifested in obedience to a will or wills not their own. Such
oversight, or such discarding of facts, whichever it
may have been, caused those writers to so restrict
their stores of intelligent agents having more or
less access to and power over man, as to put outside

20

of their own reach and vision the actual producers
of witchcraft phenomena. This self-imposed or self-
retained restriction forced upon them necessity for
efforts to show that mere children possessed gigantic
physical and mental powers and brains which concocted and executed schemes that shook to their very
foundations the strong fabrics of church and state —
yes, forced them to ascribe mighty public agitations
to insignificant operators.

Tituba, on the other hand, by a simple statement
of what her own interior self saw, heard, felt, and
did, — by a statement of what she actually *knew*, —
designated the genuine and the obviously competent
authors of witchcraft marvels, and explained their
advent rationally. She, therefore, by far — very far
— outranks each and all of those historians as a competent and authoritative expounder of the authorship, origin, and nature of Salem Witchcraft. Her
" something like a man " — her *tall white-haired man
in serge coat* — was its author. That man was a spirit,
and his works were Spiritualism of some quality.
Opposition revealed his possession of mighty force.
And, whatever his motive, the result of his scheme
was the death of witchcraft throughout Christendom, and consequent wide emancipation from mental
slavery.

Some statements made and published by Robert
Calef not long subsequent to 1692, wear on their
surface the semblance of impeachments, or at least
of questionings of the value of Tituba's testimony.
He says, " The first complained of was the said
Indian woman named Tituba ; she confessed *the devil*
urged her to sign a book, which he presented to her,

and also to work mischief to the children," &c. We fail to find in Corwin's report anything like a *confession* of any such things; she there states distinctly that *The Devil tells her nothing*, and also that the book was offered to her, and that the urgings to hurt the children were made to her by "something like a man " — by " *the man.*" She had no idea that the devil was her visitant, and never confessed that he tempted her.

Calef goes on and says, " She was afterward committed to prison, and lay there till sold for her fees. The account she since gives of it is, that her master did beat her and otherwise abuse her to make her confess and accuse (such as he called) her sister witches; and that whatsoever she said by way of confessing, or accusing others, was the effect of such usage." This is credible, and is probably true. Such proceedings on the part of Mr. Parris are not inconsistent with the character which he bears. Tituba's other master, the white-haired man, had charged her " to say nothing; " she perhaps, therefore, was in fact induced to utter " whatsoever she said by way of confessing or accusing others," by beatings she received from her visible master. But what did she say by way of confessing or accusing? Nothing, really. She merely stated facts known to her; and such statement should not be misnamed either confession or accusation.

Corwin's record of that slave's testimony excites an apprehension — yes, generates belief — that Calef unconsciously made misleading statement when he wrote that " she *confessed* the *devil* urged her to sign a book." We have met with no indication that she ever made what should be called *confession*. We repeat, that she quite fully narrated that she had seen, held conversation with, and been forced to obey, a white-haired *man*, and also that the women Good and Osburn were at times her companion operators when the man was present. That frank statement of facts constituted her only confession, so far as we perceive. Had this been made by an intelligent witness who comprehended how the public mind would interpret it, there might be plausible reason for saying that she or he "*confessed*." But with Tituba it was a simple statement of the truth.

We suspect that Calef, under the prevalent habit of his day, unwittingly wrote *devil* where Tituba, according to Corwin, said "the man." If he followed Cheever's report of the trial, he seemed to have authority for doing so. That Tituba regarded the devil and "the tall man" as two distinct individuals is very obvious. When questioned, she admitted that the devil *might* hurt the children for aught she knew, but she had never seen *him*, nor had *he* ever told her anything. She had no acquaintance with that personage. While the questions related to *his* doings she could give no information; but as soon as opportunity was given her to introduce her "tall man" she was ready to speak of him freely and instructively. The people around her, not interiorly illumined, applied the name *devil* to any disembodied intelligence that acted upon, cr whose power became manifest to, their external senses; not so did either Tituba or any of her clairvoyant sister sufferers or sister *accusers* either. Throughout the whole of her two days' rigid examination she persistently called her strange visitant "the man."

And it is a significant fact that all the mediumistic ones then, both accusers and accused, escaped ever falling into the prevalent habit of accusing THE DEVIL. Other agents met their vision.

Fear of Mr. Parris may have forced Tituba to tell her true tale, which but for him she might have withheld. But is there probability either that he dictated any part of her testimony, or that she fabricated anything? We see none. The fair and just presumption is, that though forced to speak, she simply described what she had seen, and narrated what she had experienced. The apparent promptness, directness, and general consistency of her answers, strongly favor that presumption. In her judgment, as in ours, what she said was no confession of familiarity with the devil, for she disclaimed any knowledge of him ; and therefore she made no confession of witchcraft as then defined, and no accusation of it against the other women.

Calef imputes to her a subsequent position which may be so construed as to indicate that she declined to stand by her previous statements. He says, " her master refused to pay her " jail " fees," and thus liberate her from prison, " unless she would stand to what she had said." In that quotation is involved all that we find in the older records which wears even a semblance of impeaching her testimony, or suggests any reason why we should distrust its intentional accuracy in any particular. The master did not pay the fees. She " lay in jail thirteen months, and was then sold to pay her prison charges." (Drake. Annals, 190.) But what did her master require her to " stand to "? Calef says he beat her " to make her confess, and accuse [such as he called] her sister witches ; and that whatsoever she did by way of *confessing* or *accusing* others, was the effect of such usage." What she may have confessed to having done, or what she may have accused others of doing, at other times than when she was under examination, we do not know. Her statements then, as she then meant, and as we now understand them, fell far short of confessing familiarity with the devil, or of laying that crime to any others ; therefore she neither made herself nor her companions *witches.* Still her master, no doubt, as did the recorder Ezekiel Cheever and the court, understood her as meaning *devil* when she said " the man," though she herself did not so mean. Even Corwin, apparently, as judge, put the prevalent construction upon her words, though his fidelity as a recorder caused him to write " the man " when she said " the man." This general habit of understanding *devil*, when some other personage was both named and meant, enables us to see that there may have been subsequent dispute between her and her master as to her real meaning, and that he made it a condition for her liberation that she should put his construction upon what she had said, rather than her own. It is an open question whether she ever refused to stand by her own meaning, or the true meaning of her own words. Perhaps she did refuse to stand by construction which the faith and habit of the day led most minds to put upon her words unjustifiably; but we doubt whether she refused to stand by the literal and intended meaning of what she had said.

Poor Tituba! Because of your forced connection with a scheme and works which entirely baffled your comprehension, because of your forced disclosure of things you had witnessed and experienced behind the vail of flesh, your own body was imprisoned thirteen months, and two innocent women were doomed to death. Guileless and innocent, so far as connected with witchcraft, you was borne on by mighty forces to seem to act voluntarily, though in fact unwillingly and perforce, a prominent part in one of the most fearful scenes in human history. Man's ignorance of spiritual agents and forces in your day, together with the prevalent hallucination devil-ward, made you a humble and pitiable martyr to simple truth-telling. Some seeds in your simple story now gathered from out the chaff that has covered them for nine-score years, may soon be scattered over New England soil, from which, we trust, you above, and men below, may gather wholesome fruits of justice and truth.

SARAH GOOD.

Tituba's sister witch, as that slave's master called Sarah Good, may not have been regarded in her generation as possessor of any large amount of such qualities as her name is commonly used to designate. Still her neighbors doomed her to lasting fame by selecting her as the first person to be put under examination on suspicion of being a producer-of Salem witchcraft. As a facile tool in supernal hands she may have been, and probably was, good in quality as well as name.

Indications that her spirit-form was susceptible of either easy elimination or wide radiations from its material counterpart, are contained in the facts that on January 20, 1692, the inner eye of Tituba saw this Sarah; on February 25, Ann Putnam, and on the

28th, Elizabeth Hubbard saw her apparition, or her spirit-form.

Man's "natural" or physical optics do not discern a spirit. Spirit, when not materialized, is discernible only by our inner or spirit-eyes; spirit is "spiritually discerned." The spirit forms, however, of embodied, living men and women, are not all equally discernible by clairvoyants. Generally, only such among flesh-clad spirits are readily seen by inner optics as are able to slip, or are liable to be drawn, or to radiate out, from one's ordinary integuments of flesh, or, at least, those only whose integuments are transparent of spirit-light. Only few, relatively, can either see or be seen readily and frequently by spiritual eyes. Eagles exist as well as owls and bats. And clear perception of objects by the former amid light that blinds the latter, is no proof either that the vision of eagles is perverted, or that the objects they behold are but creatures of fancy.

Mediumistic Sarah Good, because she was highly mediumistic, would naturally be a brilliant and attractive object in the field of vision which the inner eyes of other mediumistic ones might be able and attracted to survey. Distance is of little or no account in connection with vision by the inner eye. Persons and objects, scores and hundreds of miles away, are practically near to the inner optics. Spirit-forms are, perhaps, thought-forms, and, like thought, can traverse oceans and continents in the twinkling of an eye.

It is not our purpose to multiply pages by largely quoting minute accounts of what transpired at the examinations and trials of those who were suspected of witchcraft; and yet it may be well to present rather fully one sample of the proceedings of the courts. This first case which the civil authorities gave attention to may serve that purpose as well as any other.

The arrest of Sarah Good was made February 29, and on the next day, Tuesday, March 1, 1692, her examination was commenced, and was continued, in connection with that of Sarah Osburn and Tituba, through the remainder of that week. On Monday, the 7th, these three were sent to jail in Boston. On the 30th of June Mrs. Good was put upon trial, which resulted in her conviction, and on the 19th of July she, together with others, was executed.

We copy first Ezekiel Cheever's account of her examination. Cheever was temporary clerk or scribe employed by the examining magistrates to take minutes of the testimony.

" 'Sarah Good, what evil spirit have you familiarity with?' *Ans.* 'None.' 'Have you made no contract with the devil?' Good answered, 'No.' 'Why do you hurt these children?' *Ans.* 'I do not hurt them. I scorn it.' 'Who do you employ, then, to do it?' *Ans.* 'I employ nobody.' "

This question was doubtless based on belief then held, that one who was in covenant with the devil had, by the terms of the covenant, received power to command the devil and his imps to execute any desired mischief.

" 'What *creature* do you employ, then?' *Ans.* 'No creature, but I am falsely accused.' "

Her statement that she employed *nobody*, seems not to have covered all classes of possible servants in

such business. Therefore she was asked what *crea-*
ture she employed. This question suggests the probable supposition by the magistrate that such dogs,
cats, birds, and hairy nondescripts as Tituba saw,
might be subservient to the commands of a witch.

" 'Why did you go away muttering from Mr. Parris's house?' *Ans.* 'I did not mutter; but I thanked
him for what he gave my child.' 'Have you made
no contract with the devil?' *Ans.* 'No.' "

The magistrate then "desired the children, all of
them, to look upon her and see if this were the person that had hurt them; and so they all did look
upon her, and said that this was one of the persons
that did torment them. Presently they were all
tormented."

" 'Sarah Good, do you not see now what you have
done? Why do you not tell us the truth? Why do
you thus torment these poor children?' *Ans.* 'I do
not torment them.' 'Who do you employ, then?'
Ans. 'I employ nobody. I scorn it.' 'How came
they thus tormented?' *Ans.* 'What do I know?
You bring others here, and now you charge me with
it.' 'Why, who was it?' *Ans.* 'I do not know but
it was some you brought into the meeting-house with
you.' *Response.* 'We brought you into the meeting-
house.' *Reply.* 'But you brought in two more.'
'Who was it, then, that tormented the children?'
Ans. 'It was Osburn.' 'What is it you say when
you go muttering away from persons' houses?' *Ans.*
'If I must tell, I will tell.' 'Do tell us then.' *Reply.*
'If I must tell, I will tell. It is the commandments.
I may say my commandments, I hope.' 'What com-
mandment is it?' *Ans.* 'If I must tell, I will. It is

a psalm.' 'What psalm?' *Statement by reporter.* 'After a long time she muttered over some part of a psalm.' 'Who do you serve?' *Ans.* 'I serve God.' 'What God do you serve?' *Ans.* 'The God that made heaven and earth.' "

Comments by the reporter. "She was not willing to mention the word God. Her answers were in a very wicked, spiteful manner, reflecting and retorting against the authority with base and abusing words, and many lies she was taken in. It was here said that her husband had said that he was afraid that she either was a witch or would be one very quickly. The worshipful Mr. Hathorne asked him his reason why he said so of her; whether he had seen anything *by* her. He answered, no, *not in this nature;* but it was her bad carriage to him; and indeed, said he, I may say with tears that she is an enemy to all good."

Reason for asking the children to look upon the accused, Cheever says, was, that they might "see if this was the person that hurt them." That statement fails to cover the whole ground. According to Cotton Mather, belief then prevailed that "when the party suspected looks on the parties supposed to be bewitched, and they are thereupon struck down into a fit . . . it is a proof that the accused is a witch in covenant with the devil."

In many subsequent examinations and trials, these magistrates required the accused to look upon the afflicted ones, and special note was taken of the apparent action of the supposed evil eye upon the sensitive children. Belief was held and acted upon by these examiners, that, if the accused were guilty, the guilt might be revealed by observable effects of emanations from the witch's eye upon those whom she had been bent upon tormenting. Possibly human experience and observation had gained knowledge of facts which furnished substantial foundation for such belief. The eye of the powerful mesmerist is very potent in action upon those whom he has been accustomed to subdue to his will. If the children quailed and suffered under the gaze of the accused, inference might be drawn that they had previously been brought into servitude by imperceptible forces proceeding from that person. Forces of that nature probably go forth more profusely from the eye than any other part of man, though that is not their only point of egress. Any part of the body may let them out. This fact, no doubt, was assumed of old by would-be witch detectors, for they often required the accused to touch their accusers, or the reverse. And generally the contact was attended by convulsions, spasms, pains, or other distress, or by cessation of annoyances. Such results are moderate evidence that forces pertaining to departed spirits were then operating upon the disturbed ones; for emanations from such source are frequently more agitating and agonizing, or more calming and pleasurable, than any that come forth from the simple mesmerizer. One reason for this augmented effect, as given through mediumistic lips, is, that the greater remove of properties of freed spirits from homogeneousness with those of flesh-robed ones, than exists between the properties of any two mortals, naturally causes either greater commotion or greater calmness when the disembodied ones effect contact with those robed in flesh, than ever occurs upon the confluence of streams exclusively mundane. It should be remembered that spirits, when in rapport with mortal forms, have power not only to will agonies and motions therein, but also to command and efficiently use appliances needful to produce them. Where Tituba's tall man with white hair was controller of performances, all such sufferings and antics as history describes may have occurred at trials for witchcraft, and yet few of them may have been willed to come forth by any mortal. Vailed from external perceptions, that powerful operator shaped the speech, the actions, and the sufferings of all the impressible ones, whether accused or accusers, at his sole pleasure. What his object and his motives were are not matters for consideration at this stage of our investigations.

The examining magistrates, John Hathorne and Jonathan Corwin, subscribed to the following account of this examination.

" Sarah Good upon examination denieth the matter of fact, viz., that she ever used any witchcraft, or hurt the above-said children, or any of them.

" The above-named children, being all present, positively accused her of hurting them sundry times within this two months, and also this morning.

" Sarah Good denied that she had been at their houses in the said time, or near them, or had done them any hurt. All the above-said children then present accused her face to face, upon which they were all tortured and tormented for a short space of time ; and the afflictions and tortures being over, they charged said Sarah Good again that she had so tortured them, and *came to them* and did it ; although *she was then kept at a considerable distance from them.*

"Sarah Good being then asked, if that *she* did not hurt them, who did it? And the children being again tortured, she looked upon them and said that it was one of them we brought into the house with us. We asked her who it was. She then answered and said it was Sarah Osburn; and *Sarah Osburn was then under custody, and not in the house.* And the children, being quickly after recovered out of their fits, said that it was Sarah Good and also Sarah Osburn that then did hurt and torment or afflict them, although *both of them at the same time at a distance or remote from them personally.*"

The Italicized lines show that the magistrates attached importance to the children's statement that the two women had access to them and hurt them, even while the outer forms of the women were remote from the girls. Precisely how Hathorne and Corwin viewed such facts we do not know. Perhaps they deemed them strong evidence that the women were helped by the devil. The fact, if it be a fact, — and it probably is, — that those girls actually received painful sensations from forces coming to them from out the forms of those two women whose bodies were at the time distant from their own, was marvelous when it occurred, and remains so now to all such as are unacquainted with some instructive things which modern Spiritualism has been bringing into view. To entranced persons, to the spiritually illumined, to the clairvoyant, distance and material objects become nearly obliterated. Between such, also between spirits and such, when their inner powers are in the ascendant, mind acts directly upon mind, without aid from external senses and organs, and whatever then is done to the mind or spirit of the incarnated, whether it be painful or pleasing, reaches and affects the body of the earth-clad one from within, and thence works outwardly. All sensation pertains to the mind or spirit. The body, when life leaves it, at once becomes absolutely insensible. All hurts of the body, come whence and as they may, are felt by the spirit only — never by the body. Therefore when the spirit from within is pinched by a spirit directly, the hurt, though the physical body has not been touched from without, is felt precisely as it would be if fingers had nipped the flesh. One's bruised spirit acting outwardly may discolor portions of the body precisely as would an external pinch, grip, or blow. The accusing girls may have actually perceived and positively *known* that pain-producing forces issuing. from the forms of the accused women, were distorting. and convulsing their own bodies and the bodies of other sensitive ones, while yet the women's wills may not have sent the forces forth ; those accused ones may have been but the wearers of bodies, or possessors of God-bestowed organisms and temperaments through which either Tituba's tall. man or some other spirit, or even some impersonal natural force, gained access to the spirits of the girls, and, through their spirits, caused their bodies to manifest signs of intense sufferings. Spiritualism is inviting physiologists and psychologists into new and interesting fields for exploration.

The foregoing facts and views invite to very lenient

322   WITCHCRAFT MARVEL-WORKERS.

judgments, whether pertaining to the accused women
or to their youthful accusers.

Many things during the examination of Sarah Good
were culled from Tituba's statements, and used with
design to show that Sarah Good was a witch.   Tituba
charged that woman with hurting the children, and
of being one of five who urged her to do the
same.   Good rode on a pole with the latter to Mr.
Putnam's, and then told the slave that she must
kill somebody.   She came and made Tituba deaf
at prayers.   She had a yellow bird which sucked
her between her fingers ; also she had a cat, and
she appeared like a wolf to Hubbard.   Tituba saw
Good's name in the book, and the devil (no, the tall
man), "told Good made her mark."   Even her
own little daughter, Dorothy Good, testified that her
mother "had three birds, one black, one yellow, and
that these birds hurt the children and afflicted persons."

Deliverance Hobbs saw Good at the witch's sac-
rament.

Abigail Hobbs was in company with, and made
deaf by her, and knew her to be a witch.

Mary Warren had *the book* brought to her by Sarah
Good.

Elizabeth Hubbard, Mary Walcott, Ann Putnam,
Mercy Lewis, Sarah Vibber, and Abigail Williams
(all of them members of the necromantic *circle*),
were afflicted by Sarah Good, and *saw her shape*.

Richard Patch, William Allen, John Hughes, had
her appear to them apparitionally.

This long array of names of impressibles existing
in the Village at so early a time as the very first

attempt to find a witchcraft-worker there, indicates that Tituba's visitant had been an expert selecter of a spot for operation. He began his work in the midst of abundant and fit materials with which to carry out a purpose to obtain close approach to, and to put forth startling action upon and among embodied mortals. It may be learned in the hereafter that he was suggester of the visible as well as of the invisible CIRCLE which met at the parsonage; and learned, also, that his forces magnetized the members of each. That so many mediumistic ones, a large proportion of them wonderfully facile and plastic, were hunted up in " the short space of two months," among the five hundred scattered inhabitants of that Village, is surprising. Only keen eyes and active search could have found thus many in so short a time. Germs of prophets must have been abundant there, and must have developed rapidly under the culture of the supernal gardener who discovered their abundance and quality, and took them under his special watch and care.

While under examination, Sarah Good said, " None here see the witches but the afflicted and themselves; " that is, none but the afflicted and the accused; none but the clairvoyant. By witches she meant spirits and semblances of mortals and spirits; and she said in substance none others but we who behold with our internal eyes see the hovering and operating intelligences and forms. This unschooled woman then announced a great and instructive truth. She taught that the two classes — the tortured accusers and the accused both — possessed powers of vision which other people did not; that they possessed such clair-

21

voyance and other fitful capabilities and susceptibilities as pertained to only a quite limited number of persons, and that these physical peculiarities were the source of the existing mysteries.

It should be ever borne in mind that the powers which Mrs. Good had reference to are generally very fitful in their operations. Those who sometimes see spirits and spirit scenes are seldom able to do it at will, or with any very long continuance without interruption. The most of them might, every few minutes, say with Tituba, "I am blind now, I cannot see."

Having stated that the accusers and accused, and only they and others constituted like them, could see the hidden persons and forces which were there acting, acted upon, or being employed in putting forth mysterious inflictions upon the distressed girls, Sarah Good forthwith charged her fellow-prisoner, Sarah Osburn, with then "hurting the children." The fair inference is, that she saw the spirit or the apparition of her companion then seemingly at work upon the sufferers; and Mrs. Good may only have described what her inner optics were then beholding. Virtually she was confessing that she was herself clairvoyant, and consequently very near kin to a witch, if not actually one in that dreaded sisterhood. But clairvoyance pertained to the accusers also, and both sets of clear seers, if their powers were a crime, deserved like treatment.

"Looking upon them" (the afflicted children) "at the same time and not being afflicted, must consequently be a witch." The above is from the records of her examination. Apparently she was looking

upon the children while alleging that the then absent
Sarah Osburn was there present and was occasioning
their sufferings, while yet Mrs. Good was not herself
afflicted ; this was deemed proof that she was a witch.
What unstated premises led to that conclusion we do
not know. Our fathers had many notions pertaining
to witchcraft that are now buried in oblivion, and
it is often very difficult to find the reasons for their
inferences. We are baffled here, and can say only
that indication is furnished that under some circumstances a woman's failure to become bewitched was .
proof that she was herself a witch — because she did
not catch a special disease, she must already be having it.

Constable Braybrook, who had charge of her during
the night between the first two days of her examination, deposed that he . set three men as a
guard to watch her at his own house ; and that in
the morning the guard informed him that "during
the night Sarah Good was gone some time from
them, both barefoot and barelegged." From another
source he learned that on "that same night, Elizabeth Hubbard, one of the afflicted persons, complained
that Sarah Good came and afflicted her, being barefoot and barelegged, and Samuel Sibley, that was one
that was attending (courting) of Elizabeth Hubbard,
struck Sarah Good on the arm, as Elizabeth Hubbard
said." — *Woodward's Historical Series*, No. I. p. 27.

Braybrook's statement presents a side incident at
a time when none of the performers who had been
trained in the historian's famous high school for girls
were present — an incident which rivals in marvelousness anything in the main tragedy they are charged

with enacting. When the tricksy girls were all absent, when men alone stood guard over and were with this prisoner, she became invisible by them. No one of the magic-working band of girls and women was then at hand. Testimony that she disappeared is distinct; the guards reported in the morning that "she was gone some time from them." The constable so stated, and the statement was supported by two assistant guards, Michael Dunnell, and Jonathan Baker. We shall not stop to ask them how they knew that she was "barefoot and barelegged" when she was invisible. They perhaps saw her stockings and shoes when she was not to be seen. Also she was without such garments when seen that night by Elizabeth Hubbard and her lover in that girl's distant home.

An intelligent, sagacious, and reliable man, Dr. H. B. Storer, of Boston, whom we know and have long known personally, and whom we respect as being distinctly high-minded, honorable, and adherent to facts and truths, gave, in the Banner of Light, January 9, 1875, an instructive account of his recent observations at the residence of Mrs. Compton, a medium, at Havana, N. Y. We extract the following from his statements. He says that on Monday morning, December 28, 1874, —

" By my request, Mrs. Compton acquiescing without a murmur, my lady friends, entering her bedroom, saw her completely divested of clothing, with the exception of two under garments, and then had her draw on a pair of her husband's pantaloons. The basque of her alpaca dress, without the skirt, was then put on, after careful search to render it certain that no extra clothing could be secreted. Then, in my presence, the basque was sewed by its points on each side to the pantaloons, and a ribbon, which I tied with two knots closely around her neck, was sewed through the knots, and each end of the ribbon sewed to the collar of the basque. So she had on a closely-fitting coat and pantaloons sewed together, and so attached by a ribbon around the neck that the clothing could not be drawn up or down. A pair of black gloves were then drawn upon the hands and sewed tightly around the wrists. I then put around her waist a piece of cotton twine, , tying it in two hard knots behind, and the same piece of twine was tied by double knots to the back of the chair in which she sat."

On Saturday Dr. Storer had seen come forth from the cabinet, as Dr. F. L. H. Willis also had on a former occasion, "a weird phantom, bearing the semblance of a woman, and clothed in a flowing costume of white. Over her head was thrown a vail of delicate texture, and in one hand she carried a handkerchief that looked like a bit of a fleecy cloud. Her dress was exceedingly white and lustrous, without a wrinkle or a fold in it." That description by Willis is called by Storer " perfect," and is adopted by him. This "weird" personage was called Katie. Dr. Storer, after fixing the medium in the cabinet on Monday, as above described, says, —

"Very slowly the door [of the cabinet] opened, and soon her [Katie's] entire form was seen dressed exactly as before — trailing skirts, vail, and mantle, but with a belt which she gathered in her hands and rubbed together that we might hear its silken

rustle.   Standing by the door, she addressed me,
saying that when she had walked entirely away
from the cabinet, she wished me to go in quickly,
and, without moving the chair, feel after the medium,
and all about the cabinet, and see if I could find her.
She stepped out about five feet into the room, and at
once I sprang into the cabinet, felt in the chair, swept
the floor and walls thoroughly with my hands — but
— not *a vestige of medium* or *anything* remained."

The italicizing is ours.   We design to imitate
the doctor in both frankness and wisdom — to re-
state and accept his facts — but make no attempt at
explanation of them.   We adduce the case because it
parallels in marvelousness the statements of Braybrook.   What happens now may have had its like
before to-day.   The modern case out-marvels, perhaps, the ancient one ; for we know not whether the
guards felt for their prisoner or only failed to see her.
How they ascertained that she was gone is not told.
Dr. Storer felt the chair into which he had bound
Mrs. Compton, felt the floor and the ceiling all over,
and could find nobody in the little cabinet, which
was but a triangle partitioned off at the corner of the
room, whose inner sides were only five feet each in
length, so that a man, without changing his position,
might touch any part of it, unless the ceiling overhead
was above the man's reach.   Shortly afterward, says
Dr. Storer, " the cabinet door was opened, and in the
chair, tied as we had left her, without the breaking
of a thread, or the apparent movement of her person, or in any respect differing from her appearance
when last seen, sat the medium, in that fearfully
lifeless trance, from which nearly a half hour was

required to arouse her. I will not give any speculations of my own upon this most marvelous exhibition. I submit the facts and vouch for their entire
accuracy."

Were Braybrook's statements true as to the main
fact? They may have been. If they were, we do
not apprehend that the physical body of Sarah Good
was either removed from the vicinity of her guards,
or seen by Elizabeth Hubbard that night. Invisibility
may have been wrapped around her body, and yet not
around her shoes and stockings; perhaps her spirit-
form was the only one seen by the distant observer.
We hesitate to fix limits to possibilities. Spirits to-
day frequently manage, as they say, and as results
indicate, to render particular material objects lying
within the embrace of auras or emanations of some
mediums, invisible temporarily by the keenest of keen
external eyes, even when such eyes are surrounded
by light sufficient for seeing other objects in the vicinity with distinctness. That which is done now
may have been done formerly. And since such phenomena now seldom occur excepting in the near
vicinity of persons susceptible to spirit influences, the
fair conclusion is, that Sarah Good was a medium.
Elizabeth Hubbard saw the spirit-form of Sarah Good;
which fact argues that Elizabeth was a clairvoyant,
unless Sarah Good's spirit was then materialized.
Each and every one of the afflicted girls is so repeatedly reported to have described perception of what
external sight could not see, external ear hear, nor
external touch feel, that the mediumistic susceptibilities of each and all of them are manifest.

The susceptibilities and endowments of both ac-

cusers and accused were exceptional and yet alike in
kind. The spiritual perceptive faculties and the receptive capabilities of both classes could be brought
into such action as would out-work results perceptible
by the external senses of common people. Also, and
especially, each class could be made to serve as *mere
tools* of invisible beings. As such they were handled,
their users employing them severally as afflictor or as
afflicted, at their pleasure, within the permissions of
psychological laws.

The choice, which selected certain ones to be implements by which to afflict, and others to be the subjects of afflictions, was made by dwellers in spirit
spheres, familiar with psychological laws, and competent to determine in which capacity each impressible
one could be most serviceable in advancing the ends
of the supernal operators. Such a view, when its
correctness shall have been confirmed, will work out
vast amelioration in the world's judgment of that
band of girls and women in Salem Village who have
long borne its scorn and detestation, and will thrill
every kindly heart with joy. When it shall become
apparent that some inborn physical peculiarities involved the controlling reasons why certain persons
rather than others were charged with being Satan's
devotees, then none can fail to see that it was not
roguery, not artifice, not malice, not grudges, not
family or neighborhood or parochial quarrels, not disputes about property, nor any social, moral, or religious eminence or debasement, — no, not any one of
those base motives of the normal intellect and heart
which lively fancy has pleased itself with conjuring
up and imputing, — no, it was not any one of those

reprehensible and damning motives, but was innate susceptibility of being easily controlled by psychological forces; especially it was a constitutional liability to be more readily seen, heard, and felt by persons similarly endowed than was the great mass of people around them.

Ann Putnam, Jr., the keen-sighted pioneer of the clairvoyant witch-detectors, saw the apparition, and felt the distressing influences of Sarah Good, on the 25th of February. Her depositions were numerous; there were but few of the accused whose apparitions had not met her vision, but few who had not harmed her in ways and by forces unperceived by external senses. The character and general purport of her testimony, and also of most of the testimony from members of THE CIRCLE, is well presented by the first deposition we find on record; which is as follows: —

"The deposition of Ann Putnam, Jr., who testifieth and saith, that on the 25th of February, 1691–92, I saw the apparition of Sarah Good, which did torture me most grievously; but I did not know her name till the 27th of February, and then she told me her name was Sarah Good. And then she did pinch me most grievously; and also since; several times urging me vehemently to write in her book. And also on the 1st of March, being the day of her examination, Sarah Good did most grievously torture me; and also several times since. And also on the first day of March, 1692, I saw the apparition of Sarah Good go and afflict and torture the bodies of Elizabeth Parris, Abigail Williams, and Elizabeth Hubbard. Also I have seen the apparition of Sarah Good afflicting the body of Sarah Vibber.   ANN ᵐᵃʳᵏ₊ PUTNAM."

That deposition furnishes a fair specimen of the kind of evidence sought for, admitted, and applied to prove probable compact with the devil. All of the above pertains to the first examination made at Salem, and it reveals the opinions then prevalent relating to covenantings with the Evil One, to powers and dispositions thence derived, and to then existing legal methods for proving such compacts. There is little indication that experiences at Salem, during the spring and summer of 1692, gave either the examining magistrates, or the court, much, if any, new light or any increase of wisdom or humaneness. Whatever modification of processes of procedure subsequently took place, and whatever change of decisions as to the value and admissibility of spectral evidence occurred, was for the worse rather than the better. The creeds and laws conformed to then were not formed and adopted for that occasion, but had prior existence, and were here applied with strenuous vigor by firm hearts and clear heads. Amid all the excitement, frenzy, infatuation, delusion, and credulity then abounding, logic retained its power and guidance, and held courts and juries to the requirements of the wholesome statutes of the English Parliament, pertaining to witchcraft and to Christendom's witchcraft creed. Old laws and faiths were here tested by strong men. They held for a time, and wrought woeful effects, but finally were broken.

Sarah Good was wife of an inefficient husband, "William Good, laborer." The family was very poor, having at times no home excepting such as charity granted them temporarily. She is spoken of by Calef as having "long been accounted a melancholy or distracted woman." Upham says that "she was a forlorn, friendless, and forsaken creature, broken down by wretchedness of condition and ill repute." We find no reason for dissenting from that writer's statement when he says elsewhere, that "she was an unfortunate and miserable woman *in her circumstances and condition;*" but we doubt the fitness of calling her "forlorn" and "broken down." She may have been so; but the spirit and energy generally manifested by her words and acts indicate the probability that she was rather a heedless, bold woman, free and harsh in the use of her tongue, and not very sensitive to or regardful of public opinion, but yet strong and not despondent. That she may have long been deemed, as Calef says she was, a "distracted" woman, is very probable, for many simply mediumistic persons, and even more of us who at this day solely because we believe in the advent of spirits, both good and less good, have long been accounted *crazy.*

We have met with no indication that she was physically weak or mentally despondent. She seems to have borne up well under long, tedious horseback rides daily to and from Ipswich jail, nine or ten miles distant, whither she was nightly sent ever after the time of her becoming invisible to her guards. Her keeper on the way says, "she leaped off her horse three times, railed at the magistrates, and endeavored to kill herself." That attempt, if she made one, to take her own life, was scarcely less likely to spring from the angry mental mood then prompting her to

rail against the magistrates, than from despondency
or forlornness.

When under examination, her answers were about
as direct, explicit, and to the point, as most other suspected ones were able to give to the perplexing questions which were put; and some of hers have more
snap than we usually find in words from lips of the
" forlorn and broken down."

It is not probable that her previous life had won
much public favor; yet no evidence has been met
with that her neighbors generally cherished hostile
feelings towards her, or possessed sentiments which
would prompt them to rejoice at her prosecution. We,
as has already been made apparent, ascribe her arrest
to other causes than the lowness of her character and
condition. That was not the primal incentive to her
being "cried out upon." Her organization, and the
then existing condition of her faculties, made her
either a convenient channel through which to trans-
mit, or a fountain from which to draw, forces into the
systems of certain other sensitives, which forces might
act therein for either the annoyance and suffering, or
the pleasure and relief of the recipients, according to
either inherent properties of the forces themselves, or
to the purpose of some intelligence who should inflow
and manipulate them. The sensitive girls might, and,
if well unfolded mediumistically, would unerringly
trace back such forces as acted upon themselves to
their mundane point of emanation, and in good conscience and good faith accuse the person from whom
the forces issued of being their tormentor; if clairvoyant they could see, if clairaudient could hear, and,
if not specially unfolded for seeing with the inner eye

and hearing with the inner ear, could *sense* the person from whom the foreign and disturbing influences came forth.

A bold spirit and prophetic glance pertained to this woman at the close of her mortal life. When near the gallows, and about to be executed, Mr. Noyes, the clergyman at Salem proper, told her "she was a witch, and she knew that she was a witch." She promptly retorted, " You are a liar. I am no more a witch than you are a wizard ; and if you take away my life, God will give you blood to drink." Subsequently that man "died of an internal hemorage, bleading profusely at the mouth." (*Hist. of Witchcraft*, vol. ii. p. 270.) Gleamings of what will be often meet internal or mediumistic eyes ; and such probably did those of Sarah Good at that instant, and authorized her prophetic utterance.

DORCAS GOOD

has already been presented in the reports of evidence against her mother ; but in those she was called Dorothy, and was reported as testifying that her mother " had three birds, one black, one yellow, and that these birds hurt the children, and afflicted persons." Such testimony, of course, supported the side of the accusers. The little one's words were damaging to her mother, and helpful to the mother's oppressors. But, from some cause, she soon fell under suspicion of belonging to the class of bewitchers. As early as March 3, Ann Putnam saw the apparition of this child ; and on the 21st of March, Mary Walcott did the same. This, of course, was regarded as evidence

that she was a witch; and on or near March 23d she
was arrested, examined, and soon after sent to jail.

Yes, little Dorcas, daughter of mediumistic Sarah
Good, not five years old, "looking well and hale as
other children," was definitely, in legal form, accused
of witchcraft; was arrested, and brought before the
civil magistrates for examination. In presence of the
magistrates the exhibiting graduates from the school
of "necromancy, magic, and spiritualism" — the afflicted girls — accused the little child of biting them
then and there, and "also of pricking them with pins,
with pinching and almost choking them." In proof
of all this they exhibited marks upon their flesh, just
such in size and form as matched her little teeth.
Also pins were found under their clothing precisely
where they asserted that she pricked them.

Such facts as imprints upon the arms of the girls,
corresponding precisely with such as the child's teeth
might make, and the invisible pinchings, prickings,
&c., are not outside of nature's permissions, and therefore were not impossible. Those girls, at their circle
meetings, *or elsewhere*, had obviously become very
facile instruments in spiritualism, had become usable
by spirits as subjects for impressions, and psychologically induced sensations. From the mediumistic little
daughter of a mediumistic mother, forms and forces
could be made to emanate which might act upon the
plastic mediumistic sufferers in exact accordance with
such experiences, and producing such results as the
girls described or others witnessed. The senses of
the annoyed ones could distinctly perceive that the
agonizing forces issued from that little girl. The accusers probably stated only facts which they knew as

well as any witness ever knew his facts when describing what his own senses had brought him knowledge of. Whether things seen and felt by the spirit senses be deemed objective or only subjective, they are alike real to the consciousness of the person that takes cognizance of them. The statements of the girls were probably true. The possibilities in heaven and earth, and along where their border-lines come in contact, are not recognized by some historians. There are some persons at this day who hold even as contracting and misleading philosophies, as Cotton Mather and the men of his generation did. Modern wisdom (?) prompts some to discredit any actual occurrence of any extra-marvelous facts — any facts *seeming* more than natural — and to impeach the accuracy or the truthfulness of any and all who attest to such, rather than admit that the bases of their own philosophies can be improved by expansion. Such persons, when attempting to account for many facts in human history, are, though it may be unconsciously to themselves, like mill-horses tethered to an unchanging center, and made to move within a fixed circumference. Habit soon brings loss of desire, if not of courage, to turn the eyes outward and look upon facts whose producers work from outside the beaten rounds in which some theorists travel. This makes it bad for many facts, such facts as are popping into view through avenues deemed anomalous. There are writers who do their best to enforce upon such facts the Mosaic command, "Thou shalt not suffer a witch to live." But facts are immortal; buried ones often reappear, and demonstrate their own former occurrence.

Two centuries ago, the claim of great marvels to be

objective facts was generally conceded. But at that
time the hidden workers of wonders were woefully
slandered as to parentage: men deemed them *all* to
be both imps of the malignant ruler of the darkest
regions of realms unseen, and his emissaries from pandemonium to the abodes of man.

Faith in the genuineness of witchcraft facts, though
in Dorcas Good's day it hid a multitude of sins, failed
to make the arresting of a mere infant witch a desirable operation. For some reason the officious marshal,
Herrick, sent forth constable Braybrook to encounter
and capture man's great enemy when that wily one
had ensconced himself in an infant's form. But the
deputy scavengered up and sub-deputized somebody
else to fight that battle for God and Christ. His
menial went the needful two or three miles north
through the woods to Benjamin Putnam's house, and
executed the daring feat of bringing on his back, or
in some other way, a "hale and well-looking" girl
of less than five years into court, a culprit because of
co-laboring with and being a covenanted servant of
witchcraft's devil! The darkness of delusion which
such an arrest failed to illumine must have been thick
indeed! But the creed of the day, devil-ward, the
creed of the fathers, the creed of Christendom, so deluded the public judgment that it demanded the blood
of a witch even though she were an infant.

The condition of the public mind only a very short
time subsequent to the irrational, unkindly, barbarous
arrest of that child has been depicted by Upham, vol.
ii. p. 112, in sentences more graphic, spirited, and
eloquent than our own powers could possibly put
forth, and differing considerably from what we would

essay to give were our rhetorical abilities equal to his.
He states that —

" The proceedings of the 11th and 12th of April '
produced a great effect in driving on the general infatuation. . . . 'Twas awful to see how the afflicted
persons were agitated. . . . Those girls, by long practice in ' the circle,' and day by day before the astonished and wondering neighbors gathered to witness
their distresses, and especially on the more public occasions of the examinations, had acquired consummate
boldness and tact.   In simulations of passions, sufferings, and physical affections; in sleight of hand, and
the management of voice and feature and attitude, no
necromancers have surpassed them.   There has seldom been better acting in a theater than they dis-
played in the presence of the astonished and horror-
stricken rulers, magistrates, ministers, judges, jurors,
spectators, and prisoners.   No one seems to have
dreamed that their actings and sufferings could have
been the result of cunning or imposture.   Deodat
Lawson was a man of talents, had seen much of the
world, and was by no means a simpleton, recluse, or
novice ; but he was totally deluded by them.   The
prisoners, although conscious of their own innocence,
were utterly confounded by the acting of the girls.
The austere principles of that generation forbade with
the utmost severity all theatrical shows and performances; but at Salem village and the old town, in the
respective meeting-houses, and at Deacon Nathaniel
Ingersoll's, some of the best playing ever got up in
this country was practiced, and patronized for weeks
and months at the very centre and heart of Puri-
tanism, by ' the most straitest sect ' of that solemn
22

order of men.   Pastors, deacons, church-members,
doctors of divinity, college professors, officers of state,
crowded, day after day, to behold feats which have
never been surpassed on the boards of any theater;
which rivaled the most memorable achievements of
pantomimists, thaumaturgists, and stage-players, and
made considerable approaches toward the best performances of ancient sorcerers and magicians, or modern jugglers and mesmerizers."

The brilliancy, fervor, and literary finish of that
description of the public enthusiasm and bewilderment
are truly worthy of admiration, while the picture is
not, and probably could not be, overwrought.   Still
we must doubt the competency of the alleged authors
of the excitement to perform the bewildering and
frenzying acts ascribed to them.

We have heard from of old, and could quasi believe,
that mountains in labor brought forth mice.   But it
is only rarely one has earnestly and fervently sought
and striven to entice the reading public to admit conviction that a dozen *enceinte* mice could enwomb and
give birth to a vast and terrific volcano.

One must needs look in wondering astonishment
upon that keenness of vision which, at the middle of
the nineteenth century, penetrating through mold and
debris which have, through a century and three
fourths, been gathering over momentous events, sees
clearly that they were the genuine offspring of youthful " cunning and imposture," even while the owner
of such vision himself perceived that neither the
learned, talented, and keen Deodat Lawson, nor any
other one of all the many able and sagacious men who
were lookers-on at the amazing feats while they were

transpiring, *dreamed* that the actings and sufferings could have been the results of cunning and imposture. The day of Lawson and his companion observers was too near the facts for any dreams about them. It required a peculiarly plastic modern brain, and the intervening lapse of eightscore years, for the generation and birth of such a *dream*. The reason of its non-appearance in 1692 is very plain. Known facts then left no vacancy in the brains of that day for storage of the fictions of dreamland.

We return to little Dorcas Good. · The creed devilward had hoodwinked all eyes. All things were in a terrific and bewildering whirl. Calm reflection and deliberate reasoning upon anything new were impossible. If perchance a mind asked itself whether an infant was competent to bargain with the devil and thence become a witch, it had no time to respond to its own inquiry. In open court, mysterious bitings were perpetrated by the teeth of this little girl, because the marks fitted her set and none other. The marks were made by the accused girl's teeth. Ocular demonstration, therefore, was proving her to be the devil's instrument; for otherwise she could not invisibly bite, nor could her teeth be made to bite, those who were off beyond her reach.

Standing upon what we said in the last chapter relating to the passing of hurts through the spirit to its outer body, we hold that spirits may have so applied the spirit teeth of little Dorcas to the spirit limbs of the afflicted girls, as to have left the marks of her teeth upon their flesh. ·

Woefully did the creed of that time not only permit, but call for the arrest of that infantile girl, solely because, under the operation of natural laws of generation, she inherited properties or capabilities which rendered her, from the time when she was conceived, ever onward, very susceptible to psychological influences. The judges, observing what were but legitimate and necessary outworkings of her inborn properties, being ignorant of their true source and nature, deemed them such a crime that the court sent her to Boston jail a prisoner, there to keep company with the mother from whom her peculiar properties had been derived, by whose milk they had been nourished, and in whose magnetisms they had unfolded. The present century is learning facts which teach that inborn properties and susceptibilities, and not compacts with the devil, constitute *witches* — some of whom are very lovely. An infantile witch is no great marvel now. Such can be found in many a family, " through whose lips angels speak " to-day, as they did through Emanuel Swedenborg's when but a child, and who, born in January, 1688, was precisely a cotemporary of Dorcas Good.

SARAH OSBURN

was companion prisoner of Sarah Good and Tituba on the memorable first week in March, 1692. Thirty years before, she had been married to Thomas Prince, and at the time of her arrest was wife of Alexander Osburn ; consequently she was well advanced in years. She also had long been an invalid, confined during long periods to her bed. Her worldly circumstances were comfortable — she and her family were neither poor nor rich — were neither very low nor very high on the social scale. *But she had heard words coming forth from unseen lips.* And on February 25, her apparition appeared to and annoyed Ann Putnam. Nothing has been noticed in the records which indicates that Ann ever spoke of any perceptions by her inner senses prior to that date, or that any member of the circle, excepting Tituba, preceded Ann in having opened vision. The latter saw " the tall man, with white hair and serge coat," as early as January 15. But Tituba's voice, had she have spoken, would have been powerless. Ann's position in society was high; she belonged to a family of wealth, culture, influence, and high respectability. Her mystical words were potent. In four days subsequent to her first reported vision of apparitions, three women were under arrest for witchcraft, and Ann's father was one of the very efficient advocates of prosecutions for that crime. Feeble, " bed-ridden " Sarah Osburn, of whom Upham speaks as one whose " broken and disordered mind was essentially truthful and innocent," and whose residence was at least a mile and a half north from Mr. Parris's home, and quite distant east from Ann's, on a road not likely to be often traveled by her, was among the marked and blasted three. Why? None now, perhaps, can tell with certainty. Probabilities alone can be adduced. Our supposition is, that at the moment when Ann's keen and far-sweeping inner sight was opened, and spirit substance, instead of material light, became her medium of vision, the most brilliant objects to meet her gaze, in all the region far around, would be one or more of the mediumistically unfolded persons dwelling there. From those among that class whose systems were fountains of emanations which at the time impinged upon her sensibilities, and did not harmoniously coalesce with her elements, and therefore acted as quasi acids upon her alkalies, or as alkalies upon her acids, produced painful effervescences which might ensue naturally, apart from the aid of any manipulating intelligence; or, if some intelligent being were observant of the currents and conditions of spirit magnetisms or forces then, and disposed to either intensify, abate, or modify their natural action, he might do so, and also could manipulate them to furtherance of his own ends, whether beneficent or malignant. Then and there, even high benevolence in one whose vision swept the far future, might take such primal steps as short-sighted mortals must look upon as necessarily altogether harmful in both immediate and remote results.

Such natural laws as reign supreme in spirit-realms may have led to the selection of secluded, inoffensive, "essentially truthful, and innocent" Sarah Osburn, as one of the tormentors of the girls, who were either schooled in magic by their own elected study and practice of it, or were constitutionally fitted for fitful enfranchisement of their inner perceptive organs while yet dwellers in their mortal forms, and whose bodies could become tools for other minds to use. If she was simply the voluntary actor out of her own "cunning or imposture," little Ann Putnam, twelve years old, brightest among the bright, and member of one of the most intelligent and religious families of the Village, she also must have been herself a *devil*, and so devilishly a devil, that even Cloven-foot might feel it a duty to pass his scepter into her hands. But grant that she was a medium through whose form other minds and wills could act, as she in fact was, and then we can regard her physical form as simply an instrument through which an intelligence other than herself manifested action to human senses; and thus we can deem *her* guiltless, whatever shall be our judgment of the intruding performer upon her "harp of a thousand strings."

Parts of the testimony in the case of Mrs. Osburn reveal her possession of mediumistic susceptibilities. As with Joan of Arc and many others, so with this woman; the inner ear could hear voices from some source impalpable by external senses.

"(It was said by some in the meeting-house that she had said that she would never be tied to that lying spirit any more.)

" Q. 'What lying spirit is this? Hath the devil ever deceived you and been false to you?'

" A. 'I do not know the *devil*. I never did see him.'

" Q. 'What lying spirit was it, then?'

" A. 'It was *a voice* that I thought I heard.'

" Q. 'What did it propound to you?'

" A. 'That I should go no more to meeting. But I said I would; and did go the next Sabbath day.'" — *Woodward's Hist. Series*, No. I. p. 37.

Although the timid prisoner said only that she *thought* she heard a voice, the reader will notice that she made no denial that she had previously said "that she would never be tied to that *lying spirit* any more;" therefore by fair implication she conceded that she had once, if not many times, heard

a voice which she had openly spoken of as having
been that of a *lying spirit;* and also that she had
more or less been instructed by and followed his,
her, or its advice. The fact that she was enjoined
not to go to meeting any more, argues nothing either
against the spiritual source of the advice, or the
good intent of whoever gave it. She had long been
a sickly, bed-ridden woman; therefore such advice
might have been given by any wise Christian physician. We are not concerned with either the moral
or religious states of invisible actors and speakers,
but are looking specially for some of the more distinct evidences that invisible intelligences of some
quality enacted Salem witchcraft, and, therefore, looking for the peculiar properties of both the embodied
persons through and those upon whom they directly
acted.

Sarah Osburn, though a secluded, respectable, inoffensive woman well advanced in years, was an early
victim before the sweeping blast that rushed over the
Village. Too feeble to endure the hardship of prison
life, she died in jail before the day for her trial. She
who heard voices from out the realm of silence,
possessed inner faculties in fit condition to permit
effluxes that reached and annoyed the mediumistic
children, who traced them back to her, and made
statements which brought her under suspicion of
being a covenanter with the devil. Such capabilities constituted her crime — her witchcraft — and incited a devil-fighting people to persecution which
hastened her exit to the realm from which the ad-
visory voices had come upon her ears.

MARTHA COREY.

Soon after the commencement of prosecutions, suspicion alighted on one of more refinement, intelligence, efficiency, godliness, and respectability than the females first arrested. Martha, wife of Giles Corey, — aged, prayerful, but bright; disbeliev-. ing in any witchcraft; doubting the existence of any witches; discountenancing searches for any, — said that the eyes of the magistrates were blinded, and that she could open them. She possessed spiritual and theological knowledge uncommon in her day and vicinity, and must have held beliefs and convictions derived from other sources than those at which her neighbors obtained their supplies. She was aloof from the prevalent delusion devil-ward.

Though a church member, a woman of prayer, of reputed, and doubtless of genuine, piety, Martha Corey was very early *sensed* by the Anns Putnam, mother and daughter, as the source of emanations which tortured them. Therefore she must be a witch. Grounds for such conclusion were not necessarily fanciful and fallacious. When and where natural outworkings from mediumistic properties and conditions were mistaken for symptoms of witchcraft, Martha Corey might easily be convicted of diabolism. We credit the allegation of Ann Putnam the younger that she was annoyed and afflicted by Mrs. Corey even while the two were miles apart. But we decline to admit that Mrs. Corey necessarily or probably had any voluntary connection with the girl's sufferings. Either unintelligent natural forces attracted the woman's effluvia to Ann, or else Tituba's

"tall man," or some other hidden intelligent being, formed connections and applied processes which
brought elements of these two persons into conjunction, and thus produced in the girl intense physical
disturbances and sufferings, and attendant liberation
of her inner perceptive faculties.

Ann's uncle, Edward Putnam, together with Ezekiel Cheever, because of the girl's repeated outcries
upon Mrs. Corey, only just one week after the sending of Tituba, Sarah Good, and Sarah Osburn to
jail, concluded to make a call upon sister Corey,
who was "in church covenant" with them, and
learn from her own lips what she would say relative
to the suspicions that had been raised concerning
her.

These just and considerate men, — for they were
such, — probably seeing the possibility that the child
might be mistaken as to the person who was causing
her to suffer, very properly called upon Ann when
they were about to start on their way to the
woman's residence, and asked the suffering girl to
describe the dress Mrs. Corey was then wearing.
Their obvious design was to test the accuracy of the
child's perceptions. But that purpose was not accomplished. The child pleaded inability to see, and stated
that blindness was put upon her just then *by the accused woman herself.* The sequel indicates that Mrs.
Corey foresensed the visit she was about to receive,
imbibed knowledge of the intended test, and of
action to thwart its success. Though dwelling and
being miles apart as physical persons, those two females
may have then been practically together as spirits,
and have mutually sensed the thoughts, acts, and

conditions of each other as far as each avoided intentional concealment. All of Ann's statements may have been in strict accordance with facts actually witnessed and experienced by her inner self. There is no need to assume that she feigned or falsified at all, even if no invisible personal operators were concerned in what then transpired; and certainly not, if Tituba's "tall man" and his associates were then present and acting, as they may have been. Perhaps invisible actors, holding both of these impressible subjects under psychological control, either imparted to, or withheld from either of them, just such knowledge and perceptions as would further the purposes of the operators — which may have been either simply a manifestation of their own powers, or an intimation to the adroit men that they were undertaking to deal with something which it would not be easy to outwit or thwart. Also other and very different purposes may have actuated them.

Some spirits, at some times, have ability, through some mortal lips, to express their thoughts to the embodied, and to wreathe their own emotions over faces they borrow, even while the spirit, the selfhood, of the mortal form usurped is conscious of what is being done through it. Remember that the form of the conscious Agassiz was, against his own will, made to obey Townshend's mind. Perhaps Madam Corey's expressions of thoughts and emotions were sometimes prompted, and at other times modified by an unseen intelligence temporarily cohabiting with her own.

When the two brethren of the church, going forth on their solemn, self-imposed mission, had arrived at her home, Madam Corey welcomed them *with a smile;*

notwithstanding she possessed and expressed very
exact knowledge of the ominous nature and the purpose of their call. Her saluting words were, "I know
what you are come for. You are come to talk with
me about being a witch; but I am none. I cannot
help other people's talking of me." This probably
had reference to Ann Putnam's saying that she was
afflicted by this speaker. She soon asked the men
whether Ann, whose accusations had prompted their
call, "had described the clothes she then wore."
Learning that her dress had not been described, "a
smile came over her face." Somebody's consciousness
of power, issuing from her form, to obscure the child's
vision, probably expressed itself in that smile; and
the reflection that the child was operated upon by
forces within or action through Mrs. Corey's own
form, and therefore not necessarily by the devil, and
inference thence that the girl was not necessarily bewitched, was followed by her saying, "she did not
think there were any witches." She knew enough
of spiritual things to enable her to observe the broad
distinction, overlooked by her cotemporaries, that may
exist between some spirits and the devil; and also
between persons whose inner senses were cognizant
of spirit presence and action as naturally as the outer
eye was of the sunlight, between these and such other
human beings, could there be any such, and she
thought there could not, who made a covenant with
the devil, which covenant was a necessary preliminary to being a witch. "She," very reasonably,
"did not think there were any" such "witches;"
and only *such* were sought for by her visitors and
the startled public.

This woman was intelligent, courteous, and devout — was capable of understanding that *witch*, as then defined, necessarily meant a person who had voluntarily entered into a distinct compact with a factitious devil. Her *sensings* in spirit spheres found no native-born monstrosity there, and she could say in good conscience that she did not believe there existed any *such* witches as her visitors and fellow church members were on the hunt for. At the same time she may have known, probably did know, that her own spirit and the spirit of little Ann Putnam could come into such communings as would give them accurate and conscious mutual perception of many unspoken thoughts and experiences in each other.

Mrs. Corey, as we view her, was very mediumistic, and was also a woman whose habitual aspirations were after things true, pure, and excellent. But no amount of good or bad moral and religious qualities either constitutes or nullifies ability for mutual visibility and rapport between mediumistic persons. All such are impressible more by virtue of their organisms and native properties, external and internal, than by any intellectual and moral acquisitions, whether good or *bad.*

Properties issuing from Mrs. Corey's system probably pinched and otherwise tortured Ann Putnam; the girl knew their special mundane issuance, and innocently gave utterance to the knowledge. She did s) innocently and in good faith. But the divulgence of facts often brings fearful sequences.

When clear-headed logicians, being also conscientious and true men, as well as holders of undoubting faith that none but covenanted devotees to a wily devil could obtain knowledge and work harm by mysterious processes, — when such men took this case into careful consideration, the facts stated by the girl were to them proof that Mrs. Corey was the devil's minion, and therefore must be consigned to a witch's doom — death.

Edward Putnam and one other complained of her.

The warrant for her arrest was dated March 19, just one week after the visit of Putnam and Cheever. She was examined on the 21st; sentenced, September 9 ; executed, September 22. The questioning at the examination was discursive and protracted, spreading beyond inquiries as to who hurt the children, and how they were tormented, because of the prisoner's alleged disbelief in witchcraft; disapprobation of efforts to detect it; declarations that the magistrates, ministers, and others were blinded, and that she could open their eyes. She denied all knowledge as to who hurt the children, all knowledge of the devil, and repeatedly asked permission to go to prayer ; but this privilege was denied her. She behaved like one conscious of innocence of the things laid to her charge, and manifested much intelligence, self-possession, and tact.

While on trial, one feature in her demeanor, already indicated on a previous occasion, strongly attracts notice. Notwithstanding the terrible fate that was standing before her, and the unflagging persistency of the magistrates and all others present in assuming her guilt, she was several times accused of *laughing*. Those laughs may have been simply hysterical, but possibly they were widely different from such.

" Why did you say the magistrates' and ministers' eyes were blinded," and " you would open them ? She laughed, and denied it."

" Were you to serve the devil ten years ? She laughed."

" Why did you say you would show us ? She laughed again."

As previously stated, when Edward Putnam and Ezekiel Cheever made their call, although she knew the solemn object of the visit, they report that " in a *smiling manner* she said, ' I know what you are come for.' With ' eagerness of mind ' she asked them, ' Does she tell you what clothes I have on ? ' And when they replied that Ann had said, ' You came and blinded her, and told her that she should see you no more before it was night, that so she might not tell us what clothes you had on,' she seemed to *smile at it as if she had showed us a pretty trick.*" These men obviously were prettily tricked. But who was genuine author of playful proceedings at a time when the business was so grave and solemn ? And whose emotions mantled her face with smiles in the stern and frowning presence of " authority " ? Her calm and pleasant deportment, while others were agitated or solemnly stern, was very like what is often manifested through some human forms by intelligences whose condition places them beyond the reach of man's frowns, laws, prisons, and scaffolds, and who, dwelling aloof from storms of human passion, can smile amid scenes that make humanity shudder.

Calef states, that " Martha Corey, wife to Giles Corey, protesting her innocency, concluded her life with an eminent prayer upon the ladder." Upham (vol. ii. 458) sums up her character thus : " Martha Corey was an aged Christian professor of eminently devout habits and principles. It is indeed *a strange fact*, that, in her humble home, surrounded, as it then was, by a wilderness, this husbandman's wife should have reached a height so above and beyond her age." The strangeness of the fact argues strongly in favor of our position, that she was so unfolded as to receive instruction directly from supernal teachers, or sense it in amid supernal auras. " But," continues the historian, " it is proved conclusively by the depositions adduced against her, that her mind was wholly disinthralled from the errors of that period. She utterly repudiated the doctrines of witchcraft, and expressed herself strongly and fearlessly against them. The prayer which this woman made 'upon the ladder,' and which produced such an impression upon those who heard it, was undoubtedly expressive of enlightened piety, worthy of being characterized as 'eminent' in its sentiments, and in its demonstration of an innocent heart and life."

All her history suggests that this worthy woman, whose ways and powers were somewhat peculiar, was one of those rare individuals whose interior perceptives become so unfolded while in the body as to sense in knowledge by processes, and in some directions to extent, beyond the possible reach of man's outward intellect. Because of such blissful unfoldings her age condemned her, hastened her exit from among a creed-bound people, and her entrance to the home of freed spirits.

GILES COREY.

As renowned as any one among all sufferers under persecutions for witchcraft — a hero in the band —

was Giles Corey, husband of Martha, more than fourscore years old, but still strong and resolute. He may
have been wild and rough in youth and early manhood, but was efficient in business, and before the
close of life was possessor of a very handsome estate
for those times in that region. When the witchcraft
prosecutions commenced, he sided with the multitude
for a time ; was vexed that his wife would not do the
same, and, in his excitement, perhaps gave free vent
to such hard epithets as his tongue had been allowed
to put forth freely in his earlier years; some of which
were soon brought to bear against his good dame,
while she was subjected to examination. From some
cause his sympathy with the prosecutors subsided
when he saw his good wife maligned by them, and
soon the witch detectors were after him also. He was
arrested and imprisoned. His keen penetration perceived that acquittal, as things were going, was impossible, unless the accused pleaded guilty; which
plea truth, honor, and manhood forbade him to make.
To be tried and condemned would involve a forfeiture
of his property, and take it from his children. But
no trial could be had, and of course no condemnation,
unless he should plead either guilty or not guilty to
the indictment. His decision was soon formed. Taken
into court, he closed his lips, and no power there could
open them. Neither *guilty* nor *not guilty* could be
wrung from them. The large, strong, old man stood
in calm majesty before the court, his silence challen-
ging the whole civil power of the province to shake
his purpose. English custom in such cases — and he
probably knew it — was to subject the recusant to
lingering torture, trusting that pain or prostration
23

would wring out a plea of either guilty or not guilty.
Order was given by the court to lay this old man
prostrate, pile over him heavy weights, and put him
upon starvation diet for the purpose of bringing his
stubborn will to subjection. But neither oppressing
weights, the pangs of hunger, nor both combined,
weakened the hold of that strong will upon its purpose. His only utterances then were, " More weight,
more weight ! "

Corey himself testified at his preliminary examination, and the court tried to make it evidence of diabolism, that, twice at least, when attempting to pray,
there was more or less stoppage of his utterance.
Whether this was caused by the action of some outside intelligence bringing spirit forces to bear upon
him is not apparent. The case as stated will hardly
justify the presumption, though it suggests the possibility that it was. The dumbness that was formerly
imposed upon the prophet Ezekiel and priest Zacharias, and that which frequently befalls mediums in
our own age, teach that unseen intelligences sometimes can and do temporarily prevent the use of vocal
organs by their legitimate owners.

The conclusive evidences which led to his commit-
ment were spectral. His apparition had been seen by
many, and had harmed them. Ann Putnam's sharp
eyes were first in this case, as in most others, to see
the witch. She saw this old man's apparition April
13 ; Mercy Lewis did on the 14th ; and subsequently
he was seen as a specter by, and gave annoyances to,
eight other females and two males, who severally gave
in depositions to that effect.

Was their perception of him nothing more than the

product of the imagination of the witnesses? Were all the declarations false? Possibly — but not probably; for both imagination and perjury are often charged with doing what clairvoyance legitimately sees and authorizes.

He was examined April 19, five days after his apparition was first seen. Calef states that "Sept. 16th Giles Corey was prest to death." In a footnote, p. 260 of *Salem Witchcraft*, we read that "Giles Corey was *executed* Sept. 19, 1692, about noon." Perhaps these statements permit the conclusion that he was subjected to pressure from some hour of the 16th, Calef's date, till noon of the 19th, or about three days, when, according to Fowler, he died. "In pressing," Calef says, "his tongue being prest out of his mouth, the sheriff, with his cane, forced it in again when he was dying."

Corey's endurance and call for "more weight," says Upham, ii. 340, "for a person of more than eighty-one years of age, must be allowed to have been a marvelous exhibition of prowess, illustrating, as strongly as anything in human history, the power of a resolute will over the utmost pain and agony of body, and demonstrating that Giles Corey was a man of heroic nerve, and of a spirit that could not be subdued." Hutchinson closes his account of this case with the remark that, "in all ages of the world, superstitious credulity has produced greater cruelty than is practiced among Hottentots, or other nations, whose belief of a deity is called in question." And why "*greater* cruelty"? Nowhere outside of Christendom was so cruel a devil conceived of as within it. And therefore greater incitements to cruelty were called up in those fighting against his minions than in any other men anywhere at any time. The creed devil-ward, and not general "superstitious credulity," evoked in strong, good men, true to their ancestral and the *Christian* world's faith, more than SAVAGE CRUELTY.

Rebecca Nurse.

The deluding and heart-steeling power of false conceptions of the devil, combined with clear faith that he could get access to external things only through human covenanters with himself, and also with belief that it was an imperative duty of Christian men to slay such persons as even spectral evidence or statements of clairvoyants pointed to as being in league with him, is perhaps manifested as strikingly and sadly in the case of Rebecca Nurse, as in that of any other person tried and executed at Salem — or indeed anywhere, in any age. The spirit-form or apparition of this venerable lady — venerable not only for years then bordering upon fourscore, but for a long life of active beneficence ; for strong good sense ; for Christian graces ; for being the good wife of one and mother and mother-in-law of several as good, respectable, and useful men as the Village contained. Character and domestic connections so shielded her that nothing short of mighty power could fix upon her a blasting crime.

Her spirit-form or apparition had been seen by several members of the circle, and charged with having tempted them to evil and tormented them prior to the 22d of March ; on the 24th she was brought before the magistrates and subjected to examination. The occasion was well fitted to put to severe test existing fealty to a fearful creed. Well might the magistrate then say to the prisoner, as he did, " What a sad thing it is that a church member . . . should be thus accused and charged." Especially *sad* it must have been in this case, because the accused had long been, and well deserved to be, regarded as one of the most venerable and esteemed of all the " mothers in Israel " residing in the region there and round about. Some sympathy was on her side, for when she said, " I can say before my Eternal Father I am innocent, and God will clear my innocency," the magistrate responded, " There is never a one in the assembly but desires it."

This venerable matron was then, and for scores of years had been, beloved and respected wherever known for her beautiful domestic, social, and religious course. Even such a one, however, was drawn in and crushed by the fierce and whirling zeal that was impelling community into headlong and frenzied fight for God and Christ against the *Devil*. Age and virtue were insufficient to arrest or divert the rushing storm which hallucination devil-ward then generated and propelled. A benighting creed, like a huge nightmare, lay down upon, and held down, both reason and all the kindlier sentiments, while it evoked and allowed free play to harsh and murderous propensities. Whither either natural brilliancy or natural attraction drew clairvoyant eyes most intently, thither were the accusing girls swayed to lead the whelming force. Why should they lead to, or rather why fix upon, the beloved and venerated Mrs. Nurse ?

We may not find in the old records as full and distinct evidence that she was constitutionally impressible by either mesmeric or spirit force, as many others are now seen to have been — we may miss conclusive *proof* that she was a magnet either drawing to or emitting from itself psychological forces unconsciously, and thence either becoming herself psychologized or yielding out substances from her own system which might cause, or be made instrumental in causing, marked changes in other human organisms. Still, several facts indicate that she may be assigned a place among the sensitives.

Mrs. Nurse, Mrs. Easty, and Mrs. Cloyse — three sisters — whose maiden name was Towne, were eminently intelligent, efficient, respectable, and respected matrons, and yet were all accused, tried, and the elder two were executed because their spirit-forms or apparitions had been seen by clairvoyants. The records contain a statement made at the time, in these words: " It was no wonder they were witches, *for their mother was so before them.*" Often " blood will out " whatever its quality. Three noble daughters bespeak a good mother, and yet, for some reason, Mrs. Towne had been called *a witch.* The properties of the parent reappeared in her children, and rendered them visible by the inner or clairvoyant sight of others. Perception of their spirit-forms and of influences thence emanating caused the accusing girls to name these good women as their tormentors. Visibility as spirits or apparitions, and effluxes from their systems, were their crimes.

Though members of the accusing circle had been demonstrative for several weeks, and probably had attracted to their bedsides or homes nearly every person in the town who could move abroad, yet, at the time of her examination, Mrs. Nurse had not been to see any of them. Her age and infirmities alone might well have excused her. But when asked why she had not visited the sufferers, she added to a statement of her years and debility, that "by reason of *fits* that she formerly used to have," she had not been to see them. Remembrance of her own past fits — not recent — not impending fits — but fits which "she *formerly* used to have," deterred her from going to the presence of the fit-afflicted. The question was repeated thus : "*Why* did you never visit these afflicted persons?" *Ans.* "Because I was afraid *I should have fits, too.*" Why afraid of such result? Obviously she felt a secret apprehension that her coming in contact with emanations from these mysteriously fit-afflicted ones, or into close sympathy with them, would bring upon herself again such fits as "she formerly used to have." From this comes forth spontaneously the inference that she suspected that the nature and source of her own former fits, and of those then transpiring in youthful forms, were so nearly allied, that under the general law which makes like produce its like, she was liable to have again generated within herself, in her old age, such sufferings as she had experienced some time in previous years. In our view she was correct in her supposition that she herself was constitutionally liable to just such handlings as the jumping-jack girls were receiving. Her own fears bespeak the probability that Mrs. Nurse was very impressible by mind not her own — that she was highly mediumistic;

and we ascribe her persecution to her impressibility.
Natural law led to designation of both this woman
and her sisters as the devil's covenanted servants.
Their creed blinded her persecutors to moral perceptions in certain emergencies, and made them rea
son falsely concerning the source and purport of
spectral data. The presumed mediumistic properties
of her mother, together with her own apprehension
that presence with the girls might bring renewal
of her own old fits, indicate that she probably was
quite mediumistic. There is, however, no clear indication that she was at any time so far developed as
to see or hear spirits or specters, nor that her own
selfhood ever yielded up to another's use her physical organs of speech or action.

Mr. Parris, who, by request from the magistrates,
took minutes of the questions and responses at the
trial of Mrs. Nurse, states that the tumult in court
was very disturbing, and intimates that it was difficult
to furnish a very reliable account of the transactions.
Also Mrs. Nurse was quite deaf and otherwise infirm,
so that it is doubtful whether she always correctly
understood the questions put to her, or that she held
her mental faculties under such control as enabled
her to give pertinent answers at all times. She is
reported as expressing belief that the accusing girls
were " not acting against their wills." Therein, if
she was correctly understood, she differed from the
court and most beholders of the children. Then the
court remarked, " If you think it is not unwillingly,
but by design, you must look upon them as murderers." Probably all others made that inference, and yet
the accused did not. She distinctly denied that she

looked upon them as *murderers*, and only called them
"distracted." Crazy, and yet voluntary, seems to
have been the view she took of the girls; they were
voluntary, but not responsible actors. Their own
wills, guided by their own intellects in disordered
condition, produced the fearful allegations. This was
her charitable view.

The power of human will to resist fits like those
which the afflicted endured is brought up for consideration when we find enfeebled Mrs. Nurse afraid that
visiting the suffering girls might induce recurrence of
such fits as she "formerly used to have." She seems
to have surmised the probable existence of such contagion in the air surrounding the sufferers as in her
weak state she might be unable to ward off; and it is
possible that memories of her own success when she
was strong, in baffling fit-producers may have persuaded her that young persons possess power to withstand such operators, whether intelligent or merely
physical, even though the old may not.

What human wills can do deserves most careful
notice, and was well illustrated in the case of little
Elizabeth Parris. She was only nine years old, and
was one of the first, if not the very first, to be distressed by fits and pinchings at the Village, — was the
one whom Tituba loved, and was specially unwilling,
and yet was forced, to pinch. Upham says, "She
seems to have performed a leading part in the first
stages of the affair, and must have been a child of remarkable precocity." Drake, in vol. iii., Appendix,
says, "Parris appears to have been very desirous of
preventing his daughter Elizabeth from participating
in the excitement at the village. She was sent by her

father, at the commencement of the delusion, to reside at Salem, with Captain Stephen Sewall. While there, the captain and his wife were much discouraged in effecting a cure, as she continued to have sore fits. Elizabeth said that the great Black-man came to her and told her, that if she would be ruled by him, she should have whatsoever she desired, and go to a *golden city*. She related this to Mrs. Sewall, who immediately told the child it was the devil, and he was a liar, and bade her tell him so if he came again; which she did accordingly. . . . The devil . . . unaccustomed in those days to experience such resistance . . . never troubled her afterwards." It is generally true, that if one strenuously resist the visitings of any spirit, whether it be Gabriel or Beelzebub, the spirit cannot long maintain close access. If the account just given, relating to Elizabeth Parris, be correct, she both saw and heard what she, the actual and unsophisticated observer of his form and features, called the " black man," — who, as Mather states clairvoyants generally say, " resembles an Indian." But Mrs. Sewall, adopting the usage of the time, ignorantly called this semblance of an Indian "THE DEVIL." Yes, the little girl, after her removal from home and *The Circle*, and no doubt without young confederates, continued to have sore fits, and also to see and to hear with her inner organs of sense during quite a long time. " The captain and his wife were much discouraged in effecting a cure." The discouragement shows that the process of cure was slow and prolonged; eventually, however, the desired result was reached. The remedy is indicated. Will-power wrought out the cure. The patient's own will was aroused and armed with a resolute purpose to close up, and to keep constantly and firmly closed, her own spirit loopholes through which only could she see or hear the black man, or be influenced by him. A strong will, steadily set against the entrance of a disembodied spirit, or against perception of such, generally, though not always, effects its purpose. The wills of companions and advisers, if working in harmony with the resisting one, greatly increase its resisting power. Mrs. Sewall, and the captain too, no doubt kept their wills set against the visiting black man, till will-force generated an aura whose outgoing waves he could not breast, and by which the girl's inner perceptives were firmly bandaged and made dormant. Were the fits and visions which the isolated child continued to have for a time after she was sent from home nothing other than her own voluntary pranks and feignings? She was not author of them. The black man, or Indian, then acted through and upon her till it was no longer in his power to perform mighty works there because of unbelief, which had grown up and hardened into an impervious wall of seclusion.

Knowledge, gained by our personal observation in 1857, enables us to state distinctly that the late Professor Agassiz, a man strong in body, mind, and will, (while arrangements were being made for himself and several associate professors for an investigation of spirit manifestations at the Albion in Boston,) demanded for himself at the very outset, and was granted, exemption from obligation to sit in a circle. Through all the sessions which followed he kept most of the time on his feet, walking vigorously back and forth, and manifesting symptoms of great uneasiness.

We then had heard that he formerly had been mesmerized, and therefore suspected that he feared that if he sat quietly down in the presence of mediums, he "should have fits too." His own account of his experiences under the hands of Rev. Chauncy Hare Townshend we have given at length in a recent work, published by Colby & Rich, Boston, entitled "Agassiz and Spiritualism." We now gladly use what seems fitting occasion to state our own belief, that his demand for personal exemption from compliance with a rule which it was customary, fair, and important to enforce upon every person present at a seance, and that his restlessness and disturbing movements all sprung from a motive much more in harmony with the high character and principles of that illustrious man, than are disparaging ones which have often been ascribed to him. In our judgment, *self-protection* was his motive, and not design to disturb harmony, and thus frustrate manifestations. His former experience had taught him that even over his firm mental resistance another's mind had entered his body and taken it out from under his own control; therefore he well might apprehend that, if not very cautious, he again "might have fits," or might become "a Saul among prophets."

We have already substantially said that the blinding, infuriating, and bloodthirsty beliefs of former days are perhaps in no case more distinctly and deplorably manifested than in the lawless, barbarous treatment to which good Rebecca Nurse was subjected by a court and people who sought to do, and believed that they were doing, acceptable service to God, or, at least, offensive service to the devil. Spectral evi-

dence against her, and that alone, was allowed to out-
weigh the merits of a long and beneficent life. The
jury first brought her in *not* guilty. This verdict, surprising the court, induced it to express apprehension
that the jurors had not given due weight to certain
expressions which the prisoner had uttered; whereupon *the jury itself requested permission* to retire and
hold further deliberation; and even such a privilege
was granted them! They retired, reversed their verdict, pronounced her *guilty*, and she was sentenced to
be hanged. Afterward the governor of the province
granted her reprieve; and yet he soon revoked his
own clement act. Probably neither jury, nor the governor, was convinced that she was guilty of the crime
charged; nevertheless, both were forced by popular
demand to let the reputation and life of this eminently
good woman fall a sacrifice before infatuation and
frenzy which the erroneous creed of the times engendered. .

MARY EASTY,

a woman of strong character, good common sense, and
capable of comprehending both the dangers besetting
any one then accused of witchcraft, and also the purport and bearings of such questions as the court was
accustomed to ask, is presented in the following
account.

"The examination of Mary Easty, at a court held
at Salem Village, April 22, 1692, by the Wop. John
Hathorne and Jonathan Corwin.

"At the bringing in of the accused, several fell into

fits. 'Doth this woman hurt you?' Many mouths were stopt, and several other fits seized them. Abigail Williams said it was Goody Easty, and she had hurt her; the like said Mary Walcot and Ann Putnam. John Jackson said he saw her with Goody Hobbs.

" ' What do you say; are you guilty?' *Ans.* 'I can say before Jesus Christ I am free.' *Response.* 'You see these accuse you.' *Ans.* 'There is a God.'

" ' Hath she brought the book to you (the accusing girls)?' Their mouths were stopt.

" ' What have you done to these children?' *Ans.* ' I know nothing.'

" ' How can you say you know nothing, when you see these tormented and accuse you?' *Ans.* 'Would you have me accuse myself?' ' Yes, if you be guilty. How far have you complied with Satan whereby he takes this advantage of you?'

" ' Sir, I never complied: but prayed against him all my days. I have no compliance with Satan in this. What would you have me do?'

" ' Confess, if you be guilty.'

" ' I will say it, if it was my last time: I am clear of this sin.'

" ' Of what sin?'

" ' Of witchcraft.'

" (To the children.) ' Are you certain this is the woman?'

" Never a one could speak for fits.

" By and by, Ann Putnam said that was the woman: it was like her; ' and she told me her name.'

" (The court.) ' It is marvelous to me that you should sometimes think they are bewitched and sometimes not, when several confess that they have been guilty of bewitching them.'

" ' Well, sir, would you have me confess what I never knew ? '

" Her hands were clenched together, and then the hands of Mercy Lewis were clenched.

" ' Look : now your hands are open, her hands are open. Is this the woman ? '

" They made signs, but could not speak. But Arn Putnam, (and) afterwards Betty Hubbard, cried out, ' Oh, Goody Easty, Goody Easty, you are the woman ! '

" ' Put up her head ; for while her head is bound, the necks of these are broken.'

" ' What do you say to this ? '

" ' Why, God will know.'

" ' Nay, God knows now.'

" ' I know he does.'

" ' What did you think of the actions of others be-fore your sisters came out ? Did you think it was witchcraft ? '

" ' I cannot tell.'

" ' Why, do you not think it is witchcraft ? '

" ' It is *an evil spirit ;* but whether it be witchcraft I do not know.'

" Several said she brought them the book, and then they fell into fits.

" Salem Village, March 24, 1694.

" Mr. Samuel Parris, being desired to take in wri-ting the examination of Mary Estie, hath delivered it as aforesaid.

" ' Upon hearing the aforesaid, and seeing what we did then see, together with the charge of the persons

then present, we committed said Mary Easty to their Majesty's jail.   JOHN HATHORNE, ⎱ *Assists.*'"
                                  JONATHAN CORWIN, ⎰

Among the records of examinations and trials for witchcraft in 1692 we have met with none other more commendable in its apparent spirit on both sides, and in its continuous decorum, than the above; none other, also, which reveals more clearly extreme depth of public conviction that the prevalent witchcraft creed was sound to the core, and belief that spectral evidence alone might legally prove the crime charged. From aught that appears, there was something pertaining to Mrs. Easty, probably her whole general character and her intellect, which held back both court and spectators from rudeness in treatment of her, and even frequently tied up the tongues of the accusing girls. The spectacle presented by that examination was most rare and wonderful. We feel, when reading the records, that magistrates, populace, and the accusers, all — all longed for her acquittal; that none desired to, because none did accuse her of anything but having been seen as an apparition, and of being the cause of the fits which the girls were enduring. The girls named her as the cause of their fits, but seemingly with less alacrity than they did most others in like circumstances. But sympathy and respect must yield before belief; her fit-producing emanations at that day proved her to have covenanted to serve the devil. Having done that, she was *witch*, and therefore must die.   ·

Her clear head perceived that the sufferings of the girls must owe their existence to some occult power

outside of themselves, and ascribed it to "an evil
spirit." Such an origin, however, did not prove to
her satisfaction that the doings were witchcrafts, that
is, acts performed either at the instigation or by aid
of some mortal who was in covenant with the devil.
She was enough in advance of her times to suspect
that a spirit might work upon and among men without having formed such connection with a mortal ally
as would prove one's operations to be witchcrafts.
She perceived that the girls were wrought upon by
some spirit, and she deemed it an evil one.

This noble woman was wife of Isaac Easty of Topsfield, fifty-eight years old, and mother of seven children. After her conviction and sentence, and when
hope of escaping the dire penalty had fled, she addressed an admirable letter to those then in power.
The same inborn susceptibilities which made her a
victim may also have permitted a free influx of uplifting power which raised her above narrow, selfish, and
domestic views, and prompted her, in moods generous
and lofty, to appeal, in behalf of the whole people of
the land, for a stop in the course which the civil authorities were pursuing. We judge the letter to be
her own production, and deem it indicative of good
mental powers and of elevated philanthropy.

" *The humble petition of Mary Easty unto His Excellency Sir William Phips, and to the honored Judge and
Bench now sitting in judicature in Salem, and the reverend Ministers, humbly showeth,* That, whereas your
poor and humble petitioner, being condemned to die,
do humbly beg of you to take it into your judicious
and pious consideration, that your poor and humble

24

petitioner, knowing my own innocency, blessed be the Lord for it! and seeing plainly the wiles and subtilty of my accusers by myself, cannot but judge charitably of others that are going the same way of myself if the Lord steps not mightily in. I was confined a whole month upon the same account that I am condemned now for, and then cleared by some of the afflicted persons, as some of Your Honors know. And in two days' time I was cried out upon (by) them, and have been confined, and now am condemned to die. The Lord above knows my innocency then, and likewise does now, as at the great day will be known to men, and angels. I petition Your Honors not for my own life, for I know I must die, and my appointed time is set; but, the Lord he knows it is, that if it be possible, no more *innocent blood* may be shed, which undoubtedly cannot be avoided in the way and course you go in. I question not but Your Honors do to the utmost of your powers in the discovery and detecting of witchcraft and witches, and would not be guilty of innocent blood for the world. But *by my own innocency I know you are in the wrong way.* The Lord in his infinite mercy direct you in this great work, if it be his blessed will, that no more innocent blood be shed! I would humbly beg of you that Your Honors would be pleased to examine these afflicted persons strictly, and keep them apart some time, and likewise to try some of these confessing witches; I being confident there is several of them has belied themselves and others, as will appear, if not in this world, I am sure in the world to come, whither I am now agoing. I question not but you will see an alteration in these things. They say, myself and others having made a league with the devil, we cannot confess. . . . The Lord above, who is the searcher of all hearts, knows, as I shall answer it at the tribunal seat, that I know not the least thing of witchcraft: therefore I cannot, I dare not belie my own soul. I beg Your Honors not to deny this my poor humble petition from a poor, dying, innocent person. And I question not but the Lord will give a blessing to your endeavors."

Calef says, that, "when she took her last farewell of her husband, children, and friends," she "was, as is reported by them present, as serious, religious, distinct, and affectionate as could well be expressed, drawing tears from the eyes of almost all present." We can readily credit that account to its fullest possible import; for her deportment and language, throughout all the scenes in which she is presented, bespeak a strong, clear, discriminating intellect, a true and brave heart, elevated and generous sentiments, firm faith in God, and broad charity toward man. A most welcome child found entrance to some bright home above when her tried spirit gained release from its mortal form.

Susanna Martin.

The person bearing the above name was a widow residing in Amesbury, who had been tried for witchcraft more than twenty years before, and therefore obviously in 1692 was well along in life. Her answers in court, however, bespeak a prompt, self-possessed, shrewd, and seemingly merry prisoner. A few of her replies, together with the questions which elicited them, are as follows: —

"Ann Putnam threw her glove at her in a fit.
'What do you laugh at?' said the court. *Ans.* 'Well
I may at such folly.'

"'Is this folly to see these so hurt?' 'I never
hurt man, woman, or child.'

"'What do you think ails them?' 'I do not desire to spend my judgment upon it.' 'Do you think
they are bewitched?' 'No; I do not think they are.'
'Well, tell us your thoughts about them.' 'My
thoughts are mine own when they are in; but when
they are out they are another's.' 'Who do you think
is their master?' 'If they be dealing in the black
art, you may know as well as I.' 'How comes your
appearance just now to hurt these?' 'How do I
know?' 'Are you not willing to tell the truth?'
'He that appeared in Samuel's shape can appear in
any one's shape.'"

One R. P., dated Salisbury, August 9, 1692, and
forwarded to Jonathan Corwin, a document ranking
among the ablest on record against the legal proceedings of that day, in which he says, "I suppose 'tis
granted by all that the person of one that is dead cannot appear, because the soul and body are separated,
and so the person is dissolved, and so ceaseth to be;
and it is certain that the person of the living cannot
be in two places at one time." That writer conceived
that man's personality ceased at death; therefore he
logically inferred that the personality of the prophet
Samuel had gone out of existence, and said, "The
witch of Endor raised the DEVIL, in the likeness of
Samuel, to tell Saul his fortune." We find in many
places the cropping out, in those days, of the same
idea. Susanna Martin indicated her belief that it was

the devil who appeared to the woman of Endor, and
not the glorified Samuel. Premises deemed valid by
some men in 1692, would, if applied in that direction,
support the conclusion that the Moses and Elias who
appeared to Jesus and others on the mount of transfiguration were nothing but the devil in the shapes of
those old prophets. Belief that the devil personated
Samuel is to us no more unphilosophical than is Upham's conclusion, that "by the immediate agency of
the Almighty the spirit of Samuel really arose." Paul
taught that there *is* — not that there is to be hereafter, that there is now — "a spiritual *body*." All
clairvoyants to-day can see such a body belonging to
a human form, and sometimes see it being far away
from the form to which nature attached it. Each human being now possesses both a natural or physical
and also a spiritual *form*. That position of R. P. and
Susanna Martin was unsound which held that the
physical body was essential to personality. Also, since
the Almighty originally infused through nature, elements and forces which admit of the return of spirits
by natural processes, it is as unphilosophical to hold
that Samuel was raised by the immediate agency of
the Almighty, or miraculously, as it would be to
ascribe an American traveler's return home from
Europe to the *immediate* agency of the same Being.
Natural laws and forces permitted, under possible conditions, the return of Samuel himself. Such conditions
existed often in and around the hospitable and sympathetic woman of Endor, who was no *witch*, in the
now common meaning of that word; who was not
called such in the Bible, — but only a person who had
a *familiar* spirit, that is, a spirit so constantly present,

and having such ability of communion with her, as
made the spirit seem to her like one of her family —
her familiar. A spirit thus attendant on a mortal may
be either good, bad, or indifferent, and may be cognized by those persons whose constitution and development are such that their inner senses can report to
their external consciousness. The existing properties
of that woman, which permitted some special spirit to
frequently dwell and commune intelligibly with her,
and be cognizable by her inner senses as a dweller in
her household, as her familiar, — such properties would
enable her to perceive the form and hear the voice of
another spirit, who might be called to her presence for
an urgent purpose, as naturally as the outer eye which
sees one external form is competent to see another.
Samuel, when wanted, came and was seen by the
clairvoyant woman, but not by the external eyes of
either Saul or his attendants. The case was very like
what occurred at the first examination under an accusation for witchcraft at Salem Village. Sarah Good
then said, "None here see the witches" — that is, none
see spirits — " but the afflicted and themselves," —
that is, none but the afflicted and the accused, of
which she was one. In other words, the actual doers
of the marvelous works, the spirits, are seen only by
the accusers and the accused — the clairvoyants here.
It is true that in the more modern instance the spirits
seen were often, though not always, those of living
persons. But this does not affect the principles of
explanation. Those persons who are so unfolded as
to see spirit-forms can sometimes see them, whether
they be still attached to the outer ones or be liberated.
Spirits, both some who had been entirely liberated

from the flesh, and other flesh-clad ones whose encasements were translucent, could be seen by members of
the accusing "circle," and by some others of like combinations, even when the court and the mass of attendants upon it might fail to see anything of the
kind. The horses and chariots of fire were as clearly
seen by Elisha on the hills of Dothan, while his servant was blind to them, as they were after the young
man's inner eyes were opened so that he too saw the
helping and protecting hosts. The change was in the
young man himself, and not up on the hills. Departed
spirits are where they feel our aspirations for their
presence, and the opening of our inner sight, at any
time or in any place, might render them visible.

Returning to Susanna Martin, we find that one
William Brown, of Salisbury, made deposition in 1692,
" that, about one or two and thirty years ago, his wife
met Susanna in the road, who ' vanished away out of
her sight,' . . . after which time the said Martin did
many times appear to her at her house, and did much
trouble her. . . . When she did come, it was as birds
pecking her legs, or pricking her with the motion of
their wings; and then it would rise up into her stomach with pricking pain, as nails and pins, of which
she did bitterly complain. . . . After that it would
up to her throat in a bunch like a pullet's egg; and
then she would turn back her head and say, ' Witch,
you shan't choke me.' "

Much more testimony was adduced to show that
this woman's apparition was very frequently seen;
and not only seen, but was a source of exceeding sufferings to many people. This argues nothing against
her character, but plainly hints that the relation of

her inner to her outer form was such that the former could be seen and felt by many persons who either constitutionally or from sickness, or both, were very sensitive. Such persons often saw her spirit-form, and suffered from its psychological action. That peculiarity perhaps made her so luminous as to be observable, and therefore accused, by " the circle," and the accusation brought her to the gallows.

MARTHA CARRIER.

The faculties and manifestations which nearly two centuries ago were deemed to constitute witchcraft, and the mode of eliciting proof of that crime then, stand forth very conspicuously in the history of the wife and children of Thomas Carrier of Andover.

The Examination of Martha Carrier, May 31, 1692.

" *Q.* Abigail Williams, who hurts you? *A.* Goody Carrier of Andover.

" *Q.* Elizabeth Hubbard, who hurts you? *A.* Goody Carrier.

" *Q.* Susan Sheldon, who hurts you? *A.* Goody Carrier; she bites me, pinches me, and tells me she would cut my throat if I did not sign her book. Mary Walcott said she afflicted her, and brought the book to her.

" *Q.* What do you say to this you are charged with? *A.* I have not done it. Susan Sheldon cried, she looks upon the black man. Ann Putnam complained of a pin stuck in her. *Q.* What black man is that? *A.* I know none. Mary Warren cried out she was pricked. *Q.* What black man did you see? *A.* I

saw no black man but *your own presence.* *Q.* Can
you look upon these and not knock them down?
A. They will dissemble if I look upon them. You
see you look upon them and they fall down. *A.* It
is false; the *devil is a liar.* I looked upon none
since I came into the room. Susan Sheldon cried
out *in a trance,* I wonder what could you murder
thirteen persons! Mary Walcott testified the same:
that there lay thirteen ghosts! All the afflicted fell
into intolerable outcries and agonies. Elizabeth Hubbard and Ann Putnam testified the same: that she
had killed thirteen at Andover. *A.* It is a shameful
thing that you should mind these folks, who are out
of their wits. *Q.* Do not you see them? *A.* If I
do speak you will not believe me. You do see
them, said the accusers. *A.* You lie; I am wronged.
There is a black man whispering in her ear, said
many of the afflicted. Mercy Lewis in a violent fit,
was well, upon the examinant's grasping her arm.
The tortures of the afflicted were so great that
there was no enduring of it, so that she was ordered
away, and to be bound hand and foot with all expe-
dition; the afflicted in the mean while almost killed,
to the great trouble of all spectators, magistrates,
and others.

"*Note.* As soon as she was well bound they all had
strange and sudden ease. Mary Walcott told the
magistrates, that this woman told her, she had been
a witch this forty years."

The foregoing record shows the fearful ordeal to
which any one might be subjected upon whom an
accusation of witchcraft fell, and the hopelessness

of escape where spectral evidence was admitted and
held to be reliable. Here was a woman who, it seems,
had been conscious of spirit presence with her for
" forty years," and her constitutional properties which
permitted this were so luminous in the spiritual atmosphere, or medium of vision by inner eyes, that
the clairvoyant girls readily caught sight of her,
readily felt influences from her, and therefore accused her of tormenting them.

The general character and deportment of this
woman prior to her arrest may not have won public
approbation. When in presence of the magistrates
she was self-possessed and not lacking in boldness ;
for otherwise she would not have told the judge
that his own presence was the only black man she
had seen there. She told her examiners that it was
shameful for them to mind " these folks, who are
out of their wits." She said to the girls, " You lie ;
I am wronged." Her presence permitted extraordinary visions, contortions, sufferings, and outcries, and
probably emanations from her were special helps to
the unwonted outflow.

In trance, one saw thirteen dead bodies, and charged
the accused with having murdered them. It was *in
trance* that this was seen and said. If *entranced*,
was the girl, then, a voluntary seer and speaker ? No.
Supermundane force was in action there. Entrancements and obsessions came upon all those youthful
accusers fitfully — and the forms of the girls generally were tools operated by wills entering from
outside. The tongue of that entranced accuser, like
Ann Cole's, probably was " improved to utter thoughts
that never were in her own mind."

Four of Mrs. Carrier's children were brought into court in company with herself, either as accused ones or as witnesses against some members of the family. "Before the trial," says Drake, ".several of her own children had frankly and fully confessed not only that they were witches themselves, but that their mother had made them so." The artlessness and simplicity of their *confessions* render them not simply entertaining, but more instructive than almost any other statements made at the examinations and trials. Little Sarah was asked, —

"How long have you been a witch? *A.* Ever since I was six years old. How old are you now? *A.* Near eight years old; brother Richard says I shall be eight years old in November next.

"Who made you a witch? *A.* My mother; she made me set my hand to a book. How did you set your hand to it? *A.* I touched it with my fingers; and the book was red; the paper of it was white. She said she never had seen the black man . . . that her mother had baptized her, and the devil or black man was not there, as she saw. Her mother said, when she baptized her, ' Thou art mine for ever and ever. Amen.'

"How did you afflict folks? *A.* I pinched them. She said she went to those whom she afflicted — *went*, not in body, but in her spirit. She would not own that she had ever been at the witch-meeting at the Village."

The *confessions* (?) are beautiful and precious; they are robed in all the appropriate naivete of any school-girl's *confession* that herself was a — *pupil.* Not a tinge of shame, sorrow, or humiliation is visi-

ble anywhere about them.   Not a sign appears, that,
in little Sarah's comprehension, there was anything
more censurable, as in fact there was not, in her
being a witch, than there is in the child of to-day
being a Sunday school scholar.   Disclosure of common occurrences at her home, which inborn faculties
there as naturally brought into view, as other faculties there and elsewhere cause the limbs of childhood to expand and its intellect to unfold, constituted
her confession of the witchcraft that pertained to her
mother and herself.

The common mind, if not cautioned, will almost
perforce attach meanings to the testimonies of Martha
Carrier's children which never belonged to them.
The detailings of facts and experiences not rare in
that mediumistic family, were no confession of anything like what the public in any age has been
accustomed to designate by the term witchcraft.   In
biblical times the occurrences might have been called
prophecies — true or false — and to-day they would
be regarded as spirit manifestations, or near kindred
to such.

The little girl's *confessions* are *precious* as well as
beautiful; they are instructive comments upon the
creed held by the adults of her day; they give some
support to the position that compact with some spirit
was an element in preparation for working marvels.
Her mother baptized her, and made her virtually
sign a book, and then claimed her own child as hers
"for ever and ever, Amen."   The little child herself seems to have regarded this ratification of her
mother's spirit claims upon her spirit as having made
herself a witch; but such a witch as she was not

ashamed to be, and saw no harm in being. Indeed,
how can any other than perverted vision see harm
in the girl's filial compact? Her clairvoyant and
other mediumistic faculties had become so unfolded
when she was about six years old, that she and her
mother, as freed spirits, could, in conscious compan-
ionship, roam in spirit realms; and she, no doubt, felt
that forces emanating from the mother aided in her
unfoldment, and continued to have much sway over
her in her mental journeyings and operations. She
might with much propriety say that her mother
made her a witch. And her case shows that the
process for producing a witch might be much simpler
and much less horrifying than the public in her day
had any conception of. Indeed, witchification was
then, and now is, a growth or unfoldment from
God's plantings much more than a manufacture by
the devil's or any mother's hands. She saw no
devil, no black man — but only her own mother
was concerned in making her a witch; and the
mother probably made her a witch by processes as
natural and legitimate as those by which she had
previously made her a child.

The girl's power for afflicting was mental; her
journeyings and pinchings were mental; and yet,
no doubt, her grip was as sensibly felt by the nerves
of those whom she pinched as would have been firm
graspings of their flesh by her fingers of bones and
muscles. It is the spirit only which feels hurts of
the body, and a pinched spirit imprints the hurt
on the flesh it is animating. This little girl's statements confirm Tituba's, and give credibility to the
many declarations of the accusing girls that they

were pinched, bitten, and tortured by persons whose outer forms were remote from them at the time. We live amid mysteries which one by one are getting revealed as time rolls on.

An instructive instance of the warping force of these prevalent beliefs in shaping the diction of the most erudite describers of witchcraft facts, is found in Lawson's summary of events, where, when commenting upon testimony like that given by little Sarah, he says, " Several have *confessed* against their own mother, that they were instruments to bring them into *the devil's covenant.*" But the girl's testimony mentioned a covenant with her mother *alone*, saying that the devil was not there, as she saw. It was Lawson, and not the girl, who brought the devil into this case.

The same writer further says, " Some girls of eight or nine years of age did declare that after they were so betrayed by their mothers to the power of *Satan,* they saw *the devil* go in their *own shapes* to afflict others." But the statement of Sarah is, that she herself went forth and afflicted in her spirit-form, and not that the *devil* went in her shape. The cultured of that generation had *devil on the brain* so severely, that they persistently brought him in even where the facts as presented by the witnesses plainly excluded him.

Richard Carrier, eighteen years old, son of Thomas and Martha, was examined.

" Have you been in the devil's snare ? — Yes.

" Is your brother Andrew insnared by the devil's snare ? — Yes.

" How long has your brother been a witch? — Near a month.

" How long have you been a witch? — Not long.

" Have you joined in afflicting the afflicted persons? — Yes.

" You helped to hurt Timothy Swan, did you? —
Yes.

" How long have you been a witch? — About five
weeks.

" Who was in company when you covenanted with
the devil? — Mrs. Bradbury.

" Did she help you afflict? — Yes.

" Who was at the Village Meeting when you were
there? — Goodwife How, Goodwife Nurse, Goodwife
Wildes, Proctor and his wife, Mrs. Bradbury, and
Corey's wife.

" What did they do there? — Eat, and drank wine.

" Was there a minister there? — No, not as I
know of.

" From whence had you your wine? — From Salem,
I think it was.

" Goodwife Oliver there? — Yes; I knew her."

Statements by this witness, and also his probable
circumstances and condition, seem worthy of special
note. Frankness glows on all that he said. He was
stating facts, which, in his apprehension, were harmless, and why should he not let them out? He knew,
probably, that his mother had all through his life been
accustomed to see and act through other than her
physical organs, and was conscious that during the
last five weeks at least himself had been doing the
same. The abilities came unsought into action —
were outgrowths from the natures of his mother and
himself, and were not crimes. His long familiarity
with the ostensible workings of such powers through

his mother had shown him that they were neither diabolical nor censurable ; and why not admit possession
of them, and the acts they produced, whether through
himself, his mother, or any one else ? Neither the
mother nor children in that family were afraid of
ghostly beings, because able to confer with them intelligibly and sympathetically ; and the ready admission by Richard that he had aided in hurting Timothy
Swan, and been at a great witch-meeting, where they
ate, and also drank wine, was no confession of any
crime, but simple statement of facts. He was a medium, and also a frank and truthful witness.

He granted that he had been in the devil's snare.
How much did this import ? He and his brother Andrew both had been caught in it — one about four,
and the other five, weeks prior to his statement. As
certain atmospheric and other physical conditions
often produce epidemic or wide-spread physical health
or disease either, and certain public mental and moral
states often act powerfully upon many minds, the
great public excitement engendered by the arrest and
prosecution of witches may well be deemed adequate
to have unfolded latent mediumistic susceptibilities
very widely ; and it is not surprising that the children
of a Martha Carrier should have such susceptibilities
suddenly brought to their own cognizance, nor that
they should as suddenly become well-fledged clairvoyants competent to wing their way widely and rapidly in the airs of a world in which spirits dwell ; nor
that they should be psychologized by spirit beings,
and made to take part in any work, malignant or benevolent, which their controllers were bent upon executing. By being caught in the devil's snare, they

probably meant neither more nor less than that they became mediums. All conditions like theirs the public was charging the devil with producing, and the young Carriers assented to that being done in their own case. Most things not of the earth, earthy, were then charged to the devil; and the mental powers' of these children were not competent to show that their slippings out from their hampering bodies were effected without his aid.

Frequent mention occurs of witch-meetings at Salem Village, on the Green, or the minister's pasture, near Deacon Ingersoll's.

If any accused one had been seen in the company of assembled witches there, the fact was excessively damaging. Richard Carrier acknowledged having been there, and freely mentioned what persons were in the assemblage — but did not see a minister.

The records have not led us to suppose that Mrs. Carrier ever stood very high in public estimation. It is not improbable that influences from outside of her had often, during the forty years through which she had experienced them, made her life eccentric, and many of her actions mysterious. Even the aged and charitable Francis Dane said, "That there was a suspicion of goodwife Carrier among some of us before she was apprehended, I know; as for any other persons, I had no suspicion of them." We must infer from that statement that she was noted for some peculiarities which were not universally regarded with favor; suspicions hung around her.

She was accused by one of causing grievous sores in himself, of sickening his cattle, and working many injuries; by others also of hurting and bewitching

25

them, and of having attended a witch-meeting. The accusing girls, as seen above, were most excessively agonized when in court with her. She may justly be regarded, we think, as being socially among the lower class of persons then accused; and yet we have met with nothing which will justify an inference that she was altogether unworthy of esteem, or even that she was emphatically bad in any respect. Mather called her *rampant hag*, and hence much of Christendom has been influenced to contemplate her with aversion. But whatever may have been her character, the sufferings of herself and family draw forth our sympathies.

If she said she had been a witch forty years, she meant only that for "forty years" she had been conscious of the ongoing of occult processes within and around herself. We doubt whether she applied the word *witch* to herself, but can readily believe that she confessed to such experiences and performances as were in her day often called witchcrafts. That she detailed some experiences to Mary Walcott, which the latter termed witchcrafts, is highly probable. Neither the accused nor the accusers were accustomed to speak of seeing the devil; but it was the black man, or some other defined spirit, — not the devil, — according to their own statements. Yet when recorders and reporters undertook to give us either the substance of what was said, or a nearly verbatim report, they generally substituted devil for black man, or for any other unseen occult operator, whatever his, her, or its moral purpose or character. So, too, all specially marvelous works were called witchcrafts.

The little Carrier children were very instructive witnesses. Too young and inexperienced to do other-

wise than answer simple questions directly in such
language as was common, they show us of to-day, better than do older witnesses, what was probably common application of some terms of very frequent use
in descriptions of things marvelous. When by implication charged with being themselves witches, their
answers conceded the truth of the charge. One of
them, eight years old, said she had been a witch ever
since she was six. Another, eighteen years old, had
been a witch about five weeks, and said that brother
Andrew had been such " near a month." Little did
these frank and no doubt truthful young confessors
of family and personal experiences deem that they
were exposing themselves, and their mother also, to
punishment by death. What they confessed to were
frequent sights and sounds in their home, which came
as naturally and innocently before them as the visits
and ·words of friends and neighbors. Community
called such matters witchcrafts, and why should not
these children do the same ? Their mental powers
were not expanded enough to even entertain the
slightest apprehension that what they were saying
could imply that they had made a compact with the
devil, or that a simple, true statement of their unsought experiences could bring harm to themselves or
any one else. Equally incompetent were such little
ones to comprehend the nature of that devil who
existed in the conception of the magistrate when he
asked whether the devil had insnared the witness and
brother Andrew. They, no doubt, held the common
notion that any worker whatsoever from realms unseen by the external eye was the devil ; and having
had experience — at least one of them had — that her

own spirit had gone forth from her body and pinched certain persons, she understood that she had performed a part in works which were imputed to the devil. Still neither of these children confessed, or could be " insnared " to own, that they had seen *the devil.*

They, obviously, and their mother, we do not doubt, often as naturally and innocently beheld spirit forms and scenes, and just as innocently held converse with spirits, as they surveyed the scenes and forms of the outer world, or went in company with embodied people to their congregations in the meeting-house or elsewhere. The words of babes and sucklings, at a witchcraft trial, revealed the existence of finer natural laws and forces, and their operation also, upon and through some human beings, than science then dreamed of, or is yet quite ready to recognize. Very much in witchcraft times was charged to the devil which should have been credited to God. The erroneous entry of many heavy items on the great account-books, in the days of the fathers, calls for immense labor and study for their proper and equitable adjustment now. Martha Carrier and her children were probably posted on the wrong side of the moral Ledger when Cotton Mather labeled her " Rampant Hag ; " and there they have stood ever since.

REV. GEORGE BURROUGHS.

Having come to the last of the accused whose case our leading purpose induces us to notice at much length, we present here a specimen of indictment for the crime of witchcraft.

" THE INDICTMENT OF GEORGE BURROUGHS.

Essex ⎱   *Anno Regni Regis et Reginæ Willielmi et*
ss. ⎰   *Mariæ. Nunc Angliæ, &c., quarto.*

" The jurors of our sovereign lord and lady, the king and queen, *present* — That George Burroughs, late of Falmouth, in the province of Massachusetts Bay, in New England, clerk, the 9th day of May, in the fourth year of the reign of our sovereign lord and lady, William and Mary, by the grace of God, of England, Scotland, France and Ireland king and queen, defenders of the faith, &c., and divers other days and times, as well before as after, certain detestable arts, called witchcrafts and sorceries, wickedly and feloniously hath used, practiced, and exercised, at and within the township of Salem, in the county of Essex aforesaid, in, upon, and against one Mary Walcutt, of Salem Village, in the county of Essex, single woman ; by which said wicked arts the said Mary Walcutt, the 9th day of May, in the fourth year abovesaid, and divers other days and times, as well before as after, was and is tortured, afflicted, pined, consumed, wasted, and tormented, against the peace of our sovereign lord and lady, the king and queen, and against the form of the statute in that case made and provided.

" Witnesses :   MARY WALCOTT, SARAH VIBBER,
              MERCY LEWIS, ANN PUTNAM,
              ELIZ. HUBBARD.

" Indorsed by the grand jury, *Billa vera.*"

Three other similar indictments accompanied the above, for witchcrafts practiced by Burroughs upon Elizabeth Hubbard, Mercy Lewis, and Ann Putnam severally.

S. P. Fowler, in the edition of " Salem Witchcraft "
edited by him, says, on page 278, —

" The trial of Rev. Geo. Burroughs appears to have
attracted general notice from the circumstance of his
being a former clergyman in Salem Village, and supposed to be a leader amongst witches."

Fowler adds, that —

" Dr. Cotton Mather says he was not present at any
of the trials for witchcraft; how he could keep away
from that of Burroughs we cannot imagine.   His father, Dr. Increase Mather, informs us that he attended
this single trial, and says, ' Had I been one of George
Burroughs's judges, I could not have acquitted him,
for several persons did upon oath testify that they
saw him do such things as no man that had not a
devil to be his familiar could perform.'

" Burroughs was apprehended in Wells, in Maine ;
so say his children.   They also inform us that he was
buried by his friends, after the inhuman treatment of
his body from the hands of his executioners at Gallows
Hill, in Salem.

" He is represented as being a small, black-haired,
dark-complexioned man, of quick passions and great
strength.   His power of muscle, which discovered
itself early when Burroughs was a member of Cambridge College, and which we notice in the slight re-
butting evidence offered by his friends at his trial,
convinces us that he lifted the gun, and the barrel of
molasses, by the power of his own well-strung muscles, and not by any help from the devil, as was supposed by the Mathers, both father and son.   Alas,
that a man's own strong arm should prove his ruin ! "

We shall show shortly that this commentator here

overlooked an important point. Burroughs himself
made statement, in his own defense, that an Indian
stood by and lifted the gun; therefore the chief question is not whether Burroughs was himself strong
enough to lift it as alleged, but whether he told the
truth when he said that he had help. The chief question bears upon his veracity, not upon his strength.
The Mathers believed him on that point.

The allegations in the indictment were for witchcrafts invisibly practiced upon members of the famous
CIRCLE, and not for visible feats of strength. All the
girls testified to seeing and suffering from his apparition. Also some who confessed to having been *witches*
themselves (for some accused ones were over-per-
suaded to speak of their own clairvoyant observations
and experiences as witchcrafts, and therefore of themselves as witches), — some such testified thus, as
Mather says (p. 279, *Salem Witchcraft*), "He was accused by eight of the confessing witches as being head
actor at some of their hellish rendezvous, and who had
promise of being a king in Satan's kingdom now going
to be erected; he was accused by nine persons for
extraordinary liftings, . . . and for other things, . . .
until about thirty testimonies were brought in against
him."

Mather's account of the witchcraft at Salem was
drawn up at the request of William Phips, then governor of the province; and two prominent judges at
the trials indorsed it as follows: —

"The reverend and worthy author having, at the
direction of his Excellency the governor, so far obliged
the public as to give some account of the sufferings

brought upon the country by witchcrafts, and of the trials which have passed upon several executed for the same:

"Upon perusal thereof, *we find the matters of fact and evidence truly reported*, and a prospect given of the methods of conviction used in the proceedings of the court at Salem.

WILLIAM STOUGHTON,

SAMUEL SEWALL."

"Boston, Oct. 11, 1692.

Manifestation of one class of phenomena presented at those trials has not been noticed in the preceding pages; viz., the appearance of the spirits of particular departed ones to many of the accusing girls. It is obviously true that those clairvoyants were very much oftener beholders of the spirits of those still dwelling in mortal forms than of those who had escaped from thralldom to the flesh. Still there were then some cases in which the spirits of some who had been known in that vicinity, and whose bodies were moldering beneath its soil, were both seen and heard. Among others, two former wives of Burroughs were named. Mather says (p. 282), " Several of the bewitched had given in their testimony that they had been troubled with the apparitions of two women, who said they were G. B.'s two wives; and that he had been the death of them. . . . Now, G. B. had been infamous for the barbarous usage of his two successive wives, all the country over. (p. 286.) . . . 'Twas testified, that, keeping his two successive wives in *a strange kind of slavery*, he would, when he came home from abroad, pretend to tell the talk which any had with them; that he has brought them to the point of death

by his harsh dealings with his wives, and then made
people promise that, in case death should happen, they
would say nothing of it; that he used all means to
make his wives write, sign, seal, and swear to a covenant *never to reveal any of his secrets;* that his wives
had privately complained unto the neighbors about
frightly apparitions of evil spirits, with which their
house was sometimes infested," &c.

Some of these allegations probably rested on firmer
bases of facts than have generally been perceived.
Though we regard Burroughs as having been one of
the kindest and best of men, we do not entirely withhold credence from the general import of such allegations regarding him. They point both to extraordinary
unfoldments within him, and to probable handlings
and control of his outer form at times by some intelligence not his own. "*Strange kind of slavery*" would
naturally result, in those days, from a husband's telling
his wife, on returning to his home, what conversation
she had held with others during his absence, *if his
statements were true;* but if not true, the wife would
only laugh at his pretensions, and make no complaints
to neighbors. If both true and oft repeated, such
mysterious utterances might well enslave, worry, and
bring close to death's door a sensitive wife; and the
husband, however affectionate and kind, may at times
have been as powerless to shape his course of procedure as is the dried leaf when whirled onward by
strong autumnal breezes. Acts not his own the world
would hold him responsible for; and no wonder that,
in his age, a spiritualistically unfolded, an illumined
man, and one also whose form might be moved, as was
that of Agassiz, by will not his own, should strive in

all possible ways to prevent wives, and any other
people who knew them, from revealing any of his
peculiar and marvelous *secrets;* no wonder that he
sought to make his wives "write, sign, seal, and
swear" never to do it; because the noising abroad of
such powers as he possessed, and such performances
as were attendant upon him, if publicly known, would
be profaned, would destroy his usefulness, and endanger, if not take, his life. Thanks that, in our day,
danger of a hangman's rope does not threaten one because of his high spiritual illumination.

George Burroughs was graduated at Harvard College in 1670; had been a preacher for many years
prior to 1692, and, during some of them, ministered
to the people at Salem Village. But before the outburst of witchcraft there, he had found a home far off
to the north-east, on the shores of Casco Bay, in the
Province of Maine, where he was then humbly and
quietly laboring in his profession, but not in impene-
trable seclusion. Clairvoyants are masters of both
seclusion and space to a marvelous extent. Throughout a region far, far around, wherever the special light
pertaining to the mediumistic or illuminated condition
revealed its possessor and put forth its attractions,
there the opened inner vision of the accusing girls
might make them practically present. Emanations
from one residing at Falmouth or at Wells might readily meet and blend with those from sensitives at their
home in Salem. Thought flies fast and far. With
equal speed, and quite as far, can the unswathed inner
perceptives of an entranced or illumined mortal be
attracted. Old memories and undissolved psychological attachments may have operated in this case. One

of the accusing girls had lived for a time in the family
of Burroughs while he resided at the Village. Chains
of association are never broken and rendered forever
unusable, though they often become exceedingly at-
tenuated, and cease to retain recognition in our ordinary conditions. Several of the accusing girls alleged
that Burroughs was one, and a leading and authoritative one, in the band of apparitional beings from whom
their torments came. He was "cried out upon," arrested, tried, condemned, and executed.

The opinions of different writers as to the real character and worth of this man have been very diverse.
While some have accounted him an hypocritical wizard, others have deemed him a man of beautiful and
beneficent life. Mather regarded him with aversion,
and says, "Glad should I have been if I had never
known the name of this man." Afterward the same
author charged Burroughs with "tergiversations, con-
tradictions, and falsehoods." Sullivan, in his History
of Maine, says, that "he was a man of bad character,
and of a cruel disposition." Hutchinson asserted, on
insufficient grounds, that when under examination,
"he was confounded, and used many twistings and
turnings." But Fowler says, "All the weight of
character enlisted against him fails to counteract the
favorable impression made by his Christian conduct
during his imprisonment and at the time of his execution." Calef says, that, the day before execution,
Margaret Jacobs, who had testified against him, came
to the prisoner, acknowledging that she had belied
him, and asking his forgiveness; "who not only for-
gave her, but also *prayed with and for her*." The
same adducer of "*Facts*" states that, "when upon

the ladder, he made a speech for the clearing of his
innocency, with such solemn and serious expressions
as were to the admiration of all present; his prayer
(which he concluded by repeating the Lord's prayer)
was so well worded, and uttered with such composed-
ness and such (at least seeming) fervency of spirit, as
was very affecting, and drew tears from many, so that
it seemed to some that the spectators would hinder
the execution. *The accusers said the black man stood
and dictated to him.* As soon as he was turned off,
Mr. Cotton Mather, being mounted upon a horse, addressed himself to the people, partly to declare that
he (Burroughs) was no ordained minister, and partly
to possess the people of his guilt, saying that the devil
has often been transformed into an angel of light;
and this somewhat appeased the people, and the executions went on." His prayers, and his whole deportment and spirit during these last trying scenes, indicate his possession of a calm, strong soul, which bore
him, on the wings of innocence and piety, into a
region of serenity which his traducers and murderers
were unfited to enter and knew not of. The brief
account which Upham's researches enabled him to
furnish of this man's life prior to the witchcraft mania
presents still further evidences of his sterling worth.
That author says, "Papers on file in the State House
prove that in the District of Maine, where he lived
and preached before and after his settlement at the
Village, he was regarded with confidence by his neighbors, and looked up to as a friend and counselor. . . .
He was self-denying, generous, and public-spirited,
laboring in humility and with zeal in the midst of
great privations." Land had been granted to him,

and when the town asked him to exchange a part of it for other lands, " he freely gave it back, not desiring any land anywhere else, nor anything else in consideration thereof."

Scanning Burroughs as well as accessible knowledge of him now permits, we judge that he was a quiet, peaceful, persistent laborer for the good of his fellow-men, — a humble, trustful, sincere servant of God, — a rare embodiment of the prevailing perceptions, sentiments, virtues, and graces which haloed the form of the Nazarene.

Why did the people of his time take his life? What were the accusations against him? In addition to the testimony that he was felt by many of the girls as a tormenting specter, he was accused of putting forth superhuman physical strength. Cotton Mather says, —

" He was a very puny man, yet he had often done things beyond the strength of a giant. A gun of about seven feet barrel, and so heavy that strong men could not steadily hold it out with both hands, there were several testimonies given in by persons of credit and honor, that he made nothing of taking up such a gun behind the lock with one hand, and holding it out like a pistol, at arm's end. In his vindication he was *foolish enough to say that an Indian was there, and held it out at the same time ;* whereas, none of the spectators ever saw any such Indian ; but they *supposed* the black man (as the witches call the devil, and they generally say he resembles an Indian) might have given him that assistance."

That paragraph is very instructive. All subsequent historians, beginning back with Calef, have ·

mentioned, what is no doubt true, that Burroughs
was a small man, and yet was constitutionally very
strong — was remarkable for physical powers even in
his college days ; and they have fancied that on that
ground they have satisfactorily accounted for his marvelous exploits ; they seemingly overlook the fact that
it was Burroughs himself, and not other people, who
said that "an Indian," invisible to others, stood
by and held the gun out. Historians have explained
the good and true man's seeming physical feats at
the .expense of his *veracity*. Heaven help the innocent when in the hands of such traducing commentators. The question is not what Burroughs
could have done unaided, but it is whether *he told
truth* when he said an Indian helped him. His
whole character and life argue that he would not
have spoken as he is alleged to have done, unless
he had been conscious of the presence of an Indian
within or by himself, putting forth, in part at least,
the strength which raised and supported that heavy
gun. He said that such was the fact. What though
all spectators failed to see the Indian ? It was a
disembodied Indian — a spirit Indian — and therefore necessarily invisible by external eyes. The
non-perception of him by other men standing by
is no evidence that the spirit Indian was not there ;
for spiritual beings are discernible by the inner or
spirit optics alone, and not by the outer ; so taught
Paul.

The fact that bystanders supposed the devil helped
Burroughs, or performed the lifting feat through him,
implies that they, as well as he, believed that something more was done than mere human strength

accomplished. In the present day, when spirits are very often putting forth strength through forms of flesh which executes performances quite as marvelous as any which were alleged to have been enacted through Burroughs, his assertion that a foreign, hidden intelligence worked within and through his form, conjoined with the belief of beholders that some spiritual being was operating therein, any array of facts now, proving, even to perfect demonstration, that the little man was enormously strong, though it may indicate that he did not require foreign aid to lift and hold out the gun, does nothing toward impeaching his own veracity when he said he had help. Surely one *can* have help in the performance of what he could do alone. If any man says he had help in a particular case, his ability to have performed the special feat alone affords no indication that his statement is untrue ; and yet the spirit of witchcraft history implies that it does.

Prove Burroughs to have been constitutionally as strong as the strongest mortal that ever lived, — yes, as strong as the strongest of all created beings, — ay, as strong as the Omnipotent One himself, and even then you have done nothing which shows or tends to show that another intelligent worker may not have co-operated with him in the performance of marvelous feats. We say again that the question raised by his statement is not whether he, in and of himself, was competent to his seeming feats, but it is whether an Indian spirit did or did not help him. Burroughs says he had help from such a one. Bystanders supposed that the devil helped him ; but he who sensed the helper's presence called him

an Indian; and he was a much more trustworthy
testifier as to that helper's proper classification in
the scale of being, than a combined world of men
devoid of spirit-vision, putting forth only their inferences regarding an unseen personage. Imputation
of this man's liftings to his constitutional strength
solely is an imputation of false testimony to the
truthful man himself, and historic arguments, if
valid, make him a liar.

Who helped the little clergyman lift and hold the
heavy gun? He says it was "an Indian." But
Mather says, "none of the spectators ever saw any
such Indian; but they *supposed the black man* (as
the witches call the *devil*, and they generally say
he *resembles an Indian*) might have given him that
assistance." That sentence illumines many a dark
spot in our ancient witchcraft. The witches, or
clairvoyants, whether accusers or accused, were not
accustomed to speak of seeing *the devil*. It is fairly
questionable whether any one among them ever
spoke of seeing *the devil*, or of having any interview with *him*, or knowledge of *him* obtained by
personal observation. It was *man* whom they saw.
They spoke of the black *man*. Mather says that
was their name for *the devil*. We doubt it. What
they saw failed to present a semblance of Cloven-
foot, with horns, tail, and hoofs, and did not suggest
to them an idea of *the devil*. The substitution of
devil for black man, or the regarding the two as
synonymous, was Mather's work, and not that of
the clairvoyants. And who was *the black man?*
Mather informs us that those whose optics could
see him "generally say he *resembles an Indian*."

If he resembled an Indian, is not the inference very fair that he was an Indian? Yes. "Black man" obviously was applied by clairvoyants to designate any Indian spirit, and spirits of human beings probably were the only spirits whom their inner vision ever beheld. Thanks to you, Mather, for recording that explanatory sentence. The devil you fought against was your brother man — was earth-born — and when seen and conferred with not very formidable. Your clairvoyants, or witches, saw and heard occult men, women, children, beasts, and birds, but never spoke of seeing your ecclesiastical devil. The human beings whom they beheld varied in size from little children to tall men, and in complexion from black to white — even up to glorious brightness. Your informants never used the word *devil* in their descriptions. You misreported them, as Cheever did Tituba; Calef followed your lead, and subsequent historians have copied from both you and him.

You also state that Burroughs was "*foolish* enough to say that an Indian" helped him. Was it foolish in him to state the truth? Your own witnesses en masse say his helper *resembled* an Indian — he said the assistant *was* an Indian. Why didn't you take the words of your own witnesses as corroborative of the man's statement? They surely were so, and they give us a true presentation of the case. The reason of your course is obvious; the creed of your times deemed any spirit visitant or helper to be the devil himself.

A subsequent charge against "G. B." (George Burroughs) was, that "when they" (the accusing

26

girls) "cried out of G. B. biting them, the print
of his teeth would be seen on the flesh of the com-
plainers; and just such a set of teeth as G. B.'s
would then appear upon them." As in the case
of little Dorcas Good, here we have it charged
that indentations on the flesh of complainants cor-
responded to the size and shape of the teeth belonging to the person who was accused of biting. If
G. B.'s spirit-form or apparition was made to approach and bite the accusers, — and it probably was,
— his spirit-teeth would naturally, and, as we apprehend, necessarily have the exact size and form of his
external ones.

Another charge is embraced in the following quotation: —

"His wives" (he had buried two) "had privately
complained unto the neighbors about frightly apparitions of evil spirits with which their house was
sometimes infested; and many such things had been
whispered among the neighborhood."

We have previously quoted but did not comment
upon the above which relates to the appearance of
apparitions. That statement may as well indicate
that the wives themselves, or any other persons resident in his house, were the attracting or helping instrumentalities for producing the "frightly" sights, as
that Burroughs himself was, provided only that some
one or more of them were mediumistic. But the probabilities are, that the elements emanated from him
which rendered such presentations practicable.

His telling the purport of talks held in the house
during his absence indicates that his inner ears were
opened to catch either the spirit of mundane sounds,

or sounds made by spirits, as could those of Margaret Jones, Ann Hibbins, Joan of Arc, and many others. The same power in him is indicated in the following extract : —

"One Mr. Ruck, brother-in-law to this G. B., testified that G. B., and he himself, and his sister, G. B.'s wife, going out for two or three miles to gather strawberries, Ruck, with his sister, the wife of G. B., rode home very softly " (slowly) " with G. B. on foot in their company. G. B. stepped aside a little into the bushes. Whereupon they halted and hollowed for him. He not answering, they went homewards with a quickened pace without any expectation of seeing him in a considerable while. And yet, when they were got near home, to their astonishment they found him on foot with them, having a basket of strawberries. (Philip was found at Azotus.) G. B. immediately then fell to chiding his wife on account of what she had been speaking to her brother of him on the road. Which when they wondered at, he said he *knew their thoughts*. Ruck, being startled at that, made some reply, intimating that the devil himself did not know so far ; but G. B. answered, My God makes known your thoughts unto me."

True and luminous fact ! The humble, pious, intelligent, illumined Burroughs, far-looker into the realm of causes — an observer of things behind the vail which bounds the reach of mortal senses and pure reason — stated that *God* — not the devil — made known to him the thoughts of other and absent people. In other words, his intended meaning probably was, that God's worlds and laws provide for legitimate inflowings, to some minds, of knowledge of the thoughts and purposes of other minds, even though far distant in space. The character, or rather the actual qualities of this man, if we read him correctly, were truthfulness, humility, and piety. When such a one deliberately said to a brother-in-law, under such circumstances as stated above, "*My God makes known your thoughts unto me*," he indicated his consciousness of possessing self-experienced knowledge of the existence of an instructive and momentous fact pertaining to human capabilities. Only few persons, relatively, have had proof by personal experience of the extent to which the inner perceptives of embodied mortals may reach forth and imbibe knowledge by processes common to freed spirits, and in the realms of their abode. What the unfoldings of Burroughs permitted him to do and know is possible with many others while resident in mortal forms. If he could, some others may, come into that condition in which thought itself shall be heard speaking itself out to them, in which they shall be listeners to "*cogitatio loquens*" — self-speaking thought — which Swedenborg says abounds in spirit spheres; in which thought from supernal fonts shall make itself known to the consciousness of an embodied man, and become matter of knowledge with him. Others, and more in number, may have the inner ear opened and hear the words of spirits.

With ears competently attuned, the meek and truth-loving Burroughs was occasionally able to receive not only knowledge of the thoughts of mortals in ways unusual, but also, as we judge, to receive spiritual truths copiously from purer fountains than his cotemporaries generally could get access to ; and he thence obtained such truths as relaxed in him many credal bonds which firmly held most of his cotemporary preachers to the creeds forms, ordinances, and customs common in the churches then. Many questions put to him at his trial were, obviously, designed to draw forth evidence of his lax regard for and inattention to the accepted ordinances of religion. He admitted both that it was long since he had sat at the communion table, and that some of his own children had not been baptized. We presume that he was inwardly, wisely, and beneficently prompted to walk somewhat astray from the narrow and soul-cramping paths then trod by most New England clergymen. The spirit of the Lord was giving him more liberty than most of his cotemporaries felt privileged to exercise. Using his greater facilities than theirs for instruction in heavenly things, he probably advanced far beyond his brethren generally in sinking the *letter*, that is, sinking the forms, and ceremonies, and ordinances of religion beneath its divine spirit, and his less illumined brethren suspected him of an abandonment of religion itself, and of alliance with the great enemy of all goodness. Some among them apparently looked upon him as a combined heretic and wizard, withheld all sympathy from, and exulted over the doom of, this double culprit.

But this victim may have been, and probably was, as high above most of his crucifiers as freedom is above bondage, as the spirit above the letter, as light above darkness, as sincerity above hypocrisy. The blood of such as Martha Corey, Rebecca Nurse,

Mary Easty, GEORGE BURROUGHS, and probably
many others who in company with these took their
exit from life shrouded in witchcraft's blackening
mists, may go far toward making Gallows Hill a
Mount Calvary — a spot on which zeal urged on the
worse to crucify their betters in true godliness —
betters in all that fits immortal souls for gladdening
welcome into realms above.

SUMMARY.

1648. MARGARET JONES manifested startling efficacy of hands and medicines, consternating keenness
of perceptives, predictions subsequently verified, and
the presence of a vanishing child. Such was her
witchcraft; and for this she was executed.

1656. ANN HIBBINS comprehended conversation
between persons too distant from her to be heard normally, . . . and was hanged.

1662. ANN COLE had her form possessed and
spoken through by either the devil or other disembodied ones, and by them made both to express
thoughts that never were in her mind, and to further
the conviction and execution of the Greensmiths.

1671-2. ELIZABETH KNAP'S external form was
strangely convulsed and agonized by an old man, and
also spoken through by one who called himself a
pretty black boy.

1680. WILLIAM MORSE, in his home, where lived
his good wife, who had been called a witch, saw pots,
andirons, tools, and household furniture generally,
seem to take on wills of their own, and rudely play
many a lively gymnastic game.

1688. John Goodwin saw four of his children subjected and tortured immediately subsequent to the scolding of one of them by a wild Irish woman; and the same one afterward was made to play the deuce in Cotton Mather's own house. Mrs. Glover was hanged for bewitching; and also she *continued to torture the same children after her spirit had left its outer form.*

The above cases occurred prior to the holding of " The Circle " at Salem, before the establishment of a school at which the arts of " necromancy, magic, and spiritualism " might be learned. Generally the performers named thus far had no visible confederates. If sole actors, their geniuses were vast, and the fonts of malice or of benevolence in some of them were both very capacious and copiously overflowing.

1692. Tituba, the slave, avowed having been forced by something like a man, and his four female spectral aids, to pinch the two little girls in her master's family at the very time when they were first mysteriously afflicted. She furnished strong evidence that a tall man with white hair and serge coat, invisibly to others, frequently visited her, compelled her aid, and kindled and long kept adding fuel to the fires of witchcraft at Salem Village. For this she was imprisoned thirteen months, and then sold to pay her jail fees.

Sarah Good was seen as a specter, was accused of hurting by occult organs and processes; became invisible by those standing guard over her; announced to the magistrates the great explanatory fact that none but the accusers and the accused, that is, none but clairvoyants, could see the actual inflictors of the pains endured. Also she fore-sensed a fact that occurred when Mr. Noyes died in an after year. She was hanged.

DORCAS GOOD, not five years old, was big enough to have her specter seen, to have her spirit-teeth bite, and also to see clairvoyantly. The little witch was sent to jail.

SARAH OSBURN was sighted by the inner optics of the accused, and she heard voices from out the unseen. This feeble one was sent to jail, and soon died there.

MARTHA COREY was charged with afflicting; also she avowed heresy pertaining to witchcraft. Though interiorly illumined far beyond her accusers and judges, and enabled to smile amid their frowns, she was executed.

GILES COREY, seen as a specter, and accused of harming many, would make no plea to his indictment. Pressure, applied for forcing out a plea, extorted only his call for "More weight, more weight," — and his life went out.

REBECCA NURSE, venerable matron, daughter of a mother who had been called a witch, and conscious of personal liability to then prevalent fits, was seen by, and accused of hurting, members of The Circle. Therefore she must be hanged — though jury first acquitted, and then, under rebuke, called her guilty; and though governor pardoned, and then revoked his clement act. Fealty to witchcraft creed in that case triumphed, though nearly defeated twice.

MARY EASTY, noble woman, sister of the above, and daughter of the same witch-blooded mother, once arrested and discharged, and then re-arrested, because seen by inner eyes and accused of bewitching, rose sublimely above thoughts of self and dread of death, and appealed to the magistrates, in clear, strong, and forceful language, to change their course of procedure, to spare the innocent, and become wisely humane.

SUSANNA MARTIN, spectrally seen, and a reputed witch during more than a score of years, bravely faced the dangers besetting an accused one, was self-possessed before the magistrates, was spicy, shrewd, and keen in her answers to their questions, but failed to descend to confession, and died on Gallows Hill.

MARTHA CARRIER, having been a clear seer for forty years, and long visible by others similarly unfolded, was brave, self-possessed, and ready with pointed retort. Because hard to subdue, accusations came thick and heavy upon her from "The Circle" almost *en masse*, and she too was doomed to mount the ladder.

SARAH CARRIER, daughter of the above, eight years old, stated instructive facts in her experience as a clairvoyant, and notably said that her own *spirit* could go forth to others and hurt them; also that her mother's was the only spirit with which she entered into the compact that made her a witch.

REV. GEORGE BURROUGHS, sometimes supernally strong physically, because, as himself asserted, an Indian, invisible by others, helped him; able, by God's help as he claimed, to read his brother's thoughts; a freer and less formal religionist than most clergymen of his day, because of his high spiritual illumination; a humble but beneficent Christian — was, like his exemplar, made to yield up life at the call of such as cried, "Crucify him! crucify him!" If he was luminous, and spoke like an angel of light in the hour of his departure, he was not Satan transformed, but George Burroughs unvailing his genuine self.

1693. MARGARET RULE, the first of afflicted ones
noticed in our pages, endured her strange experiences
last. The evening before her fits came on she had
been bitterly treated and threatened by an old woman
whose curings of hurts had put her under suspicions
of witchcrafts. Margaret was not a graduate from
the Salem school, but was self-taught, if taught at all;
and yet she saw many specters — saw, in the night, a
young man in danger of drowning who was miles
away from her; was lifted from her bed to the ceiling
above in horizontal position by invisible beings; fasted
nine days without pining; and saw and heard one
bright and glorious visitant who comforted and heart-
ened her much. She, under the special watch and
care of Cotton Mather, was held back, mainly perhaps
by his advice, from any divulgences which should
endanger the lives of others. No blood was shed
because of her afflictions.

Twenty persons were put to death in Essex County,
by the direct action of government officials, between
June 9 and September 23, 1692. Nearly or quite two
hundred were accused, arrested, imprisoned, and many
more than the executed twenty were convicted. Numerous arrested ones perished under the hardships of
prison life and gnawings of mental anxieties. Others
had health, spirits, domestic ties, and worldly possessions shattered to pieces, and the condition of their
subsequent lives made most forlorn and wretched.
Neither tongue nor pen can possibly tell their tale in
its fullness of horrors. Most excessively frenzying
and woeful must have been the privations, sufferings,
heart-wrenchings, agonies of nearly all the scattered
residents of the then wooded region at and round

about Salem Village, when Christendom's mighty and malignant witchcraft devil was believed to be prowling and fiercely slaughtering in their midst. No blood, nor any other mark, on the door-posts would effectually warn the fell destroyer to pass by and leave the occupants within unscathed. Mysterious and fearful dangers flocked above, below, around, before, and behind : they lurked here, there, and everywhere continually, so that none could ever be at ease.

And now we ask, whether common sense admits that such credulity and infatuation ever pervaded any hardy, energetic, and intelligent community, in any county of Massachusetts or New England, in any age, as that girls and old women, aided by a very few insignificant men, however bright, cunning, roguish, playful, self-conceited, greedy of notice, or resentful and malicious the leaders might be, could possibly so perform as to induce Rev. Mr. Whiting, Samuel Willard, William Morse, Cotton Mather, Deodat Lawson, Samuel Parris, Rev. Mr. Hale, and scores upon scores of other intelligent, sagacious, and leading men, to present to the public, in writing, such narratives as they did, and to essentially vouch for their own belief in the positive occurrence of such "amazing feats" as they described ? We ask also, whether such frail enactors as a band of mere girls and a few women must have been, could possibly devise and manifest such tricks, and put forth such accusations, from any motives whatsoever, as would cause the leading minds throughout a large section of the state to regard the accused ones as allies of beings rising up from regions of darkness, and making malignant and most baneful onslaught upon the children of God and

Christ, and upon the families and possessions of men, in such numbers and with such force, that the civil power of the land was urged and helped to put the gallows in use upon every one whose specter was said to be seen and to torment? The amazing feats are well attested. The more amazing deviltries both of the accusers and of courts and executives, no one can doubt, if all the feats were offspring of mere juvenile and senile cunning, fraud, and malice.

In the cases of Margaret Jones, Ann Cole, Elizabeth Knap, John Stiles, and Martha Goodwin each, there is distinct mention of the presence, the speech, or the action of some spirit. We found Tituba distinctly stating that she saw, heard, and was made to help a nocturnal visitant whose doings indicate that he was the originator of the vast Salem Tragedy: that visitant was a spirit. Mr. Burroughs said, in explanation of his feats of strength, that an Indian, invisible by others, was his helper. Margaret Rule, as had Mercy Lewis the year before, saw, and each was infilled with bliss by, a most glorious bright spirit. In our own day, in every city, town, and hamlet of our land, as well as on the opposite shore of the Atlantic, spirits are widely recognized as the authors of performances alike strange and amazing in themselves, as those described in the seventeenth century, which are there called witchcrafts. The primitive records of American witchcrafts show that portions of it, and especially that Salem witchcraft feats, were devised in supermundane brains, and enacted under their supervision.

THE CONFESSORS.

WHEN persons arraigned for specific offences plead guilty, their pleas generally are deemed conclusive evidence that the accused have performed the special deeds set forth in the allegations. Many of the accused in witchcraft times made statements which have ever since been called *confessions*. Inference from that has long been general and wide-spread, that nearly such witchcraft as the creed of our fathers specified had positive manifestation in their day. But we seriously doubt whether any record of statements made by an accused one exhibits distinct admission that he or she had entered into covenant with that devil which one must have been in league with to become such a witch or wizard as the laws against witchcraft were intended to arrest. Such confessions as were recorded may have been true in the main, but they fall short of confessions of the special crime alleged; they amount to little, if anything, more than admissions and statements that the confessors had seen, been influenced by, and had acted in company with apparitions or spirits all of whom were of earthly origin, and were members of the *human* family; they confessed only to being, or to having been at times, clairvoyants. The circumstances under which even such confessions were generally made, need to be carefully viewed before just estimate can be placed upon the worth and significance of the recorded statements.

Hutchinson supposed that "those who were condemned and not executed, all confessed their guilt," . . . and that "the most effectual way to prevent an accusation" (of one's self) "was to become an accuser." Strange — strange — and yet obviously true. An accused one, then, could look for escape from death — the legal penalty of witchcraft — only by pleading guilty to the charge. Confession of guilt, and nothing else, then, purchased exemption from capital punishment. This becoming obvious, all natural instincts for preservation of one's life, and all possible entreaties, urgings, and commands of friends and relatives, forcibly tended to extort confession even from the innocent. Husband or wife, children, parents, brothers, sisters, and trusted advisers, often all conspired in urging an accused one to plead guilty — yes, even a condemned one, for that plea was as efficacious after conviction and sentence as before. It is said that many did confess. Confessed to what? Never to having made a covenant with the great witchcraft devil nor any formidable imp of his, but generally to clairvoyant visions, to mental meetings with the specters of friends, neighbors, and other embodied mortals, and to some compacts and co-operative labors with such personages, — *never with the devil.* They did not confess to witchcraft itself *as then defined.* The clear-headed Mary Easty besought the magistrates " to try some of the confessing witches, I being confident there is several of them has belied themselves and others." Her clear and calm brain perceived the broad distinction existing between clairvoyance, and witchcraft. So, too, did Martha and Giles Corey, Jacobs, Proctor, Susanna Martin, George Burroughs, and others; these, and such as these, did not confess, while many weaker and more ignorant ones did.

Little Sarah Carrier, only eight years old, whose testimony we adduced in part, when presenting the case of her mother, throws much light upon some *confessions* of that day. *Simon Willard,* who wrote out and attested to " the substance " of her statements, heads his record, " Sarah Carrier's *Confession,* August 11th." The girl's confession? No; it was simply a frank statement of facts in her own experience, which lets us know that when she was about six years old her own mother made her a witch, and baptized her. But " the devil, or black man, was not there, as she saw," when she was made a witch. She afflicted folks by pinching them; went to those whom she afflicted; but went only " *in her spirit.*" Her mother was the only devil who bewitched her, and the only being whom her baptism bound her to serve. Such was her witchcraft. That plain statement is refreshing and valuable. It shows that when about six years old this mediumistic girl had become so developed that her spirit could commune with her mother's, independently of their bodies. She then became a conscious clairvoyant, and could trace felt influences, issuing from her mother, back to their source. Thenceforth mother and daughter could conjointly place themselves on the green at Salem Village, ten miles off, or in any pasture or any house whither thought might lead them. The mother's stronger mind had but to wish,

and the child must go with her and do her bidding; and when
the two were in rapport, any stronger spirit controlling the mother
could make the child co-operative in pinchings or any other inflictions of pains. Because the little girl had set her hand to a red
book presented by her own mother, and thus, by implication, bound
herself to be obedient to that mother, her statement of the fact
was labeled *a confession* of witchcraft, and deemed damaging to
her mother. Three or four other children of Mrs. Carrier were
able to sense spirit scenes. Her home was a domestic school of
prophets, and her own children were apt pupils in it. Her moral
character and influence do not here concern us.

Abigail Faulkner was condemned, and two of her children,
"Dorothy ten, and Abigail eight years old, testified that their
mother appeared and made them witches." That mother was
daughter of Rev. Francis Dane of Andover, some of whose
other children and grandchildren were accused, which suggests,
though it fails·to prove, that much medianimic susceptibility was
imparted through either him or his wife, or both, to their offspring.
His descendants attracted the notice of clairvoyants. Hutchinson
states that Mr. Dane himself "is *tenderly* touched in several of
the examinations, which " (the tenderness?) "might be owing to a
fair character; and he may be one of the persons accused who "
(the accusation of whom) "caused a discouragement to further
prosecutions.". "He," being then "near fourscore, seems to
have been in danger." Internal luminosity and copious radiations
from their interior forms probably rendered Rev. Mr. Dane, Rev.
Samuel Willard, Mrs. Hale, wife of the minister at Beverly, Mrs.
Phips, wife of the governor, and many others of high character
or standing, visible by mediumistic optics, and presentible apparitionally where spirits were wont to congregate, consult and
manipulate instruments for acting out — not for learning — the
" wonders of necromancy, magic, and Spiritualism."

Witch meetings, as they were called, or congregated spirits or
apparitions on the green, or in the pasture of the minister at
Salem Village, are mentioned more frequently and with more
particularity and concordant specifications, than would naturally
be looked for if they had no basis on fact. That spirits in vast
crowds have more than once been seen in modern times by a seer
looking up from High Rock in Lynn, can be learned by perusal

of A. J. Davis's visions there. But he was the observer of departed
ones only, while the apparent personages at witch meetings of old
were partly either the spirits of embodied persons or their apparitions. The fact of apparitions being present thereat in those
days proved the persons themselves apparitionally seen to be
the devil's allies. Some confessors of witchcraft intended to
verify the truth of their statements by describing whom they had
seen, and what they had observed at such meetings. And it is
not without interest that some people now read confessions like
the following from Ann Foster of Andover, viz.: " That she was
at the meeting of the witches at Salem Village when about twenty-
five were present ; that Goody Carrier came and told her of the
meeting and would have her go, and so they got upon sticks and
went the said journey, and being there did see Mr. Burroughs the
minister, who spake to them all ; . . . that they were presently at
the Village," when they rode on the " stick or pole " ; and that she
heard some of the witches say that there were three hundred and five
in the whole country, and that they would ruin that place — the
Village. Also that there was present at that meeting two men
besides Mr. Burroughs, the minister, and *one of them had gray
hair.*

Not without interest are such things read, because they prompt
to fancyings of things possible in an unseen sphere which hangs
over and enfolds all mortals. Could Ann Foster's gray-haired
man have been Tituba's white-haired visitant — the originator
and enactor of Salem witchcraft? Who knows? Could not he
and such as he have searched out and numbered many persons
in the land who were adapted to be facile instruments for his
use, and found three hundred and five in all? Had not his will
power to call instantly together, that is, to arrest and concentrate
the attention of as many of them as were at the moment impressible by him, either directly or through other plastic mortals,
from any part of the region between the Penobscot and the Hudson, or even further, and thus collect a band, that is, arrest and fix
the attention, of twenty-five of them, more or less, to whom inklings of his plans for the future might be given, and whose relative
rank, efficiency, or importance could be foreshadowed? Through
either unconscious apparitions or conscious spirits of mortals,
or of both classes commingled, might he not enact scenes

which it pleased him to have certain witnesses behold, and to proclaim, so far as he judged best, his purposes, his doctrines, or aught else it should be his pleasure to divulge or enforce? Possibly. Those witch meetings may have been much more than mere fictions.

We will look now at other and quite different confessions, or rather at what reputed confessors afterward said in explanation and defense of their own admissions. Six well-esteemed women of Andover conjointly subscribed to the following account : —

"We were all seized, as prisoners, by a warrant from the justice of the peace, and forthwith carried to Salem. And, by reason of that sudden surprisal, we, knowing ourselves innocent of the crime, were all exceedingly astonished and amazed, and consternated and affrighted even out of our reason. And our nearest and dearest relations, seeing us in that dreadful condition, and knowing our great danger, apprehended there was no other way to save our lives, as the case was then circumstanced, but by our confessing ourselves to be such and such persons as the afflicted represented us to be : they " (our friends), " out of tenderness and pity, persuaded us to confess what we did confess. And indeed that confession, that it is said we made, was no other than what was suggested to us by gentlemen, they telling us that we were witches, and they knew it and we knew it, which made us think that it was so ; and our understandings, our reason, our faculties almost gone, we were not capable of judging of our condition ; as also the hard measures they took with us rendered us incapable of making our defense ; but said anything and everything which they desired, and most of what we said was but, in effect, a consenting to what they said. Some time after, when we were better composed, they telling us what we had confesssed, we did profess that we were innocent and ignorant of such things. . . .

" MARY OSGOOD,   ABIGAIL BARKER,
MARY TILER,   SARAH WILSON,
DELIVERANCE DANE,   HANNAH TILER."

That document no doubt describes very accurately the mental condition and pressing circumstances under which a very large

27

number of the confessions were made. There existed some cases, however, which differed from the above. Samuel Wardwell, represented in some accounts as insane, confessed, and afterward recalled his confession, and was executed. Margaret Jacobs, perhaps under pressure and bewilderment as great as those attendant upon the Andover women, made confession, in which she accused both her grandfather and Mr. Burroughs; but compunctions of conscience forthwith came over her, and she most fully and humbly recalled her confession, choosing rather to die on the gallows than not to confess and repent before the God of truth.

THE ACCUSING GIRLS.

One more case — not of an accused one, but of a chief accuser, Ann Putnam, the younger — merits careful attention. She was only twelve years old in 1692; but was the eldest child in a family of at least nine children, both of whose parents died while they were all young; and this eldest continued to live at the homestead, caring for the younger ones, during many years. In August, 1706, fourteen years subsequent to the scenes in which she was eminently conspicuous, she made the following confession before the church, and thereupon was admitted to membership in it.

" The confession of Anne Putnam, when she was received to communion, 1706.

" I desire to be humble before God for that sad and humbling providence that befell my father's family in the year about '92; that I, then being in my childhood, should by such a providence of God *be made an instrument* for the accusing of several persons of a grievous crime, whereby their lives were taken away from them, whom now I have just grounds and good reason to believe were innocent persons; and that it was a great delusion of Satan that deceived me in that sad time, whereby I justly fear I have been instrumental, with others, *though ignorantly and unwittingly*, to bring upon myself and this land the guilt of innocent blood. Though what was said or done by me against any person I can truly and uprightly say, before God and man, I did it *not out of any anger, malice, or ill-will to any person,* for I had no such thing against one of them; but what I did was ignorantly, being deluded oy Satan. And particularly as I was a chief *instrument* of accusing Goodwife Nurse and her two sisters, I desire to lie in the dust, and to be humbled for it, in that I was a cause, with others, of so sad a calamity to them and their families; for which cause I desire to lie in the dust, and earnestly beg forgiveness of God, and from all those unto whom I have given just cause of sorrow and offense, whose relations were taken away or accused.

(Signed)   ANNE PUTNAM.

" This confession was read before the congregation, together with her relation, August 25, 1706 ; and she acknowledged it.

" J. GREEN, *Pastor*."

In that confession she speaks very pointedly of herself as having been used as an *instrument*. Any mortal may perhaps properly do so in relation to each and every act performed. But her history induces inquiry whether Ann was not very strictly an instrument; whether her own will, or whether some other intelligent being's will, used her lips when they put forth accusations of witchcraft. The latter may have been possible; for once, while we were in conversation with a lady who applied disparaging remarks to a particular gentleman who was a prominent medium, we, in reply, expressed our belief that the doings which annoyed her were not the man's voluntary acts, and also that his consciousness that such deeds were alleged by truthful and trustworthy persons to have actually been performed through his physical organism made the acts even more grievous to him than to any one of his acquaintances. She doubted, while we maintained, the possibility of one's mortal form being thus subjected to a will outside of itself. Not many minutes had elapsed — not much argument having been presented on either side — before her own lips were set in use for putting forth a warm defense of Victoria C. Woodhull, a person upon whom our colloquist looked, and of whom she was accustomed to speak, with very decided disapprobation. She was a conscious listener to the words that rolled from her own lips, and experience taught her that our defense of the censured man might be admissible; for, in spite of herself, her own lips were made to bless whom her sentiments were inclining her to curse. Baalam *could* not curse whom his Lord did not. That lady is a *conscious* medium —

conscious that her physical organs, without her consent, and in
spite of her resistance, are sometimes temporarily borrowed and
used by an intelligence outside of herself. As such she is representative of many others. Of course, in these days, she is so informed as to see that actions and words of spirits are imputed to
her as being her own because performed by use of her organs,
while they are, in fact, no more hers than are the acts and utterances of her neighbors. But we doubt much whether any one in
1692 or 1706 had attained to knowledge that some human forms
could be thus filchable and usable; no ground had then been discovered on which one could stand and credibly say, "Though my
own lips spake thus and so, another's will put forth the utterances
in spite of me." Firm ground for that has now been found; it is
not a new formation, but existed, though then unknown, in 1692.
Ann Putnam's form may have been used by another's will in each
and all of her imputed accusations for witchcraft, and she, as far
as then concerned, have been absolutely a will-less *instrument*.

There are other classes of mediums. We call to mind at this
instant four ladies, all of them respectable and excellent, whom we
know and have known for years, whose lips often give utterance to
facts, opinions, and beliefs while the ladies are absolutely unconscious; and sayings then which seem to be theirs are often wide at
variance with what either their knowledge or their sense of right
and truth would permit their own wills to announce. These are
unconscious mediums; not responsible for, because absolutely ignorant of, what their physical forms are being made to say and do.
These persons are representatives of a large class of good mediums.

One phrase in Ann Putnam's confession indicates to us that she
probably belonged to the mediumistic class here presented. She
had been, years before, as she says, an *instrument* not only ignorant,
but *unwitting*. In childhood, Ann was brightest among the bright;
and, in the absence of evidence to the contrary, it is fair to presume
that when reaching the age of twenty-six she was an intelligent
woman, capable of knowing the fair import of any statements to
which she gave deliberate and solemn assent. We apprehend that
her confession was drawn up very carefully, and in consultation with
her intelligent and excellent pastor, Rev. Mr. Green; also that
every word of it was carefully weighed. She seems then to have
been stretching forth a hand soliciting acceptance and friendly

grasp by representatives of some whose blood had been shed because of accusations from her lips; and we feel forced to presume
that then she was in mental and affectional moods which would
make it her duty and her choice to take upon herself all the blame
for her share in the witchcraft transactions which facts and truth
could possibly permit. Her confession is special. It all pertains
to her *instrumental* share in accusing innocent persons of what was
then deemed grievous crime, and thus · in bringing them to death
upon the gallows. Her declaration is as distinct as words can
make it, that the doings through her were "not out of any anger,
malice, or ill-will to any person" on her part; and this renders
Upham's supposition, that family, neighborhood, and sectional quarrels, disputes, rivalries, &c., were motives in her, very improbable.

Also her statement is very distinct, that whatever she did in that
respect was done, so far as she was concerned, both "*ignorantly*
and *unwittingly.*" We are aware that those two words are sometimes used synonymously, or very nearly so. But when the first
occurs in a carefully constructed sentence, the other, if added,
should be deemed to have been inserted for the special purpose of
expressing something beyond what the first usually imports. The
whole had not been told when she had said she acted ignorantly.
To express the remainder, she added — *unwittingly.* When that
word was thus applied, she cannot fairly be supposed to have meant
less than that she acted *unknowingly* — that is, without either
knowledge or consciousness that she did thus act. An *unwitting*
instrument — an instrument not knowing that it was being used —
enfolds within itself a silent but most potent plea for the world's
lenient regards. When consciousness has taken no cognizance of
acts performed by the tongue or the hand, — when memory can
find no record of them, compunction cannot gnaw deeply, nor conscience be a stern accuser. Often, conscience may be at peace, and
God may approve, where man blames. Testimony from without
may force mental conviction that one's lips and limbs must have
been used in doing excessive harm, though consciousness of the
fact be entirely wanting. Conviction even thus generated will naturally and almost necessarily create apprehension that the world is
regarding the owner of those lips and limbs as having been guilty
of very great crimes. That apprehension may create sadness over
all one's subsequent days. Public opinion bridles the tongue then;

for a denial of guilt, however honest and true, can receive no credence where external senses have perceived knowledge to the contrary.   Ann's relations to society may necessarily have been
saddening during many years, even though she of herself had done
nothing offensive either to her own conscience or to God.

Imagination can scarcely picture the sadness which must have
come upon the accusing girls when, a year or two later, public
opinion and favor, which at first buoyed them up and favored such
use of their organisms as has been depicted, began to turn against
them and to brand them as murderers of the innocent and good.
We have no means to trace many of them through their subsequent
years.   Could we do it, we should expect to find them weighed
down, depressed, and made forlorn by the great change of estimation in which the doings were afterward held, in which they had
appeared to be prominent and most disastrous actors.   Few of
them probably had inherent stamina enough to enable them to
stand erect, and move about firmly poised, under the burdens of
obloquy, pity, hatred, resentment, &c., which the wounded hearts
of the families of murdered ones would lay upon these seeming
authors of their losses.

It is pleasant to find that the sensitive and bright Ann Putnam,
as prominent as any one in the band of accusers, survived such
pressure, continued long to care for her orphaned little brothers
and sisters, and, after the first and most crushing effects of the
change in public opinion had been endured for a dozen years or
more, held out her hand in friendly beckoning to those who had
most seeming cause to blame her, and who perhaps in turn had
imposed her heaviest burdens, and seeking to thus open the way
for her unopposed admission to the church, and to fellowship with
the kindred and friends of those whom her tongue had been used
to defame and bring to ignominious death.   Her life experiences
were hard, but perhaps fruitful of good to man beyond what words
can express.   Possibly it is her blessed privilege now to see that
her form was used as an *instrument* for effecting Christendom's
emancipation from monstrous error, and putting an effectual stop
to executions for witchcraft everywhere.

THE PROSECUTORS.

The first warrants for arrest for witchcraft at Salem were issued on February 29, 1692, on complaint preferred by Joseph Hutchinson, Thomas Putnam, Edward Putnam, and Thomas Preston, that Sarah Good, Sarah Osburn, and Tituba had by witchcraft, within the last two months, done harm to Elizabeth Parris, Abigail Williams, Anne Putnam, and Elizabeth Hubbard.

Complaint of Martha Corey was made by Edward Putnam and Henry Keney, March 19.

Edward Putnam and Jonathan Putnam complained of Rebecca Nurse ; and

Jonathan Walcott and Nathaniel Ingersoll, against Elizabeth Proctor.

Perusal of the records shows that very many of the most intelligent, influential, highly respected, and trusted men of the Village were complainants; and shows also that, as early as February 29, when the first complaint was entered, there were four afflicted ones: two in the family of Mr. Parris ; one in that of Thomas Putnam, living more than two miles north from the parsonage ; and one in that of Dr. Griggs, dwelling more than two miles east from the same. Thus much had the trouble spread before the law was invoked to aid in its suppression. The homes of the minister, the doctor, and the parish clerk — a capable and good one, too — were the first invaded. Not mean abodes housed, nor low-lived people cared for the first afflicted ones. Men of the highest standing there were leaders off in the impending conflict with the devil. Two were most prominently and persistently active, viz., Thomas Putnam and Mr. Parris. And why? If any people then and there knew what the emergency required, these two would be among them: none were more competent than they to perceive and perform the duties of such an hour. They, too, and theirs were the chief sufferers. No other active men there had motives pressing as theirs to work for prompt relief in their households ; and we will notice these two as representatives of the prosecutors.

Thomas Putnam deservedly held high position among the inhabitants there, and possessed the esteem, respect, and confidence of the whole community around him. How came it that this very intelligent, influential, and useful citizen, then a little more than forty years old and in the full vigor of manhood, was prominent among the foremost and most pertinacious prosecutors? Why was such a one an enterer of complaints against neighbors, whether high or low, good or bad? Our response is, that in his home a loved and loving wife, cultured, refined, and of acute sensibilities,— a daughter, twelve years old, bright and charming, — and also Mercy Lewis, a young domestic, were all so mysteriously tortured at times, that no doubt existed in a mind which comprehended the creed of that day, that the devil was author of the abnormal torments. That enemy must be getting access to these innocent and loved ones, the creed said, through some neighbors — at least some living mortals — who had made covenants with the Evil One, and thus become his agents. Imbued and bound by the creed of his day, this husband and father could cherish no expectation that his wife and child could be shielded, or that comfort, tranquillity, and peace could come to him and his dear ones, so long as such covenanters were allowed to live. His creed — the general creed of the times — called upon him to invoke the law's aid, since by help from no other source could he hope to reclaim wife, child, and domestic from the clutches of hell's sovereign, and save his own fireside from continuing on indefinitely a frenzied pandemonium. The higher his manhood, and the deeper his love for wife and children, the more vigilant, resolute, and untiring would be his purpose and his efforts to use any and every available means for delivering his family from the hell which had been thrust in under his roof.

The sufferings of his dear ones, then necessarily operative upon his mind and affections, we presume were the chief prompters of his course and incentives to his perseverance in it. Defense and protection of wife, children, and all within his household are incumbent on any one worthy to be called a *man*. Think not the worse of Thomas Putnam because of his resolute purposes and speedy as well as prolonged efforts to rescue from sufferings and perdition wife, child, and domestic. Because a prominent sufferer, he became a prominent prosecutor — yes, the most prominent. Though that fact stands boldly out on the pages of history, no one in his time or since, so far as we have noticed, ever imputed to him an unworthy motive, or annexed a disparaging epithet to his name. Perhaps he, as well as Mr. Dane of Andover, was "tenderly touched" because of "a fair character."

In part the same can be said in defense of Rev. Samuel Parris as we have adduced in defense of his co-sufferer and co-laborer for relief. During the weeks from January 20 to the end of February, both his little daughter and niece, under his own roof, were so strangely and sorely tormented that he and his whole household must have been wearied, agitated, and rendered miserable. When medical aid and kind nursing had proved abortive, and medical authority announced the working of an *Evil Hand* there, who can wonder, knowing the creed of the day and place, that Mr. Parris sought the law's aid for bringing relief to the little sufferers and to all beneath his roof? Samuel Parris and Thomas Putnam, the minister and the clerk of the parish, were both the first and the greatest sufferers affectionally at the oncoming of invasion by mysterious tormentors, and both have fair claims to be judged of tenderly in their connection with witchcraft prosecutions. The chief apparent action of the minister was as scribe or reporter for the courts, and this because he was more competent to that work than any other person obtainable there. Such action is surely not censurable. His position and abilities, however, were such that it was quite as much within his power to have stopped the whole proceedings as in that of any man then living; and they, no doubt, had his sanction and efficient support. And yet we find no ground from which inference either must or can fairly be drawn that the motives of the minister's actions *pertaining to that special matter*, both at its commencement and in its subsequent progress, were other than those common to the most enlightened and best members of the community. Still we have not learned to like the *man*. Selfishness, and disposition to rule harshly over his parish and individuals, if not resentfully and even maliciously, are made too manifest in the records for us to hold him in high esteem.

As servants of God and Christ, which they professed and believed themselves to be, the prosecutors entered upon and long followed up war, bloody war,— not against neighbors and men, but against the Devil— the great enemy of God, Christ, and all good Christians. They were true, earnest, resolute, strong, fearless men, waging their fight in good conscience.

The community at large, in which those men lived and held prominent position, was not below most, if below any other of equal numbers on the continent. Intellect there was keen, and

morality high. Upham's "History of Salem Village," admirable
for its research, its thoroughness, its prevailing accuracy, and its
extensive charms, clearly shows that the five hundred people, more
or less, residing there in 1692, could scarcely be surpassed by the
residents of any other locality in intelligence, mental keenness,
moral strength, personal courage, and firmness of purpose and
resolve to live up to their convictions of truth, right, and duty.
Salem witchcraft was born in the homes of intelligent, brave, honored men, — who, in co-operation with their wives, children, and
domestics, contributed to its growth, and elicited its vast and awful
power to startle, frenzy, and desolate the region round about. The
world at large has never been kept well instructed as to the circumstances amid which that great *delusion* made its entrance on the
field of human vision, nor as to the high standing, intelligence, and
character of its first escorts and sponsors. Its victims, too, as a
whole, were very respectable. Some of them, it is true, were not
high on the social scale, but the most of them were well up, and
quite a number ranked high among the intelligent, virtuous, and
saintly. The wide-spread and long prevalent notion that the dark
doings there were little else than outgrowths from tricks played by
a few artful and mischievous girls upon some low-lived and bed-
ridden old women, has no foundation on the facts in the case. This
most monstrous child of Christendom's creed had begetting and
birth, in 1692, amid as reputable circumstances and people, and as
religious opponents of Satan, as any marked revival of religion
which has anywhere transpired since that memorable day when the
leading men of Salem Village, being challenged to defense of their
homes, armed themselves with civil law, and bravely, long, and
forcefully fought for God and His against the Devil.

WITCHCRAFT'S AUTHOR.

What personality or persons, and of what rank in the scale of
being, was or were primal and chief in originating and enacting the
famous Salem Tragedy? If, as the generation then living believed,
it was a specially great controller and commander of all invisible
foes to God, Christ, and Christians everywhere, and who, having
been effectually baffled in Europe, resolved to keep America from

passing into the control of his enemies, God and Christ, and to thoroughly banish the hated intruders from these his more exclusive and prized domains; if it was that being, his strategy seemingly was to "beard the lion in his den," to make bold and fierce attack on one of the strongest fortresses of Christians, presuming that capture of such a post would lead to easy expulsion of all trespassers from the whole of his broad lands on this side the Atlantic. His apparent policy, judged of by the place and circumstances of attack, was to subdue the strongest first, and thus so intimidate as to frighten all others back to their former homes or the homes of their fathers. But *such* a devil was not there. Many beliefs prevalent two centuries ago are now obsolete. Such a devil as witchcraft was imputed to, and who was believed to put forth greater power over all Indian and heathen lands than God exercised there, receives cognition in few brains to-day. Nevertheless, faith in the presence, power, and malignity of such a being, present and at work among them, was the main force that enabled his contestants to unwittingly put an end to faith in the existence of any one special foe to all goodness, whose power and dominion over the earth and its inhabitants very nearly rivaled those of the Omnipotent One, and whose malice was a near counterpoise to complete supernal benevolence.

Reason demands that the creature shall be inferior to its creator, that devil shall be less than God; and she in most persons refers all things and all events, in the ultimate analysis of causes and agents, back to One Great Over-Soul — one God.

If an all-wise and omnipotent One, being full of mercy too, proposed to subject an erroneous and enslaving human creed to a strain which should shatter it past restoration to strength, and thus to set its subjected holders free, highest wisdom may have seen that bright intellect, true courage, firm nerves, unfaltering devotion to sense of duty, and strong faith heavenward, were needful instrumentalities for best accomplishment of the design. The abode of people than whom none elsewhere were better prepared, more able, or more willing to fight the devil himself promptly, unfalteringly, and persistently, may have been a spot where supernal prescience saw that men, as blinded instruments, could best be made to effect their own and the world's emancipation from a time-hardened and disastrous public error. The mental and moral strength, and other good *fighting* qualities of its occupants generally, may have caused the Village to be fixed upon as the most favorable battle-ground available for the projected struggle.

Neither God nor the devil, however, was author in any sense pertinent to the present inquiry. Our *ifs*, and the sentences which follow them, cannot meet the demands nor the needs of modern readers. Faith, in direct personal action upon either individual human beings or communities and nations by any incomprehensibly vast and ubiquitous intelligent being either malignant or benevolent, is not as prevalent now as it was in many generations past. God, or a mighty devil either, as constant, immediate, and personal performer on humanity's stage of operations, is not extensively recognized by the deep thinkers of our age.

Indeed, modern thought has come very low down in its search for witchcraft's author. Turning from God and the devil, the reputed workers of great marvels in ages long past, our interpreters of America's earlier wonders have fancied that they find the former existence of little girls whose powers to sway the human mind and agitate a land, so approximated those of omnipotence, and whose malignities so perceptibly equaled his of Cloven Hoof, that they of their own wills concocted and enacted scenes of simulated pains, distortions, losses of sight, hearing, and speech; and also mimicked the movements of birds and beasts, and performed such impositions and tricks innumerable as made their homes and neighborhood a horrid pandemonium; in doing which they manifested such prodigious power, skill, and perfect acting, that these little untaught and untrained ones outled in skill, all the world's most expert tricksters, and, in malignity, the most devilish human monsters our world ever contained, in any age or land.

Somewhere between the extremes of strength and weakness, of benevolence and malignity, we perhaps can find beings more likely to have directly produced the marvels in question than either God, devil, or little girls. Consciousness and experience indicate to most persons that an all-dominating power exists, and bounds and hedges in the spheres of freedom and ability which are occupied by finite beings. Something above and beyond all finites says to each of them, " Thus far, but no farther, canst thou go." Within spheres thus limited there abide many grades of intelligent and affectional beings, ranging in differences of powers and dispositions as widely as any mortal's thoughts can conceive. Vast, countless hosts of intelligences, though vailed from our outer vision, may be, and evidences are very strong that such ever are abiding dwellers above, below, around, and in the midst of earth's corporeal inhabitants. Within their unperceived abodes such ones may actuate the forces which evolve many less marked events, as well as all special providences, special judgments — miracles so called, and such marvels generally as were formerly imputed to either God or the devil as *immediate* author. We have no faith that either of the two had any closer or more special connection with witchcraft matters than with the ordinary doings of man.

The undefinable source of all things which are contained in the vast creation, emitted all forth subject to laws, and surrounded and infiltrated by forces which enable the world's progressing inhabitants, visible and invisible, to purchase, through study, toil, absorptions from enfolding auras, and other furnished helps, both knowledge and powers just as fast and great as their advancements and growing needs from time to time call for more light and for augmented powers.

Finite beings naturally gravitate to where every instrumentality needful to their highest well-being can be obtained by the co-operative efforts and aspirations of finites, seen and unseen, for learning laws and manipulating forces which pervade their places of residence. Generations upon generations, whose mortal forms long centuries ago moldered away, may still be active laborers in and about the men of to-day, and may be, and may always have been, the immediate manifesters of all supernal intelligence and marvelous force issuing from regions which the eye of flesh lacks power to scan. One of the old prophets of a prior generation made known to John the Revelator what he recorded; and agents of like nature, that is, departed human spirits, may have been the only revealers of supernal truths, facts, and visions to man, and the only workers of the signs or extra-marvelous manifestations of force and knowledge which have been deemed credentials from the Omniscient and Omnipotent. We believe in God and in the issuance of knowledge and force from him to man, but have not faith in his immediate personal putting forth of either, in accomplishment of such events as are often called special providences. Such events occur — they often come both uncalled for and in response to prayer — to yearnings "uttered or unexpressed;" but the prayers and yearnings reach, stimulate, and help both ambient forces and ascended spirits to let in or to confer the needed protection or restoration. The air all around us is alive with hearers of prayer, and no humble and fervent aspiration for help to come forth from the mystic abodes of spiritual beings and occult forces ever fails to bring aid and elevation. The purer and humbler the aspiration, the nearer does it penetrate toward the Great Source of being, life, and bliss, and the more powerful and beneficent are those whose responses and emanations can reach and aid the petitioner.

The same forces and laws which permit the sensible action of good spirits among men, just as freely and extensively permit the presence and action of malicious ones. God aids the good and restrains the wicked just as much and no more on the other side of the grave than on this. Freedom, whether to comply with or to contend against either natural or moral law, is as great in spirit spheres as in our midst on earth. Any spirit, either benevolent or malignant, is as free to use the forces and laws which permit spirit manifestations, as any navigator is, be he morally good or bad, to avail himself of winds, currents, tides, and the like, for passing over seas to a land not his own, and acting out his characteristic purposes there.

Our position, fortified by the facts and reasonings in the preceding pages, is, that spirits — departed human beings — generated and outwrought Salem witchcraft. That is our answer to the question of its authorship.

THE MOTIVE.

Thus far questions pertaining to the character of the main motives operating in the authors of acts called witchcraft, have purposely been avoided. The actors and their doings have been sought for, irrespective of morality. But the *cui bono*, the what good? must have been asked over and over again by the reader. Why did any intelligent being, whether mortal or spirit, thus woefully invade and disturb the homes of able, honored, worthy Christian men? and especially why perpetrate such agonizing cruelties upon bright, lovely, and promising children?

The spirit-world, as well as ours, holds inhabitants differing widely one from another in character, tastes, propensities, and occupations — it contains yearners to recommune with surviving kindred at the old material home — contains its rovers, its explorers, its scientists, its seekers after novelties, facts, and principles ; after new places, scenes, and peoples to visit; after new routes and appliances for travel, and after new applications of known powers and forces. The motives for acting upon and through mortal forms may vary from worst to best, from best to worst.

The moral character of motives can neither invalidate nor confirm what has been adduced. The motives, having been either good or bad, may be ascribed to spirits as well as mortals. and to mortals as well as spirits, for both good and bad beings dwell in mortal forms now, and both classes have left their outer forms behind, and passed into the abiding-place of spirits — have become spirits, and that, too, without necessary alteration of their moral states. Motives in different cases and with different operators were doubtless quite varied. Correct presentation of their qualities in connection with the several cases adduced in the preceding pages is obviously beyond our power. Though conscious that we must probably be mistaken in some instances, we yet are willing to state some of the thoughts which facts and appearances have suggested.

Perhaps no unseen intelligences aided or acted through either Margaret Jones or Ann Hibbins; and, if any did, their performances in and of themselves were never perceptibly harmful to the public. We apprehend, however, that if the whole truth were known, man would now see that kind physicians, who had bid farewell to earth, continued to practice the healing art through the brain and hands of Margaret Jones.

The users of Ann Cole's vocal organs furnished no distinct indication that they were either specially benevolent or the reverse. We are constrained to regard them as having been low, ignorant, willing to excite consternation among men, and very willing to help the lewd Greensmiths on, by the halter's use, to speedy entrance into conditions in which themselves could confer with these debased ones more familiarly than was possible while they remained encased in flesh. Such a view need not imply that they were malicious. Desire to hold closer connection with one's affinities is natural, and not necessarily bad. Communicators from the other side of death's portals generally decline to call any spirits *bad;* they speak of many as being low, ignorant, benighted, undeveloped, &c., but seldom call any one bad. They seem to regard many much as we do green fruits. One omits to call the half-grown apple bad, however sour or crabbed, and says only that it is immature, unripe, &c., implying that, though in its present condition not good to eat, time may come when it will be palatable and nutritious.

Elizabeth Knap's visitant — the one to whom she said, "What cheer, old man?" — who presumably was the chief operator through and upon her form, and lingered about her for at least three years, we regard as a sort of recluse spirit, who kept mainly aloof from other disembodied ones, and found his chief enjoyment in retaining or resuming as close alliances as possible with the outer or material world, and from a selfish desire to secure permanent possession of this instrument, strove through torturings to reduce her to subjection; and this, perhaps, without desire to injure her, but mainly with a view to gratify his own selfishness. The other one — the pretty black boy — of a more lively disposition, found pleasure in playfully bantering the grave clergyman, and probably strove, in playful mood, to teach the honest and good man some lessons in charity and demonology. We see no reason why he may not be regarded as a genial good fellow, desiring to make some gloomy portion of mankind more cheerful and happy.

At Newbury there possibly was nothing more than a playful and self-gratifying exercise of constitutional powers by a band of spirit gymnasts — not malicious, but playful and rude; curious also, it may be, to see how far they might be able to frighten mortals and arouse consternating wonder, while they should be pleasurably exercising their own faculties. We view them as neither specially good or bad, but as heedless and rude in their frolic.

Appearances are different when we look at the Goodwin family. There an embodied old wild Irish woman's spirit was the first to put forth psychologizing power over the children. She was moved by anger, or resentment, or both; her guardian or kindred spirits no doubt helped her, and from motives like her own. Perhaps we may properly call both her and her aids bad. Yet we hear no call to apply that word emphatically. Little Martha had just charged the old woman's daughter with having stolen some of the clothes which the latter was employed to wash; and, if that charge was false, or even presumed by the old woman to be false, she, who was obviously fiery and ignorant, may not have been excessively diabolical in using any process of mental or emotional retaliation which was at her command. Perhaps ignorance and instinctive retaliation were quite as operative in her as malice.

Martha's form, subsequently, when she was residing with Cotton Mather, was often used by one or more spirits who seem to have been bent upon showing the learned man that sport might exist and be enjoyable beyond the confines of mortal life, and that denizens there were disposed to make some at his expense. They soon showed him that linguists unseen could comprehend his meaning, whatever the language he might use for expression of his thought; and also thumped the sectarian by disdaining to read books which he approved, and by reading with ecstatic delight such as he condemned. Nor was this all; they exhibited in his presence feats of strength and agility, and many marvelous antics, which were suited to cause a thinker and scholar to hold on to his belief that others than the guileless miss took part in the performance of such marvels. While amusing themselves, they were exhibiters of instructive facts. Nothing bad in their purposes becomes apparent.

The case of most special interest and chief importance pertains to Salem. Upham, vol. ii. p. 429, says, "If there was anything supernatural in the witchcraft of 1692, if any other than human spirits were concerned at all, one thing is beyond a doubt; they were shockingly wicked spirits." *Beyond a doubt?* Perhaps not in some minds. But if any disembodied spirits whatsoever, even *shockingly wicked* ones, were mainly performers of the convulsing operations at Salem, the historian's theory of explanation is not only baseless, but is lamentably cruel and unjust toward the human instruments through whom the spirits acted. If specific doings prove their authors, if spirits, to have been shockingly wicked, the same having mortal authors, would prove the latter to have been just as shockingly wicked. We do not like to apply that defamatory phrase to all those girls and women who are set forth as the chief accusers. Were all those youthful females

28

shockingly wicked? We hope not, and think not. God rules
alike in the invisible and visible world, and often moves in mysterious ways for executing benevolent designs.

The motive of Tituba's "tall man with white hair," whom we
regard as prime mover in the most momentous witchcraft scene
the world has ever witnessed, is difficult to comprehend satisfactorily. The deliberateness indicated both by his visit to Tituba
five days in advance of practical operation, and by his then
appointing a special time and place for entering upon his intended
processes, bespeaks a definite and abiding motive of some marked
quality. Judging from the earlier and more perceptible effects of
his doings, the world must almost necessarily regard him as a
deliberate tormentor of innocent children; as a disturber of domestic, social, religious, and civil peace; as an immolator of the innocent and the virtuous; as hell's sovereign acting out his fiendish
pleasure upon the inmates of a Christian fold. Infernal malignity,
at the first glance, seems to have actuated this intruder at the
parsonage. World-wide experience, however, has learned that
many things are "not as they seem." We have been taught to
recognize One being, and there may be many others in spheres
unseen, in whose sight "a thousand years are as one day." Teachings of history and observation show that the overruling power is
attended and guided by far — very far — reaching prescience; and
also that many of man's greatest blessings are educed from temporal evils of vast magnitude. The malice of man nailed Jesus
to the cross. What wears every appearance of wicked motive
is often used as helpful, if not needed, instrumentality in procuring man's deliverance and redemption from debasement and
oppression.

When John Brown made his raid across the border line of freedom, not only the invaded South, but a large portion of the North
regarded him as a ruthless and malicious invader of the rights
of our fellow-countrymen, and therefore worthy of a felon's doom.
A cannon soon sent to Fort Sumter the comments of the South
upon what Brown had done, and war, carnage, and horrors of varied
forms and vast dimensions soon spread over the broad nation, from the
St. John to the southern gulf, and from the Atlantic to the Pacific.
John Brown was no felon, no malicious invader, but a philanthropic
planner to strip the chains of slavery from four millions of his

brother men ; and his step, though a seeming evil then, led directly
on to the emancipation of all for whose good he went forth in seeming malice.

When plagues of various kinds were invoked and brought upon
the Egyptians by and through the mediumistic Moses and Aaron,
what Egyptian would have deemed that the motives of the unseen
intelligence who counseled and controlled them could be benevolent? Plague, pestilences, and sore afflictions for a long time, and
finally death of the first born, were imposed upon each Egyptian
household. The motive to those inflictions is deemed to have been
deliverance of the children of Israel from bondage. Egyptians
being judges, it must have been a shockingly wicked spirit who
acted upon them through Moses and Aaron.

History, on most of its pages, shows that war — war, — that
ruthless trampler upon the innocent scarcely less than upon the
offending, has ever been a very common, if not the chief, instrument by which oppressed people have gained deliverance, and
through use of which the depressed have come up to higher stand-
points. If our world has, through all its past ages, been wisely
and beneficently managed by some intelligence higher than man,
then far-reaching wisdom — supernal wisdom — has often seen
that the good of the many — nay, the good of all — required the
coming of suffering, sacrifice, and anguish upon the few. Has
the Great Permitter of the many sufferings which war has engendered been " shockingly wicked "?

The chains of old enslaving errors often become invisible and un-
felt by those on whom they were early placed by a mother's kindly
hand, and the like to which all associates wear as supposed helps,
and never as suspected hindrances, to expansion and health of
mind and heart. Nothing short of a most strenuous conflict —
nothing short of a struggle for life and all that makes life valuable and dear — is competent in some cases to awaken perception
that such chains are and ever have been cramping their wearers,
and holding them back from such expansion and freedom as their
Maker fitted men to attain to and enjoy. We regard the witchcraft
creed as having been such a chain.

Looking carefully at the methods by which the power that over-
rules all terrestrial affairs has almost invariably led man to break
away from thralldom and oppression, can one reasonably entertain

belief that any purely peaceful measures, any preachings, arguments, appeals to the reason of men, could have brought Christendom, at any time after the twelfth or thirteenth century, to perceive
that its witchcraft creed was enslaving its mind, and thwarting its
proper expansion heavenward? We apprehend not; and also we
surmise that in 1692 supernal intelligence saw that opportunity and
power existed, which, if then availed of, could put mortals into a
conflict which would reveal to them the inherent falsity and barbarity of the witchcraft creed, and thus let such light into their minds
as, in time, would lead them to cast off the chains in which they
were bound, attain to clearer and more accurate views of their relations to God and the spirit-world, and rise to higher and freer
manhood.

If such were the case, we can readily conceive that supernal wisdom and benevolence might permit and foster the oncoming of an
appalling and terrific struggle which should bring into vigorous
action man's every latent energy, sweep away in its course many
erroneous beliefs, hampering customs, and ruts of thought, and
thoroughly overturn much which had long been deemed immovable
truth. Such a course might be the most beneficent possible, even
though it involved destruction of the comfort, peace, and lives of
many innocent and most estimable inhabitants at the place and
vicinity where the battle should be waged, and that, too, whether
the war itself should be the ostensible offspring of revenge and
malice, or a brave conflict for preservation of one's altars and fireside in peace.

Some amusement, and little else perhaps, may be furnished by
presentation of what a spiritualist's fancy, prior to careful study of
facts narrated by Tituba, had become accustomed to deem not only
possible, but probable. She was a slave dwelling among oppressors
of her kindred and race — oppressors of the negro, the Indian, and
of those generally who were "guilty of a skin not colored like their
own," and of worshiping gods different from their own. What
more natural than that departed ones, whom the whites had de-
frauded, injured, and oppressed while dwellers here, and whose
surviving kindred were still being treated in like manner, should
embrace an opportunity which the mediumistic qualities and the
abode of Tituba furnished, for perpetrating retaliation whence woes
had been received? True Christian morality may denounce such

action as being "shockingly wicked," but the more prevalent morality in the world — in the more resolute portions of it at least,
and especially in the less enlightened — may be as ready to commend as to condemn it, and to applaud as to censure those whose
fire and pluck induced and enabled them to pay over upon their
oppressors wrong for wrong, even augmented with interest at the
highest rates which their altered circumstances allowed. It having
been discovered that Tituba's form was a portal for spirit return,
fancy saw the spirits of her ancestral race, and hosts of ascended
aborigines of Massachusetts soil, eagerly coming back through her
helping properties, disposed and eager to cast their impalpable
arrows and tomahawks at any members of the wronging race who
might be vulnerable by such weapons. Scouts swiftly and widely
spread over the spirit hunting-grounds knowledge of the glorious
opportunity for retaliation and revenge which had come, and hosts
of volunteers rushed thence with lightning speed to the alluring
scene. Quick havoc ensued, and the great consternation, bewilderment, devastation, slaughter, disturbance of peace, and agonizings
of terror and awe, which the invasion produced, gave keenest pleasure, satisfaction, and joy to the assailants. Possibly Indian spirits
might then begin to cherish hopes of expelling all whites from the
land of their fathers, and of re-acquiring and leaving the whole a
legacy to red men's heirs.

But the whites, not less than the darker-skinned, were under the
supervision of spirit guardians, friends, and helpers, who, though
probably taken by surprise and at disadvantage, were by no means
disposed to leave their wards, kindred, and loved ones to be long
thus harassed and abused. Invisible hosts soon mustered, and
warred against other invisible hosts over and around th- Village;
and when the struggle had been waged far enough to sever witchcraft's chains, the laws of the *Highest* permitted the guardians of
the Christians to conquer a lasting peace whose balm would heal
the wounds inflicted, and whose fruits would be emancipation from
cramping errors, and consequent expansion and elevation of mental
powers.

As, perhaps, appropriate sequent to our fanciful views, we next
present something which was not born in our own brain, and which
may or may not be statement of ancient facts. We have devoted
but little time to directly seeking information from spirits relating

to the subject upon which we are writing, and yet have seldom entered into conversation with any good clairvoyant, at any time during the last year or two, without receiving description of one or more spirits then in attendance, and manifesting desire to have us recognize them. In most cases they have shown their names. In this manner Cotton Mather, more than any other one, signifies that interest in our present work draws him near to us. Mather's mother, also Martha Goodwin, Rebecca Nurse, and others, have presented their cards through persons ignorant that individuals bearing such names ever lived. But Mather has done more. On two or three occasions, using a medium's organs of speech, he has entered into conversation with us upon his connection with witchcraft. He is not now well pleased with his blindness when in his physical form, and urges us to be more severe in our criticisms upon his course than historic facts permit us to be.

February 9, 1875, he was in control of a medium, and we inquired as to his present views of George Burroughs. At once and cordially he described Burroughs as one of the brightest of all spirits whom he had seen, and as "illumining whatever sphere he enters." We asked Mather if he had ever learned who the spirit was that came to Tituba and started Salem witchcraft. He had not. Had he met Tituba? "Yes." "Can you not," we asked, "find him through her?" "Probably," was his response; "and will try, if you wish it." "Well, then," we said, "two weeks from this day and hour we will meet you at this place." This was arranged through an *unconscious* medium, who never receives into her consciousness any knowledge of what her lips utter while she is entranced, and she was on that occasion. We did not inform her, nor did any other mortal than ourself know, that we arranged for a subsequent meeting with Mather.

We called upon the medium February 23, when forthwith, in her normal and conscious state, she said that she was then seeing at our side two spirits of very strange aspect, and of race or races unknown to her. One of them she described as a male, uncouth in aspect, having large piercing eyes, a very wild look, and as being clothed in a sort of blouse, beneath and below which were short pants tucked into the shoes; also his teeth were very large. The other was a female of unknown race, and of a race different from that to which the male belonged; her complexion was dark, but she was neither negro nor Indian, and exhibited the letter T.

This medium may have known, and probably did, that we were engaged in writing upon witchcraft; but she is not conversant with its history, nor did she know the names of individuals concerned in it, nor the parts any had severally performed.

Very shortly after having given the above description, the medium was entranced; soon Cotton Mather, speaking through her, signified that he had brought with him both Tituba and her nocturnal visitant when she was slave of Mr. Parris; also, he stated, that, since they were not accustomed to giving utterance through borrowed lips, he proposed to speak for and of them. . The statement relating to the man was substantially as follows : —

"His name was Zachahara; he was of Egyptian descent, but a Ninevite, or dweller in Nineveh. His time on earth was somewhat before that of Moses. Not long after his death, he, a spirit, observed that a spirit by the name of Jehocah — not Jehovah — was working strange marvels, and enacting cruelties among the race from which himself had sprung, through one Moses, and was thereby acting out a spirit's purposes toward man through a mortal's form. At once he, Zachahara, felt strong inclination and desire to exercise his own powers in the same mode. The desire clung to him tenaciously, and ever kept him alert, to find a mortal whom he could use with efficiency rivaling that which Jehocah manifested through Moses. No one of his many trials, however, was very successful until he put forth his skill and power upon and through Tituba. His ruling motive was desire to ascertain how far he, being a spirit, could get and keep control of a mortal form, and what amount and kinds of wonders he could perform with such an instrument. The motive was devoid of either malice or benevolence ; it essentially was that of the scientist seeking new knowledge of nature's permissions. To keep Tituba in good humor with himself, he freely made promises to bestow upon her many fine things ; and, to please her, he would say and do anything he thought might add to his power over her, and, through her, over other mortals."

Such was the account ; and, while it was coming upon our ears, it carried us back to familiar accounts of marvels of old, and we felt that the acts of Jehocah through Moses, and those of Zachahara through Tituba, bespoke motives so much alike in apparent barbarity, that, if either actor was blameworthy, it might be difficult to see why equal blame should not be meted out upon the other.

Mather, speaking of and for Tituba, said, that "when the man first came to her and sought her service and aid, he was very bright and pleasant; but that, when she declined to comply with his wishes and demands, he became awfully dark and terrible." Briefly, Tituba herself managed the medium's vocal organs, furnished a simpering confirmation of Mather's statement, and said, with a shrug and shiver, "he was awful! awful!"

Subsequent conversation at the same seance elicited from spirits their belief, that, as soon as a door of access to men through Tituba was discovered, numerous Indian spirits were able and eager to rush through and lend a helping hand to the old Ninevite, and were devoid of any strong desire to help gently; indeed, they were very willing to molest the whites on their own responsibility. Soon, when unimpassioned search for knowledge of what ability spirits possessed or might acquire to revisit and again act amid terrestrial scenes was too much attended by agents willing to enact, and actually enacting, havoc too severe to be longer tolerated, wise and compassionate spirits brought power to bear which soon put a stop to what was producing most agonizing consequences. Spirits claim that they did much in the way of changing the views of mortals, and preventing a renewal of prosecutions at the next term of court. Perceiving that enough cruelty had been enacted to make mortals ready to ask whether both humanity and God were not belied by the creed Christians were enforcing, they turned the minds of men to more rational and humane views.

Some time during the winter of 1874–5, Rev. G. Burroughs having poured out, through a medium's lips, a few sentences redolent with charity and heavenly grace, we asked him what he now deemed the motive which primarily induced some spirit to inaugurate the operations which brought himself and many others to untimely end? His response was, "I suppose it was the natural and proper desire of some spirit to resume communion with its dear ones on earth." No spirit has ever indicated to us a suspicion even that the spirits whose acts evolved witchcraft were either malevolent, censurable, or in any sense *shockingly wicked.*

Did supernal prescience select and post agents peculiarly fitted to perform the witchcraft tragedy? Perhaps so : and possibly Sir William Phips was not governor by mere chance. Some statements by Calef indicate that Sir William when young, perhaps while but

a learner of ship-carpentry in Maine, received a written communication which led him to go to Europe and obtain means whereby
to seek for a wreck, the finding of which brought him fortune and
title. He long and carefully preserved the prophetic paper, and,
when flush in means, paid the writer of it more than two hundred
pounds. From the same or a similar source he fore-learned his
becoming a commander, governor of New England, and other
events of his life. Information of that kind usually comes to such
as are mediumistic enough to be susceptible of guidance, or at least
of swayings, by the intelligence from whom the prophecy issues.
Sir Phips may have been himself mediumistic. The probable fact
that the accusing girls named the governor's wife as one from whom
they received annoyance bespeaks probability that she too had
place in the class of impressibles. Therefore, one inclined to pros-
ecute such speculations is here furnished with a basis on which to
argue that the Infinite Prescience which permitted the advent of
Salem witchcraft, also embraced fit instruments in fit position for
controlling its course, and also for putting a stop to it as soon as it
should have outwrought enough of seeming evil to beget the good
which Infinite Benevolence purposed to bestow upon mortals.
Spirits take to themselves much credit for the part they performed
in changing the opinions and course of the authorities and people
here in the autumn of 1692, and the early months of the following
year.

The adjournment of the court, and no law permitting another
session for months, gave opportunity for reflection. Also the
actual and contemplated arrests of many of high standing and most
estimable character were matters of sobering influence, so that
reason resumed its sway; no more were tried for witchcraft, and
all prisoners were set free. This may have occurred either with or
without special action of spirits upon the public mind.

We now regard the primal motive as nearly or quite devoid of
moral quality. It probably was either a natural and proper desire
to get access to dear ones left on earth, or some experimental or
some scientific impulse to test the power which a spirit could
exercise over those encased in mortal forms. When, before the
days of ether, good Dr. Flag had fixed his forceps firmly on our
raging tooth, and given a long, strong pull till out of breath, our
pains, our agony, our heavy blows upon his hand and arms, failed

to make him let go. He was shockingly wicked at that moment,
for he not only held on and kept us in torture, but pulled again
without success; and even then he would not let go, but pulled yet
once more, and the tooth came out. Spirits, getting access to
mortals, may have judged that only through transient evils and
sufferings could man get relief from severe chronic maladies, and
that, when opportunity occurred, their kindest possible treatment
of men was homœopathic — was the curing like with like — curing
evil by inflicting evil. They may have been so shockingly wicked
as to do that.

Spirits may often, and generally explore and operate from motives not perceptibly different from such as actuate their human
counterparts. The devoted vivisectionist seldom shrinks from
entering upon, or gives up pursuit of, knowledge because the
scalpel agonizes his living subject. So, too, a spirit in pursuit of
knowledge — if, either casually or by intended experiment, finding
himself controlling the will and organs of Tituba or some other
impressible mortal, and thus opening up a new field for exploration
— might be strongly inclined to see how far and efficiently he could
wield forces of nature so as himself to sway the forms and affairs of
embodied men. Each gain in power or skill for acting amid terrestrial beings, scenes, and objects, would naturally thrill him with
pleasure, and incite him to follow up researches in the spirit of
science. That spirit is prone to look upon sufferings which its own
processes occasion, as but temporary incidents, and of little account
in comparison with the beneficent results which its triumphs will
procure. Extension of their own fields of knowledge and influence
was perhaps among the chief motives which prompted spirits to
perform the wonders that startled, frenzied, and agonized the subjects and observers of their operations in 1692. Another may have
been self-gratification by revisiting well-known scenes; and yet another, beneficence to man by opening for his use a new source of
knowledge and wisdom.

Realms unseen are the abodes of sympathetic as well as of scientific beings; and as soon as a false creed had been forced to disclose
its falsity, the former may have seen occasion to dissuade the latter
from acting further upon benighted dwellers in mortal forms, until
time should bring man to calm reflection and retrospection, and to
possession of such mental freedom as would embolden him to meet

unawed, strange visitants from unseen realms, and extend to even such a friendly hand. The lapse of a hundred and fifty years brought such mental freedom to us, purchased by the sufferings of our fathers, that, undeterred by fears of the halter, we now can invite to our earthly homes the loved and saintly ones who have passed on to realms above, hold blissful and uplifting communings with them, and learn their justification of the wonderful ways of God both to and through the children of men and in all nature.

Whatever the ruling motive of the chief direct producer of Salem Witchcraft may have been, the resistless power which moves all things, including malignant motives, onward toward the production of ultimate good, caused the fierce conflict we are considering to soon put an effectual stop to prosecutions for witchcraft throughout all Christian lands, and shattered to fragments a pernicious creed which had long enslaved the Christian mind. Costly as that struggle was in pains, sicknesses, tortures, anguish, physical exhaustions, domestic distresses, social alienations, church discords, languishments in prison, fears, frenzies, and even life, the price may not have been high for the wide-spread and abiding blessings of mental·freedom which it obtained.

LOCAL AND PERSONAL.

Members of the First Parish in Danvers, and all residents on the soil of Salem Village: —

About three years since it was my privilege to speak briefly concerning the marvels of 1692, on the spot where they transpired. Courtesy then required brevity, and some vagueness of statement resulted : my remarks on that occasion are embraced among the addresses appended to Rev. Charles B. Rice's admirable " History of the First Parish in Danvers, 1672–1872 " — a production of much more than ordinary merit.

The present occasion is embraced to point out a misprint. On pages 186 and 187 of those bi-centennial offerings, I am made to say that " the little resolute band of devil-fighters here in the wilderness became, though all *unwillingly*, yet became most efficient helpers in gaining liberty for the freer action of nobler things than any creed," &c. — I never cherished a thought so derogatory to them as that they *unwillingly* became efficient helpers in gaining liberty. My spoken words were, that they *unwittingly*, that is, without knowing it, were being made instrumental in gaining mental freedom, or deliverance from the chains of error ; and I believe that a large part of the preceding pages tends to make the truth of my actual statement apparent, while it shows the falsity of the one imputed to me.

The soil beneath you long has been and long will be either consecrated or damned to fame ; damned, hereafter, if prevalent modern views of former actors there be correct ; consecrated, if the ostensible actors be viewed as chosen combatants and instruments on witchcraft's last and most widely renowned battle-field.

Many of you know that I first drew breath and also received my earlier training and unfoldment on the soil of your town. My relations to witchcraft soil were not of my own choosing, and I feel no responsibility for them — feel no sense of gratulation, and none of shame, because of them. Still, no doubt, they increase my desire to set forth the merits of former dwellers at the Village as having been as great and noble, and their faults as few and small, as authenticated facts fairly demand; and this not because of anything done or suffered by any one of my personal ancestors, no one of whom, so far as I have learned, was either accuser, accused, or witness in any witchcraft case. There, however, has been transmitted orally from sire to son what possibly indicates that one of them was exposed to arrest. Immediately after the prosecutions ceased, Joseph Putnam, father of General Israel, was a firm and efficient opponent to Mr. Parris's retaining position as minister at the Village. Tradition says that when rage for arrestings was high, he, being then only twenty-two years old, and his still younger wife, kept themselves and their family armed, their horses saddled and fed by the door, day and night for six months. This was preparation for either resistance or flight, as circumstances might render expedient in case an arrest should be attempted there. Opposition to prevalent beliefs, therefore, may not be a new feature in the family history. The heretic to the notions of many to-day, may have had an ancestor heretical to the witchcraft creed in 1692.

But if heresy has come by inheritance, charity combines with it; for my heart is gladdened by each newly discovered indication that Joseph's elder half-brother, Thomas Putnam, the great and impartial prosecutor, and Ann, daughter of Thomas the great witch-finder, — also that Mr. Parris and many other former villagers, — never, any one of them, acted any part in relation to witchcraft that was not prompted by devotion to the relief and good of their families and neighbors, or forced upon them by unseen and irresistible agents.

Your trusted teachers upon the subject — Upham, Fowler, Hanson, and Rice, all well informed in most directions, and well-intentioned — have severally favored the view that neither supermundane nor submundane agents were at all concerned in producing your witchcraft scenes. Their course throws tremendous and most fearful responsibilities upon both the fathers and daughters of a former age; and not responsibilities alone, but also accusations of deviltry upon the children, and of stupidity and barbarity upon the fathers, which make them all objects of aversion, and a stock from which any one may well blush to find that he has descended.

No one of these teachers went back to the commencement of the strange doings, and scanned the testimony of Tituba, that personal participator in them, and the best possible witness. No one of them used, and probably none but Upham had at command, her simple but plain statements, that a spirit came to her and forced her to help him and others pinch the two little girls in Mr. Parris's family, at the very time when their mysterious ailments were first manifested. The keen and exact Deodat Lawson states that the afflicted ones "talked with the specters as with living persons." Mention of spirits as being seen attendant upon the startling works is of frequent occurrence in the primitive records. Therefore, facts well presented and authoritative have been left unadduced by your teachers. They, however, are a part, and a very important part, of things to be accounted for. Any theory of explanation that fails to embrace such is essentially faulty, misleading, and not worthy of adoption. Fair respect for historic facts, and especially for the reputation of those men and young women who were prominently concerned in its scenes, very properly and forcefully demands a widely different and less humiliating and aspersory solution of your witchcraft than such as has been proffered in the present century.

My reading in preparation for this work failed to meet with either distinct mention of any meeting of a circle at Mr. Parris's house, or with any statement which had seeming reference to the existence of such a one, till I got down to Upham, who dwells much upon it and its influences, but omits mention of the source of his information. Since the publication of his Lectures upon Witchcraft, many writers have followed his lead.

Knowledge of the locality and of the relative positions of the homes of those girls, and of their positions in those homes, is perhaps kept more steadily in view by a writer whose young days, and parts of his manhood, were passed there, than by others not so long familiar with the region; and perhaps he holds firmer conviction that gatherings, with the frequency and to the extent which are claimed, for the purpose of learning the arts of necromancy, magic, and spiritualism, under the roof of such a man as Mr. Parris, were very much nearer to an impossibility, than most others do who have of late had occasion to consider *who* enacted Salem witchcraft. If current assumptions, that the accusing girls, by study and practice, rendered themselves able to concoct and enact the vast and bloody tragedy imputed to them, and if their own minds and wills were properly authors there, — if the prevalent explanation of witchcraft be much other than fanciful, — then the magical skill and powers, and the brutal acts there manifested, loudly call for admission that wolfish fathers had begotten foxes, and were beguiled and spurred on by their own wily vulpines to commit such horrid havoc as must fix unfading and ineffaceable stain of infamy upon the spot where they prowled.

The blackest smooch on the pages of your history was dropped from the pen which virtually made the Village daughters incarnate devils, and their fathers gullible, stupid, and brutal mistakers of what their own girls performed for the marvelous doings of agents possessing more than mortal powers. God save the parish soil from the stain which modern fancy's course tends to impress upon it! Its men were never beguiled and aroused to perpetration of monstrous barbarities by the self-willed actings and words of their daughters. But genuine and mysterious afflictions of their children found the sires ready to fight manfully and unflaggingly for God and the deliverance of their families from mundane hells, and that, too, with such force and persistency as never before was equaled in witchcraft's long history, and with such success that no extension of that sad volume has since been possible.

That was most emphatically a time that tried men's *souls*; and the souls then there proved to be brave enough to wage conflict against the mightiest and most formidable of possible enemies, and strong and persistent enough to force him to such struggle as strained his vitals, and paralyzed his power to molest grievously in any future age. The Unique Devil of Witchcraft left that field of fight a Samson shorn of his locks; the source of his strength was there cut off, for the intensely indurated encasement of the delusion which centuries before had begotten him, and had ever since been feeding him abundantly, was then so thoroughly cracked, that its contents went the way of water spilled upon the ground, and he famished.

Blush not for the fathers. They were heroes, true to their creed, their families, and their neighbors; true servants of their God — true foes to their devil. And their fight purchased the freedom which lets me now speak in their defense, devoid of any fears of the hangman's rope; and purchased, too, your no less valuable freedom to let me now speak without molestation, — which would be impossible were the creed of the fathers now prevalent, and if you equaled them in devotion to *Faith*, — because then my methods and processes for gaining knowledge would require you to hang either me or those through whom loved and wise ones speak back from beyond the grave, impart their hallowing lessons of experience in bright abodes, and their instructions in righteousness. Thank God yourselves that you hold no creed calling you to perpetrate such barbarity! Hutchinson's statement, that our witch-prosecutors were more barbarous than Hottentots and nations scarcely knowing a God ever were known to be, involves a very significant comment upon the witchcraft creed. That creed made our fathers more barbarous than any tribe of men outside the Christian pale; and were that creed yours to-day, and were you true to it, you would be equally barbarous as they. Their struggle purchased for you and all Christendom exemption from their direful condition.

Adopt the view — and we believe it correct — that the accusing girls were constitutionally endowed with fine sensibilities and special organisms and temperaments which rendered their bodies facile instruments through which unseen intelligences acted upon visible matter and human beings, the supposition that God made them capable of being good mediums — good instruments for use by other

minds and wills than their own, and that their bodies, either apart
from or against their own minds and wills, were concerned in the
enactment of witchcraft, and then you may look upon each and all
of them as having been as pure, innocent, harmless, sympathetic,
and benevolent as any females in that or in this generation; and
no descendant from them need fear the cropping out of specially
bad and disreputable blood thence inherited, and each may regard
his or her native spot as deserving to be consecrated rather than
damned to fame, because there true, conscientious men fought manfully and legitimately for rescue of both their own homes and the
community from direst of all conceivable foes, while living instruments of rare efficiency existed there, by use of which the Christian
world was delivered from dwarfing and hampering slavery to a
monk-made devil. What other battle, of any nature, ever fought
on American soil, purchased choicer freedom, or effected mental
emancipation more widely over Christendom, than did your fathers'
conflict with *their* devil? May the year 1892 deem the spot worthy
of a commemorative monument!

Your last historian poetically says, that your "witchcraft darkness is a cloud conspicuous chiefly by the widening radiance itself
of the morning on whose brow it hung." Shining traits, qualities,
and deeds of New Englanders in the seventeenth century, including
the dwellers at the Village, no doubt gave widening radiance to the
morning of our nation's day; and the abiding brilliancy of that
morning may be what makes your "witchcraft darkness" far more
conspicuous than any in other lands. But it surely required far
other than begulled fathers and beguiling daughters to emit the
rays of a morning of such widening radiance as would make darkness more conspicuous there than elsewhere. That morning owed
its brightness to far other traits than beguiled and beguiling ones.
Clear perceptions of the demands of a creed, of duty to God, of
duty to one's family; prompt, vigorous action in obedience to God's
direction and the king's law when the devil invaded one's home;
fearless and untiring conflict with man's most powerful and malignant foe; — these, and other powers, qualities, and acts kindred to
these, emitted the radiance which made the blackness of witchcraft
more conspicuous at Danvers than elsewhere in the broad world.

No. Witchcraft did not rage with most marvelous fierceness,
and enact its death-struggle, on your soil because of the weakness,

but because of the strength of your fathers; not because of their cowardice, but of their courage; not because of their heartlessness and barbarity, but of tenderness toward their agonized families; not because of lack of faith in God, but because of faith in him so strong that it could put humaneness down, and keep it down till God's call to put a witch to death could be obeyed.

Such properties gave to the morning of the Village an inherent brightness which first extinguished witchcraft's dismal day, and now harbingers a brighter one, in which, no civil law molesting, spirits hold mutually helpful communings with mortals. That momentous and most valuable privilege was essentially won on your soil in 1692. Nation after nation, taught by results at the Village, has repealed its obnoxious statutes, and broad Christendom is the freer and more elevated because of light widely radiating forth from your " witchcraft darkness."

METHODS OF PROVIDENCE.

Our planet, Earth, is yet crude. Its soil, products, emanations, and auras are coarse and harsh. Though meliorated much since it first gave birth to man, it is not now fitted to nurture beings as refined as it will be centuries hence. It is being constantly softened, and is ever progressing toward the present ripened condition of older planets, whose embodied inhabitants easily and constantly commune with wise departed kindred, from whom they receive such instructions and aids as cause them to live in close harmony with the laws of animal health, and therefore nearly free from sickness and pains, and, when ripened for release, to pass painlessly out from their grosser integuments. From the days of remotest history, and our world over, spirits have often been transiently visible and palpable by some mortals. But the atmosphere in which humans live is measurably uncongenial and oppressive to most, and espe- cially to purer and more advanced spirits; still it becomes less so from century to century, is ever gaining such conditions as lift a little higher its incarnate inhabitants, and is less oppressive to those disrobed of flesh. Its modifications prophesy that time will be when mortals and spirits may here more comfortably than now intercommune constantly and with mutual benefit. Terrific mental

. 29

conflicts — moral tornadoes, agitations to the depths of society, are used as instruments in advancing earth and its inhabitants to states which will permit spirits to be our constantly recognized attendants, and our helpful advisers and guides along the paths of spiritual progression.   Progress is hastened through intense tribulations.

Great changes and advances of either a material, mental, political, social, or spiritual world are, like births, generally outwrought through anguish and sufferings.   Even the entrance of spirits into mortal forms is usually painful to both parties.   First and earlier reincarnations are almost necessarily attended by psychological action which forces spirits severally to manifest, and, moderatedly, to undergo, again their special sufferings during their last hours of earth-life.   Mortals, too, shrink from, and are agitated by, and afraid of their nearest friends, if disrobed of flesh.   Such fears are repulsive forces, making spirit approach arduous and often impossible.   The boon of return, in most cases, is at the cost of suffering — but of suffering which pays well — suffering which purchases joy for both those who come and those who welcome them.   Our earth and all who are born upon it receive or earn many of their greatest blessings through the sweats of convulsive throes or severe toil. The abolition of a wide-spread obnoxious creed was terrific in 1692.

In civilized lands extensively, and especially in Protestant Christendom, possibility of the return of departed good souls from their invisible abodes has for centuries been doubted.   Therefore a most copious source of valuable instruction and help has been unused. Resort to it has, or had, become horrific; it has been deemed by men the devil's pool exclusively.   But not so by spirits.   Wise and friendly ones, unseen, have long and often sought and labored for such recognition and welcome, by survivors on earth, as would render demonstration of spirit presence widely practicable.   Spirits have sought this because they have been seeing that free and extensive intercommunings between dwellers in flesh and enfranchised ones might greatly facilitate the advance of both classes in beneficence and happiness.   The immense aid which the earth-embodied living, and only they, can give to many unhappy ones whom they call dead, is not yet dreamed of by the public.   Knowledge that many departed ones are obliged to get aid from earth ere they can make an efficient start up the ladder heavenward, opens a wide and interesting field of labor to those who have carefully sought to learn the mutual dependences of the seen and unseen worlds.

The possible advent of instruction from unseen realms is now for
the first time receiving practical demonstration among a people,
who, as a whole, are able and disposed to scan carefully the nature
and qualities of the intelligences who impart it. Prior to 1692, the
Christian world had long been shrinking from conferences with
unseen colloquists, deeming all such diabolical in purpose and influence. Ignorance was mother of its fears. The present age, more
enlightened, more disposed to investigation, more prone to believe
in the reign of law always and everywhere, asks the hidden teachers
who they are, and whence and why and how they gain access to
our homes. Their responses affirm, and each lapsing year of non-
refutation confirms the allegation, that they are spirits now, but
once were mortals robed in flesh; and that they come, some from
this motive, some from that, — some for fun, frolic, and even revenge and wrong; but more of them to give and to receive the
pleasure and happiness which visits to their former homes and
friends will generate, and especially to make known to their loved
ones here the course of life which will best fit them for joy and
happiness in the mansions and scenes of the world to which they
all must come.

The methods of Providence have ever been homogeneous; and
now that they have brought peoples to the dawn of a day when
human hospitality is entertaining angels, not always unawares, but
often consciously and joyfully, the beneficence of the witchcraft
scenes at Salem Village, whereby Christendom's thralldom to a
factitious devil was effectually broken up, becomes conspicuous.
Lapsed time reveals probability that the barbarisms of that day
were availed of as instruments for procuring the freedom which now
permits instructive, helpful, and gladdening intercourse between
millions of devout and truth-seeking mortals and bright, beneficent
spirits. What though the agitation of Christendom brings its latent
iniquities and impurities to the surface? What though the counterparts of publicans, sinners, and harlots float numerously into view?
Ascent of dross and scum to the surface is usually the first product
in processes of clarification. Inexperienced observers are very
liable to regard the unsightly stuff as a sample of all that underlies
it. Others, who better comprehend the cause and object of bringing impurities into view, observe such first results complacently,
knowing that subsequent effects will be most beneficent — will pre-

sent purified, and therefore more precious views of the divine methods of bringing men to righteousness, and will furnish more efficient helps to man's upward progression than have been generally applicable heretofore.

Great reformatory truths have seldom been first offered to or received by the worldly-wise and prudent. Not rulers and Pharisees,—but common people, fishermen, humble women, publicans, sinners, and harlots were numerous among the first followers of Jesus; and these were the ones who heard him gladly. Like causes which made it thus of old, operate to-day, and the supplemental revelations and revealers of our time meet with like reception as did those centuries ago. It is well. Wide popularity and affectionate fondling might sap an infant *ism* of its best health-giving and reformatory powers. Comprehensive wisdom lets it harden and strengthen through buffetings with the leaders of prevalent theological and scientific decisions, opinions, and fashions. The boundless intelligence, which ever acts for good, is patient and long forbearing. It waits for seeds of reforms to take deep root in the masses, and thence, in time, pushes onward the force which overturns dynasties, hierarchies, and all effete institutions, creeds, and customs which are no longer fruitful of food suited to cultured man's existing needs.

Savage and barbarous nations, everywhere and always, attain to more or less faith in the presence and help of ancestral spirits; they seek instruction from the departed. Broad and perpetual belief in a particular fact is far from weak evidence of its positive existence. Uncultured minds admit witnessed facts to be positive occurrences, and affect no need to comprehend how they are produced before giving assent to their verity. But the cultured are prone to deny the manifestation of any events whose transpiration is not referable to the permission of some law whose operations are familiar. They cannot account for a fact, and therefore it does not exist, or, as Agassiz said, "it is not in nature." The greatest of human scientists, however, falls far short of acquaintance with all the forces and permissions enfolded within boundless, unfathomable, incomprehensible *nature.* It is dogmatism — not science — which says that facts observed by the senses of man continuously from the birth of his race down to now, have had no positive existence.

Law reigns; and we know no law which permits return from

beyond the grave; therefore departed spirits cannot revisit their survivors on earth. Such is often the position and argument of theology, science, and culture. But our question to them is, Are you sure that you are acquainted with all the laws, forces, agents, and permissions in the broad storehouses of nature? Have you explored all realms in the universe, and qualified yourselves to maintain that you have definitely learned that no forces anywhere exist by which things anomalous to human science can be manifested to human senses? Practically you say, Yes. And doing thus, you foster and fast extend belief in non-immortality.

Are the results of your course to be lamented? Perhaps not. The oozing out and disappearance of an old belief, and a consequent state of non-belief, may be arranged for in the methods of Providence, because the latter state may be the best possible for the induction of belief founded on demonstration, where one previously lived which rested upon dogmatic authority.

The skepticism of our generation pertaining to a future life is an offspring of general and advanced education which asks for proofs as the only proper foundation for belief. That education has fitted the thinking masses to demand that teachers shall grapple with and either refute or adopt sensible facts widely witnessed. Millions upon millions of Christendom's inhabitants are having sensible demonstration, day by day and hour by hour, that the spirits of departed mortals make known their veritable presence among their survivors in mortal forms. They say to the world's leading minds, —spirit return is a fact in nature: it is made manifest to our physical senses; we know it to be true. Therefore, ye sticklers for law and scientific methods, prove to us our mistake if we are dupes.

During more than five and twenty years we have been putting forth that call, and you have thus long omitted to give any other response than dogmatic assertion that the appearances we witness are the productions of fraud, fancy, delusion, and the like. That is not satisfactory. Our claim is, that departed spirits of men are working marvels on the earth. That claim is good till it be shown that the marvelous events witnessed are the productions of other agents. Each lapsing year strengthens that claim. And if a check to such materialism as argues that man is devoid of any property which will consciously survive the death of his body, and if a positive demonstration of man's survival beyond the tomb, be matters

which the methods of Providence are employed to advance, then
the unwonted numbers of returning spirits recently and now, and
the frequency of their advent, together with the consequent daily
and palpable demonstration of a life beyond the present, come to
man most opportunely — come to him both when vast masses of
mortals are prepared to meet and welcome them as friends and
kindred, and also, and significantly, when their presence impairs
the power of bright and leading minds to cause the thinkers of our
age to anticipate annihilation of themselves, their kindred, and their
race, and to suffer loss of the incentives and joys which attend
anticipations of a heaven in advance.

So welcome, efficient, and salutary an advent of invisible actors
and teachers as we witness to-day, seemingly would have been impossible, had the witchcraft creed of our fathers retained abiding
hold upon their descendants. The methods of Providence seem to
have embraced both the abolition of that creed, and a sufficient
lapse of time for the nurture and culture of a people up to such
elevation that a large portion of it would be fitted and disposed to
welcome back departed ones just when their proved presence would
be the great fact at man's command which would effectually deter
advancing and beneficent physical scientists from inferring and
teaching that life's emigrants all take a plunge into the rayless
abyss of nonentity.

A continuous thread of the methods of Providence seems traceable through many of the darkest and most shocking scenes of
human history. Many of man's greatest advances have been outwrought through anguish and tortures whose inflictors we reprobate.
Is it too much to say that such a thread ropes in, as instruments
of good, Pharaoh, Pontius Pilate, Witchcraft, and many other
notable personages and scenes, which have been made to further
the deliverances of oppressed and suffering mortals? Permission
of sins, sufferings, and wrongs comes from the Infinitely Benevolent.

Fit instrumentality existed at Salem Village for demolishing that
special creed of Christendom which closed and barred the gates
that nature hinged for furnishing a way of egress back from beyond
the grave; and wisest and kindest dwellers above were in mood
then to let suffering and anguish enough come upon mortals there
to awaken them out of their deep delusion, and sway them to set
those special gates ajar. They broke the bars; but dust and rub

bish long made a wide opening difficult and arduous. A century and a half was needed for such liberation of mortals from the crampings of delusion, and for such exercise of free thought in a land of free schools, as would educate a nation up to courage which could calmly ask any mysterious visitant whatsoever, who he was, whence he came, and what he wanted. In the fullness of time, this could be and was done. When culture and science were broadly producing conviction that there is no hereafter for man, one came forth from the land of the departed, knocked on cottage walls, gained the ear of common people, allured hosts of other spirits to follow him to human abodes ; and the numerous band of returning ones is now the only host which can effectually stop the hope-crushing advance of materialism, and furnish the world palpable demonstration of an hereafter for the souls of men.

In 1692, an unprecedented strain in its application effectually broke up Christendom's long cherished and indurated delusion that devils unfleshed and devils incarnate are the only beings who can act and commune across the line dividing this from the life beyond. That rupture set Christians free to learn that duty called them to " try the spirits." In time a generation came who met that duty. Spirits of God — good spirits — as well as others visit human abodes, and their presence itself is proof positive of man's survival beyond the grave. Their widely conceded advent seems divinely opportune, for it occurs when their presence tends forcefully to check, and promises to stop the prevalent strong tendency of science and culture to divine that man's doom is drear annihilation. The beneficent intensity of a special strain upon a specific delusion, nine score years ago, is due to the strength of faith, character, and action, and to the unwonted extent and excellency of medianimic instrumentality then existing at Salem Village, whose conspicuous action and use there made that spot lastingly memorable ; and we deem it just to regard it as a point from which influences emanated whose fruits to-day are eminent blessings to the Christian world. The methods of Providence often educe choicest good from most direful evils.

APPENDIX.

CHRISTENDOM'S WITCHCRAFT DEVIL.

CHRISTIANS, when New England witchcraft occurred, generally believed that it originated with, emanated from, and was controlled by *one* vast malignant personality, possessing frightful powers, aspects, and efficiency. A fair comprehension of what that being was then conceived to be is needful to anything like accurate knowledge of the origin, growth, sway, exit, and genuine character of occurrences which outwrought as dire strifes, horrors, bloodshed, and heart-wrenchings, as any courageous, intelligent, and conscientious people ever aided forward or suffered under.

Christendom, in the day of our Puritan forefathers, believed in a devil peculiar to a few centuries — in one who was of more modern birth than the Bible or other ancient histories — who was very different from any being characterized in either Jewish or heathen records of antiquity, and has no parallel, we trust, in any creed to-day.

Probably many malicious, as well as benevolent, unseen personages exist, who may often act upon men and their affairs. There may be powerful *evil ones*, in realms unseen, who there rule over hosts of like dispositions with themselves. Neither the existence of many devils, nor intermeddling by them with man's peace and welfare, is called in question.

Authors of the Bible, when using the terms devil, Satan, and others of similar import, generally designated, as our own age extensively does, beings very unlike *such* a devil as was conceived of and dreaded by Christendom from two to five hundred years ago. Prior to and during the days of Jesus and his apostles, such terms were often applied to whatever, in either the visible or the unseen world, tempted or forced men to wrong-doing. or hindered their

459

progress in goodness. Jesus said to a disciple, "'Get thee behind me, *Satan;*" and this, simply because Peter was giving him advice more carnal than spiritual, and which was designed to dissuade Jesus from following the course which his conscience was prompting him to pursue. The mere giving of unwise advice made Peter a *Satan.* Turning to 2 Sam. xxiv. 1, you may read that the LORD, being angry, moved David to number the people. Turning again to 1 Chron. xxi. 1, you will find a description of the same transaction, in which it is said that "*Satan* . . . provoked David to number Israel." Therefore, in biblical language, even the LORD, when angry, was equivalent to Satan. Any accuser, in a court of justice or equity, might properly have been called a Satan, in the days of the prophets, for then that term was applicable to any adversary or opponent, of whatever grade or nature.

Very much later than David's day the word *devil* frequently had a much softer meaning than it usually bears now. Jesus said (John vi. 70), " Have not I chosen you twelve, and one of you is a *devil?* " Having previously called Peter " Satan," Jesus here called Judas a *devil.* Thus highest Christian authority spoke of unwise and treacherous men as being Satans and devils, and thereby showed that those words anciently were sometimes applied, by the pure and wise, to other beings than one special great malignant spirit. The devil of modern *witchcraft* was unknown by Jesus and by all biblical authors.

Whence, then, since not from the Bible, — whence did Christians of the seventeenth and some earlier centuries obtain those peculiar conceptions of him, which made the devil almost counterbalance, in malignity and monstrosity, the benignity and beauty of the Infinite God ? Where did they find him ? So far as we perceive and believe, his like was never recognized, either outside of Christendom, or prior to the dark ages. No being verily like him was ever dreaded as an enemy by any other people than Christians, and not by them till within the last thousand years. About all that we know is, that he had become huge and frightful at the time of the Reformation; and our belief is, that morbid fancy, in the cloisters and monasteries of Europe, through several centuries plied her limnistic verbal skill, and thereby outlined and blackened piecemeal her most *outré* conceptions possible of the lineaments and expressions of a being as monstrous in shape, as powerful, wily, and malicious, as imagination could fabricate, and thus gave the Christian world a monk-made devil — a hideous personification of evil, Lapsing time eventually caused this cloister-born scarecrow to be looked upon as vitalized malignity incarnate — as an immortal, ubiquitous personality — as a living fiend of awful sway and force, who should be watched, feared, and fought by every God-serving man. We look upon him as a production of human fancy. But not so did our predecessors. They assigned to their devil of horrid form and huge dimensions a very different origin and nature.

Where born, and what his nature, according to the belief of those who imported him to New England shores, are important questions the appropriate answers to which must be comprehended before one can obtain just appreciation of the position in which their creed placed our forefathers, and the direction and force it gave to their action whenever seeming diabolism not only fearfully disturbed private firesides and social relations, but threatened tenure of lands, and continued existence of church and state throughout the colonies.

Their Author of witchcraft was conceived of, believed in, and set forth in language, as having been heaven-born — a glorious angel once, but apostate and banished from his native skies; — as one mighty, maliguant personality, almost ubiquitous, almost omniscient, second in power to Almighty God alone, and nearly His equal. As quoted by Upham, vol. i. p. 390, Wierius, a learned German physician, described the devil as being one who "possesses great courage, incredible cunning, superhuman wisdom, the most acute penetration, consummate prudence, an incomparable skill in vailing the most pernicious artifices under a specious disguise, and a malicious and infinite hatred toward the human race, implacable and incurable." — "He was," says Appleton's N. A. Cyc., "often represented on the stage, with black complexion, flaming eyes, sulphuric odor, horns, tail, hooked nails, and cloven hoof." Many of us now living have seen him pictured nearly thus in some old illustrated editions of the Bible.

But the gifted Milton's comprehensive fancy and lofty diction, exempted, under poetic license, from adherence to fact or creed, or other enfeebling restraint, put forth, in masterly and acceptable manner, lineaments and features appropriate to an embodiment of his highest possible conceptions of combined majesty, might, and maligni'y, and thus allured his own and future ages to bow in awe before a devil who in grandeur far surpassed any which monkish powers had been able to fabricate and describe. He imputed to Satan "eyes that sparkling blaz'd; his other parts, besides prone on the flood, extended long and large lay floating many a rood," . . . "unconquerable will, and study of revenge, immortal hate, and courage never to submit or yield," . . . "resolve to wage by force or guile eternal war, irreconcilable to our grand foe, . . . ever to do ill our sole delight, as being the contrary to his high will whom we resist: If then his providence out of our evil seek to bring forth good, our labor must be to prevent that end, and out of good still to find means of evil." Such was the great poet's "Archangel ruined;" nearly such was the prevalent perception of him by the general mind of Christendom. He was one mighty Evil Spirit — monarch of all fiends, and an untiring operator for harm to both the body and soul of man.

Such conceptions were general alike in Europe and America. But still another view, quite as appalling as any of the foregoing, and appealing more directly to the temporal interests of men, operated in *America*, and made it specially needful for all property holders here to contest the devil's advances. Cotton Mather called the arch mischief-worker "a great landholder;" and he was spoken of as though conceived to be temporal as well as spiritual ruler over all Indian tribes and their lands, and also as being a contester against God and Christ for empire over each and every part of the American continent where Christians encroached upon his sable majesty's domains. God and devil — each was a vast and powerful spirit, exercising sway and dominion widely, as the other would let him; and these two mighty spiritual Rulers were often struggling in sharp conflict of doubtful issue for empire over particular portions of the earth. The Devil — and such a devil too — occupied much space not only in the theology and philosophy of the learned, but also in the daily and worldly thoughts of the common colonists.

Upham has forcefully and truthfully said (vol. i. p. 393), that our fathers "were under an impression that the devil, having failed to prevent progress of knowledge in Europe, had abandoned his efforts to obstruct it effectually there; had withdrawn into the American wilderness, intending here to make a final stand; and had resolved to retain an undiminished empire over the whole continent and his pagan allies, the native inhabitants. Our fathers accounted for the extraordinary descent and incursions of the Evil One among them, in 1692, on the supposition "that it was a desperate effort to prevent them from bringing civilization and Christianity within his favorite retreat; and their souls were fired with the glorious thought, that, by carrying on the war with vigor against him and his confederates, the witches, they would become chosen and honored instruments in the hands of God for breaking down and abolishing the last stronghold on the earth of the kingdom of darkness."

This mighty Devil, commander-in-chief of the countless hosts of all the devils, demons, satans, Indians, heathen, sinners in, above, upon, or around earth, — this mighty contester for dominion with God and Christ and all good Christians, was conceived to be author of all works called witchcrafts, producing them through human beings who had voluntarily made a covenant to serve him, and who resided in the midst of the people whom he molested; for we shall soon see that the philosophy of those times permitted him no other possible access to man than through persons who were in covenant with himself.

Any covenanter with such a devil, that is, any wizard or witch, could be regarded by the public as nothing less formidable than a voracious wolf burrowing within the Christian sheepfold, who, if not at once unearthed and slain, would either actually devour, or frighten away from their pasturing grounds, all those with their descendants who had crossed the ocean to feed on the hills and vales of America. Our fathers felt that the possession and value of their homes and lands, as well as the temporal peace and prosperity of the community, its religious privileges, and the salvation of human souls, were at stake in a witchcraft conflict. Their faith, their interests temporal and spiritual, their manhood, and all that was brave, strong, and good in them, called upon them to face boldly even such a devil as has been described above, and to fight him by any processes which had been tried and approved in Europe; the chief of which was, to seize his covenanted servants — his guns — and silence them promptly and permanently. Witches must die!

LIMITATIONS OF THE DEVIL'S POWERS.

Creed-makers before the Reformation conceived, what is probably true, that natural barriers at all times have effectually debarred even the mightiest devil, as well as each and all of his disembodied imps, from coming directly into such close contact with a human body, or any other material object, as enabled them to produce effects perceptible by man's physical senses. Being themselves spirits, whether primarily earth-born or foreign, devils could effect direct access to, and could harm the minds and souls of men, and, unaided by mortals, could incite human beings to evil actions and self-debasement, while yet, so long as they were unaided by voluntary human alliance, they were absolutely unable to act upon matter — unable to subject human forms to fits, twitchings, tumblings, transformations, sicknesses, pains, &c., such as the bewitched of old experienced, and such as await many mediumistic persons to-day. Devils, formerly, and spirits now, to make the effects of their powers observable, or to make themselves felt by men's external senses, usually must act first and directly upon the equivalent to such nervous fluid or aura as enables man's mind to actuate his own body. Any disembodied spirit, of whatsoever grade or character, may be, and probably is, seldom able to command that intermediate aura — or that *something* — excepting when in or near an animal organism which possesses those properties or conditions, whatever they are, which render a person mediumistic. Constructors of the witchcraft creed probably had learned that nature always and everywhere makes matter intangible by spirit directly, and they thence inferred that the devil could never get into close contact with human bodies without the aid of some spirit, or of appendages to some spirit, who holds living alliance with matter, and consequently has in or around itself nervous fluid, or its equivalent, which is usable by mind not its own — is loanable, or at least liable to be abstracted.

Transpiring observation now quite distinctly perceives that control of human organisms by disembodied spirits is usually attended by conditions fundamentally analogous to an antecedent covenant. The old creed-makers may have reasoned from facts of experience and observation much more generally and logically than the present age imagines. No special desire is felt, and we do not see that any special obligation rests upon us, to palliate the doings of those monastics who in dark ages both fabricated and shackled the devil of witchcraft. Still we do not begrudge them such justification as may flow out from passing facts. We have already stated the probability that nature makes physical man intangible by spirits directly. Because of protracted observations of their doings, we assume that spirits are able to read at a glance the properties of each form to which they give special attention, and are at no loss to determine what organisms are controllable by them when conditions are all favorable. One and an important condition is, absence of resistance to control by the mind to which the susceptible organism pertains. The genuine owner generally *can* withhold his or her nervous fluids, or auras, or those properties, of whatever kind or name, which a spirit must use in the controlling process; and, consequently, *a quasi agreement*, amounting at least to acquiescence on the part of the medium, is generally a necessary preliminary to any modern spirit-manifestation, especially with mediums not much accustomed to be controlled.

When and where belief prevailed that all disembodied spirits who ever actuated human forms were the devil or his imps, the inference that those whom he and his controlled had entered into an agreement with *him*, was natural and almost necessary. For an agreement or consensus between a controlling spirit and the will of the person controlled is very common now, and, no doubt, has been in all past ages. The assumption, however, which seems to have been prevalent formerly, that such consensus involved eternal reciprocal obligation between the devil and a human soul, or the sale of that soul to the Evil One, could not be required or suggested by any facts perceivable by modern observation. No doubt each successive use of properties of a particular body by an intelligence from outside itself, generally enables the foreign spirit subsequently to manage that body with increasing ease to itself, and with more satisfaction probably to both parties; and the practice, if mutually pleasurable, renders prolonged co-operation probable; but co-operation for a time imposes no obligation or necessity that the parties shall remain forever conjoined. Common use of the same magnetisms, nervous elements, or whatever they use in common, may tend to make a spirit and a mortal assimilate in their tastes, emotions, motives, and characters. This co-operation may evoke such sympathy between them, that each may often be drawn to the other's aid, and conjointly they may manifest both physical and mental powers which neither could put forth alone. And it is possible that a liberated spirit may be so linked in sympathy with numerous other spirits, that the joint powers of many are at his service, so that through a single human form there may be manifested to the outer world the effects of the combined forces of legions of ascended spirits, either good or bad, in one accordant band.

Obviously, spiritual beings, of whatever quality, are generally dependent, for any manifestation to the outer world, on one or more of a class of mortals possessing special properties or susceptibilities. Nature seems to impose such necessity. She does not let even man's own spirit act upon his stable body directly, but through something evanescent before microscope and scalpel.

COVENANT WITH THE DEVIL.

Perhaps, and probably, the direst and most disastrous of all deluding misconceptions by our forefathers — the one which engendered, nurtured, and intensified the greatest evils of witchcraft — was, that neither their huge devil, nor any subordinate fiendish spirit, could get access to external nature and human bodies through any other avenue than some man, woman, or child, who had already *voluntarily made an explicit agreement with him or his to be his obedient and faithful servant, in consideration of helps and favors which the devil promised to bestow in requital.* When such a covenant had been ratified by signature in the devil's book, written with the blood of the mortal party, then forthwith the devil and his hosts thereby became subject to his new servant's call, and the servant to the devil's summons, so that either could command the powers of both for co-operation in the execution of any malice or deviltry whatsoever, and upon any designated individual. The assumed fact that the devil could use the faculties and properties of no human being who had not expressly covenanted with him, conjoined with belief that he must have the voluntary help of some human being whenever he molested men, was the specially murderous ingredient of faith which impelled good and humane men on to copious shedding of innocent blood. The making of that covenant, and thereby opening an aperture for the devil's entrance through nature's barrier, and thus admitting a wolf into the Christian fold, who otherwise could not possibly have entered, constituted the essence of the crime of witchcraft. That covenanting act made the covenanting man or woman a wizard or a witch; and God had said, "Thou shalt not suffer a witch to live."

THE DEVIL'S DEFENSE.

The custom is humane and equitable which permits the accused to be heard in their own behalf. It is a common saying, that even the prisoner now at our bar is always entitled to his due; and we cheerfully grant him opportunity to defend himself. Under his alias, Satan, and using a cultured Englishman as his amanuensis, he has recently favored the world with his autobiography; in which he says, —

"I am a power. I am a power under God, and as such I perform a task which, however unlovely and however painful, is destined to put forward God's wise and benignant purposes for the good of man. . . . I am an image of the evil that is in man, arising from his divinely-given liberty of moral choice. That evil I discipline and correct, as well as represent; and so I am also a divine schoolmaster to bring the world to God. My origin is human, my sphere of action earthly, my final end dissolution. Evil must cease when good is universal. While, then, I cannot boast of a heavenly birth, I disown fiendish dispositions. Worse than the worst man I cannot be. I am indeed a sort of mongrel, born, bred, reared, and nurtured of human fancy, folly, and fraud. As such I possess a sort of quasi omnipresence and a quasi omniscience, for I exist wherever man exists, and, dwelling in human hearts, know all that men think, feel, and do. Hence I have power to tempt and mislead; and that power, when in my worst moods, I am pleased to exercise. . . . I am a personification of the dark side of humanity and the universe. . . . I exist in every land, and occupy a corner in every human heart. . . . I am the child of human speculation: I came

30

into existence on the first day that man asked himself, ' Whence this world in which I live and of which I am a part?' " *

The frankness, perspicuity, definiteness, and point, taken in connection with the calm, earnest tone, and gentle, candid spirit in which his then placid Majesty dictated that account of himself to his Reverend scribe, win our credence, and induce us to believe he utters only the simple truth when he describes himself as " a personification of the dark side of humanity and the universe," — as one who " cannot boast of a heavenly birth," but was " born, bred, and nurtured of human fancy, folly, and fraud," — as possessing " a sort of quasi omnipresence and a quasi omniscience," existing " wherever man exists, . . . dwelling in human hearts," knowing " all that men think, feel, and do," having power " to tempt and mislead," and, in his " worst moods, is pleased to exercise " that power. Such a Satan, or devil, no doubt exists. But, though we admit that he was a mighty impersonal power in the midst of witchcraft scenes, he was vastly different from the heaven-born " Archangel fallen," whom the good people of New England believed in, feared, and supposed themselves to be fighting against.

A personification of the principle of evil, or " of the dark side of humanity and the universe," is the only devil who is simultaneously present with the whole human race. But hosts of unseen personalities — earth-born, expanded, wily, malignant, and powerful — may act upon man, and bands of such may be subservient to some abler ones of their kind, who reign over them as princes of the dark powers of the air. Malignant departed mortals are the only disembodied personal devils who molest mankind. We believe in *many* devils, but not in Christendom's witchcraft chief *One*.

The devil of our fathers, though but a fiction, was chief cause of witchcraft's woes, and therefore merits attention first, in any attempt to subject that matter to new analysis.

DEMONOLOGY AND NECROMANCY.

Demonology — intercourse with demons — implies dealings with spiritual personalities; but these may be either good or bad, and

* The Autobiography of Satan, edited by John R. Beard, D. D., London, 1872.

may consist wholly, or only in part, of departed human beings, provided there be any other grade of spirits residing in, or able to enter, earth's spirit spheres : probably there are not.

In earlier ages, these demons were often deemed to be intermediate messengers and links facilitating intercourse between mortals on earth and most eminent gods above. That idea, somewhat qualified, is having revival now in the minds of those who are receiving from their departed friends instructions and influences which allure humans heavenward. In the olden faith, demon was used to designate a spirit who might be good; and demonology, then, far from being branded as DIABOLISM, or dealings with one great Devil and his special devotees, was generally deemed not only innocent, but helpful ; — as much so as man's communings to-day with either his disembodied kindred and friends, or with benighted, forlorn, and anguished souls who seek needed encouragement and solace, which they can obtain from none other than an earthly source, are deemed helpful by those loving and philanthropic men and women who take active part in similar demonological interviews now. Bad as demonology seems at this day, when the word has come to suggest dealings with bad and demoralizing spirits alone, time was, when both it and necromancy, or intercourse with the dead, could be legitimately applied to such interviews as Jesus had with Moses and Elias on the Mount of Transfiguration ; and therefore then might have imported communings that would spiritualize and elevate whoever experienced its operations. Strictly, there are no dead. Moses and Elias were living personages when seen by Jesus. Socrates, and many another ancient and wise teacher, drew much profound wisdom and inspiration from out the vailed recesses of demonology and necromancy, and the example of such wise and good men of old has practical imitation by the spiritually-minded and philanthropic disciples of modern communicators living in supernal spheres.

BIBLICAL WITCH AND WITCHCRAFT.

VERY great difference existed between the witchcraft of Bible times and that of Christendom fifteen hundred years after John recorded the Revelation. The difference was almost as marked as that between the devils of those two periods.

The word witch seems primarily to mean, "a *knowing* one," and perhaps has always hinted at knowledge or power acquired by some mysterious method. Witch has generally meant, not only a *knowing one*, but also any person who gets knowledge or help by processes which are mysterious. Witchcraft has been the utterance of knowledge, or the application of power, thus obtained. But neither all such utterance, nor all such application of force, was, in biblical times, called witchcraft. Far, very far different from that. Daniel, Ezekiel, and John the Revelator, all obtained knowledge mysteriously from the lips of departed men; their promulgation of it, however, was not called *witchcraft*, but the *word of God*.

Neither do the Scriptures speak of the woman of Endor as a witch or practicer of witchcraft, though she had both a familiar spirit, and such clairvoyant powers that at her call Samuel rendered himself visible by her ; and he either used her organs of speech, or impressed her to use them, in utterance of rebukes to Saul and prediction of his coming fate. This was not biblical *witchcraft;* though, departing from biblical precedent, the modern world has fallen into the habit of calling the woman of Endor a *witch*, while that epithet is not applied to her in the Bible.

His lawgiver said to Moses, "Thou shalt not suffer a witch to live ;" but if that teacher furnished any very clear definition of either witch or witchcraft, it has not come down to us. Tempting to *spiritual whoredom*, so far as we can determine, constituted the crime of witchcraft among the Jews. The people of Israel were regarded as being *wedded* to the God of Abraham ; therefore persons who by *signs*, by marvelous utterances and acts, tempted Jews to be false to their marriage relations with their God, were witches. The crime of witchcraft was not involved in simply putting forth knowledge, signs, and wonders by the help of familiar spirits, because prophets and apostles often did that when they put forth "the word of God." Witchcraft was application of supernal knowledge and powers for the special purpose of seducing and tempting people to worship Moloch, or some other god of the heathen. (See Lev. xx. 5, 6.) Bible witchcraft was *use of mysterious acquisitions in teaching* HERESY.

PROTESTANT CHRISTENDOM'S WITCH AND WITCHCRAFT.

In the seventeenth century, much of the biblical import of witch and witchcraft, as well as of demon, had been either perverted or dropped, and belief was prevalent, especially outside of the Catholic Church, that none but *evil* spirits could come to men; and also that "the days of miracles, or special manifestation directly from the Almighty, had ceased." Then, too, a personal devil, heaven-born but apostate, and perhaps also myriads of other heaven-born but rebellious and banished angels, could, and only such base spirits could, get access to our external world; and they could effect entrance only through human beings who voluntarily consented and agreed to co-operate with them. It will be apparent on future pages, that any spirit then seen by clairvoyant eyes, whatever the sex, form, features, complexion, or aspect, was either the devil himself, or some apparition formed and presented by him or his, and he was held responsible for its presentation. Our fathers attained to and held firm conviction that all channels for inspirations and mighty works, available since the days of Jesus and his apostles, were avenues for the influx of none but poisonous waters. This was a sad mistake ; for, could they have perceived the groundlessness of their faith that supernal springs of truth, purity, and benevolence had been dammed against the emission of good waters earthward, — groundlessness of their belief that the possibility and feasibility of such works and inspirations as they called miracles had ever been restricted by anything but natural conditions, — that perception would have rendered it apparent to themselves that they ought to make wizards of Abraham and Lot, of Moses and Samuel, of Daniel, Ezekiel, and John the Revelator, since each one of those communed with spirits.

Our American predecessors in the seventeenth century believed

It impossible that good spirits could come to man from bright abodes, — doubted perhaps,. perhaps disbelieved, that departed men and women ever did return to earth, excepting " by the immediate agency of the Almighty ; ". and their writings and actions justify us in saying, that with them, *witchcraft was injection of occult forces and teachings upon man, through consenting mortals, for malicious purposes solely, and by invisible intelligences.*

SPIRIT, SOUL, AND MENTAL POWERS.

Perplexing diversity prevails among users of English language in their application of the terms spirit and soul. Some regard spirit as only a fine, invisible robe of the essential man ; while others speak of soul as the robe and spirit as the man who wears it. Our own custom has been to regard soul as *the man*, and spirit as his under-garment during earth-life, and his outer one, if he shall have more than one, when he shall put off his present outer. This view is not novel. The sometimes clairvoyant Paul stated that there is a natural or outer, and a spiritual or inner body — yes, *body.* Opened inner eyes to-day often see spirit-forms pervading the outer forms of people around them. Their observations are in harmony with the apostle's declaration.

The essential nature of spirit is all unknown by us. Whether matter, spirit, and soul are but different combinations and conditions of like primal elements, we are utterly incompetent to determine. Practically we accept, what is probably a common notion, that matter and soul differ fundamentally; and, having done that, we are unable to identify spirit with either of them elementally. Therefore, without any definite conceptions as to its inherent alliances, we speak of it as possibly something between the other two — *a tertium quid.* Thought regards it as the substance of worlds unspeakably finer than material planets. Spirit, in mass, is not a living, conscious entity, any more than matter is; but is a finer than gossamer substance, capable, like matter, of becoming organized, and growing into a living enrobement of the soul — enrobement of that which constitutes the on-living man through all changes of vestiture. Such is our present conjecture.

We apprehend that a world whose elemental substance is spirit, both pervades and surrounds this material one — a world, we will say for the purpose of indicating our thought, composed of spirit matter. The invisibility and impalpability of such spirit substance are no conclusive refutation of its existence in and around us perpetually. Who sees electricity, magnetism, gravitation, attraction, cohesion, repulsion? Who sees either mind, or the force by which an aching toe reports to the brain and excites the sympathy of the whole organism? Many things are about us, and yet known only in their perceptible phenomena. Spirit substance may be all about us; the spirit world may be in, through, upon, and around the material one. Many manifestations hint at the existence of an all-permeating something, which — since the word is shorter than atmosphere, and not so liable perhaps to be suggestive of palpable matter — we will call *aura*, that contains and furnishes the elements out of which spirit *bodies* are formed, elements of the solid globe on which spirits live, and also is the medium of sight, sound, touch, and all sensation to man's spiritual or inner organism even now and here. A soul, encased within a body elaborated from and within that aura, may, when and where conditions favor, live, move freely, and be happy, whether near the fireside of its former earthly mansion, in earth's atmosphere above and around us, in the earth below our feet, under and in the waters of ocean, in the heavens over us, or *wherever thought can go*. It gives body to thought itself. Brick walls and granite mountains may be no hindrances to its movements, or its freedom and power to see, act, and enjoy. All such powers and privileges probably pertain to us as spirits, even while residents in these outer forms, provided only we can effect temporary disentanglements from the outer, as is often done by or for the highly mediumistic. And yet, so long as the two bodies of a human being retain their ordinary conjunction, something not yet well understood, generally either keeps the spirit senses from cognizable contact with what is conceived to be their native aura, and therefore holds them seemingly embryonic, or it keeps the exterior consciousness of most persons from perceptions of many things which inner senses may be latently experiencing.

A broad survey of mediumistic phenomena raises the question, whether the inner powers of· mediums — now in this life, and daily — see, hear, and learn any more of spiritual things than do the inner powers of others, or whether the chief difference between the mediumistic and others is that the inner faculties of mediums are enabled, in consequence of some peculiarity in relative strength between the outer and inner or in the attachments between the two sets of organs, to report to the outer consciousness, and thus let their outer faculties perceive and report what the inner have cognized, while in the mass of mankind such process is not cognized.

The young servant of Elisha (2 Kings vi. 17) was unable to see spirit hosts upon the hills about Dothan, which were visible to his master; but "Elisha prayed, and said, LORD, I pray thee, open his eyes that he may see. And the LORD opened the eyes of the young man, and he saw; and, behold, the mountain was full of horses, and chariots of fire round about Elisha." The prophet did not ask that his young man should be endowed with any new organs of vision, but only for the opening of such as he already possessed. As soon as those visual organs in him, which could be reached and illumined by spirit aura, came into action of which he became conscious, the young man beheld spiritual beings; which beings, since the prophet had been seeing them all the time, were obviously as near and as visible before as after the prayer. Some spirit perhaps ejected spirit force upon the young man in such way as helped internal perceptions to impress themselves on his external consciousness. Spirits frequently throw some invisible aura with perceptible force upon the external eyes of modern mediums, when these sensitives are being brought into condition for conscious discernment of spirits. Whether the object be to awaken new vision, or simply to impress existing internal vision upon the outer consciousness, is yet an unanswered question. Perhaps each in different cases.

Possibly an actual discernment of earth-emancipated intelligences by our inner organs, especially in our hours of sleep, occurs frequently with most human beings; that is, the "inward man," or inner consciousness, of each mortal may be well acquainted now with many spirits and spirit scenes, so that, upon liberation from the flesh, emerging spirits may find themselves among acquaintances and at home. With some individuals — especially with prophetic and otherwise mediumistic ones — their knowledge, gained through sensations experienced by the inner faculties, is sometimes brought to and impresses itself upon the outer consciousness, and becomes so palpably operative that those individuals are deemed inspired, for they speak as never *man*—that is, as the outward man—spake. Either physical peculiarities, or peculiar relations between the outer or natural and the inner or spiritual bodies, more than the quantum of either mental or moral developments, seem to be the requisites for facile mediumship. That view is often set forth in statements made by spirits, and is rendered probable by observation of many facts. Mediumistic proclivities run much in families, about as much as musical ones do; and the capabilities for either mediumistic or musical performances are measurably constitutional and transmissible. Moses, Aaron, and their sister Miriam, all prophesied, or were mediums of communications from the realm of spirits. In our antecedent pages it appears that four children of John Goodwin,—that three noble, adult, and married sisters, Nurse, Easty, and Cloyse, living apart from each other, whose mother had been called a witch,—that Sarah Good and her little daughter Dorcas, five years old,—that Mrs. Ann Putnam and her daughter Ann, and that Martha Carrier and four of her children, were mediumistic. We can add to the list seven sons of Seva, and four daughters of Philip, in apostolic times. Constitutional properties, combinations, or endowments, differing from such as are most common in the make-up of man, pertain to such persons as are or can be the most plastic mediums. In many people, the organized properties of their physical or mental structures, or of both these, and the relations of such properties to each other, and their mutual action, become, at times, so modified by severe sickness, proximate drownings, protracted fastings, sudden frights, intense griefs, by use of anæsthetics, narcotics, and stimulants, and from many other causes, that those to whom the properties belong become temporarily mediumistic, though they be not observably or consciously such in their more normal states. The most common, and the more mildly acting agents or instrumentalities of such change, and those which produce the more abiding effects, are magnetic emanations and psychological influences from the positively mediumistic acting upon relatively negative systems. Such emanations may be seed originating new, or fertilizers quickening and expanding existing, inward growths.

Emanuel Swedenborg was, prior to and independently of his marked spiritual illumination late in life, one of the most erudite and illustrious scientists of the last century, and, being a truthful, conscientious, devout man, trained to accuracy of observation and statement, he was admirably fitted for a reporter to the external world, of facts which came under his observation as an observer in spirit realms; and we take from his works the following short extracts, which have some bearing upon the topic just presented.

"Man loses nothing by death, but is still a man in all respects. . . . Many are bewildered after death by finding themselves in a body, in garments, and in houses, . . . some had believed that men after death would be as ghosts, specters of which they had heard."

"The will and understanding . . . are two *organic* forms, . . . forms organized from the purest substances. It is no objection that their organization is not manifest to the eye, being interior to sight. . . . How can love and wisdom act upon what is not a substantial existence? . How else can thought inhere?"

Two Sets of Mental Powers.

Teachers unseen, speaking back to the world they have gone from, often say that, when here, they possessed two *bodies* — one of which is entombed below, while in the other they went forth and still abide; they say also that they possessed two mental systems and a double consciousness, one only of which survives. Quite recently, science, pressing forward in explorations, obtained perceptions of this latter fact. In his eighth lecture on the "Method of Creation," given May 1, 1873, and reported in the New York Tribune, the eminent Agassiz spoke as follows : —

"Are all mental faculties one? Is there only one kind of mental power throughout the whole animal kingdom, differing only in intensity and range of manifestation? In a series of admirable lectures, given recently in Boston by Dr. Brown-Séquard, he laid before his audience *a new philosophy of mental powers.* Through physiological experiments, combined with a careful study and comparison of pathological cases, he has come to the conclusion that there are *two sets*, or a double set, of mental powers in the human organism, or acting through the human organism, essentially different from each other. The one may be designated as our ordinary conscious intelligence; the other as a superior power which controls our better nature, solves, sometimes suddenly and unexpectedly, nay, even in sleep, our problems and perplexities, suggests the right thing at the right time, acting through us without conscious action of our own, though susceptible of training and elevation. Or perhaps I should rather say, our own organism may be trained to be a more plastic instrument through which this power acts in us.

" I do not see why this view should not be accepted. It is in harmony with facts as far as we know them. The experiments through which my friend Dr. Brown-Séquard has satisfied himself that the subtle mechanism of the human frame, about which we know so little in its connection with mental processes, is sometimes acted upon by a power outside of us as familiar with that organization as we are ignorant of it, are no less acute than they are curious and interesting."

Many persons, including the author of these pages, more than twenty years ago found among " phenomena called spiritual," many which seemed imperatively to demand a broadening of the base of any mental philosophy which the world at large had presented to their notice, and apprehended that light was dawning amid the dark work of spirits, which might reveal to man more knowledge than he had ever obtained both of his own mysterious structure, and of his relations to and possible intercourse with his predecessors on earth. Many, perceiving this, have held on prosecuting such observations, and drawing such conclusions as their opportunities and powers permitted, undeterred by sneers and cold shoulders ; and such now spontaneously hail with joy the arrival of the world's most advanced scientists at " *a new philosophy of mental powers;*" such a philosophy, too, as manifestations well scrutinized have long been indicating would some day be based on the firm foundation of proved facts, and become a blessing to our race. Both spiritualism and science, by distinct routes, have reached a common point, and each testifies to the other's discovery of a new world *in* man.

" The subtle mechanism of the human frame, about which we know so little in its connection with mental processes, *is sometimes acted upon by a power outside of us as familiar with that organism as we are ignorant of it, . . . acting through us without conscious action of our own, though susceptible of training or elevation.*" Such is the conclusion of Dr. Brown-Séquard, which is

indorsed by Agassiz. Backed by such authority, one may very
courageously move forward in efforts to show that the very structure of man through all ages may have permitted certain human
forms to have been controlled and used by intelligent powers outside of themselves, and without conscious action of their own, that
is, without consciousness on the part of the individual minds to
which those bodies naturally pertained. Such facts are guide-
boards designating pathways along which producers of prophetic,
witchcraft, and spiritualistic phenomena can reach standing-points
for speech and action perceptible by men's external senses; these
facts are keys, too, that will unlock many chambers of mystery, and
we have used them in searches among the records of witchcraft.

Those eminent savants do not state, and therefore we shall not
maintain, that the outside power they refer to is spirits of former
occupants of human bodies; but since that power "is as familiar
with the human organism as we are ignorant of it," the language
surely implies reference to *some intelligent* power, for its familiarity
with the organism is that of *knowledge*, the acquisition of which is
contrasted with our *ignorance*. To whom can they refer, if not to
spirits of some grade?

The nature of things contains provision for temporary reincarnations of some departed spirits in the physical forms of some peculiarly organized and endowed human beings. This fact is important,
and should be borne in mind during a perusal of the present work.

MARVEL AND SPIRITUALISM.

We are reluctant to use the word "miracle" because of its liability to be construed as designating not only an act performed
directly by an Almighty One, but also that, in performing it, He acts
"contrary to the established constitution and course of things;"
which course we believe was never adopted. Therefore we shall
use "marvel," to designate all works which have seemed to require
more than human power, and have been understood to be "more
than natural."

Such A MARVEL *is a result from application of powerful occult
forces which man neither comprehends nor can manage.*

SPIRITUALISM is phenomena resulting from use of occult forces
and processes by invisible, departed human spirits.

Most genuine spiritual phenomena are marvels; but there may be, and may have been in witchcraft-scenes, marvels which spirits did not produce. We left out from the definition of marvel, necessity for an *intelligent* operator. Impersonal influxes to many mediums may at times produce many things which are often ascribed to personal spirits.

Our broad definition lets the word marvel cover all supernal revelations and inspirations from any god, spirit, or the impersonal spirit realms, — all angel or spirit presence ever perceived by man, — all mighty works, signs, and wonders ever wrought through prophets, apostles, magicians, sorcerers, and the like, — all promptings, helps, and works by spirits called "familiar," — all necromancies, witchcrafts, &c., &c. As a natural philosophy, our subject embraces all these. Its moral or religious aspects do not come under special consideration in the course of inquiry which is pursued by us. Spiritualism — as evolvements by finite unseen intelligences, using none other than natural forces, however occult, acting in subserviency to natural laws and nice conditions — has its rightful place with whatever has come forth from action of intra-mundane or supra-mundane forces and agents.

Hidden intelligences in all ages and lands have had credit for performing in man's presence many "mighty works," and for making revelations from the world unseen. Over the whole earth formerly, and over the larger part of it now, such intelligences have been and are deemed to be of all characters and grades, from very unfolded, pure, and benevolent beings, down to the ignorant, corrupt, and malignant. But our Puritan ancestry on this continent had inherited and brought hither with them a firm, unqualified belief that no other spirits but evil ones could, or at least that none but such would, operate among the Christian dwellers on New England soil. The mysterious workers and their doings were here excessively diabolized by the monstrous creed previously described, which prevailed all through Christendom during the seventeenth and some prior centuries, so that signs, wonders, and mighty works among our ancestors assumed forms, characters, and horrors which were never known among Jews, Christians, or heathen of old, and do not revive in our own times. There was then lacking here any conjecture that the same laws which in Job's time permitted Satan to mingle in company with the sons of God, might permit a son of

God — a good spirit — to traverse the paths along which the sons of the devil — bad spirits — made approaches to the children of men. Moses, Elias, Samuel, and John's brother prophet were forgotten. We apprehend that facts of history teach beyond all successful refutation that spirits of some quality acted upon and through many persons in the American colonies during the latter half of the seventeenth century. Our fathers were not mistaken as to that fact; but their inhospitable and fierce slamming of doors in the faces of these visitants provoked terrible retaliations. One leading object of this work is to refute the position of intervening historians, that no disembodied spirits whatsoever had any hand in producing American witchcraft.

Indian Worship.

The historian Hutchinson said, " the Indians were supposed to be worshipers of the devil, and their powows to be wizards." Such supposition by the mind of Christendom intensified fears and ruthless acts on American soil more than elsewhere, whenever suspicion of witchcraft was engendered. America was then understood to be peculiarly the domain of the Evil One, and all its pagan inhabitants were regarded as his devoted adherents. Thence his followers here were deemed to be more numerous and formidable than elsewhere, and therefore his invasion was more to be dreaded on this than on the other side of the Atlantic.

We must impute a considerable portion of witchcraft horrors to such narrow and cramping religious views and feelings among our fathers, as made all men everywhere seem to them not only outcasts from God, but also associates with Satan, who did not possess heir special creed, and worship by their processes. They practically forgot that all men, of all nations and tribes, are the offspring of the Unknown God, whom Paul declared to the Athenians; and also that his paternal beneficence extends to his children everywhere, and draws them toward him by methods suited to their circumstances, capacities, and needs, and consequently that all religious creeds and all modes and forms of worship may be helpful to those who possess and use them.

History, literature, and public belief, pertaining to the religious practices of North American Indians, so far as we remember, have very uniformly ascribed to them something closely resembling communings and consultations with invisible intelligences. Such religious services are, and ever have been, rendered in all those primitive tribes the world over concerning whom we have attained to anything like accurate knowledge. (See Primitive Culture, by Edward B. Tylor.) Ethnology proves that belief in the presence of spirits — and, generally, belief in the access of ancestral spirits — exists among man everywhere in the nations lowest of all in culture, and survives in them as they rise in development. Dr. Bentley declared that "the agency of invisible beings, if not a part of every religion, is not contrary to any one." Hutchinson, as quoted above, says, "The Indians were supposed to be worshipers of *The Devil*, and their powows to be wizards."

No question is raised that such a supposition pertaining to Indian worship was prevalent in the New England mind down to the close of the seventeenth century. Nor can we doubt that untruthfully the Puritans charged the aborigines with worshiping the one great Devil of Puritan Diabolism, because of our conviction that the red men were in fact communing with their ancestral and numerous other friendly spirits. The white man's erroneous conception that his devil was the red man's god, had no small influence upon public action in witchcraft times. The idea that their devil had for backers all the aborigines of the continent, made him a more formidable foe than he otherwise would have been, and intensified the ruthlessness of the whites in their persecutions of those of their own complexion and households who were believed to have made a compact to serve the Evil One. Perhaps a modern instance may exhibit with much clearness the real nature of Indian worship in former ages.

We quote from the Washington Chronicle, early in the year 1873, what is there ascribed to General O. O. Howard, who is often called the *Christian Soldier*. He, as commissioner from the American government, had, unarmed and with but two attendants, penetrated the fastnesses of the mountains, made his way to the home of the Appache Indians and to the presence of their fierce chief, Cochise. After council with the Appaches, "they had," as General Howard writes, "an Appache prayer-meeting, ... one Indian after another would pray or speak. ... Cochise's talks were apparently the most authoritative ; ... I could hear him name Stagalito, meaning Red

31

Beard.   I knew from this that our whole case was being considered
in their way *in the Divine Presence* either of the God of the earth,
or of His spirits; and surely these were solemn moments, . . .
fortunately the spirits were on our side." These words indicate
very clearly the nature of that devil whom modern Indian powows
worship: they make him on one occasion neither more nor less
than the ascended chief Stagalito, associated with other spirits of
the same nature.   Can there be a doubt that Hutchinson misrepre-
sented the fact, if he meant to call the Indian communings with
spirits a worshiping of that monstrous being whom the word
" *Devil*," uttered through clerical lips, or recorded by intelligent
pens, in early colonial times, was intended and understood to describe ?   We think not.   There was neither truth nor justice in the
supposition that the red men were devil-worshipers at the times
when they were consulting departed spirits ; nor in the presumption
that their mediums — their powows — were wizards.   False epithets
do not convert any sincere worship, performed even by the rudest
of the rude, into a bad act.   Those Indians of two centuries ago,
as judged by us now, had truer conceptions and better knowledge
of spirit intercourse with mortals, and of the fit methods of obtaining useful incentives and help from spirit realms, than had their
Christian neighbors, who misunderstood and blindly maligned the
devotions offered to the Great Spirit by his children in the forests.
The Indians, to the best of their ability, worshiped Him who is the
common Father of all men of every hue and condition.   They
sought access to the Great Spirit, our God as well as theirs, through
communings with their ancestral and other spirits.   But the supposition that they worshiped such a being as the devil of Christendom,
is obviously incorrect.

Cotton Mather said that "the Indians generally acknowledged
and worshiped *many* GODS : therefore greatly esteemed and revered
their *priests*, powows or wizards, who were esteemed as having
immediate converse with the gods."   Rev. Mr. Higginson, of
Salem, said the Indians in that vicinity " do worship two gods — a
good and an evil."   Mather and Higginson are better authority on
this point than Hutchinson.   Those denizens of the impressive
forests were nature-taught spiritualists communing with their ancestral spirits, and through them were lured and helped on to worship the Great Spirit of Nature — the Omnipresent God.